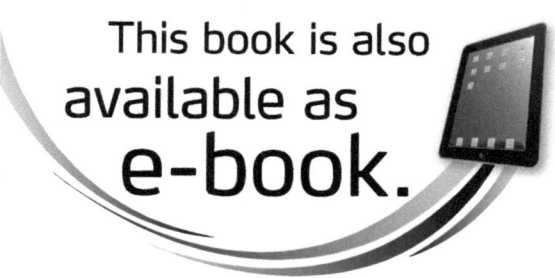

This book is also available as e-book.

www.novum-publishing.co.uk

© 2021 novum publishing

ISBN 978-3-99107-412-0
Editing: Ashleigh Brassfield, DipEdit
Cover photos: Mariusz Lubkowski, Volodymyr Byrdyak, Janinearnold22 | Dreamstime.com
Cover design, layout & typesetting: novum publishing

www.novum-publishing.co.uk

Jay W. Ess

SOME STAY,
SOME DIE

novum ▲ pro

Dedication

For my beloved Nancy – she has shown me patience and tolerated me for half a century

A Tribe Lost, somewhere in southern Africa

This book is a work of fiction, but it does cover events that happened, if not identically, then certainly similarly. The time period is specific: the 1970's and 1980's. It is written for those people involved at the time, mostly white but not exclusively so, who tried first to protect an old order and then tried to make a new order work. It was a time when a country was lost by idealists who believed that change would be necessary, but whose masters were unable to change. The tribe endured a change from one group of political diehards, who remained intractable, causing the death of a nation, to a group of political lightweights, who could only flex their all powerful personal selves and forgot to nurture the baby nation's needs. It was a question of bottle-feeding from the start; the breast was never an option, so there was no real bond formed. Nevertheless, those tribe members who did remain did so mostly to be part of a new-born nation and help it grow to maturity. They, after all, had an inherited privilege – that of education – so were at the vanguard to help the new-born survive its first years, whilst a larger, more equal force of carers was developed. The tribe cautiously waited out the early muscle flexing of the politicians' muscles, themselves inexperienced, and indeed the unruly infant began to develop. To their chagrin, towards the end of the 1980's, once again an event occurred which would lead the politicians to plan an exacting revenge on their own child for its disobedience in failing to give the politicians absolute power. The lost tribe began to die at that time, though they did not realize it at the time. The politicians took absolute power anyway, but quite deviously, fooling many, even lulling the near teenage nation into believing things were improving. Then the politicians moved the goalposts and the tribe did die, slowly at first, but as history has subsequently recorded, the tribe became more or less extinct by the time the nation reached adulthood.

The characters I have portrayed are themselves fictional, but are at least to some degree, composites of various people I had personal experience of in those times, added to by the experiences of close friends. The stories I have heard through friends of friends also figure in the narrative; indeed, the tribe may not have known all its members individually, but invariably they would all know someone who knew any member, and it is that knowing someone which typifies the tribe. The events I have portrayed, with some licence on occasion, did largely happen, and maybe that reflects the turbulence of the times, good and bad. My sentiments may ultimately betray me, but this story is fictional – or is it? Perhaps, it is not itself part of any folklore of the time, but more a snapshot of those times.

As history has recorded, the tribe is indeed lost, as almost all of its kind have been in other parts of Africa, and specifically, that new nation, now approaching middle age, has suffered from the excesses of absolute power driving it into those unending pits of despair. To those few of the scattered remaining members of this almost extinct particular tribe: I salute you and assure you that you will be remembered.

The other characters that make up the story are not men, but elephants. Though the book remains fiction, there is a serious aspect to it; that is, ivory poaching. In a way, I decided that their survival is perhaps more important than the snapshot of the times, and indeed we as the tribe can adapt to another life, an option not available to the elephants. I hope there may be a message there.

Jay W. Ess, 2020

CHAPTER 1

1985

Jasper waited until the plane began its taxi run carrying his latest, hopefully satisfied, customers back to the capital, where they would all be able to catch their connections to Europe and the East. His baby, Osprey Safaris, had built a superb and well-earned reputation for providing fascinating encounters with game, excellent fishing experiences and that hint of danger which clients deemed necessary to fulfil their fantasies. He watched from the baggage shed and saw the usual ritual of the old army Land Rover driving down the runway before the plane's take-off, to scare off any game, mainly kudu or impala. The airstrip had been carved out of the bush thickets just beside the lake many years ago, at first as a military strip during the region's birth pangs when the individual countries that made up the Protectorate gained their independence from the Empire. The lake itself was a creation of the Empire, meant as both a conservation area and as a power source for the region by the damming of one of Africa's greatest rivers. Indeed, it was a massive lake, the world's biggest reservoir at the time, 140 miles long by 20 miles wide. Jasper sometimes wondered whether anybody could imagine the ecological damage that would happen to the southern African region when the dam broke. The governments must have some sort of crisis plan, he guessed, but who really knew what damage the sudden release of 200 billion tonnes of water would do on its 800 mile rampage to the Indian Ocean.

He heard the whine of the plane's engines building up to a crescendo as it turned onto the runway, and off it went without stopping. The pilot must have had a hot date in town that night and wanted to get back to the capital as early as he could – good luck with that. The plane lifted off and rose quickly into the late afternoon sky above the glistening waters of the lake and swung south towards the capital before landing an hour later in time for those international connections. Jasper turned, striding round the side of the baggage shed towards the parking area, past two Chinese gentlemen in their Mao type suits, clearly suffering a little in the humidity. He thought that was odd; they were clearly waiting for someone, but the normal meeting point would be just inside the tin-roofed "shed" that served as the terminal. He greeted them and asked if he could help, perhaps deliver them to the local town, but they ignored him and hurriedly turned their backs on him. What bad manners, he thought, but then perhaps they did not understand him. Jasper crossed over to where his Land Cruiser was waiting with Henry, his trusted lieutenant in his business. Henry was a Matabele, the minority tribe, and therefore not a favourite of the ruling Shona tribe. He had first met Jasper years ago, in an elite branch of the military, after having been a game guide for a conservation organisation. Jasper spoke to Henry, asking him if he had seen the two Chinese men; Henry nodded and replied rather less complimentarily that they were not Chinese, but Korean. He pointed to the airport's entrance and Jasper saw a government-plated vehicle swing in, scattering gravel and going straight to the baggage shed where the two Koreans were waiting. The Koreans appeared to berate the driver until an army officer, a brigadier it seemed, stepped out of the Mercedes S 320, at which point everybody was all smiles. Henry commented, almost questioningly, that the brigadier was a Matabele, to no-one in particular. The driver collected their bags and put them in the boot before getting back into the car and then speeding off, no doubt to stay in one of the luxury, air-conditioned hotels in the town. Henry asked if he wanted to go for sundowners in town, as it would be dark in half an hour.

Jasper was thinking of their early start tomorrow, and said "No, let's go home."

Home was a villa, a 240-acre plot in the Charara safari area that he had got a hundred year lease on from the government. The orange sun was turning the sky red and would soon drop below the skyline, bringing that special kind of blackness that you can only experience in Africa. It enveloped you like a cloak, yet was clean, vibrant, and given life by the noises and silences that permeated it. In the gathering gloom the lights had come on at the front of the 'terminal', which was in reality a plain agricultural shed, and already moths were playing around the lights. When the night came it would seem as if every insect in the country had come to play in the light. The lake had a large preponderance of small, sardine-like fish called kapenta, which, like krill, were the bottom of the food chain, sustaining not only the other lake fish but also the human population both locally and at large. The local tribes had boats with big, saucer-like nets which were lowered into the black depths on their derricks. Just above the centre of the net a powerful light was shone, and like the insects at the airport lights, the kapenta collected in their thousands, a silvery throbbing mass, before they were literally scooped up and out of the water. The boats were strung out across the lake, and their fishing lights gave the impression of a pearl necklace spread out in a curve.

Henry started the Cruiser and drove off towards the main road. He turned right and travelled three and a half miles before heading right again onto the Charara bush road, which led to the fishing camp and the two or three settlements at the very eastern end of the lake. The main, metalled road led from the Kariba Dam wall, the border post, through the town of Kariba, past some black marble workings, then the airport on the right, on past the bush road leading to Jasper's holding and to an escarpment, about 30 miles away. There, it met the main A1 road between the capital and Chirundu, one of the two border crossing points over the Zambezi to Zambia, the northern neighbour. The lake road met the main road at Makuti on top of the escarpment, the crossroads being marked by a garage and a colonial-style motel called Clouds End. This was also about 30 miles from Chirundu, and so served travellers to and from Zambia and as a watering hole for safaris going into the Zambezi valley or to the lake. The road from the lake to Makuti followed old elephant trails, and it would not be unusual, especially at night, to come across several of these pachyderms strolling along stretches of the road – wonderful for the tourists, but sometimes annoying if you had to follow a lumbering elephant for a half mile or more before they cut off into the bush again. Still, that was part of the deal you made when you came to live in this part of the world, along with the heat, the mosquitos and the tsetse flies. All had to be endured. Sure enough, just a couple of hundred yards from their turn off, Jasper and Henry had to crawl along behind a small group of elephant and, as luck would have it, the four females and one calf turned onto the bush road. Fortunately, they cut off into the bush alongside the track, but Henry kept his distance for a minute to make sure they did not turn back onto the track. It was pitch black now, and occasionally the eyes of animals could be seen as the Land Cruiser rounded bends. Twenty minutes later they turned towards the lake and just past the pineapple farm found the entry to their plot, Osprey Safaris, drawing up to the centre portion of the villa. After the five-day safari down the Zambezi flood plain, Jasper knew Henry would be keen to see his family, so he did not hold him back and Henry quickly disappeared to the cottages just a short way off the villa. Jasper was greeted by his houseboy Francis with a cold beer and told his supper would be ready 'now now'. This could mean anything from 5 minutes to 30 minutes – it was African time – so Jasper knew he had time to get into the shower and at least begin to feel civilised again. After his shower, Jasper sat on the stoep eating the meal Francis had brought, along with another cold Castle beer, watching the kapenta boat lights strung out across the lake. He could hear the generators on board working, but then other sounds began to take over; there were various chatters of animals, like they were talking to each other, the persistent high pitched buzz of the cicadas, and the odd territorial hippo altercation, usually ending in a rumbling run and a splash as the vanquished one ran into the safety of the lake. Now and then came the almost mournful muted roar of a lonely lion. Jasper himself was feeling a little lonely, missing Sophie, his partner of the past four years. He was close to counting off how many 'sleeps' he had left till she returned. Unfortunately, that was still two weeks off.

The villa was built some 100 yards from the estimated highest possible lake-line, but the water had not been any nearer than double that distance in the last 10 years. It was a gentle gradient down to the jetty at which Jasper had made a small inlet, a 'posi', where his cabin cruiser *Osprey* lay. The villa was a kind of opened U shape, without the curves, and both wings pointed diagonally towards the lake, wrapping round a generous swimming pool. One wing held three bedrooms, all en-suite (at least shower and toilet), and the other wing had a kitchen, utility room, toilet and office whilst the centre wing had a large split-level lounge and small bar. Close to the kitchen wing Jasper had built the carports, standalone freezer room, and a small room which housed a generator to provide electricity to the villa, mainly for air-conditioning, and half a dozen rondavels in which clients would stay before safaris began. Each rondavel was fairly luxuriously appointed, with their own connected shower and toilets. Mosquito nets were standard around the four poster beds and large overhead fans provided at least a little cooling effect. All meals, which were to a high, home-cooked standard, were served at the villa, with all drinks being included during the client's stay. Indeed, Osprey was well known for its outstanding wines, mostly South African ones. Behind the villa were several buildings which served as housing for the few families that stayed on the property, employed one way or another. The remainder of the plot was used to grow vegetables and some maize to support the working families and clients alike, with meat and fish either caught or bought in. It was not possible to keep livestock, apart from some poultry, because of the tsetse flies and cattle's susceptibility to trypanosomiasis, the sleeping sickness, which first weakens then kills cattle and people. It is often called the curse of the African subsistence farmer, but in truth Jasper was glad of the flies' presence in Charara and the Zambezi valley. The tsetse flies kept the nomadic farmers from cultivating and therefore rapidly shrinking the area for the wildlife. It was a ridiculously small area, considering the size of Africa and the low population densities outside of the cities. In fact, there were now generations of youth who were not interested in farming anyway; but nevertheless, Jasper and the other safari operators would occasionally sabotage the Ministry's attempts to maintain tsetse fly traps in the valley by burning them.

All in all, Osprey Safaris was a superb centre for its activities, both game viewing and fishing on the mighty Zambezi or the lake. For the adventurous, there was a canoeing trip down the river to Mana Pools, with 2-3 nights camping on the riverbanks and an added bonus of moonlight walking safaris at Mana Pools if there was a full moon. Alternatively, there was daylight walking within Charara, and of course a separate four-day fishing trip on the lake to catch the famous tigerfish – though Jasper always thought the river fish were the better prize, despite being smaller than their lake brethren. He considered the lake tiger to be lazy and potbellied, having life too easy, swimming open mouthed through the shoals of kapenta, whereas the river tiger had to be constantly swimming against the river and foraging for its prey, making it a more streamlined fish. His canoeing concession, the last addition to the business, was for a safari from Chirundu to Mana pools, with two or three nights being spent on the riverbank using the luxury mobile overnight camp system. Jasper and Henry had built shower and ablution blocks at the three sites, with 3 thatched 'A' frames under which a crew would put up self-contained tents and beds. The Unimog crew would also erect tables and chairs for a cooked meal at night, as well as breakfast in the morning. The clients had to do nothing but eat, drink, have a shower and stare at the panorama of the sky, whist listening to the cacophony of sounds around them. It was not unusual to hear the roar of lions and try to guess how far away they were, or the chittering of jackals and the chattering of hyenas, often likened to laughter. After the canoes left in the morning, the crew would pack up the site into the two cruisers and trailers and move on to the next night's stop-over site and perform the same operation. When the safari had reached Mana, and if there was a full moon, guided night walks were added on for an extra night in the bush before returning to Charara by the Land Cruisers.

Jasper used his cabin cruiser for fishing safaris, the first mainstay of his business, around the eastern basin and central part of the lake. There were a couple of bedrooms with bunks below the main deck, but most clients preferred to sleep in the open on the upper deck. The boat captain and another galley boy could look after 6 clients comfortably. As with the canoeing safaris, all meals and drinks were included. Most clients came from overseas and were charged in US dollars. As part of the terms of his concession, Jasper had to allow about 3 months of the lake fishing for the local people, charged in local currency but at the equivalent rate to the US dollar. Even so, Osprey Safaris would net around half a million USD a year, and local dollars were useful for local purchases. Jasper was entitled to keep half of all USD earnings, so it was a nice little business.

CHAPTER 2

Pre 1973

Jasper Jackson, predictably, 'JJ', was one of a pair of twins born in 1948 to Marika and Frank Jackson in the resort town of Umhlanga Rocks, several miles north of Durban on the Indian Ocean coast of South Africa. His sister Jade was actually first born, so Jasper did brag he had an elder sister. Their mother, Marika, was from a well-known Natal sugar plantation family, the Jouberts, but had studied gemology and had a thriving jewellery business, hence the names of the twins. Father Frank was a Scottish anthropologist who had been studying the Zulu culture when he met Marika. He was a bit of a dreamer but had become something of an authority on the Bantu people's southwards migrations. He had been invited by the Commonwealth Crown Office to document and research the tribal cultures of the peoples that would be displaced by the proposed building of the Kariba Dam, the 1953 idea which became a reality with the formation of the Federation of Rhodesia and Nyasaland. So, in 1953, the Jackson family moved into a large rangy house on Churchill Avenue in Salisbury, South Rhodesia, opposite the grounds of the University of Rhodesia, which was Frank's base. Jade went to the Dominican Convent school as a day pupil, whilst Jasper was enrolled as a day pupil in St George's College. This suited Mum, as she had started a small jewellery factory from one of the spare rooms in the house and was soon in great demand from local jewellers. Jade finished her education at the convent and studied medicine, learning a lot about trauma medicine and qualifying as a doctor by 1973. She was soon married to a visiting English medical lecturer and left for Scotland with him when his year was done. Jasper had only got into the Jesuit run St. George's because Dad had been from a Catholic family, though he was a non-practising Christian, and

St. George's judged the young Jasper to be a very bright boy. He was a big boy for his age and the staff saw him as a future national rugby wing forward and possibly a fast bowler. Jasper proved to be bright and very good at sports, especially rugby, and went on to study his father's subject, anthropology, then chose a combined botany/zoology course and graduated in 1971. He spent a lot of time with his father during his holidays up in Kariba and the Zambezi valley and became fairly proficient at bushcraft and animal tracking. As he was eligible for army service, and by now the 'Chimurenga' or black war of Independence was in full swing, he was drafted into psychological operations and intelligence. During this time Jasper got to know Andre Rabie, the first regular tracking instructor of the Selous Scouts. He was so impressed with young Jasper that he suggested to his colleagues that they had a natural on their hands regarding bushcraft. The main training base for this elite force was about an hour from Kariba, in an area that was restricted but whose general topography Jasper already knew through his trips with his Dad. At the Wafa Wafa camp, Jasper became part of an intake of 130 men from various army units both black and white. The Scouts were an integrated unit with a ratio of roughly 2 black scouts to 1 white. They were encouraged to speak in either Shona or Ndebele. JJ had been pretty much fluent in Shona since the age eight, and also had gained a useful vocabulary of the two toed Tonga people who were indigenous to the Kariba and Zambezi valley, so that was a bit of a doddle. The identification of plants, trees and animal spoor also came easily to him, though the discomfort of what amounted to extreme camping without any equipment or hygiene was harder, but not overbearing. Things began to get really tough when the dehumanising began; firstly, with no rations except water, and then made to forage for rats, snakes, and baboon meat. Some 30% to 40% left the training at this, but JJ became inured to it. He even managed to drink water from carcasses and strain the stomach contents, learn to eat rotting meat, grasshoppers, lizards – literally anything to survive. By now the original intake of 130 men had been reduced to 30 odd, and still the pain was heaped on. In their starved condition the men still had to do marches of 20 miles in under 3 hours, made increasingly difficult by having to carry a sand bag for the last 7 miles; and all this in hot, humid conditions. Only those who were mentally strong could survive this treatment, and by the last few days only 21 recruits remained. There were more lessons: making fires without matches, using string made from bark to make snares, bush medicines such as marula as anti-histamines; everything designed so that they could survive alone in the bush because they had developed second nature within any environment. The much vaunted test of being dropped off in the bush, with a gun, 20 rounds, a match, and a raw egg, amongst lions, hippos and elephants, and having to emerge the next morning for inspection with a hardboiled egg, was almost a pleasure. JJ had survived the intake, being one of only twelve to do so. He was maybe 30 pounds lighter and a very lean and much meaner machine, ready to take his role as a tracker. At six feet two inches and 190 lbs weight, well bronzed by the sun, he was a handsome man, but his ever-present smile was now much more thoughtful. He had been quite explosive in his school days, but clearly the environment of war and death had tended to mute his quick tongue. Jasper was seconded to the Kariba eastern basin and the Zambezi valley from Chirundu to Kanyemba, a border town where Zambia, Mozambique, and Rhodesia meet. He, together with Nkomba, with whom he had struck up a close, life-long friendship during training, would spend weeks in the bush hunting down terrorist spoor and calling in the infantry or air force for strikes against any infiltrating groups they considered too big to deal with themselves. As the war went on and became more intense, Jasper became hardened – not so much with the killing of what after all was an enemy who was equally likely to kill him, but with the demonising and cruelty these groups subjected their own people to. While he had been and still was proud of the Selous's badge, the Osprey, he could no longer wear it openly, since he had to maintain as much anonymity as possible as to what his role was in the bush war.

CHAPTER 3

Pre Independence Times

The bush war had escalated by 1975, and Jasper was either in the Zambezi valley with his partner Nkomba for their 6-week plus tours or recovering for a month, off-duty, so to speak. He still kept a room in his parents' house in Churchill Avenue, which was now his. Frank and Marika had returned to Durban in 1965; Frank then completed his various theses the Zambesi Valley's tribes. The Federation of Rhodesia and Nyasaland had breathed its last in 1963, with what became Zambia and Malawi going their own ways, followed by the Unilateral Declaration of Independence in Salisbury 11th November 1965 which created Rhodesia. At that time Frank Jackson's contract was modified, in that the Colonial Office had to cut ties with the UDI state. By then, Frank had a mountain of collected information and he and Marika left Salisbury, returning to the La Lucia home and being installed as a professor in anthropology at the University of Natal. Jasper stayed and the title of the rambling mansion was transferred to him. He managed to let out the 6 remaining bedrooms to students to keep the house going. His mother also left him the ownership of the Jewellery Creations business and its assets. This business pretty much became dormant, but he managed to sell off the stock, giving himself a nice nest egg.

It was Friday night and he was with a couple of old school friends, Tom and Tony, in the Park Lane hotel bar. The plan was to down a few beers, move on to have piri-piri chicken at the Coimbra, and then hit the Archipelago nightclub in Baker Avenue. Tom West was from his parent's farm, not far from Salisbury out on the Old Mazoe Road, and was spared the draft because he was a food producer; instead he had to serve in the police divisions.

He was an Inspector in the Intelligence division and was involved mostly in co-ordinating potential contact risks amongst farm workers in the north west sector of Salisbury. Similarly, Tony Chapman, possibly because of being a lawyer, had gone into psych-ops with the police, working out of Karoi, just south of the Kariba/ Zambezi valley area where Jasper himself operated. Their paths crossed occasionally, when JJ was either on his way in and needed the latest information as to the terrorist infiltration or as he ended his tour, being debriefed in Karoi. The boys were joined by another friend, George Smith, who had recently qualified as a doctor, and was about to start as a field surgeon with the RLI on the eastern border with Mozambique. The bar was now getting into full swing with 'squaddies', and sensing the usual Friday night brawl amongst the army men home for R&R was now imminent, the boys left and drove the short distance along Jamieson Avenue, turning right up 7ᵗʰ Street and then left into Selous Avenue to the Coimbra. As always, they sat out in the garden, having starters of Beira prawns before the famous main event of piri-piri chicken. More Castle and Lion beers were needed to mollify palettes and throats after the fiery piri-piri sauce. Well-fortified, Tom, Tony, George, and JJ were now ready for the Archipelago nightclub and its promise of vast female availability which had arisen as a result of the war. This apparent imbalance of ladies to men was not due to any loss of men in combat, but because of the number of men out in the field. Given that the whites were around 4% of the total population, with the menfolk pretty much away for 6 months, it was hardly surprising to find a very high divorce rate. It was great odds for a good night out if you were one of the relatively few men in town. By midnight, maybe slightly afterwards, all the boys were with their favoured belles for the night, so Tom used his rank and influence and 4 constables were delegated to drive the boys four vehicles home to Churchill Avenue for the party to continue. It was empty; being the weekend, JJ's student lodgers were off home for a long weekend and to get fed properly. JJ kept a full time domestic, Rarios, to at least keep the house clean and the garden tidy. He was available to cook up some breakfast later on, but tonight he was sent back to bed until the morning proper.

When JJ woke, his partner had already left, along with Tony's, but had left him a note with her phone number. He and Tony languished in the pool, nurturing a *babelas* (hangover), and both realised they would probably meet in Karoi on Monday, as both were to begin a tour in their respective roles for the security services. As Rarios brought breakfast and much needed tea, they sat on the pool patio under the thatched cover, which seemed to have become home to a bat. Tony told JJ that there had been a recent spike in activity amongst the native TTL's around Karoi. The Tribal Trust Lands were where the terrorists who crossed the Zambezi from Zambia, headed for. There they tried to hide and sustain themselves before moving closer to the nation's capital, mostly by terrorising the local natives in whose name they claimed to operate. Largely they would choose soft targets, such as the more outlying farms. This was not as easy as it may seem as first: the large black workforce resided in villages on the farm with a clinic and a school for the children, and the workers were not keen to lose their employment security and meal ticket. Secondly, the farm "agri-alert" system operated very well; farmers were well-armed and their neighbours could be on site within minutes. Tony reckoned that JJ would have an active time on this tour, as it was clear more infiltrations were taking place. He had heard the team that was in the Mana area had been shot up, with one seriously wounded before his partner managed to return fire and call in support. JJ would no doubt be briefed together with Nkomba on Sunday when he arrived at camp, RLI (Rhodesian Light Infantry) South Salisbury. They would then be further briefed in Karoi as to the latest info on sightings and activities. JJ could not discuss anything about where and when he would be deployed, partly because he was not sure himself and mostly because the fewer people that knew, the safer it was. Tony was not offended. After lunch, the guests left to their respective homes and JJ turned to preparing himself to leave first thing Sunday to the pickup point at Kingsway.

Arriving at the RLI depot before 0800 hours, he went to his section's gym for a session of karate, with an instructor who told him he was slipping and not worthy of his dan status, then on to the armoury where he handed in his personal weapon, a .44 Magnum Special, for an AK 47 assault rifle, the most likely terrorist weapon, a CZ 75 pistol chambered for 9mm ammunition, and a huge 10 inch bowie knife, to which he added a crossbow with about 20 bolts. The rest of his rucksack was filled with a couple of claymore mines. JJ test fired his weapons and cleaned them thoroughly before going to the canteen for lunch. In the briefing room he met up with Nkomba and was brought up to date with Nkomba's family news. They then double checked each other's weapons; Nkomba used the same AK 47 and the CZ 75 pistol, but instead of the crossbow he carried an SVD sniper rifle. Despite the racism, however benevolent, that existed in Rhodesia, none was allowed or tolerated in the Selous Scouts between black scouts and white scouts. The need to trust each other in their activities was absolute, so whilst they were obviously aware of differences in colour and culture, neither considered himself or the other inferior. They were "boets" or brothers. The proud motto of these elite was simple, 'Pamwe Chete' – Together Only. They would bunk together tonight before being helicoptered up to the police compound in Karoi. There would be a final briefing as to the latest sightings or known activity before being dropped off at point X-ray Charlie 483.

Jasper turned to Nkomba and said, "Henry, best we pray to Nyaminyami for his protection." Nkomba nodded.

CHAPTER 4

1982 Osprey and Sophie

Jasper woke in the early light, having slept on the veranda, to what he called a heavy dawn. He heard that particular cry that some say is the call of Africa, the fish eagle. It was a handsome raptor with its distinct white head and neck and an absolute joy to watch as it would swoop down from the sky and seemingly just pick a fish out of the water before flapping its wings to gain height, levelling out to find a suitable perch to eat its spoils. It was October, the first of the two 'suicide' months when the humidity got a whole lot worse before the annual rains. Looking to the north, towards Zambia, he could see a few thunderheads building, so there well could be an odd downpour later, though he thought that unlikely. He jumped into the pool and did a few lengths before getting out. Despite the humidity he was almost dry by the time he walked the few yards back to the villa, and then sweaty again. It must be 30°C already. Apparently, the suicide rate in Zimbabwe trebled in October and November; not surprisingly it would coincide with the brutal weather before the rains came. Kariba had high humidity for most of the year, though it was easier May through to August.

Francis came through excitedly, almost shouting, "Boss, you must come to the radio!"

JJ said, "Calm down, what's the story?"

Francis said it was the airport calling to say that Sophie was en route from Joburg and would be catching the 1000 hrs Harare plane to Kariba. JJ felt his heart booming dammit, he was excited like a schoolboy and thankful he could feel like this. He was at peace with himself, but it was a fragile peace, and he had fought long and hard to keep his demons from pre-independence at bay. Sophie had been a saviour for him, on hand for those nightmares, helping him to control the demons and find his emotions again.

* * *

In 1980, Jasper had to make a decision as to where he would go; whether he would go back to an academic life, joining his parents down in Durban, or make a life in a new nation. The war was lost, and the Nationalists had prevailed, gaining Independence for Zimbabwe on 18th April 1980. Rhodesia was gone. He had escaped any serious physical injuries during the war, only getting a couple of minor flesh wounds, but once he came out of the army, he began to have occasional nightmares, demons in his dreams, disturbing periods when he would remember the senseless brutality of war. Officially, he was army and all records of Selous Scouts were suddenly 'lost' to prevent retribution, but nevertheless several of the well-known majors/colonels were advised to leave the new country. Jasper had not chosen the hierarchical route, despite having it offered; he had chosen to stay in the bush, which was his first love. He had been involved in Operation Eland, which was a pre-emptive raid on a military camp in Mozambique in 1976, but he then remained in the Kariba/Zambezi valley operational areas because of the increasing incursion rate of terrorists. He missed, therefore, the Mozambique raids on Chimoio and Tembue camps, but was involved in the aftermath of both Air Rhodesia Viscounts being shot down shortly after take-off from Kariba in 1978. Though clearly affected by the civilian losses and the mass killings of Operation Eland, Jasper could justify his part as a war between armies. What he could not rationalize was the terrorists' brutality to very people they claimed to be fighting for. The vision of some of the injuries sustained and butchery of overwhelmingly black non-combatants by the terrorists, the grief of these families, seemed to stay with him and torture his sense of fair play. He refused to stomach the bayonetting

24

of babies or their dead bodies being filled with explosives to be carried into towns.

In the euphoria at Independence – or was it relief? – experienced by both black and white citizens, there was a genuine attempt to make the new nation of Zimbabwe work. One of his father's old friends, John H., in the Agricultural Extension Service suggested he might like to join the National Parks as a game ranger. Though tempted, when he relayed this to his mother, she raised the idea of running a safari business. He eventually went to his bank with a plan, but the astute bank manager referred him to a man who was both a jeweller and an influential manager at the Reserve Bank. This gentleman, Toby B., was very supportive and saw a safari business as an excellent option to bring in foreign currency. So, having liquidated his quite considerable assets, and with the help of Toby B., John H., and his local bank manager, Jasper ended up as the proud owner of a new safari business and the tenant of a 240 acre lot on the lake shore in Charara game reserve. 1981 was all about getting buildings erected, facilities prepared, and establishing concessions. He had bought the Osprey in South Africa, or rather, his mother bought it for him. It was a 40 foot cruiser powered by twin Thornycroft Cummins diesel engines, luxuriously appointed with 2 separate cabins with double berths, a lounge/dinette area, twin heads, a holding tank, heating, battery chargers, an inverter, shore power, hot and cold water, a separate shower, a galley with a fridge, freezer and microwave, a twin helm with full instrumentation, a fish finder, radar, an echo sounder, a brand new sat nav, vhf, and autopilot. There was a small river boat with a 60hp Mercury motor which was tender to the cruiser. He managed to get a couple of refurbished ex-army Land Rovers locally, plus a second hand Toyota Cruiser and a Toyota 4WD bakkie, both from South Africa. Having got the villa and three rondavels built, Osprey Safaris was born, taking up to 6 guests on 5 day fishing safaris on the lake. Each safari was accompanied by a trip around Kariba town, the dam wall and the chapel built by the Italians during the construction of the dam. By the end of 1981, Jasper was in business, with a full schedule.

He sometimes went to one of the hotels, the Caribbea Bay at Kariba, to meet some drinking buddies. It was here that he met Sophie, an emergency medicine nurse, who was on holiday from New Zealand. She had finished a correspondence business management course and stayed on. She was taken on initially as a receptionist who helped to manage the bars and restaurant. She was a pretty girl, brunette with a ponytail, about five feet two inches tall, with a lively and bubbly nature. Sophie was more than capable of fending off the usual blunt attentions characteristic of young men away from home without making them feel spurned, but pity help you if she heard you refer to her as a 'crow', an unfortunate epithet, not necessarily derogatory, but sometimes used by the Rhodie male. They met one evening when she was trying to calm down an irate, slightly drunk guest who was complaining that his air conditioner was squeaking, making it impossible to sleep. It was far too hot to try to sleep without it. Despite the assurances Sophie was trying to give him that she would get the engineer to come and have a look, the guest was having none of it.

Jasper had a good idea what the problem might be, having experienced it several times himself, so he went over and said, "Good evening, I am an on-call engineer, what seems to be the problem?"

Sophie looked at him curiously, took onboard his wink and began to explain. The guest immediately butted in, "At last, someone local who will understand me, the bloody air-con is squeaking."

Jasper quickly asked, "Is this a regular or intermittent squeak, sir?"

"It's bloody both, going on and on then it stops for a minute, then starts all over again."

Jasper asked if he could have the guest's key and a couple of minutes, to which the guest simply said "Be my guest." He allowed himself to be steered to a chair and accepted a cold beer. Jasper asked Sophie under his breath for a can of fly-spray, and off he went. He was back in five minutes, pronounced the problem solved and invited the guest to come and check. All was well, and when he came back to reception, Sophie asked politely if he had killed the guest and hoped he had disposed of the body.

Jasper laughed for the first time in a while and with a smile said, "Very often cicadas will come into rooms and hide below the freestanding air-con units. Unfortunately, they don't move out easily and you have to spray under and around the unit."

"Well," she said, "thank you for your help, I owe you one."

Very quickly Jasper said, "Only a pleasure, can I take you out for some dinner?"

He had already been struck by the arrow, and Sophie, sensing he was no fly by night, surprisingly for her, agreed and said, "I'm off in 15 minutes. I'll meet you here in half an hour."

The next 30 minutes were hellish for Jasper. He was actually more nervous than he had ever been on ops, thinking she was only being nice to him and she wouldn't show up. Then suddenly she was there, smiling radiantly like an angel.

"Right I'm ready, where to in this one-horse town?"

She linked her arm with his and off they went to the car park and got into his cruiser with its Osprey logo. There were not many options in Kariba, so he decided to go over to the Lake View, which had a decent restaurant. As they were walking from the car park into the hotel, both realised they did not know each other's names.

Sophie nearly embarrassed him unknowingly as she jokingly said, "What's your name, because I should not be out for dinner with you let alone kiss you if we are not introduced? My name is Sophie Mitchieson from Auckland, North Island, Aotearoa, that's New Zealand to you."

He shot back "'The Land of the Long White Cloud.' My name is Jasper Jackson of ..." he thought for a moment, "... Southern Africa."

She said, "Aren't you the mystery man, but I shall beguile you," in a mock German voice. They both laughed and went into the restaurant. They probably fell in love with each other in the next hour, and she had told him all about herself and noticed that, whilst he talked freely about his parents, school and his baby Osprey Safaris, he spoke little about his army days. She didn't mind; she sensed there were some demons there and he would tell her in time.

As they left, she took his arm, cuddled into him and said, "Take me home." He took her back to the Caribbea, where he presumed she would have accommodation, but as he turned in to the hotel, she said, "No, silly, I want to see your home."

He pulled up sharply and looked at her. "It's dark, so you won't see anything, and anyway what about work in the morning?" He knew he was dithering, but he didn't want to spoil the very new relationship; his mind was made up, something like full speed ahead and damn the torpedoes. He banged the Land Cruiser in reverse and then pulled out, turning for home.

She laughed and said, "I have a day off tomorrow anyway."

On arrival, he started the generator, then switched on the lights and pulled a good South African wine out of the cooler and sat on the veranda with Sophie. They toasted each other and gazed out over the lake looking at the kapenta fishing boats and their lamps. Francis appeared out of nowhere, wanting to know if he was needed, but was firmly sent back to bed. The wine was nearly finished, though neither of them was feeling the alcohol, and without a word they went to Jasper's bedroom. They came together quite naturally and made passionate uninhibited love to each other, as if they were old lovers. They awakened passions in each other they never knew they had. Afterwards they lay exhausted and both fell into a wonderful sleep; for Jasper, his first in a long time without his demons. And that was that; Sophie had moved in and simply stayed, quickly winning over Francis and his family, and was immediately in charge of the meeting and greeting, bookings, and supplies. She also turned out to be a quick learner as to the flora and fauna and was very skilled at finding the best area for tigerfish as the year moved on, wearing its various cloaks. She took and passed her boat captaincy exams, becoming an extremely skilful handler of the boat.

★ ★ ★

Jasper was at the airport early and watched the plane come in. Sophie came down the steps, waving to him and running across the tarmac to literally jump into his arms, showering him with kisses. As he came up for air, he managed to say he had deeply missed her and was grateful and delighted to have her back, even though she was supposed to be another week away. As they waited for her bags to get to the baggage shed, she confessed she loved seeing Auckland, her parents, and her old friends, but after nearly three weeks she knew she had to get back to Jasper. The bags came and the porter loaded them into the back of the bakkie, and they set off back to Osprey.

On the way she told him she had she had spoken with friends in the travel business in Auckland, and they were keen to advertise on their behalf. He smiled and thought, we are busy enough anyway, but that was Sophie, always looking for ways to expand the business. As they entered the Osprey Compound, she saw the pleasure in his eyes as he watched two bateleur eagles playing chicken. The strikingly colourful raptors, with their distinct tail shapes, would climb to a fair height and then lock talons, spinning whilst falling back to earth, seemingly oblivious to the up-rushing ground before disengaging just in time. Francis and his wife were on hand to greet her and she quickly dug in her bags for the gifts she had bought for them.

After lunch Sophie disappeared into the office and groaned, seeing that very little filing had been done, though the blackboard did at least have bookings chalked in for both the canoe and the Osprey safaris, linked to the arrival times at the airport of guests. It took an hour to match up the info on the board with the little cards she had specially designed for the purpose. There was a few thousand ZWD and a few US dollars in the safe waiting to be banked and credited, which was unusual as mostly the safaris were paid for in advance by international bank transfers. Still, all in all the office was in reasonable shape. She then got Jasper and did an inventory check, noting that they would need to restock the freezers with food for the guests, and that the imported wines were fine but they would need beers and some soft drinks and mixers shortly. Sophie radioed through orders to their various suppliers; most were in Kariba, but the beers meant contacting Delta in Harare for the Castle and Lion beers, as well as the mixers and soft drinks. Spirits came from African Distillers at Stapleford, just outside Harare on the Churundu/Kariba road. Due to the tight foreign currency restrictions, most spirits in Zimbabwe were based on the local white spirit distilled from sugar known as cane spirit. Even whisky was 'adulterated' in that it was imported as 120 proof rebate and diluted with cane spirit and water down to 70 proof. It was now whiskey. The locals had long since found out the end product could be improved vastly by taking 2 measures out of the bottle and replacing it with sherry. You could at least pretend it was Scotch; it was actually drinkable. After two or three tots no-one really cared. Fortunately, Jasper could use his half of retained forex to import wine and whisky, or anything else, so Joburg's discount liquor stores would rail orders to Harare, which then would be delivered via Delta for final delivery to Osprey.

In 1982, largely due to Sophie's persistence, she pushed Osprey into the wider business of canoeing down the Zambezi to Mana Pools, which at first was very much full participation by guests, paddling down, carrying all their needs with them, and basic camping on the river banks. Jasper handled these trips whilst Sophie oversaw the fishing safaris. It was not long until they both realised that the canoeing safari was really only for the young adventurers, usually backpackers, so it was a limited market at the lower end of the chargeable scale. As they understood this, it became clear they should change this limited market for another for which they could charge top dollar. They would start a high-class safari, using motorised canoes to ease the paddling, and provide quality mobile camps with proper toilets, albeit chemical, and showers with good catering. All the guests would have to do was slightly exert themselves in the canoes if they wished, take photographs, fish a little, and generally learn about their environment or simply drink in the magnificence of the ambiance where life battled with nature every day. However, this would also necessitate having to find another guide, a tracker who could look after the guests, who may not always recognise the dangers of the bush. They had been lucky to find Henry, whose qualities as a tracker and bush fundi were without question, as Jasper well knew from their many ops together.

CHAPTER 5

Changing Lives, early Eighties

The problem was how to find one black man amongst an estimated 8 million – and one who would have had an incentive to keep his background in the war and tribal culture concealed. Certainly, amongst the remaining white population, which had fallen from its peak of nearly 300,000 in 1975 to an estimated 180,000 with Independence, most people knew of each other or had common acquaintances, so there was a lively 'gossip' line established throughout the country. At Sophie's urging, Jasper began to track down other ex-Selous Scouts. This was not easy as most, like Jasper himself, did not advertise themselves as having been elite troops. The same anonymity had been applied to the black Selous Scouts, for not only had they had fought for the defeated side, but Henry was also of the minority tribe. Jasper was not getting anywhere and began to talk a little of his past to Sophie. She immediately understood and assumed that his service in the Scouts had damaged him, but it was late into the night before she realised that it was the death of non-combatants at the hands of their so called brothers that inflamed her man's demons. She did have one bright idea though. It was common knowledge that most 'unwanted' white ex-army men took the hint and went to South Africa, so she suggested that maybe Jasper's mum might know someone in S.A. As it happened, Marika, through her family, did know of some ex-Rhodies who were reputed to have left as soon as it was definite that Black Independence would prevail, and there were allegedly some Scouts amongst them. Eventually Marika got a name of a black ex-officer from the scouts, who had to flee and had set up a sort of support agency for black ex-Scouts in Johannesburg.

Anticipating that, at some point, the authorities in Zimbabwe would cut off legal holding of multiple passports, Jasper had pushed ahead using his connections to change his South African passport for a Zimbabwe passport, though he was entitled to British and South African documents as well. His reasoning was that if he was to stay in Zimbabwe, he would be better off having that country's passport and citizenship for business purposes, especially the use of foreign currency. He would always have the fall-back position of being entitled to a South African passport by birth and a British one through his father. Indeed, he already held both anyway, though both were unused and actually kept in South Africa with his parents. Strangely, he first found that a Greek friend was able to get him an identity disc as a favour. Then, through a rare local client on a fishing safari who happened to 'know' another friend who knew someone in the citizenship office, Jasper duly took the oath of citizenship in the capital, which by now had changed its name from Salisbury to Harare. It was still known as Bambazonke by the people of Bulawayo, who thought it best described the attitudes of greedy 'take it all' Salisbury peoples. Bulawayo had been the first and main city in the days of Cecil John Rhodes, and the residents of Bulawayo still thought they were the nation's 'main men'. Unfortunately, even among the black population, the Ndebele did not have a favourable view of the dominant tribe, the Shona, and consequently, Bulawayo had to suck the hind tit. Having citizenship, Jasper put the old boys' network to further use and fast tracked a Zimbabwean passport, having parted with a little cash in the process. Once he had got this, he and Sophie went to the capital and Liquenda House in Baker Street, which was the headquarters of immigration, to extend Sophie's work permit for another 2 years, Osprey becoming her guarantor. This was relatively easy because she was a qualified nurse in New Zealand, and it was accepted by the immigration that this was a good thing in the safari business, particularly with the Department of Wildlife and Tourism's recommendation.

This whole exercise however became irrelevant when, outside the lobby of Liquenda House, Jasper, taken by the more impulsive nature of his youth, blurted out, "Listen, since you are going to stay, why don't we make it official?"

Sophie looked at him, and for a moment he thought the worst, before she said, "Jasper Jackson, if that is a proposal, I would have said yes that first night, but I knew you had to be sure yourself and ready. Now I believe you are, and in spite of your extremely romantic proposal, of course I'll accept, kind sir. It saves me having to ask."

He whooped with joy, picked her up, kissed her and swung her round and round, saying, "If you had asked that night, I would have said yes!"

They came back to earth realizing they had attracted an audience, who were clapping, having guessed what had transpired. Jasper knew he was blushing, but nevertheless bowed to the group and holding Sophie by the hand as if he was presenting her, announced, "Ladies and gentlemen, the future Mrs Jackson."

And that was that. He took her immediately along to Tony Chapman's offices in Third Street, and as luck would have it Tony was free, so he introduced Sophie, told Tony to get a quick wedding arranged, made the necessary changes to his will, and made Sophie an equal partner in Osprey. The boat was round at Kariba harbour undergoing its annual refit for the next two weeks, so a quick call was made to Francis to tell him they would not be back until next week. Tony was still a bachelor with a live-in girlfriend, and insisted Sophie and Jasper stayed with him and Chrissie in their home in Mount Pleasant. Chrissie came to the office and took the lovebirds home whilst Tony called in a few favours and managed to get a licence to marry in 3 days' time.

When he got home and said that Friday would be the earliest, Chrissie swung into gear, said, "We'll make a plan." Sophie would need to shop for outfits tomorrow, and Chrissie rang George at home to see if he could do the necessary blood test first thing, because Jasper would need to fly back up to Kariba tomorrow, collect some things for Sophie and himself, including birth certificates, his citizenship documents and his passport. They already had Sophie's, because of their earlier visit to the Department of Immigration. Since it was high time his parents met Sophie, he would have to get a visa from the South African Trade Mission just off Second Street, as he would use his Zimbabwean passport. It also would let him go and meet the ex-Selous Scout officer in Joburg without any questions regarding his visit to the R.S.A. Officially, Zimbabwe and the R.S.A were unhappy neighbours, with a lot of anti-R.S.A rhetoric in Zimbabwe, but between being landlocked and Mozambique in its own civil war, Zimbabwe had no option but to trade both directly and indirectly with the 'enemy'. The flights, first to Durban on Sunday, then up to Joburg and back to Harare before Friday evening, had also to be booked, but Tony's office would be able to do all the grunt work. They could be back to Kariba on the Saturday. He would have to go to New Zealand to see her parents, but that would have to be later. Sophie made it a condition that when in New Zealand, they must sort of renew their vows so that her parents would accept missing their daughter's marriage. Fair play!

* * *

Tony's people at the office had organised all the arrangements for the wedding and the flights. Chrissie sorted Sophie out, the 'blushing bride' in the smartest peach suit that Barbours could provide, plus all the accessories needed, including a hat with a feather. In front of the registrar, Jasper and Sophie exchanged the rings bought that day and became Mr and Mrs Jackson, sealed with a kiss and duly witnessed by Tony and Chrissie. Friday night was spent in the very best accommodation Harare could offer, namely the Meikles Hotel, and its Bagatelle Restaurant. Tony and Chrissie, Tom, and even George made it, with their partners and another of their friends who happened to be down from Zambia, Jonty Westhuizen and his wife Paddy, who had both mirrored Jasper and his twin, Jade, in being schooled in the Convent and St. George's, though in different years. Eventually Jonty took over the family farm in what had been Northern Rhodesia now Zambia. Funnily enough, Jonty's father had once been 'asked to leave' the Meikles, when he was in a group of wild men in from the country who all brought their mules into the lobby and organised races jumping over the reception area's couches and tables, whilst people were taking afternoon tea. This had not been considered proper behaviour, especially in the 30s. There was much partying, with Sophie the centre of attention from the prying gang. They kept the resident pianist going with requests for old tunes, and the rest of the diners joined in and partied with them. If it had been a quiet wedding, the reception turned out to be a grand affair, as more and more people joined in completely spontaneously. A kitty was started and the party continued well into the early hours, long past when the original group left for home, Jasper and Sophie to their room in the hotel.

Saturday morning was spent walking along by the flower sellers under the jacaranda trees on the bottom side of Cecil Square, and along to First Street, along Jamieson and crossing over to find the park behind the Monomatapa hotel. They had a light lunch in Sherol's and strolled leisurely, hand in hand, back to the Meikles, where they found Jonty and Paddy waiting for them. They were also staying the night at Meikles before driving back to Zambia on Sunday. Jonty had organised a table at Escargot, the exclusive restaurant in the Courteney Hotel, and insisted that Jasper and Sophie must join him and Paddy in the evening. Jasper and Sophie were driven round by Jonty and Paddy and they were shown to a secluded corner table. Jonty was obviously well known in the restaurant and he was offered prawns from Beira, certainly not on the menu, and Kingklip, a prized sea-fish and usually unavailable outside of South Africa.

Their flight was took off at 1105. The plane was half full and would fly across Mozambique until it reached the Indian Ocean, turn right and fly down the coastline to Durban and its Louis Botha airport. Over Mozambique they hit turbulence, and though they were warned to sit and belt up, there were many hijinks, trying to keep a drink in its glass, having to raise arms to the fullest, such was the scale of sudden drops in altitude. It lasted for about ten minutes, and the rest of the flight was smooth enough. As they were following the coastline and had begun their descent, the captain reported that there were whales down below, and despite their height it was possible to distinguish their shapes. A few minutes later Jasper pointed out the window to La Lucia where his parents lived. Then they went past the city and airport did a 'u-ee' over Amanzimtoti, coming into Durban's single runway from the south.

Jasper and Sophie went through Immigration and Customs and were met by Marika and Frank. They instantly took to Sophie, having really only spoken on the phone previously, though they were well aware of their son's relationship. Now all was in order and they could look forward to having grandchildren. Frank led them outside, where their driver/gardener was waiting with the Merc, and they soon headed north up the M4 coastal road, over the Umgeni River, past the Mangrove Reserve and into La Lucia and the family plot. It was several acres, dominated by a sprawling hacienda-type house, which had a superb view of the ocean. Marika's parents had bought the plot and house many years ago, and it was their wedding present to Marika. Frank had become very much the absent-minded professor type, being totally wrapped up in his books, and wanted to quiz Jasper on some of the cultural rituals of the Zambezi valley, so it was some time after dinner before Jasper was able to talk to his mother about what she had found out about the Selous support group.

CHAPTER 6

1982 Henry

Marika had used her family's not inconsiderable clout to find the support group. There was a hard-core group of white ex-Rhodesian SAS and Selous Scouts who settled around Durban; indeed some were involved in Colonel 'Mad Mike' Hoare's 1981 attempted coup in the Seychelles. From them came the information that a Captain Mzembi ran a support service for black ex-Selous Scouts, and eventually Marika made contact. She told Mzembi who her son was, and that he was looking for his partner, Henry Nkomba, with whom he had done ops in the Zambezi valley 1972 onwards. After some time, she received a phone call from one of the white ex-Scouts to phone a Joburg number at a given time. When she did, she spoke to an African, who confirmed she was Jasper's mother and then told her that they could help, but only through Jasper himself. He gave her a number to ring when she would have an idea of when a meet could be arranged. So it was agreed that Jasper would meet with whoever this person was on their way home on the Friday, then they would take the 0910 flight to Joburg and then the 1830 flight to Harare, stay over with Tony and fly up to Kariba at 1000hrs. Jasper would be contacted in Durban with details of the meet.

So, the happy couple had four days to spend with his parents, who were delighted to have that time, particularly with their new daughter-in-law. Marika got Sophie's parents on the telephone, reasonably easy from South Africa, and let her tell them of the wedding, before spending some time making friends with her new in-laws. Then it was off to La Lucia Mall to do some exclusive shopping, particularly for lingerie, which was much more difficult in Harare and impossible in Kariba. Jasper went with his

Dad to the University to meet his Dad's friends and chat about the Zambezi valley people. Both Sophie and Jasper gorged themselves on fresh sea fish, Maputo prawns, and lobster, all things that were extremely irregularly obtainable in Zimbabwe. They also took the opportunity to check out more wines, so that they would be able to improve their Osprey selections.

A man whom Jasper thought he knew arrived and who asked bluntly a few details about Wafa Wafa camp, and in particular about things that only a Selous Scout would know. In other words, he was being checked out to confirm he was who he claimed. Suddenly he remembered having seen the man in the RLI camp, South Salisbury, in the armoury.

"I wondered if you would remember me, not that it was essential, because I remembered you and your crossbow." He gave his name as Monty and gave Jasper an address for him to go to when he went to Joburg.

Thursday arrived, Marika took them up to Bothas Hill to a craft centre, overlooking part of the Valley of a Thousand Hills, for a homestyle lunch at the restaurant there, the Pot and Kettle. Jasper was glad that they would be on the move tomorrow, for he had been here long enough. He loved his parents dearly, but it was time to go.

The next morning they left early to catch the nine o'clock plane to Joburg. Jasper was a little concerned that he had not heard from Jonty, but he need not have been. As he checked in the girl behind the desk returned their tickets and boarding passes with an envelope. Once on the plane he opened it. With Sophie peering over his shoulder he read the single line, "You will be met." Jasper became a little nervous; he had intended to deposit Sophie in the airport and go alone, because he did not want to introduce her to any risks: after all, Joburg did have a reputation as a violent city. They took off at 0915 and landed in Joburg at 1000, dropped off in a bustling domestic terminal. As they came out the taxi drivers began shouting for business, some holding placards with names on. Then he spotted his man, carrying "JJ". He nodded and as they exited the building the man took their cases.

Just as Jasper was about to say he wanted to leave Sophie at the airport, the man said in Shona, "Missie will be safer with us, and you will be brought back in time for your flight to Harare."

They drove out of the car park and in the direction of the central suburbs, eventually turning towards Hillbrow and finally heading into Berea and Soper Road. The driver stopped at the Casa Mia and took them up to the third floor and into an apartment there. Once inside, a pleasant lady introduced herself as Priscilla and announced that the captain would be here presently; in the meantime, would they both like coffee and a biscuit?

Within 5 minutes a man walked in and said to Jasper, "What was your number?"

"84910070602," Jasper replied.

The man put out his hand, smiled and said, "Mangwanani, I'm Mzembi," whilst shaking his hand.

"Mangwanani, marara sei," replied Jasper.

"Now then young man, may I congratulate you on your marriage and very lovely wife. You make sure you make a good go of your safari company." He paused, then said, "I do not wish to be rude; your wife will be safe here with Priscilla whilst we go through to my office."

They went through into a small room. Mzembi motioned for Jasper to sit down and proceeded to tell him that Henry was indeed alive, but before they could meet he would need to know why Jasper wanted to contact him, and then it would remain Henry's decision whether to meet or allow contact.

Before Mzembi let Jasper speak, he asked, "Tell me, what was your remark to Henry each time you were deployed to the Zambezi valley?"

Jasper smiled and replied, "Asking for Nyaminyami's protection."

Mzembi relaxed and apologised, saying, "I know you would be aware that we have checked you out as far as possible – you would not have got to meet me otherwise – but you appreciate that given who we were, we must be absolutely sure of you, as well as protecting Henry's past. Now why do you want to contact Henry?"

Jasper gathered himself and said, "We are expanding our Safari business to include a luxury canoeing arm, Kariba to Mana, and I simply need someone who knows that area, and, above all, that I can trust. My wife has become extremely proficient in running the lake fishing and she can take clients herself, but the river run is a different story, different skills needed. I want Henry to come to Osprey Safaris, firstly to help me set the operation up and then to run it in my absence. I have a decent lodge set up, room for accommodation for his family, and work in terms of looking after guests. We are building more guests' rondavels for accommodation, so our safari camp can handle 6 clients for the canoe trips in addition to the boat business. I need Henry, and I am prepared to offer a partnership in the new business, at least. Sophie will keep the books and diaries, but the running of the canoes, overnight stops, mobile camps will be down to him. If he wants to work with me again and can cope, then he would get a half share in that side."

Mzembi leaned back and said, "I shall convey your offer to Henry through our people, and now we have to agree how we let you have his answer. I suggest we use your Kariba telex service for making enquiries from potential SA clients. We will give a text that will include the number in the party, available dates and where they want to be collected from. You would need to confirm, of course, but give us two days to get your offer to Henry and remember we need that two day time to relay messages. Agreed?"

Jasper nodded, and that was that. He did not realise they had chatted for over an hour; it was now well into lunchtime and it seemed the obvious thing to ask Mzembi if he would join them.

Mzembi said, "We are not in Zimbabwe and this is not the Scouts; we would attract attention if we lunched, and I am sure that you would understand I cannot be spotlighted down here, but thanks anyway. You can use the driver this afternoon and he will deliver you back to the airport for this evening's flight. It's been a pleasure to meet you."

And with that he was gone. Jasper re-joined Sophie, who had idly chatted with Priscilla and compared notes as to what was the latest office gadgetry available. The driver took them to Eastgate Mall by Bedfordview, then on to the Boat Centre in Kempton Park to pick up some previously ordered spares for the boat and order half a dozen 12HP motors, suitable for mounting on the three modified Canadian aluminium canoes already ordered. These would use up half of last year's earnings but would return all of that within the next year. Then back to the airport, and they landed 5 minutes early in Harare. Tony picked them up for the night and then took them back to the airport for the 1000 flight to Kariba.

* * *

Two weeks later, Jasper and his team of workers had finished a basic 3 bedroom brick and timber cottage with ABR roofing a little way behind the villa and connected it to the generator supply so that the lights, ceiling fans, and fridge could work. He hoped Henry would occupy it, but it would be needed whoever came. He saw Sophie returning from her morning run to the Post Office and wandered over to meet her to see what the mail had brought. Sophie immediately said the telex had arrived. He read it:

"Rates agreed, 4 pickup Mlibizi suggest 25 or 2."

Sophie knew it was a full day's cruise to Mlibizi, the other end of the lake, certainly 18hrs anyway. The 25th was this weekend, four days away. She said, "I have a charter on the 28th which would go on to the 1st, so that would be a squeeze. We should go this Friday."

Jasper agreed, musing on why Henry chose Mlibizi; true, he was a Matabele, and it was therefore most likely he would come from there, or at least that side of the country, but he must know what I am doing, where I am and that I have the boat.

He said to Sophie, "I should not be surprised, really, but he obviously knows what we do and that we have the boat. I wonder how much more the grapevine knows. I do hope Henry is not wanted by or known to the authorities, otherwise I cannot use him."

Sophie said quietly, "You won't know till you see him. Shall I confirm?"

He nodded, "For sure."

On Friday morning he got the boys to load some food and meat onto the Osprey while Sophie explained to Francis that they were going to check out fishing spots past Binga, so they might not be back till Monday. She left a list of jobs that Francis would have to get the boys to do in her and the boss' absence.

"Don't you worry, Madam, Francis will sort it out." He had taken to calling her Madam from the moment he was told of their marriage; previously she was Miss Sophie.

The boat was loaded and off they headed, with Jasper at the helm to keep his hand in, since he rarely did this nowadays. He had stowed his hunting rifle and his pistol in the appropriate locker, partly as a safety measure and partly out of habit, noticing Sophie had already stowed her revolver. They were licensed to carry arms for protection of their clients when out in the bush. They did not want any captain or crewmen on this trip; Sophie was a captain anyway, and more into the fishing safaris, so she pulled out the charts he would need and climbed on the top deck to read her book. He took the boat first into Marineland just before the main Kariba harbour, to fill up with diesel and water and to advise the harbourmaster that he was intending to check out fishing spots the other side of Bumi. They then got underway, passed Rhino Island, and 4 hours later were approaching Bumi, passing the Umi river and the magnificent backdrop of the Matsuadona mountains. The Bumi promontory had the high-reputed Bumi Hills lodge on top overlooking the lake, and had excellent views of the cluster of islands around Bumi and of the game and birds, but of course they were competitors to Osprey; Jasper could only hope Osprey would build as good an international reputation as them.

Sophie brought up some sandwiches and fruit and took over the wheel for a bit. As they were going through the Kota Kota narrows and into the wider Sengwa basin, she began looking the charts with a mind to find a suitable 'posi' before it got dark. Out here darkness would fall very quickly and be an all-enveloping cloak. Already the sun was low and almost hurrying, flooding the sky with a heavenly orange-red colour. They were alongside the Chete safari area and headed slowly towards shore to find a little posi where they could tie up. They found one big enough and proceeded to lay up for the night. A couple of others, also looking for posis, went by and shouted across "Howzit," waved and then were gone. As night fell Jasper started the small onboard generator for lighting, and despite the hum he could hear at least two others, probably just a couple of hundred metres away. He prepared the braai whilst Sophie put together a green salad and made a dressing with oil, mustard, vinegar, and garlic. They ate simple, steak and salad, washing it down with cold beers. They sat on the top deck, having put the insect repellent on each other; they were still at the touchy-feely stage of their relationship.

Turning the generator off, they went to bed on the top deck under the stars and a mosquito net. Shortly their neighbours switched off their 'gennies' and silence seemed to fall. Of course, this was an illusion, as the sounds of the night took over though in a tranquil manner. Even the mournful muted roars of a lion, probably as far as five miles away, was peaceful in a way, but death did move through the animal world at night. They lay on a mattress with a sheet and blanket over them while marvelling at the display above them. They spotted the flashing lights of international aeroplanes on their nightly runs from Johannesburg to Europe and even the constant light of an orbiting satellite – surely it was not spying on them with high resolution cameras. They must have drifted off to sleep when they were suddenly startled by an onrushing sound which suddenly stopped; a hippo had been running from a chasing hippo and happened to leap into their posi before realising there was a boat in it. Almost one and a half tons of animal, twisting in mid jump and then landing alongside the boat with a grunt and a massive splash; the Osprey rocked and a badly shaken Sophie, clutching onto Jasper, said, "What the hell was that?"

"Just your local hippo being seen off by the owner of this patch, he didn't expect a boat in his way for sure. Did you know that if you light a fire on a hippo's run, he will come stamp it out?" He sounded so matter of fact that Sophie clouted him and turned over.

Where nightfall is quick and brutal, the morning is a much more gentle affair, with the dawn softly increasing, getting into all the nooks and crannies chasing the night first, then the shadows left, until everything is bathed in warm bright light. As Sophie woke, she realised the boat was already backing out of the posi and beginning to move away from the land, gathering speed so that the rush of air provided a welcome freshness. Jasper called her to get her camera, cutting the engines, and pointed out in the early light towards the shore. She looked and looked and then saw three lionesses attacking a buffalo maybe 80 yards from a small herd of buffalo. One was on the buff's back and one on her throat, and when the third cat jumped up from the side onto her she finally fell, and she would not be getting up again. Sophie could not understand how the rest of the herd did not attack, but Jasper told her that particular buff was either old or ailing. Indeed, through the binoculars Sophie could see the animal was not in great condition. Now she could see the male lion trotting to the kill to claim the first meal, and then a lioness bringing the cubs out to get their share when the big boy was finished. She gently punched Jasper and said she would not stand back from her kills to let an idle man eat first.

He quickly shot back, "I'm not idle, I'm driving the boat, but you are; anyway, the lion probably asked his girls to go get him breakfast."

"All right, what do you want, an egg and bacon roll with coffee?"

"That would be perfect if we had any rolls."

Off she went, but first to shower and change, only then she ducked into the galley and prepared bacon and egg sandwiches – there were no rolls – and coffee. She also found some biltong and brought that up to the cabin as well. She got the charts for the Chete Gorge as they were about to enter and took over the helm. She had not sailed this bit before, so she turned on the echo sounder and the radar. There was a slight sense of foreboding as the Gorge narrowed to less than 400 yards. A few minutes later they were out of the Gorge and back in open water and heading for Binga. It was getting on for 4 pm when she manoeuvred the

Osprey into the fuel jetty at Mlibizi, topped up their tanks, and announced their arrival to the harbour authorities. They then parked the boat paying the fees for a one-night stopover. Jasper left Sophie to complete the log and went to the store to buy some mealie meal and bolo meat, which would be preferred by Henry and his family if they had come. He and Sophie prepared their own meal early, not knowing when or if Henry would turn up, but Jasper put a potjie on the braai and made a stew with the bolo meat, cabbage potato, carrot and onions and began to make sadza, slowly stirring mealie meal into salted water whilst constantly beating it, adding more meal until he had a stiff thick porridge. He put it aside to keep warm. Night had fallen and sure enough, just as Jasper expected, he heard what to most people would sound like some sort of animal or bird. He began to make a series of clicks and similar sounds which, at first, astonished Sophie, before she realised that Henry must be around and indeed, they were 'talking' to each other.

Suddenly a small man appeared on the jetty alongside them. Jasper said "Lotmjani," and Henry jumped onboard. The two embraced and laughed. Henry looked at Sophie and greeted her as Madam JJ, and said she looked to be worth many cows in lobola. She was not offended having been long enough in Zimbabwe to understand marriage price or lobola and that cattle were a tribesman's real worth. Sophie turned away and got some cold beers, opening them using the leverage technique of one cap on another, and discreetly moved to the bridge. It must have been an hour or more later when a woman with a young boy and a younger girl suddenly came on to the jetty, at which point both Jasper and Henry got up and helped them onboard. Jasper said Henry and his family were going to eat and had agreed to return with them tomorrow to Charara. He would develop the Kariba-Mana run with Henry. And so young Patrick and Olivia, Pauline and Henry became part of the Osprey adventure. They ate the sadza and relish Jasper had prepared, and the children, though uncommunicative, gratefully accepted some chocolate that Sophie had found. They and her mother were bedded down in the lounge area of the boat, which did have the back open to the rear deck so there was some cooling. Henry would join them later, but for now he sat up on the top deck with Jasper and Sophie for some more beer. When he left, the couple were able to lay out their mattress and get some sleep.

It was about 0430, with the first light beginning to paint its picture, that Sophie took the Osprey out of Mlibizi and set a course for the Chete Gorge. The children looked on in amazement as they saw who was driving and started to scamper about gleefully, until Sophie, with Henry's help, got them to put on the smallest lifejackets she had in the lockers. Jasper brought coffee and bacon and egg sandwiches and took to showing Henry round the boat before coming up to the bridge so that Sophie could take part in their discussions about the canoeing side. She was delighted that Henry had been one of the guides taking clients game viewing and on overnight camps from Kanzangula on the Botswana border to Victoria Falls. That meant he knew about client care already, and all that had to be done to make clients happy. As a bonus, it turned out that Pauline had been employed as a kitchen and chambermaid at the Victoria Falls Hotel, so that was perfect in regards to maintaining the Rondavels. Sophie knew now that Jasper and her dream of becoming the best safari camp operators in Southern Africa was more than possible. She opened up the engines, only slowing for Chete and the Kota Narrows, when Jasper took over and got them to Bumi by late afternoon. He asked if they should find somewhere for the night, but Sophie was on really familiar ground now, so she chose to run for home. She took back the helm and slowed as it did get dark, but they still made it back to Osprey's home in Charara by 2000. Still, it was late by the time they managed to eat and get Henry and his family settled into their building before getting to their own bed. Sophie would only have tomorrow to restock the boat and prepare for her charter on the Tuesday; she would have to let their normal captain, Barnabas, take the party out as she would be needed to keep Jasper and Henry on track. And so, Henry joined Osprey Safaris, noting immediately the significance of the name.

* * *

The next morning after breakfast, Jasper and Henry went on foot around the plot that was Osprey Safaris, leaving Sophie to get on with organising the Osprey for the imminent safari. She began planning with Barnabas for the four-day trip; where he would go so that the six people would get the best of fishing and game viewing photography, what the menus would be, drinks stocks, and all the no-noes as to whatever the clients might want to do. Meanwhile Jasper showed Henry how they had tried to protect the plot from any marauding animals, mostly buffalo and elephant, by planting a mixture of lekkerpeul, acacia and bougainvillea in a double row with a trench in between. Not a guarantee by any means, but mostly enough to put off the elephant and the buff sufficiently to go elsewhere. The most frequent marauders tended to be baboons, but by shooting a few every so often, the wild pawpaws and the workers' maize went largely untouched. The local crocodile farm was always grateful for dead baboons to use as feed. Though no local villager or tourist would agree, the WWF had persuaded Africa that the 'nilus crocodilus' was endangered and that actually killing them was a no-no. The tourists had unfortunately contributed to the dangers of crocs by dumping their rubbish overboard from their houseboats. The crocs soon learnt to associate the big, double-decker, slow houseboats with easy food sources. Crocodile farms, like the Kariba one, were allowed to collect eggs from the wild and hatch them on the condition that they released 5% of their collection back into the wild as 12-month-old stock. So, from an approximate 1% survival rate in the wild, now there was an almost 100% survival of the 5% put back as year-old crocodiles. A further 10-year moratorium on hunting recently meant that crocodiles or 'flatdogs' were once again becoming a problem for villagers, with or without livestock. Jasper was not above doing favours for the local chiefs with the troublesome flat-dogs, shooting those too close to villages. The statistics rarely showed that crocs killed up to 4 people a week around the lake, simply because there were never any remains found, unlike a death by buffalo, for instance.

Jasper then took Henry out into the local game area, Charara Safari area, for a quick recon tour to show him where they would have walking safaris. He also explained that Henry needed to get to know the area's rangers, whom he would introduce him to, as they worked closely with the Parks and Wildlife rangers, even tracking poachers for them. There was an element of consultancy in performing wildlife counts on behalf of the National Parks. Jasper was always keen to help Parks so that better wildlife management techniques could be developed.

On returning to base, Sophie collared them, and they sat down to talk over the canoeing plans and how the workload over the next months was to be achieved. Jasper was glad that Sophie took charge of the overall planning, so all he had to worry about was to organise doing the work with Henry. The three canoes and six motors would be cleared through Tony Chapman's offices next week, and they would get them onto a truck for delivery to Kariba. They would probably use the Osprey to tow the canoes from the harbour back to the lodge so that they could be fitted with the motors and tested there. The trailers, which they had for the previous canoe operation, would also need to be modified. The mobile camp was being put together round a Unimog type truck which would be driven to prearranged sites where tents, showers and toilets could be erected, together with a field kitchen to provide hot meals. Two sites had been identified and agreed on with park authorities on the riverbanks between Chirundu and Mana Pools. Once at Mana there was plenty of open space beside the facilities already provided by the Parks that they could use. The first job Jasper and Henry had to get on with would be to clear the two sites and put in steel and wood structures to serve as a shower and sit-down chemical toilets. Three 'A' frames were erected and simply thatched, under which tents could be erected, and the field kitchen would be simply a rope and tarpaulin between two trees. The idea was that the team with the Unimog would drive in on the morning of the day appointed and set up the camp, waiting for the canoes to arrive in the afternoon. A genny carried on the Unimog would provide electricity for lights, fridges and a small kettle, but cooking would be done on charcoal. There was a small freezer available in case a client caught a keep-able fish, but mostly clients were encouraged to have their photo taken with their fish, which then would be released. There was a certificate of authenticity to which the picture of the catch was attached and signed off on by a local Chief, organised by Sophie. Pure Africana, but well-loved, especially by American and German clients. After providing a hot breakfast, the team would pack up and move on to the next site to await the arrival of the canoes that evening. This would be repeated once more at the Mana Pools.

To Jasper, and Henry too, the Mana Pools were the epitome of what the Zambezi evokes in the imagination. They figured a lot in their war, so they were able to deeply appreciate the beauty and remoteness, and generally the elephants, lions, and antelope had survived well, particularly where the forest was itself untouched. Sadly, not so the rhino, and consequently the few that could be located would be darted and transferred to more secure and guarded areas. Even so the breed, especially the white rhino, was pretty much extinct along the Zambezi, from Kariba to the Mozambique border and beyond.

The name Mana means four in Shona, and there are, as the name suggests, four pools, which were in fact ox-bow lakes formed by the Zambezi, in-land from where the course of the river runs now. Before the Kariba Dam controlled water flow, this was an annual flood plain, and now the lakes are known as Pools. The most impressive one is over 2½ miles long and has remained a magnet for hippo, elephant, eland, zebra, buffalo, waterbuck, warthog, baboons, monkeys, and impala – often called the goats of Africa. The animals come out of the vegetation and down to the Pools to drink, and of course they attract the predators: lions, leopards, cheetah, spotted hyena and, of course, crocs. There was a kind of magic, almost religious atmosphere, with the vegetation up from the river to the forest on the other side of the pools allowing just enough light in between to provide a kind of almost silent yet strangely vibrant area of Albida woodland. The same forest stretches out along the old river courses, along the terraces that were formed, providing lots of the Albida fruit for the herbivores to feed on.

The birdlife was, and remains if anything even more impressive, with well over 300 species along the river, and presents many photo opportunities for the clients, so there was a chance to re-familiarise Henry with the likes of Rufous-bellied Herons and Long-toed Lapwing in the weedy areas along the Zambezi banks, and the White-fronted Plovers and the African Skimmers, which favour the open sandbars for breeding. There are bee-eaters of various types, and those that nest on the riverbanks are as noisy as African Starlings. There was always the chance of photographing fishing owls, fishing eagles, hawk eagles, bitterns, storks, hornbills, flycatchers, and sun-birds, so no client would ever be disappointed with whatever show the Zambezi chose to put on in any single day. The mighty river flows quite sedately on its way to the next dam at Cahora Bassa in Mozambique, and on into the Indian Ocean. The whole area, from Kariba to Kanyemba on the Mozambique border, and encompassing the Hurungwe safari area, Mana Pools, Sapi, Kanga Pan and Chewore safari areas, and Charara, back to Karoi, was of course the part of the country that Jasper and Henry spent the majority of their time between 1974 and 1979, though that was in much darker times.

They worked hard, got the groundwork done within two months, and then Jasper and Henry made plans for a test run, meeting up with the Unimog mobile camp kitchen crew, for the two sites.

So, one morning, they got dropped off with one fully loaded canoe and motor at Chirundu, ready to start from the launching site owned by old Piet Du Toit. Having completed their negotiations for keeping three canoes at Chirundu, they were ready to go. They were waved off by Sophie as they paddled off from just about under the Albert Beit road bridge connecting the border post with Zambia.

CHAPTER 7

Zambezi valley 1975

The helicopter, an Alouette 111, flown by a ex Ranger from Burbridge, Montana who missed ops in Vietnam so much he came to Rhodesia, took JJ and Henry and another pair of Selous Scouts who were destined for Kanyemba to the Karoi Police Camp. They were briefed about the latest intel, which suggested that six groups of terrorists, four to six strong, were due to cross over the Zambezi in the next week. They would be Zipra, who were the minority faction led by Nkomo, but were considered more dangerous than the Zanla faction, who operated out of Mozambique. It was generally held that Zipra, being Matabele, of Zulu lineage, were better fighters than the predominantly Shona Zanla. Best guess suggested Chirundu to Chiawa, with some infiltration around Kanyemba. JJ and Henry would patrol from Chirundu to Chiawa whilst the other pair would start from Chiawa and work out towards Kanyemba. They agreed their call signs, both between themselves and also back to the Karoi base.

The schedule indicated the usual 6 week deployment, and though they would have a radio, it was not for base to call them, but for them to call and warn of bigger columns of terrorists which they would be unable to take on themselves. This might involve a detachment of soldiers being brought in to deal with a moving group or a gunship, but was mostly used to report where terrorists had hidden in village compounds, whether they were welcomed or threatened the locals. A unit would be brought in to surround the village and then move in, either to capture or kill the infiltrators. JJ and Henry had previously completed two tours in the same area, patrolling the Chirundu to Mana area, and had good results in that they had neutralised several four-man incursions in ambushes, as well as having tracked a twelve-strong unit from Zambia up through Urungwe Tribal Trust Lands and alongside the A1 road back towards Karoi. The group was carrying a substantial amount of weaponry and explosives, so JJ figured they were going to start a cache somewhere or going to add to an existing dump. It seemed that this must be the reason for keeping so close to the A1, so that it was easier to mark the sites for others. JJ and Henry had their own series of caches in their patrol area, but these appeared on no maps and the actual sites were only known to themselves, specially marked so that only another Selous would recognise that a cache was nearby. Finding it would be another matter, but there would be a natural map indicating it, if you knew how to read the signs.

Once they saw that the unit had obviously cached the excess weaponry, they marked the spot themselves and prepared to continue the track but, astonishingly, the group made camp within two hundred metres of the cache. They brought in a unit of men at night and, with the terrorist camp surrounded, Henry and JJ subdued the two guards who, typically, were almost asleep themselves, whilst the unit entered the camp and, apart from two who tried to fight it out and were killed, the whole group was successfully captured and taken away for interrogation.

The cache was a big one and had obviously been supplied several times, the haul including 30 AK 47s, 50,000 rounds of ammunition, 38 grenades, and two 1 kilogram blocks of plastic explosive, but no detonators, and 2 rocket launchers with 12 rockets. The strange thing was that the terrorists were caught carrying two leopard skins, which, it was assumed, would be used to invoke spirits, and terrorise blacks in the TTLs into submission. It was a big success, and clearly this represented an unwelcome escalation of activity. It would give the intel boys a headache trying to work out or get out of the prisoners what targets were in mind.

Henry remarked that he wondered if the story that had originated in Vietnam was true. It was rumoured that 3 captured Viet

Cong had been taken up in a Huey helicopter and the American asked a question of one, who only replied rudely. He was thrown out of the helicopter at 2,000 feet. The next VC was asked the same question, and he gave an immediate reply, but he too was thrown out. The third captive was talking before he was asked anything. It was reputed that when the interrogator was asked why he threw out the second man, he replied that it was the only way he could be sure that the third man was truthful.

JJ said, "I'm sure that's just a scary story, we would not do that for sure," but he was not as convinced as he made out. Philosophically, he and Henry had seen killings and indeed taken lives themselves, but not on the brutal scale they had witnessed committed by the terrorists. Still, both of them knew there was no such thing as a clean and noble war, it was dirty, cruel, and far from good.

★ ★ ★

The Alouette, or G-car as it was known, flew JJ and Henry and their gear, including extra armaments and mines into the small army camp by the border control post at Chirundu at 1700hrs. Alouette 111s, which had been adapted as gunships, were referred to as K-cars. Welcome to Camp X-Ray 483. They unloaded and immediately entered one of the tents in the compound. The G-car took off after the supplies to the army unit were unloaded and headed back to Karoi. There was no contact between any of the army personnel and the two Selous Scouts, except for the Intelligence Officer who came to their tent. He did not have much to add to the Karoi information and was soon gone. The two settled down to what sleep they could manage. It would likely be the last truly relaxed sleep both would enjoy for several weeks.

At 0300hrs, they slipped out of the camp carrying 50lb rucksacks and an extra bag, each destined first for a cache point. They headed down towards the river in the gloom of the impending dawn so that they were beyond the bridge and on towards Jecha Point before full light. They spread out 20 yards apart, with Henry in the lead and JJ following, listening intently for any click or whistle signals that Henry may use. Despite the heavy loads, they made little or no noise, blending in to the vegetation using animal trails, and mostly covering the first 1½ miles by 0400hrs. JJ never stopped being amazed that Henry, being a small, lean, wiry man, could physically match himself in carrying the loads. This next two-mile-plus stretch of the Zambezi was fairly narrow, headed North and, apart from two hippo colonies, would be relatively easy to cross. It was, however, heavily infested with crocs, so even in dugouts or rafts the native dislike and fear of crocs meant night crossings here were infrequent. The Zambian side had various villages or settlements, so the inevitable informers paid by the Rhodesians made sure few crossings were made in this area. This brought them to an area where the river split round a large sand bar, which pushed the river entirely over to the Zambian side in two streams. From here they headed about 2 miles into the bush, away from the river, following an elephant trail in a south-easterly direction. They were in an area of scrub bush, and here they located the cache they had built previously on their very first mission. Henry took up a position where he could protect JJ's back as he began to check that their cache had remained undiscovered by man or beast, and to carefully disconnect the prepared booby trap that they had left the last time. It took him a couple of minutes to safely disarm the first claymore mine. The cache was basically a termite mound which had been treated to encourage the resident colony to move on a few yards and then dug out. It was used to store ammunition, mines and some prepared explosive devices. It was protected by a second claymore, designed to detonate if the final covers were pulled off. JJ had also added a few crossbow bolts to the cache so that he had a decent stock for the 6 weeks. They discharged their rucksacks and bags individually whilst the other stood guard, then selected what they would take with them now. They both carried about two hundred rounds of 7.62 ammo, plus three 30-shot box magazines, and 50 rounds for their CZ 75 pistols. Henry had two 10-shot box magazines for his SVD sniper rifle and Henry had 20 bolts for his crossbow. In addition, they carried big bowie-type hunting knives, water bottles, iodine tablets, malaria prophylactics, and salt tablets. For food they would live off the land, except for tea leaves and biltong – Southern African dried spiced meat similar to jerky. The equipment was rounded off by the radio phone and a pair of night-vision binoculars. Henry, this time, reset the covered in cache and its contents, so he would be the one to deactivate this cache when they returned to it. They tracked back to the river, slightly further north from where they had left the sand bar, but within sight of where the river came back to be partly in Rhodesia. It was getting on to late afternoon, so they drew back to the tree line and climbed up to suitable forks in a tree to settle for the night. Supper was biltong and iodine treated water. Six drops per litre made the water taste vile, but it would at least be safe to drink. JJ blackened his face, neck and limbs where skin showed. He would not shave, so he would be well bearded by the end of this op. Finally, he pulled his floppy hat on. The long night began. They took it in turns to monitor the other side via the binos, which gave everything a green hue. Animals were moving about, and they could see the odd prowling lioness patrolling the sand bar for any animals wishing to drink from the river. It was also evident that there were several crocs close to the water, apparently just waiting menacingly. The distinct grunts of hippo coming ashore to look for grass, and even the apex predator, the lion, moved out of the crocs' way.

It became obvious that it would be unlikely that any incursions would occur until around first light, so each took a nap whilst the other watched. Who knows who was watching them; neither JJ nor Henry were foolish enough to think that a large number of the animals didn't know of their presence, but they were absolutely sure no human knew they were there. Although the night was black and quite noisy, between the grunts and rumbles of animals and the noise of insects, like cicadas, there was an almost orchestral harmony, so it does become easy for the trained ear to pick up any disruption to the general music of the night. Around 0300 JJ clicked his tongue and received an affirmative click from Henry. They heard a new noise that was completely alien to the regular harmony and began watching the Zambian side and were soon able to pick out movement. Sure enough, two tribesmen carrying some things were quartering the ground, but as the dawn began to establish itself more and more, it was seemingly apparent that they were poachers about to set traps – for impala, probably. Then, as they drew back towards the forest line, they picked up rucksacks and weapons. Henry quickly identified military rucksacks and AK 47 rifles and gestured to JJ that they were probably more than just poachers. It was getting too light to cross over to the Zambian side to follow the two, so they knew they would have to stay through the day, as there would be no attempt to cross over till evening or the following morning. They could be just tribesmen out for meat for their families, but the military look suggested they were an advance group waiting for others to join them. Either way, JJ and Henry would need to watch, and, depending on the number in the group, they would deal with it or follow it into Urungwe TTL area, to determine where they were headed and call in a unit. They were pretty sure that it was a collection point for cadres to meet. Rhodesian security had sufficient informers on the Zambian side to ensure that any group moving down to the Zambezi escarpment would be noticed and their position relayed to the Rhodesian authorities. There were stories that that pairs of Selous operated in Zambia, though these were all black crews. This had become known by the terrorists, who eventually began to wonder why they were almost always expected south of the river and consequently had tried to minimise their exposure by breaking up groups to ones and twos. This meant they had to meet at prearranged points, which should have been away from prying eyes, but indiscipline was rife, with the ones and twos taking the easy routes by bus towards Chirundu before turning left and keeping close to the river to reach their rendezvous points. Here they would receive final instruction from men who trained them politically and came down separately, to see them off as it were, before returning to the guerrilla training camps around Lusaka.

To soldiers and trackers of the calibre of the Selous Scouts it was almost too easy to intercept the terrorist incursions at the river or, indeed, to follow them as they moved inland from the river. JJ and Henry were in a league that far surpassed any field and bushcraft that their enemies possessed and, being young, they had no doubt about their skills, almost to the point of total disregard of the dangers. The Wafa Wafa training had honed that inordinate oneness they had with their environment, together with superb survival techniques which had their enemy already in fear of them. The Selous were famed for their ability to set ambushes and draw in targets, a sort of meet and kill technique, or to simply pick off members of the terrorist unit to frighten the remainder of the group. The average black was often intimidated by ancestors and spirits, and this would be deliberately used. This was mind games at the supreme level.

Henry remained on watch, seeking what shelter from the sun he could, while JJ set off into the bush with his crossbow to seek some game. It took an hour for him to track a warthog and get within 50 yards. The animal fell without ever knowing it was hit, the bolt having gone in just behind the left shoulder and without a whimper being made. JJ quickly skinned and gutted the animal and, being far enough away from their vantage point not to be a giveaway, started a small fire in a pit and built it up with dry wood chips. He put on several stones, each a little way away from the others, then the carcass, followed by more of the stones in a honeycomb pattern. Finally, a layer of soil pretty much sealed off the pit. The wind was away from the river, so with very little smoke, the pit was no marker. He would return later and pick up the meat so He and Henry would at least have something to chew on through their night vigil. When he got back to the river-side, he had to go look for Henry and soon located him to the west side of the sand bar. Recognition clicks and whistles complete, JJ slid into the gully and realised what Henry had found. Clearly this gully had been used as a landing place before, and it was a good bet it would be used again. There was evidence of footprints shod in typical military boots, and Henry found a 7.62mm round for an AK 47 and clear drag marks of a dug-out being pulled up into the gully.

"We may have visitors tonight," said Henry.

JJ nodded, and they moved out to recce the immediate area for ambush spots. They would need to see how many were in the group that crossed before they would decide whether to 'meet and kill' or try for a capture, or even to allow the crossing and trail the group. If it was a large group, then they would follow them and bring in the Alouettes. They agreed on two places within 20 yards of each other that would give them a 360-degree arc of fire without endangering themselves in any crossfire, providing they did not fire face to face. They had minimised risk of being ambushed themselves and shot in the crossfire.

JJ said, "If there are no more than six, I say we take them as they land. I can shoot one with the crossbow before they can react, possibly two. The only place they can go is into the gulley or back into the river, but I doubt that will be an option with the crocs alerted. If we set two linked claymores at the back of the gully, any survivors will more likely go back for fear of other mines, so they will be in the open."

Henry concurred, adding, 'There will be a good moon tonight. If they use a different gully, or there are more than six, we just follow."

That covered the initial plan; though of course both were aware that it depended on the group being six or less and using the one gully, it was useless to plan all eventualities, too much to remember. If anything changed, they would withdraw before a fire-fight, follow and re-plan. JJ left Henry to set the Claymores while he returned to his pit oven, opened it up and cut enough meat for today and the morning, reburying the remainder. By the time he re-joined Henry it was late afternoon and the sun was on its way down. They ate and then returned to their ambush points. The vigil began and they saw the men over on the Zambian side actually light a fire and prepare food, which they must have brought with them because their snares were still empty. JJ thought, what a wonderful way to let the game know you were here so that there would be no game coming down to drink there. As it went from light to dark, it was clear that another two men had joined them. That pretty much confirmed that this was a enemy group. Suddenly there was a commotion, which seemed unreal, in that another two had arrived and were clearly having an argument about the fire. If the fire had not already given away their intent, the shouting would certainly let anyone know within a mile or two. JJ smiled to himself, thinking that now there would be some discord between the group, which always would be to his and Henry's advantage. Night had now spread its cloak and allowed only the noise of the night to develop. However, an enemy was to intrude, and by midnight the moon was making inroads, with its soft light reducing the black night to a dull gloom. There was an occasional slight rumble of a thunderstorm some distance off, but no visible lightening. Had it been a full moon it would have been indistinct anyway, but that would not happen for a couple of days yet. Still, there was enough light to make out the six men preparing to cross. Neither JJ nor Henry could see any dug-outs, so it seemed that the group would not be crossing tonight, but just then a boat with what probably was a bass fishing motor judging by the slight whirring noise. JJ and Henry both heard a second motor and two boats slowly came down the river as if from Chirundu, with a small light, probing the gloom on both sides of the river. One boat, a flat bottomed Vaal-type, came into view and there was only one ferryman. JJ recognised the other boat as belonging to the Zambian Border

Patrol, confirming that Kenneth Kaunda and his government did actively help the cadres, which, in itself, was not a new suspicion, but it was the first time he had seen it. So much for KK's protestations and denials of the camps in Zambia. Anyway, it was known that KK and Nkomo were related through marriage, and certainly there would be an obligation to help through the extended family system which was predominant throughout Africa. The two boats stopped by the camp and a man got off the official boat and seemed to be delivering a pack and a sermon to the six men. Finally, he got back into the Border Patrol boat and it pushed off, disappearing back the way it came. It was definitely going to be a 'meet and kill' situation and, unfortunately for the boatman, it would have to include him. It would help to build the image of invincibility the Selous' evoked in not only the cadres minds but also those who dared assist. All six men got into the boat, which, apart from seriously overloading the boat with men and equipment, was fundamentally bad tactics, in that all the eggs were in the one basket. Had they thought about it, they would have realised it was easier on the boat, and if only half crossed, then that would cause a problem for any ambush – whether to wait for all or only hit the first party. Still, that was not JJ and Henry's problem; in fact, it gave them overwhelming odds. Watching the boat slowly whirring its way across, it became apparent they were heading for the gully, and indeed they bottomed the boat at the entrance riverside. The guerrillas added to the odds against them by taking little precaution, and their weapons were not actively engaged. Two got out, followed by the second pair whilst the remaining pair began a human chain, passing equipment to their comrades already out. Within a minute the main goods were out, the remaining two got out, and the ferryman stood to pass out the last of the gear. One man bent to push the boat back into the water.

This was the moment for JJ and Henry. JJ took the ferryman as he was about to sit with a bolt from the crossbow. Simultaneously Henry shot the bent over pusher with a silenced shot from his

SVD, then took those two who stood dumbstruck, and JJ shot another who began for the gully. The boatman had keeled over and went overboard with quite a splash, immediately followed by a scream from him that meant a lurking croc had grabbed him – it must have thought it was Christmas. In the eerie moonlight, it would have possible to see the ferryman's face momentarily contorted as he was dragged under, if anyone was watching. The two remaining guerrillas made for the gully and opened fire at shadows; then came the double crump of the claymores, and silence. The boat lay stuck by its bow on the sand, with the water lapping against it. JJ and Henry stayed their positions, watching both the entry and exit of the gully carefully, though both found it unlikely that there would be any survivors – still, as their founder Major Ron Reid-Daly was fond of reminding his men, "Audacity but not foolhardiness," and then, borrowing from Confucius, "the cautious seldom err."

The whole action, from the first crossbow bolt to the detonation of the claymores, had taken less than 60 seconds, but now they would wait at least to first light before they ventured forward. Within minutes the noise of the night had returned to full volume, as if there had been no disturbance. When they did go forward, it was as expected: two mangled bodies lay in the gully and four on the sand bar. They quickly got two of the bodies into the boat and pushed it into the water, watching it float away towards the Zambian side, where the current took it to the deepest water. It would probably beach on one of the other sand bars. The remaining bodies were taken to the edge of the sand bar for disposal by scavenging crocs, which would also serve to ensure the crocs would patrol this stretch of the river.

The equipment yielded six AK 47s, two CZ 75 pistols, ammunition, and explosives, plus a RPG-7 launcher with some grenades. They also found the package they saw handed over, and upon opening it they discovered two leopard skins, which they noted to tell HQ about, but would cache in the meantime. Clearly this was a party with a mission. They would need to move these quickly out of sight before any Zambian patrols came once they found the boat. It was important to leave sufficient evidence that the group had failed the incursion into Rhodesia. The word would filter back to the guerrillas and confirm they were never safe from the dreaded 'Skuz apo', as they called the Selous.

Their own cache was pretty well stocked, and they had only used 2 bolts, 4 rounds from the SVD, and two claymores, so they would look for a new site to cache the weapons and explosives within an hour's march from the river. This would take them the next two days before they were able to get back to the river and continue their patrol down to Mana.

CHAPTER 8

1986

The motorised canoe safari venture had been going for 8 months now, and Henry had taken full charge of it, being a popular and knowledgeable guide. People had to be told politely not to drag their hands in the water for fear of crocs snatching, keep out of still water for fear of bilharzia (schistosomiasis), tip out their boots in the morning for fear of scorpions and spiders, watch where to put their feet for sake of snakes, only wear clothes that had been ironed because of putzi flies, all the things that did not allow for mistakes nor second chances. Little did clients know that he knew the area from Kariba down the Zambezi valley and on to Mana Pools better than just about anyone else in the country. Some asked about the years before Independence, but neither Henry nor Jasper would divulge anything about the past. It was and would remain the past – different times; indeed, a different country. It was sufficient that both worked for Parks and Wildlife when required. Certainly, they had built a formidable reputation for customer care and reliability, and though most clients accepted that there were no guarantees of what could happen on their trips, all felt safe. Indeed, some actually wanted the adrenaline rush that came with near misses with hippos or the closeness of buffalo or even elephants. Sadly, the valley had very few rhinos left; most having been moved to well-guarded private game farms. The trade in rhino horn for use in ceremonial daggers in the Arab kingdoms or as Chinese medicine unfortunately meant that extinction due to illegal poaching was almost unavoidable. Sophie's management of the whole business and her own speciality regarding fishing safaris on board the Osprey cruiser did not go unnoticed; in fact Jasper had become very much a stand in on the canoes or the cruiser. He had begun to spend more time on surveying wildlife in the Parks and Safari areas, becoming a consultant for the National Parks. He also took on hunting safari commissions for clients with licences and was able to ensure that animals they shot were in line with conservation policies: old animals, who would satisfy the clients trophy aspirations but were in the last stages of their lives.

Jasper came home one afternoon intending to write up a report he had been commissioned to do on the elephant population in Hurungwe (name change and dropping of TTL, as the new country's masters dictated) and Charara areas. He saw a Zambian reg 4x4 sitting at the villa and guessed it must be Jonty and Paddy down on one of their trips. Sure enough, they were sitting on the stoep with Sophie, having some tea and cake.

"Hi darling, Jonty and Paddy are staying a couple of nights," said Sophie, and shouted for Francis to bring another cup for Jasper. Seeing Jasper's look, she said, "You can wait until 5 o' clock before you open beers."

Apparently, they had come down to Harare to hospitalize Jonty's dad, who was in the first stages of cancer and needed the kind of care not available in Zambia. The father had most of his friends down in Zimbabwe, so he was not lonely during his treatments.

Jasper went and showered, flushing the bush dust off his body, and feeling refreshed, returned by way of the fridge with a couple of cold Castles for him and Jonty, putting another half dozen into an 'eskie'. He spoke to Francis and told him to bring some wine for the madams and some Willard's chips and nuts. He thought that Jonty might have an interest in canning pineapples for the Zambian farm and would like to see a farm, three miles away along the shore, run by a chap called Sid Brown. An ex-tobacco farmer, he was of the older generation and not one of the old school chums. The farm, like Osprey, was a 100 year leasehold, but also had a sponsored school for the workers' children, which was where the kids from Osprey went. Because they were sponsored, and both Sid and Jasper had also guaranteed better salaries for teachers, the school had a first-rate reputation, to the extent that several settlements around would rather send their kids there than to Kariba. Jasper got on the radio and organized having breakfast over there in the morning. Jasper asked if Paddy would like to come along, but she said she would do the Kariba run with Sophie and pick up some supplies. She wanted to see what some of the local carvings were like, having seen Jasper's personal Nyaminyami which Jasper had commissioned from Patrick Mavros, a world recognised Zimbabwean silversmith, but also the wooden carving that stood in the corner of the stoep.

The carving depicted Nyaminyami as the Zambezi River God, or River Spirit, with the body of a snake and the head of a fish. The local tribes to the Kariba area worshipped him, and when they were displaced they believed that Nyaminyami would be angry. Indeed, the dam wall was said to have separated the god from his wife, and the various seismic tremors caused by the weight of water in the dam were interpreted by the locals as attempts to break through the wall to reach his wife. It remains a belief that not only the number of deaths of workers on the wall, but also the hundred-year flood that washed away the coffer dam, were due to Nyaminyami. Furthermore, he would eventually break through the wall and restore the lands back to the local indigenous tribes. It was, therefore, partially out of respect for local culture and partially as a way of asking for the River Spirit's protection, as well as a good luck omen, that JJ and Henry would make a little prayer to him before each of their missions.

As the evening wore on, through dinner and drinks afterwards, Jasper and Sophie found out more about Jonty and Paddy's lives up in Zambia, near Mkushi. Their farm, Suma Calo (or Good Earth, in the Bemba language), was a mixed beef arable farm, which had good water available and also produced tomatoes, pawpaw, mango, watermelon, and other vegetables. Like Jasper,

Jonty was allowed to keep 50% of any foreign exchange he generated, but in return he also had to produce a quota of maize, Zambia's staple. His main export earners were soya beans and beef, through state agencies, with mangos and peas being airfreighted to Marks and Spencer in Britain. The rest of his crops and some beef were grown under contract to a food processor/cannery in Ndola or for distributors in Kapiri, Kabwe and Lusaka. They had two infants not yet at school, who, after a primary education in Zambia, possibly the American School in Lusaka or Harare, would however have to go to boarding school – maybe in Zimbabwe or Britain. The children were being looked after by Paddy's mum, who had come to Zambia a couple of years ago to help at the births and never left. Although all pointed to a good life in Zambia, the downsides were in education and health facilities, the latter being available by private plane in Zimbabwe or South Africa. There were shortages mainly of things like butter, rice and cooking oil, which was why they made frequent trips to Zimbabwe, but generally they enjoyed their lives. They sat and drank some of Jasper's whisky and set the world to rights.

The next morning Jasper and Jonty headed for Sid Brown's place around 0700. On the way out, he showed Jonty his plot and explained his business and how much Sophie actually drove it. This was why he was able to do commissions for Parks and Wildlife, and he had a few hunting clients to keep him busy. Sid, a widower, welcomed them and soon realized that he used to know Jonty's father, years ago, and was sorry to hear of his ill health. He promised to visit soon. Sid's boss boy served a hearty breakfast of pawpaw, bacon, and eggs and reminisced on his generation's penchant for the wild and stupid, such as the mule racing episode in the Meikles hotel. After breakfast, he suggested that Jasper might not want to join the on the tour of the bananas, pineapples and canning unit, and Sid could bring Jonty back to Osprey at lunchtime. That suited fine, as he would be able to work on his report regarding the elephant population and whether the range could support it.

He said "Cheers, I'll organise lunch."

When he got back, Sophie and Paddy had already left, so, telling Francis there would an extra for lunch, he disappeared into the office and began to type.

He had made a survey from Makuti down to the lake and covered both Hurungwe and Charara safari areas, concluding that overpopulation of elephants was not a huge problem, though the range was beginning to suffer. There were too many bare patches beginning to appear where the bush was not regenerating fast enough, or trees were permanently stunted, indicating that the range was not sustaining the elephant population. Indeed, there had been an increase in reports from villages outside the safari areas of elephants raiding crops. Overall, Jasper would say that the condition of elephants in the Hurungwe and Charara areas was not the best, but certainly a long way from being out of control. One item he had concluded might become a problem was that the birth of new calves was going down, based on his 5 years in the area. He did stress that the period was not long enough to make an overall judgement as to whether the habitat was being endangered sufficiently to warrant a cull, as many other factors were involved. The key factor was water; elephants need a lot of water, but even in droughts the Zambezi was well managed, thanks to Kariba, so that would not be the problem. However, drought also represses the growth of the grasses and trees that feed the herds, and wholesale damage in hard times could kill not only the elephants' habitat, but also the biodiversity needed for other species. Drought in this part of the world tended to be on a four-year cycle, but then it may seem that the sun's apparent thirteen-year cycle of sunspot activity may interfere with that. Another resulting or contributing factor seemed to link the size of Southern Africa's maize crop with El Niño variations. Jasper had, despite his scientific training, come to realise that even a 100-year period in the earth's history was far too short a time span on which to base any predictions regarding habitats and the flora and fauna supported by those habitats. Nature did move slowly, as evidenced by evolutionary theory, and when man alters basic habitats, he in effect upsets the balance of nature. Jasper had begun to subscribe to a more fatalistic viewpoint: that nature would fight back to restore balance. The philosophical side of him could see that climate change to some extent was irrelevant; it had been happening for millennia anyway. Mankind's ability to change his environment was becoming a factor that even nature could no longer control. With all the knowledge gained, the lengthening of man's lifespan through medical and technological advances had resulted in simply too many people on the planet. It was a case of the more we improved our lifestyles, the more counterbalances would appear either in new devastating diseases or natural phenomena, as Nature itself tried to find equilibrium. Even man's cultural and economic differences would increase the divisions between them and more global wars would take precedence. Jasper's experiences with both people and the bush had a profound effect on him, which changed his thinking regarding culling. He had thought originally that the only way to preserve the wild areas for the future was to control the numbers of animals in those habitats that could sustain them. Nominally this would need to be via a cull of any species that began to diminish the habitat through sheer numbers. He approved of hunting as a method of conservation not because he had a bloodthirsty streak, but because it could be controlled. With elephants, who could be destructive in their habitats and particularly their behaviour patterns, it had seemed that it was relatively easy to fix a number that could be sustained in a river ecosystem. Therefore, a number could be determined which should be culled to keep an overall equilibrium of elephant numbers to habitat. Jasper further believed that closer study of the elephants, in particular in the Kariba basin, Zambezi river and surrounding so-called "safari areas" had shown two major issues were vital to good conservation of the animals: First, the family life of elephant was a key factor for their survival. The family was normally run by the dominant female, generally an older female, or matriarch, who would serve as the teacher and disciplinarian of her sisters, for all herds were a female dominated group. Male bull elephants were ejected from a family group, as they became unruly when sexually mature. They were sent out of the herd to live in small groups before becoming largely loners. Bull elephants only visited the female herds when females came into heat. The second factor was the habitat itself, in that it was limiting sustainability of numbers by the food it could provide and its seasonal diversity. Elephants would move their habitats to secure feeding and, not being terribly efficient converters of the vegetation consumed, they would move constantly. This very movement, trekking, allowed for areas to regenerate and be available the next year. It was this knowledge of trails, food, resources, and water, together with how to care for calves, that the matriarch would be passing on to the herd, usually to her sisters. Those sisters would then undergo a dominance scenario as to who would succeed the aged matriarch when she needed to be replaced with a newer model, so to speak. Indeed, if the matriarch considered that the herd had become too large, she might well split and drive off the eldest sisters to form a new herd. If the matriarch were culled too early in her life, there would be great uncertainty in that herd and possibly no successor. The herd would become totally dysfunctional and devolve into rogue individuals or groups. There was a body of so-called experts who advocated for culling to be carried out on a family herd in its entirety, mothers and calves, to prevent rogues threatening human settlements in their drive to find food. Jasper did not subscribe 100% to this view, but it made a lot of sense. Similarly, he saw sense in not changing any habitat, even down to leaving the trees and thicket to rot where it fell. Supervised hunting of the sort he undertook at least put him in a position to determine and select animals for a client to shoot. Obviously, the first options would be old bulls and ousted matriarchs, who would be mostly favoured by clients in that they always would be the older and therefore bigger animals with longer tusks. If too many young juvenile elephants were culled, with a several-year cycle for calves to develop, it can become possible to miss generations, destroying the social structure of herds. Certainly, at the very least, Jasper believed that only professional registered hunters could be authorised for animal licences sold at auction. Then they must accompany clients when hunting the animals on those licences. Weapons used in these hunts would only be legalised hunting weapons, with no automatic weapons allowed. Of late, after monitoring herds in the Kariba areas as part of his brief from Wildlife and Parks, Jasper was leaning towards natural methods for culling – allowing the elephants to overgraze their habitats, with starvation killing off the excess numbers and allowing a natural balance to be established. This would follow the Darwinian 'survival of the fittest' theory, ensuring the best genes in the future. He thought that if you try to modify any one aspect, like a cull of a species, there must be an effect on other species who share the same ecosystem, so eventually you will have to try to cull everything. Perhaps everything should be left to nature to sort out; but then again man was the big interferer, whose effects were always short timescales as opposed to nature's longer times. He had surmised that man would kill himself off by altering the planet's overall ecology, or nature would kill off man, protecting itself. All he could do was try and slow down any alterations man made towards nature. He felt it was a pity the human race could not control itself, either in population or its ever more materialistic wants. Change, he thought, was only change, not progress, unless it produced sustainable benefit. Still, we were here and now for such a short time, so even our lifetimes were just a snapshot in planet life. He wrote his report and recommended no cull was yet necessary, but a review of the numbers and condition of the animals should be carried out in 12 months.

The girls arrived back just seconds in front of Sid and Jonty, so Francis quickly served the cold buffet and salads that he had prepared earlier. Jonty had had a bit of an epiphany; he had realised that a canning operation on site would increase the value of his fruit and veg enormously, especially the rejected fresh product for the airfreight to Marks and Spencer. Sid had let him see the equipment and given a cost estimate structure, so Jonty was itching to get home and start doing the sums. Paddy had found a carving she liked and bargained it down to a third of the original asking price, so she was happy, but Jonty was concerned with the size of it as the vehicle was pretty much loaded. After lunch, Sid said goodbye, telling Jonty he would be happy to come up into Zambia to give any advice or help if Jonty went ahead with the canning plant. Just as Sid was leaving, the cruisers bringing the latest clients back from the Chirundu-Mana canoe safari arrived. Henry showed the clients back to the rondavels to clean up, then came on up by the office to sign off on the trip with Sophie and advise what stocks and stores needed replenishing before the next one. The canoes were being returned to their Chirundu store by the Unimog, and he handed over the list of what had been used. Jasper called Henry over and introduced him to Jonty and Paddy.

"This is Henry, my boet, without whom the canoe side would not be and since the other lake fishing and the business bits depend on Sophie, these two make me redundant."

If he was looking for support, neither gave it; in fact, Sophie replied, "True," in a very serious tone, with Henry's nod making it unanimous.

They all burst out laughing, and when Paddy added, "I know exactly what you mean," the men all knew they were beat.

JJ continued, "But seriously, Sophie is the businesswoman. Henry watches my back as he has done for years; they allow me my passion of the bush and my elephant studies."

Jonty asked, "I did not know you had a thing for elephants – rather, I thought you hunted them?"

Sophie jumped in, "Jasper–" she never called him JJ, "–thinks more of the bush and his animals than he does of mankind generally, present company excepted," before adding proudly, "He was asked by government to do the survey and recommend action on the elephants in this part of the world. He is following more and more his father's passions, but with the natural side rather than the tribe's cultures."

Jonty looked curious and said sincerely, "Yes, he will make old Frederick proud."

The girls did not seem to notice the glance that passed between Henry and Jasper, but clearly, they had the same thought. Did Jonty know more about them than he let on? The reference to Frederick could have only meant Frederick Courteney Selous, a British officer of the late 1800s and early 1900s, who was a hunter and conservationist, and for whom the Selous Scouts were named.

The moment passed as quickly as it arose, and Paddy, not to be outdone, though it was not of any competition, claimed, "Jonty had a bit of a hell-raiser for a father, not like you Jasper, but he has been doing a lot with conservation groups, on elephants particularly."

Jonty tried to hush his wife, but Sophie was in there like a striking cobra, "Come on Jonty, tell all."

There was a bit of a silence, then Jonty laughed and simply said that he had acted in the past as a go-between for Zambian Parks and WWF regarding elephants in the Luangwa Valley reserve and the Zaire Demalisques de Leshwe game preserve which neighboured them. Jonty was interested in JJ's work and began to ask about patterns and behaviour regarding the elephants in that region, especially in view of the conflicts that were still simmering in the area, especially the Katanga province.

Jonty threw up his arms in mock surrender and pleaded, "I simply know some government people, and when they asked me to assist with firstly UN reps and thereafter WWF, I helped to put together some meetings, that's all."

Jasper asked, "Do you know where any scientific studies may have been done, and if I could get hold of them if they are unpublished?"

Jonty said he would ask but couldn't make any promises. Sophie had detected an awkwardness arising, so she quickly called Francis for some cold beers and wine, to which everybody cheered. Henry stayed for a beer and then, saying his goodbyes, begged to be allowed to go and see his family. Both Jonty and Paddy remarked to Jasper that he had a good man there.

"I'll drink to that," was the reply.

Later that night, when everyone had gone to bed and the gennies had been switched off, Sophie said to Jasper, "You've never told Jonty about the Scouts, have you?"

"No and I'm not convinced that the Frederick remark was entirely innocent. Come to think of it, I only know Jonty and Paddy through Tony Chapman, really; Jonty was not in my year at school, and I don't recall ever meeting him there, not that was impossible given the numbers. It is possible Tony may have said something, though I would have thought not. Anyway, I don't think it's important. I like them, and maybe he can help me with my elephant studies – but I'll have to talk to Henry tomorrow, see what he thinks."

With that they went to bed.

Next morning, after breakfast, Jonty and Paddy said their goodbyes and issued an open invite to Jasper and Sophie for them to spend a few days at their farm near Mkushi. Jonty promised to take them to Lake Tanganika for a weekend, and they left for the six to eight-hour drive home.

Jasper went for a chat with Henry about Jonty and was relieved that Henry, too, thought the Frederick remark was not a coincidence. JJ said he could only imagine that Tony may have mentioned either or both of their backgrounds. He would check, but given that neither of them had been bothered by the authorities – indeed, to the contrary, they were both keenly sought by the Parks and Wildlife people, as well as police, for their tracking skills and knowledge of the Kariba and northern areas – there was little threat.

CHAPTER 9

Dark Times 1976 Nyadzonya

When the Portuguese gave Independence to Mozambique in 1975, Rhodesia lost a friendly government and instead now faced a communist inspired Frelimo government on its eastern border. This new government gave active support to the terrorist organising camps, transport basically providing an infrastructure for them. As a result, the eastern border now had to be seriously guarded to prevent or engage incursions from Mozambique, which tied the army up even more. Similar to the Zambezi valley, where JJ and Henry operated, other Scouts formed flying columns, which would be either deployed by helicopter or, for deeper operations, by parachute via a Dakota aircraft. They would gather intelligence regarding where the camps were, numbers, general security, transportation within Mozambique and so on. It became apparent that it would be more effective to hit the terrorists in their camps, to destroy their logistics and their resources. The level of activity plus the size of the incursion parties meant two-man teams were insufficient and would be pinpricks at best. After a bad start to August, where white farms in the Umtali district were attacked by a large incursion force and the army had several casualties, the Selous were tasked with attacking a terrorist camp. The closest to the border was identified at Nyadzonya, some 25 miles across the border, and so the Selous Scouts mounted what became known as Operation Eland.

Henry and JJ were on the range at Salisbury South, firing in their weaponry before going back to Karoi. Henry was making kill shots with 99% success up to 400 yards using the SVD rifle. JJ was using his crossbow and getting kill shots up to 70 yards, but began to lose accuracy at 100 yards. When they were happy their telescopic sights were ranged in, they swapped to open sights and their AK 47's, where little time was needed. They finished off with their CZ's and, once they were happy, returned to the canteen. Their briefing had been put back to 1600hrs, so they were required to go and do some mat time for unarmed combat for an hour before they could go to the canteen. They were a bit shocked in that there seemed to be a lot of Selous about; quite unusual, they thought. There was no lack of questioning looks amongst the assembled Scouts, as it was unusual for so many of them to be in one place at the same time. Both Henry and JJ recognised others, and some were asking what was going on. Then Captain Rob Warraker addressed them in a rather crowded briefing room. They were going on a raid into Mozambique with only one objective: to wipe out a guerrilla camp of an estimated 1,000 terrorists. The plan was simple; a convoy would cross into Mozambique disguised as a Frelimo column, drive into the camp onto the parade ground and start shooting the terrorists, drive out back over the Pungwe river and into Rhodesia.

"All white members must be blackened and kept in the centre of the Unimogs, and the Ferret armoured cars away from the view of the outside with only black soldiers visible. They would all be dressed to look like Frelimo soldiers."

"We want them to know they are not safe from us, wherever they are, so you will only need your assault rifles and pistols. I will carry some plastic, as we will take out the Pungwe bridge to slow down any possible pursuit. Gentlemen, we need to send a message. We will meet back here shortly. We proceed to Umtali this evening in normal army transport and pick up our own vehicles there. We are now in a lockdown, blackout state. Good luck to all of you. Let's go."

Henry turned to JJ and asked him, "Do you think Nyaminyami knows anything about Mozambique?"

Most of the 70 or so Scouts slept on the 5-hour trip down to the army camp down in Umtali, and the five-truck convoy arrived shortly after 2200 hrs. The men had rations which they had eaten on the trip to Umtali, and were encouraged to perform ablutions. They loaded up into four Ferret armoured cars and seven Unimogs, two of which were armed with scavenged 20mm cannons. All vehicles were disguised as Frelimo, complete with Frelimo number plates, just as the visible soldiers in Frelimo uniforms. JJ and Henry were both in one of the Unimogs, JJ in the lower well along with 4 other white Scouts, all completely blackened, bush hats pulled down, whilst Henry in his Frelimo shirt was on the top well. They left immediately, crossing over into Mozambique just after midnight. They passed a couple of sentry points, who actually saluted the convoy as it drove by. JJ certainly had a few butterflies. This was a completely alien situation for him and although he trusted those around him completely, he was used to only Henry for back up; he knew how Henry thought, how he reacted in any given situation. Later he would confide in Henry and be mightily relieved to find a mutual feeling in his partner.

It was nearly 0830 when the outside Scouts tapped their feet to announce they had arrived at the camp. JJ could not see properly as his Unimog seemed to come to a stop on the edge of a field. Then he saw it was a parade area and already had a considerable number of cadres on parade. His pulse, whilst not racing, was up a little more than it normally was during an ambush, but he focussed and waited for the signal. A loudspeaker from another truck away to his left broke into Shona announcing Zimbabwe was theirs, the Rhodesians had been beaten. Cadres cheered and began to mill around towards the trucks which were stationary on all sides of the parade ground. As more excited cadres ran on to the ground the signal to shoot came. The Selous opened up and initiated a bloodbath, with very few being able to escape the slaughter. JJ and the others fired in controlled bursts so as not to overheat their barrels. There was virtually no return of fire, with people more interested in running, some even dropping weapons they had. There were piles of bodies, raked with more fire to catch those hiding beneath. JJ could see shattered limbs, white bones sticking out of blackened, minced meat, and patches of bloodied matter as the AK 47s scythed through the bodies at close range. The human body is not as strong as you are told, at least not where 7.62mm and 20mm ammunition is concerned. Each truck and Ferret had an arc of fire, and the arcs overlapped to cover the whole parade ground. It was a killing field.

At last, an eternity later, the Scouts stopped firing and a brutal silence took over. There might be questions asked of inner souls later, but right now there was nothing, not even relief at being alive. Already there was a stench of kak as several hundred sphincters relaxed in death, which began to overcome the smell of gunpowder, of spent rounds. Again, orders were barked, engines started, and trucks gathered in convoy. Not many could tear their eyes away from the abattoir they were leaving behind.

The miles rolled by before there was any banter, firstly almost a nervous laughter before the inevitable, "Well, did you get the message?" It would be sometime before they would engage each other in normal chatter, not so much because of the horror of what they had done – that would come later – but because it had been so incredulously easy.

Henry seemed to say it all; "I saw no woman or children, only youngsters, but they too have parents."

They would learn later that they had killed close to a thousand terrorists that day, losing not one of the Scouts – just four lightly wounded. Most would recover quickly, and perhaps that would be due to the small unit system of the Scouts, which allowed them to share thoughts, but recovery did not mean a cleansing. When they got back to the Umtali base, the overall mood would not have convinced an outsider that these 72 had just had a stunning victory which indeed hurt the guerrilla movements. For most, the showers at least cleaned the outside off, and that had to do. Some, very few, had life changing experiences, none committed suicide, and most understood that war was uncompromising with no good in it at all. Rightly or wrongly, that's what men did. The officers gathered their men together, but no debrief was necessary. However, the Scouts were reminded of the atrocities the enemy had committed; the bayonetting of woman and children; the rapes; the gutting of babies to hide grenades. What the Scouts had done was not nice, but it was to protect their country, and it had been efficient, not haphazard, involving only combatants. That helped, but the worst would come after Independence, when it would hit home that it didn't matter a bugger, as nothing gets resolved for long, man always finds a reason for a fight. Only the dead get rest, and they won't mind if you forget them. Perhaps the Selous' training camp's name said it best; the name *Wafa Wafa* was derived from *Wafa Wasara*. In Shona it meant 'Those who die, die – those who stay behind, stay behind.''

These attacks on the terrorist camps in neighbouring countries were initially effective, but in the end, they became no more than bloodied noses for the guerrillas. They did, however, remain in awe of the Selous Scouts in particular, as did most of the world's armed forces. Gradually terrorist camps were more widely sited and became much more fortified, so some of the audacious raids made by the Scouts and the Air Force had a lessened effect. Mostly the raids were confined to Mozambique, as the greater number of terrorists were located there, but there were some camps in Zambia. Indeed, the Green Leader raid took place within Zambia and, in its way, passed into legend. Selous Scouts continued causing mayhem, particularly in Mozambique, where they destroyed lorries carrying guerrillas to the border; they also mined roads and blew up bridges. When the Frelimo people started to use the railways for transportation of soldiers and their equipment to the eastern border of Rhodesia, the Scouts destroyed rails, locos and rolling stock so the enemy had to carry their own supplies over long distances to reach the border. However, they could only delay the inevitable.

CHAPTER 10

1986 – A Secret Meeting

Several weeks had passed since Jonty and Paddy had visited and Jasper began to take stock of himself and Sophie. Clearly, they both loved each other deeply and he knew that, although Sophie would not say it, they were running out of time to start a family. His mother was pushing to get them down to Durban to become a grandparent, and he suspected that would be the case for the Mitchiesons too. He knew his mother was in regular contact with them in New Zealand, phones being reliable down South, unlike Zimbabwe. With the business going well and the bucks flowing in, Jasper was well on the way to being a wealthy person, both in local currency terms and, more importantly, in USD offshore. Tony Chapman had put them in touch with a financial company which specialized in offshore investments. JJ figured another couple of years would realise a lifelong income for them and he was beginning to see that he was, frighteningly, getting like his dad in his passion for academia. Although he had already lived considerably more than most people in the world in his 38 years, he still thought he would seek adventure for years to come. He did realize that his was a shared life and he had to accede to his wife's wants as well. He decided they would start a family, but he would also be absolutely firm about the baby not being born here, especially Kariba. The climate was relentless and there were the dangers of the safari camp itself, malaria, sleeping sickness, bilharzia, and tick fever, so his line in the sand would be Durban for Sophie. He would pay for airline tickets for the Mitchiesons, and his parents would be only too delighted to host them. The Joubert millions would ensure the best environment possible. He was equally sure Sophie would rail against the Durban idea, but he knew that after some skirmishing, she would see the sense of it. The only problem remaining was to get the courage up to tell her. He turned his mind to another potential pressing problem, involving one of the Hurungwe elephant herds. His main contact in Parks and Wildlife, Willie Du Preez, who was based in Kariba, had asked him to drop in next time he came to into town, so he went in with Sophie on her daily post run and got her to drop him off.

He greeted Willie, "Howzit, whats up?"

Willie got him a cup of coffee and said, "It may be nothing, but I'm not so sure. You know Marta and her group, have you seen her in the last two weeks?" Marta was the biggest matriarch elephant in the region and her herd included some eight sisters, three youngsters and a calf from this season. "She should have been near Chirundu at this time, but even the Inn has not had them coming to the swimming pool."

Some tourists had been fascinated when they were sitting having Sundowners at the Inn one evening, and Marta and her group came through and found a new drinking hole – the swimming pool. It had become a feature for visitors ever since.

Jasper shook his head and said, 'No, but I have been more in Charara in the past few days. Anyway, she may have found a decent patch of vegetation and stayed on it."

"Well, maybe you can have a look, or even Henry when he goes down next, and let me know."

"OK, we'll let you know."

At that point Sophie came in and said "Hi, you all done honey?" Willie offered her a cup of coffee, but she declined, and they said their goodbyes and left for home. In the bakkie she asked Jasper what Willie wanted.

"He's missing a herd of about a dozen elephants in Hurungwe, and he's asked if Henry or myself can keep an eye out. He seems a bit concerned; I am not sure he is telling me everything."

Then Sophie said, "You know, I was thinking we hadn't seen jumbo on my last trip with the Osprey and those Americans; plenty buff, antelope, water buck, but no jumbo. Mind you, we don't always see jumbo, but you know Arthur's Creek, they are always there. By the way, Tony has sent a telex, and he is coming up to see us tonight," she said, handing him a telex. Strange, thought Jasper, especially that he was driving. When they got home, he went to see Barnabas – he knew Henry would not be back till tomorrow – and asked him if he had noticed anything about the elephant around the lake.

"Boss hapana, nothing around Sanyati, hobhos plenty around Umi but cheeky."

Jasper nodded, thanked Barnabas and asked him to keep an eye out and ear to the ground regarding elephant numbers or behaviour.

He went in and pulled his files on elephant patterns in Hurungwe, Charara, Sapi and began checking his notes. Just after 1500 hours he saw a Mercedes Estate coming up to the house and went out to meet Tony.

"Howzit," he said to Tony, and quizzically looked at the elderly man who also got out of the car.

Sophie came out and said hi to Tony. "I was hoping you were bringing Chrissie."

"Sorry not this time, but I will soon, I promise. Sophie, Ken and I need to talk to Jasper, I promise nothing bad, and certainly not to do with Osprey."

"OK, but I don't appreciate secrets."

"Neither do I." Jasper added icily.

Ken spoke for the first time, saying, "I apologise, Mrs Jackson, I am afraid it's my request to meet your husband, and I would normally not allow you to be involved, so you can stay but please do not interrupt. You can speak to Jasper after."

Sophie nodded and replied, "I'll let you say your piece, it's obviously important, at least to you. Now, tea or beers?"

They sat on the veranda, and when Francis had brought both beers and tea, Sophie said he could go off till dinnertime.

"Yes madam, how many for dinner?" he asked, but Sophie said she did not know yet.

They toasted each other and Tony began to explain. Ken was from the Central Intelligence Organisation; later they would find out he was the lead man coordinating the nation's involvement in a global effort to eliminate ivory poaching.

Jasper stopped him and asked, "Jonty is involved, isn't he?"

Ken smiled and said Tony had called it right. Jonty had realized that his Frederick reference might be picked up by Jasper and contacted Tony to warn him. Ken now took over, explaining that Jonty was a link man between Zimbabwe and Zambian equivalent of CIO. He was, in fact, a high-ranking Special Branch Officer for the Zambians, tasked with ivory anti-poaching. The Zambians had discovered and subsequently confirmed through their informants that the point of despatch for any ivory would be via the Tazara railway terminus at Kapiri Mposhi. It would be transported to the port at end of the line in Dar es Salaam. Poached ivory, some 30 tonnes from Zaire, had already been brought to a Zambian bonded warehouse in Kapiri on behalf of two Korean gentlemen, Kim A and Kim B, with definite Chinese participation. They had been identified as two of the North Korean diplomatic staff in their Zimbabwe Mission, who were also accredited to Zambia. It was suspected the Chinese are pulling the strings. The Zambians had also discovered that both Kims had been active in commissioning known Zambian gangs for ivory in the Luangua Valley, and ivory from that source is also being taken to the bond set up by the Kims.

'The common link is that our so-called friends, the North Koreans, had previously suggested, but are now demanding, ivory as payment for their support of the President in the Independence struggle, and whilst the President still believes in the ideology, he knows full well that the North Korean demands would sink the country in the world's eyes. Zimbabwe has stocks of ivory which have been confiscated, but that has all been tagged and declared through the UN. We have information that the Kims have, for a couple of years now, targeted a senior Army officer, a brigadier, who in turn has recruited some ex-combatants to poach on his behalf. Army transport will be used to bring a cache of ivory to a disused camp near Chirundu, which you will know, to be containerised as diplomatic cargo. The army officer's family have a transport business, and their trucks will be used to take the containers to the bond in Kapiri. Locals in Chirundu are already reporting that the disused camp is being guarded by what looks like army personnel, though we believe that is probably the ex-combatants."

The President had personally charged Ken and the CIO to engineer a graceful solution which would not implicate Zimbabwe with the North Koreans, or any poachers. Ken went on to say that they would take care of the army officer and his gang themselves, but they had to first get round the Kims having the diplomatic immunity in Zimbabwe.

"Before I go any further, I need to ask you: can we count on your support regarding getting the evidence we need to get ourselves out from under the Korean yoke? I am not asking for any direct involvement in any terminations, but I am in need of your special skills in the bush. You will of course be rewarded by a grateful nation, probably anonymously."

It was like a movie, but you just couldn't write a script for it. Jasper stood up slowly, would have tapped out his pipe if he had one, and said of course he would help, and he would do so for the elephants. He asked, "What about Henry?"

"Ah, your partner; it's up to you, I had not included him, partly out of respect for him, and I do not know him or anyone connected to him, whereas Tony is able to vouch for you."

Sophie chipped in, "I will go and organise rooms for you and extra plates for dinner. I will stay out for now and make sure you are not bothered by any of the staff. I'll send some more beers and snacks." With that she was gone. Ken nodded appreciatively.

"I knew you were police, of course, but you never let on about the CIO/SB," Jasper remarked to Tony.

"I wasn't involved until 1977, and really, even if I had been tempted to confide, I wouldn't wish to jeopardize our friendship. I only mentioned that I thought you may have been a Scout to Jonty when he approached me about some things to do with international law regarding the operation, enticement or even the meet and greet you guys were so good at."

The beers, biltong and nuts came, and they got down to some discussion. Ken unfortunately believed that the elephants had already been killed, and if the 30 metric tonnes from Zaire were anything to go by, Hurungwe and Sapi may have lost 200+ elephants directly.

"We know that we have lost nearly that in Hwange, and that ivory is being brought here to Chirundu in small quantities. We also know that 2 road trucks have been withdrawn from service in four weeks' time and 2 containers booked, so we assume that will be the date for transfer to Kapiri."

Jasper asked, "Anything to suggest Korean involvement either here or in Hwange?"

"Oh yes; the Kims gave notice, as required if they travel 30 miles outside their Mission, and spent a week at a private lodge bordering Hwange, ostensibly game viewing and visiting Victoria Falls. They requested their brigadier for bodyguard, and I do expect them to apply for travel permits shortly to Chirundu, because they will need to supervise the diplomatic cargo through border-post and at the bond in Kapiri. The brigadier will no doubt accompany them to the border."

For the time being Jasper decided to keep quiet about Willie Du Preez's concerns, and Barnabes' too, but he had to admit that Ken's supposition that the elephants had been killed already was probably accurate. He was at a loss to comprehend the impact on any survivors in the herd and feared that there would be a lot of undisciplined teenagers left to fend for themselves. They were probably not targeted, because they had little tusk. How could this happen, and no bush telegraph!

Ken broke across his thoughts. "If I am right, and in my business, I cannot afford to be wrong, their plan will be to travel in close proximity with the two containers to Kapiri. They will supervise the loading of the estimated six containers onto the Tazara rail, handing them over to the Chinese management before returning to Zimbabwe. Jonty's people seem to think there is a small Chinese registered freighter due into Dar around that time, and it is certain that it is there to pick up the containers."

Jasper voiced his assumption that the cargo would not be allowed to leave Dar es Salaam.

"Correct. I cannot give any detail because I don't know; there's no reason for me to know, and I can't let it slip if I don't know. I can make some guesses, as you can, but with the UN involved, they have to leave China an opportunity to condemn the poaching. It cuts China's options if one of their ships is implicated."

Jasper kept on inquiring, 'That, then, begs another question — what happens to the Brigadier and the Koreans?"

Now Ken became a notch more serious and simply said, rather chillingly, "You do not need to worry about the Brigadier, but the Kims will be expelled and sent home in disgrace. The penalties for failure are severe and will probably include their families, poor buggers. They will be written off officially as rogue elements working for themselves."

Jasper nodded and observed, "You seem to have this tied up, and so far I am no clearer what it is that you want me to do."

"OK," said Ken, "We need proof, evidence if you will, of Kim A and Kim B's involvement throughout the whole chain, particularly here in Zimbabwe." He came straight to the point, "I want you to go and find evidence of slaughter, photograph it, then find this Hurungwe camp; confirm it is the place and photograph what's going on, how many people there are, and especially to be there when the Kims arrive, along with the Brigadier. I need pictorial evidence of the containers being loaded and sealed with Diplomatic tags."

"What about the combatants?"

"Either you deal with it or you call us in."

"Well, that's to the point," said Jasper. "I suppose I have never met you and I am on my own." They all laughed and opened beers to seal the deal.

Sophie appeared and asked if they were finished, and it was Ken who said, "Not quite, but it does now involve you. I need your husband to go to Zambia and see Jonty to tie up with him, so I would suggest the two of you go up on a holiday. It needs to be next week at the latest." Then, to Jasper, he said, "Tony has some toys for you which might be of use, contacts if you want, and if you can deal with him from now on, I'll be grateful. I shall be keeping an eye out and for the record, only Tony knows who you and Henry are in relation to this case, and no-one else at this point needs to know about you at all."

Sophie smiled and said that she might even get to like Ken for making good suggestions, but he told her that she had never met him. As for the staff, she had already put the story around that it was a couple of travel agents who had come wanting to do some deals on getting more clients. With that she showed Ken and Tony to their rooms, where the showers were, and said they had a couple of hours before dinner. Tony came back with a couple of cases which he put down with a clunk. He produced a camera and a set of lenses, which he described as being high resolution and capable of taking pictures at night without flash. Then he produced an SVD, complete with silencer, and a couple of CZ 75s, night vision binos, a satellite phone, a stock of tranquilizer darts, and military maps of the Hurungwe, Charara, Sapi, and Chiwore areas. Lastly, he repeated a call-sign and a number, should JJ need to contact him for anything. He seemed almost apologetic and began to explain, he had never abused his friendship, that at least being genuine. Jasper waved him away, saying he never would have thought that anyway, and that he was actually excited at the thought of action. He hated to admit it, but he did miss the thrill of the chase, the thought of being on the good guys team. Despite the fact that they had lost a war, with all the disappointment of that, there was nevertheless a magic about the adrenaline rush one got, knowing you could become at one with, indeed part of, the bush. The satisfaction came with from being like any policeman, upholding the societal laws for the good of that society, the bush. Being part of that grand scheme did bring home both the insignificance of an individual, but also the extent of care needed to maintain the equilibrium of life. Anything that threatened that equilibrium was clearly the enemy. As they chatted, Jasper was reminded that he needed to update his will and how to dispose of assets in the event of the unexpected. His plan was to relocate Sophie to his parents in Durban, at least until he had completed the business at hand. She already knew how to access the offshore funds. He was unsure if he would be welcome or safe from any backlash that may come about, irrespective of success or failure, so he reasoned that they may not be able to return to the safari business. Tony agreed and understood why Jasper was suspicious of what might be in the future, so came up with a plan that would seem to have been in place before the events about to unfold. He made provisions for Henry to take over the business on the basis of a fictional yearly payment, and respected certain bequests to Francis and Barnabas, plus a secure job for both. As Tony explained, he could fix it so that should Jasper want to pick up the reins again, he could; if not, the business would pass into Henry's hands, with Tony's company assisting with the management of the business, but not the actual running of it. He would have to talk to Henry when he got back.

Now for Sophie: he wondered how he was going to tell her that their idyll at Kariba could be over and that he had to do this. It struck him that she might see it as a chance to start a family. He did not have to worry, of course; though she was not happy about the danger to Jasper, she understood why he had to do it, maybe better than he did himself. They sat up late while Jasper explained about his projected role of stealth photographer, and he was thinking that he wanted to bring Henry in. Sophie said forcefully that he had to have Henry as a backup, and she would create hell if he went in alone. She understood that she could not stop him, and neither should she, because although he would bend to her wishes, he would resent her for it – maybe not knowingly, but their relationship would have taken a substantial blow. She knew her man, his idealism, his love for nature and therefore his disappointment in the behaviour of man, allowing his greed to exploit his environment. That would not stop her from worrying. She also knew that their time here at Kariba was limited, and however well this turned out, it would break his heart when he realized the futility of stemming what amounted to pockets of poaching. She had heard enough to see that this strike against the bad guys was entirely politically motivated and nothing to do with the poaching. She knew that he was a bit of a dreamer, and she applauded that, but she also suspected that he knew that there would be no future in staying in Kariba, especially if they wanted a family. Her biological clock was ticking, and she had already taken the steps to give nature a chance, so she was secretly pleased that Jasper himself had taken steps to hand over the business to Henry. Maybe that was a subconscious acknowledgement on his part that Kariba was not forever. On their return from Zambia, she would dutifully go to Durban to allow Jasper's adventure, for that is what she believed it was, to play out its course.

Three days later, Jasper and Sophie packed the Land Cruiser with a few things, along with Paddy's carving, which she had left behind. Leaving Henry in charge, they headed for the border post at the Dam wall. Henry had been just as excited as Jasper at the prospect of a little bush work again and made no bones about being involved. No way was JJ going in on his own. He had told him that, yes, he had noticed a general absence of elephants, and he had heard some rumours. He had intended to pass this onto Jasper and suggest they go and have a look, but he would wait until Jasper got back, he would in the meantime he would have a foray around Charara. He was, however, not so happy at the arrangements for him to get the business and swore he would only be looking after it. After all, JJ was his boet, not some business, even though he would very likely become a wealthy man through it.

Sophie and Jasper made it through both border posts, bought the obligatory government insurance on the Zambian side and began the drive along the northern edge of the river till they came to the junction with the main road, left up the escarpment to Kafue and Lusaka, right to the border post at Chirundu. They smiled when they came to the road bridge over the Kafue, which forbade any photographs, then came across a grey covered landscape from the fallout from the Chilanga Cement Works, getting to Lusaka and the main thoroughfare Cairo Road by 1130. Following directions, he cut right at the traffic circle along Independence Avenue past the statue of an African standing with broken chains representing Freedom. Ironically, Zambia had suffered heavily when Rhodesia declared Independence, and the joke about the statue was that an African will either eat what he is given, or he'll break it. He turned left into Church and right again into the Pamodzi Hotel. Perhaps it was an omen, but the entrance to the hotel was a covered walkway, and this was littered with the tourist-y elephant carvings the baying vendors were selling. The hotel itself was a bit of a surprise, being of a high class, or at least it seemed so. The stop was more or less a comfort stop for Sophie, and anyway it was close enough to lunch time to warrant a break. After lunch they got back to Cairo Road, went to the top traffic circle and got on to the Great North Road heading for Kabwe and Kapiri Mposhi. The drive out really was depressing, with poverty very apparent. It was a shock to the system, as there was nothing like this in Zimbabwe; indeed, there had been little deterioration visible to buildings and infrastructure, with no shanty type shelters visible along main roads. Was this another example of black governments not being able to manage themselves? It was unfortunately typical of black Africa, however unfair the sentiments were. An hour and half saw them come to Kabwe, called Broken Hill in a past life, which was the centre of the silver mining for Zambia. The silver mined here was among the purest in the world and carried a premium because it needed less refining. Still, it was a mining town, with the usual disfigurements of pit heaps and discarded ore dumps, so they were glad when they once again passed into bush country. Every so often they saw signs with school names, and occasionally children skipping along in school uniforms, always the same. There were plenty of shebeens just of the road, with plenty of trucks parked and, not unsurprisingly, several burnt-out, rusting tankers just lying where they had crashed. Zambia had an oil line from Dar which terminated at the northern Copperbelt town of Ndola, and all fuel had to come from the refinery there.

The Copperbelt was just that, an extensive region with massive copper deposits that made up almost all of Zambia's exports and therefore its foreign currency earnings. In Zambia, the area stretched around the towns of Ndola, Kitwe, Chingola, Luanshya and Mufulira. Oddly Luanshya had a strange claim of its own, nothing to do with copper. Its Roan Antelope Rugby Club was recognised in the Guinness Book of Records as having the tallest rugby posts in the world, at 110 feet and 6 inches. The Copperbelt, of course, was shared with Katanga, the southern province of Zaire famous for its ore wealth. Though risky, as it was like having all your eggs in one basket, it should have been the wealth of the nation. The traditional routes of export for landlocked Zambia had been through Rhodesia, but this was closed to them with UDI and the globally imposed sanctions on Rhodesia, so they had long, expensive routes through war torn neighbours. This was only partially resolved when, with Chinese help, the Tanzanians and Zambians built the Tazara Railway from Kapiri through to Tanzania and its port of Dar es Salaam on the Indian Ocean. This only began to function in 1975, so no wealth had accrued at all to Zambia, but had left it as the only potentially viable route. The falls in copper prices, according to the commodities type mentality, meant Zambia never got out of the poor league. It was a heavy price for the fledgling country to pay in order to support the sanctions against Rhodesia.

They came to the junction of the Great North Road where it went on to Ndola but turned broadly east towards Mpulo. Once through Mpulo they continued on to the Mkushi turn, before cutting right onto a secondary road labelled D200, and in less than a mile found the entrance to Suma Calo, Jonty and Paddy's place. From Mpulo the bush was quite flat and scrub-like with small bushes and the inevitable tall towers of termite mounds. These ant hills were hard as hell and actually contained a highly complex society, but what was extraordinary was the way the hills were built using saliva and soil. The clever bit was the series of passageways and interior tunnels which gave an air-conditioning system so simple yet completely effective. The height of these towers of soil and saliva was substantial; in some cases well over 12 feet high, they dried, or perhaps baked, in the African sun to produce safety for the colonies inside. It took specialized animals, like pangolins, to break in for the rewards of fat juicy termites inside. The anthills were hard as steel, as many an off roader has found out the hard way. It took armoured heavyweights such as tanks to collide and survive. As they got to the Mkushi turn the bush began to change towards part bush, part cleared, and then to what looked like fully arable cropping land, surrounded by odd bits of fringing bush. By the time Jasper and Sophie reached the homestead of the farm, it was getting on for 1600 hrs. Jonty and Paddy were both outside waiting to greet them and make the necessary introductions to Paddy's mum and the two babes, Jonty Junior and Dorothy. The houseboys unloaded the cruiser and took their bag and Paddy's carving inside. Jonty cracked open some ice-cold beers and poured into glasses instead of the normal drink-out-of-the-bottle etiquette. He explained that, whilst the Mosi lager beer brewed locally was lekker, pretty good, he could not always say the same for the cleansing operation of returned bottles, so it was wise to check that no insects or foreign matter had found their way into the bottling operation. He was right that, taste-wise, the beer was good.

Jonty said he had organised a trip up to Lake Tanganyika, to a lodge, Ndole Bay, where they would meet a UN official and his wife, who were having a couple of days R&R from their Nairobi base. He felt that it would be good for Jasper to meet this man as he was a fellow elephant scholar, an American, but nevertheless a good 'oke'. The downside was that they had to be at Ndola Airport for the 0930 flight, which meant they would need to leave by 0800, at the very latest. Jonty managed to speak alone to Jasper and Sophie, and simply said that although Paddy knew a little of his role with Special Branch, he had not exactly lied, but rather omitted to explain the depth of it. He would rather keep it that way for as long as he could. He apologised for any deception they may have felt he had perpetrated on them but assured them it was almost a paranoia to be as unknown as possible. Jasper understood this, being an ex-Selous; indeed, the fact he could remain in Zimbabwe and operate a business depended on the anonymity of his past. Sophie realised she and Paddy may well be side-lined when they were away in Ndole whilst the men talked.

After drinks Jasper and Sophie had a shower, cleaning off the day's travel, and changed. They hardly unpacked, as they had brought little but a couple of changes, just enough to get by. Sophie had brought her newest toy, a small travel iron, so she always could iron her private things, which she preferred to wash and launder herself rather than rely on staff. When she had first arrived as a backpacker in the newly independent nation, nobody had told her about the putzi fly. Sometimes called a tumba fly, the putzi is a skin maggot fly, a species of blowfly common in southern Africa, right up to Kenya, and loves to lay its eggs on clothing hung out to dry. The eggs will hatch, and larvae then penetrate the skin and grow. It can appear horrifying to see little like spots and movement under the skin. It is extremely itchy, and though some people would cover affected areas with Vaseline to cut off air, you still have to dig them out with a pin. It can be quite painful, as Sophie found out. The cure, or rather prevention, is to iron all clothes after washing and drying, so the eggs are killed by the heat of the iron. She had begun to realise that nature was not actually all that friendly in Africa, and unless you respected nature, she would either bite, sting, poison you, stab you with thorns or horns, trample you or eat you. Dinner was served in the covered patio, which had open French doors on two sides to allow a breeze through. There was the inevitable steel bar grille on the outside of each door, as indeed on every window. This was the first-stage protection in the event of gangs, often armed, coming calling to see what could be stolen.

The dinner was prime rib roast was from the farm's own beef herd, and all the vegetables were also from what the farm grew. A tropical fruit salad of pawpaw, mango, and pineapple finished the meal off. Jasper congratulated Paddy on the beef, it was the very best he had eaten in a long time and he said so.

He saw that Jonty had installed a couple of insecutors, with their UV tubes attracting insects to them and the electric grill which emitted a satisfying zap each time and insect landed. They were effective and most commonly used in factories. It seemed a different kind of night here, just as black, but in some way more open. Jasper thought the noise of the farm was a poor symphony in comparison to that performed at home; there were no big cat rumblings, hippo calls or insect concertos here. There was almost silence. At the far side of the patio was a half sized snooker table and it reminded him that he had last played snooker at the Chalet Inn down in what was called the 'cows guts' in Salisbury, a bit further down from the Auction Rooms. He wondered if the Chalet was still there, with its snooker tables on the first floor and a decent bar menu downstairs. He made a mental note to have a look next time he was in the capital. A sudden thunderstorm blew in and with it, a typical downpour, which lasted perhaps 10 minutes, but was well in excess of half an inch of rain. With the downpour over, the French doors were once again opened and the fresh smell of the earth permeated in. There was still an intense show of lightning going on, far more intense than Jasper and Sophie were used to. Paddy said it was because of their proximity to the Copperbelt and Kabwe, which meant the higher ore concentrations in the ground attracted ground strikes. They went through to the lounge for coffee and Jonty opened a cupboard to reveal a well encased gun cabinet. He had a pair of shotguns, clearly matched and no doubt expensive, an old 450 Nitro Express, a 458WM Winchester, his own 375 H&H Winchester Safari Express, and a selection of pistols. Jasper recognised a 9mm CZ75, a .44 Magnum Ruger Night Hawk, a 9mm Sig Sauer, and an ancient Luger. Jonty said the 450 Nitro and the Luger were his father's.

"Do you actually use any of them?" asked Jasper.

"Virtually never; I do no hunting, I prefer fishing, but I have been known to have a pop with the shotguns at Egyptian geese if they are silly enough to come into range. I am issued with a 9mm Walther, which I carry occasionally, and I am entitled to a 24-hour two-man guard of the property. We have to use a private operator to prevent any association being seen with my rank. By the way, there will be an unobtrusive detachment of a protection squad at Ndole, because of the proximity to the Zaire border, and the risk of bandits, though slight, cannot be discounted especially with the UN man. Don't worry, I would never put Paddy at risk, it's purely a precaution."

"I guess I am used to just me and Henry evaluating risk, and how to counter it."

After coffee and a very fine Caol Ila 18-year-old malt whisky they called it a night and went to bed.

The next morning they were up at 0630, though Sophie, unusually, was fast asleep as he showered, he had to wake her and left her to shower while he went outside. He saw his cruiser was being washed and cleaned and smiled at how old murungu habits kept on. A man to wash cars at 0600 every morning, whether the vehicle was dirty or not, and the cook to prepare breakfast.

Jasper was hungry and, along with Jonty, had the full plate, bacon, eggs, sausage, and tomato, while Sophie and Paddy made do with coffee and toast. Then they were off in Jonty's double cab and arrived at Ndola Airport an hour later. They checked in and waited for the flight. Ndola had the same sort of small terminal as Kariba; indeed, it was slightly bigger, by virtue of a wing of what looked like old schoolrooms. The baggage handling was by a corrugated shed and tables, with all baggage collected on a hand trolley being trundled out to where the plane would stop. A second trolley waited for the luggage coming off. The flight, using a Hawker Siddely 748 turbojet twin prop, landed on time, having come from Lusaka. The four of them sat in two rows, opposite each other over the central aisle. The two girls each took a window seat to allow the boys to chat over the aisle. They had entered by the back and found the galley had been stacked up with what must have been several hundred cheeping young chickens. They waited for goats to be loaded, and then they were off. It was a good fairly long metal runway at Ndola, capable of taking Boeing 737s, but the HS748 did not need more than half to take off, both pilots' hands on the throttles to ensure no slip back during take-off. The doors to the cockpit were never closed, so you could pretty much see ahead. Everyone seemed relaxed and occasionally people would walk up to the front toilets and have a conversation with the pilots. As they got up to 12,000 feet above the ground, alarmingly there was a constant hiss of air around Sophie's window, and indeed there was a gap. Jasper immediately summoned the stewardess, a big African girl, and tried to tell her the problem but by now the hiss was as loud as to make hearing difficult. The stewardess finally nodded and went forward, literally grabbing the complementary newspapers out of readers hands. She returned, told Jasper to stand, and leaned over in front of Sophie and stuffed the newspapers into the gaps around the window edges. The hissing pretty much stopped, to the degree the cheeping chicks could be heard again. The stewardess thanked Jasper for pointing it out and wished him a pleasant flight.

Jasper sat down, dumbstruck, only to find Sophie laughing at him, and she patted his hand, saying, "Your face is a picture, nobody else was bothered so I guess it's a tried and trusted method of sealing windows."

Jasper, still bemused, could only manage an "Only in Africa," before laughing himself. The plane flew north west over a bit of Zaire, coming back into Zambia over the Bangweulu Wetlands. It was quite spectacular seeing sheets of water just glimmering in the morning sun beneath the vegetation. The heat of the day now began to take over, and it became quite a bumpy ride as the plane descended into the airport at Kasama. When they landed, they saw that it was a dirt runway, and the only tarmac was the parking area at the shed that served as a terminal. Most of the plane disembarked here at the provincial capital, including the chicks and goats, leaving only 6 passengers to go on to Kasaba Bay, on the shores of Lake Tanganyika. Apparently, it was only a bush strip at Kasaba Bay, serving the safari lodge there, and there was a weight restriction for the plane, more applicable on take-off from Kasaba Bay. Jonty knew the other couple on the plane and did the introductions. Paul and Donna Venter owned a decent restaurant in Ndola, and Paul was also a boat builder. He was a keen fisherman and kept a 25-foot cruiser up at Ndole Bay so he could literally commute by air as and when he wanted. It was a 12-hour trip by road, so once a year he would send his boys up with a cruiser and trailer with the boat, and bring it back only for its annual refit. Jonty let it be known that Paul was a world record holder for catching a tigerfish – a 32-pounder on an eight-pound breaking strain line. When he was told about Jasper and Sophie's Osprey business, he promised to take them out for a shot at Lake Tanganyika's gargantuan variety of tigerfish. He also said there were some huge Nile perch in the lake, which could be fun, over 100 pounds. The plane continued its 20-minute journey from Kasama to Kasaba Bay, but it never got very high, so they were able to see just how desolate the bush was up here. Suddenly the plane swept out over the lake before doubling back and aiming for what the passengers hoped was the runway. This was a real bush strip, and short – there was a restriction of eight passengers for take-off – so as soon as the wheels touched, everything went on: brakes, full flap was maintained, props thrown into reverse, and when they finally came to the end they were able to turn round and head to the middle, where there was a gazebo. There were no ground staff, so the stewardess released the back steps, opened the doors and invited them to disembark. As they did the heat of the sun hit them like a brick wall, and polite or not, they became quickly quite damp with sweat.

CHAPTER 11

Bad Times 1978

The heat, the brightness of the day, the desolate bush and the turboprop aircraft suddenly brought back to Jasper's mind a fateful Sunday in September 1978. He and Henry had arrived at Karoi prior to their insertion into the Urungwe TTL area for another 6-week stint. As they landed, they could sense there was an unsettled atmosphere at the Karoi post. They were soon apprised that an Air Rhodesia flight, 825, from Kariba to Salisbury had gone missing shortly after take-off from Kariba. This was what became known as the first of two shoot-downs of the Air Rhodesia Viscounts by terrorists, and was made infamous by the actions of the terrorists, who then executed 10 civilian passengers who had survived the subsequent crash. They did not know that then, and indeed the police only knew that the plane took off at about 1700 hours and that by 1710 the Captain made a mayday call to say his inner starboard engine had exploded and he was going to attempt a landing in a flat bit of bush in the region of the Whamira Hills.

Jasper and Henry were stood down and Jasper went in search of Tony to see if he was on site. He was, collating reports of the Kariba Airport radar, flight plan, and some unconfirmed reports of a plane crash, gunfire, and a bush fire in the TTL by the Whamira Hills. It was dark by now and the G-car had already gone to look for the crash site. Around midnight, Tony came and told the two that it was now almost certain that the Viscount had crashed as a result of a missile attack to the east of Kariba, probably as the aircraft was banking to the right, heading towards Karoi. The two were to be held in reserve until it had been established if there had been a terrorist attack or not, so they were left to their own devices but could not leave the camp. Next morning, the place was alive with Army personnel, three helicopters coming and going, and a Dakota was seen trundling overhead. The mood was sombre as there was no doubt that the plane had done a 'wheels up' – a euphemism for death – and it was unlikely that there were any survivors. JJ and Henry were called to the briefing room at lunch time and were told that the plane had been found burnt-out, but 3 people had been found hiding, and there was a report of 5 others having reached a village looking for water and help, but they had then apparently returned towards the site. At the crash site there appeared to be 10 bodies outside the aircraft and an initial report that 2 people had been picked up. It seemed the plane was shot down, and a number of survivors were then gunned down. No other detail was available yet, and they were told to be on stand-by. Their tracking skills would be needed. That evening Tony and another officer came and confirmed that the previous reports suggesting a massacre of 10 survivors were accurate and the slaughter had been carried out by a group of nine terrorists. 8 survivors had been picked up and were now hospitalized. It was not known whether or not the group of nine guerrillas had split up, but there was intelligence they were seen around Nyamasoka and Chitau. It was unlikely that the group would try to reach to the capital now, and it was most likely they would try for the border.

"We will drop you tonight at Chitehere. You are instructed to track the group or any part of it and neutralise it. We would like one prisoner to question, but the word that Skuz Apo got them will serve. It's up to you. I'll leave you with a report of what they did to the 10 survivors at the plane and then again a couple of hours later when they returned to loot bodies."

It was just a psychological reminder, rather crudely put, to try and ensure that the two of them would not lose focus. To be fair, at least Tony looked embarrassed, as if to say that the officer really did not understand the difference between standard army and the

Selous. He was probably himself extremely distraught at this latest atrocity; nevertheless, JJ thought, how would this man react if he saw the results of the atrocity himself? Not well, he surmised.

On the way out of the room Tony went with JJ and Henry and simply said, "He doesn't know how to put emotion to one side."

It was Henry who stopped Tony; "No matter." Tony understood no more apologies were necessary. The report indicated that, apart from executing the survivors by shooting them, bodies were bayonetted and then desecrated when they returned to loot the plane and the bodies. It would seem that a lack of discipline was present in this group and that perhaps they were already afraid of being caught.

"Absolute bullshit," said JJ, "these guys know exactly what they are doing. They revel in soft targets; they don't want to come against us." He looked at Henry and said, "I don't see how we can hope to bring anyone back. They will be travelling fast, so we are tracking this time and not carrying lots of gear. We go locked and loaded."

Tony said, "Officially, I did not hear that; unofficially, go for it. Do you want me to do anything?"

"These boys will be heading for Zambia. They won't risk Makuti itself, so they'll go probably by way of Makuti, use the Mana trail where they can, and on to Mazunga, then down the riverbed to the Zambezi. I'd guess they'll go for Chiawa to cross into Zambia; otherwise they will go for Chitsungo Mission, towards Kanyemba, and maybe go on down to Centenary. They've probably got caches to go to if they are to hit more targets." said Henry.

Tony said, "I have to guess they will go for Zambia, because they will know up in the Lusaka bases that all hell will be let loose here to search and capture, so Nkomo will not want any risk of them being caught by us. Better if he can produce heroes at the camps to encourage the others."

"Can you get us to the other side of the road at Makuti where the Mana trail is? I guess the choppers will be all tied up. We can try and get ahead of them and be ready for them going down the Rukomeshi River to the Zambezi or heading for the mission. A scout car or lorry can drop us. All I need is the AK, my pistol, and bow. Henry, you?"

"I'll take the SVD and pistol, plus some claymores. We need to leave the rest of the gear except the night eyes."

"We have arms stashed in the Urungwe area anyway."

Tony went away to see what he could organise. When he came back, he said, "Latest suggests they are headed for Makuti; a truck will take you as soon as its dark. I've organised that we will fly-over tomorrow at roughly 1500 and again on the two days following so you can radio if you need to. We would want sit reps to see which way they go. Two of your lot are being put in by Kanyemba to come down the river towards you, and another two in Guruwe, also to work towards you. Anything else?"

With that they said their little prayer to Nyaminyami, so as not to break their tradition, and were ready to get on with it.

At 1900 they were taken the half hour down the road, just beyond Makuti, and dropped off near the Mana track. The truck slowed down, and the crew knocked on the frame and they jumped out onto the verge with their equipment. They literally picked it up on the run and quickly disappeared off the road, about 20 yards into the bush. They lay down and waited for 10 minutes without speaking or moving until they were sure they were on their own. There was a small, waning crescent moon, so there was little light. Using their night vision goggles they fell into single file, checked the compass, and set off in the gloom. They found a path which had been used that day, but no evidence of a nine-man armed group. There were a few trails from Makuti into the bush, so the odds that they would be on the same trail were low. In any event, Henry thought they may be ahead of the group, because Africans did not relish the bush at night; too many snakes and groups of buffalo to be a stroll in the park. They planned to get to an area around Matsikita which was a sort of crossroads and where a lot of trails from the bush met. They should definitely be ahead of them at that point if the information that they were heading for Makuti was right. They had to skirt a couple of settlements after scanning them to see if there was any obvious sign of the group; passenger clothes, cases, bits and pieces, guards, or anything that just did not seem or feel right. Anything that stood out as being foreign in the general picture would be the giveaway, but they saw nothing so moved on. JJ would have expected that if the guerrillas had holed up at a settlement, they would not be able to keep quiet and would boast of their exploits, and a certain amount of partying would occur. That would be easily seen and that would be what Tony and his ilk would be listening for from their informers. JJ and Henry moved fast, being able to use the track, and saw no sign of them. They reached the crossroads before full light and got themselves into position on either side, settling down to wait. Nine hours later, they still had not seen any sign, and they heard the *whup-whup* of a chopper, so JJ got on the radio and gave the call-sign, saying no contact. He received the relay back that the chopper had been fired on some 8 miles back, so they should expect a group soon. Comms were broken and the chopper flew off towards the Mission. JJ moved around the crossroad, giving his and Henry's recognition signals, and slid in beside him. He repeated what the chopper had told him and suggested it would be later in the evening or early tomorrow before they would get sight of the group. They agreed that the crossroads was not an ideal place for a two-man ambush, so they would allow the group to catch up with them, then track them, getting as far ahead as they could once they were sure of which way the group was headed. If they went towards the Zambezi, then that was easier, in that they would bypass them and lay a meet and kill option at the Zambezi, when they would be less guarded, thinking they were home and dry. If they turned to the Mission, then they would track to try and identify any caches and settlements that helped them. Hopefully they would meet up with the pair of Selous coming from Guruwe and set up an ambush there at a cache.

Around 1900, with darkness falling with its usual speed, there was a couple of brief interruptions to the low level of insect noise which then re-established itself. The level of noise would be missed by nearly all, but certainly not by a Selous Scout, and indeed it announced an arrival, first of a single combatant, who led the eight others by ten yards. They all turned towards the river and clearly were in a bit of a frivolous mood, in that they were wearing women's lingerie items around the heads and carrying bits and pieces of luggage, as well as the Air Rhodesia Captain's hat. It was very hard for JJ not to lob a couple grenades and start firing close bursts, as he had done in the Nyadzonya raid over two years ago, but he controlled that urge and drew back to join Henry in the bush on the other side. They motioned and pulled further back so they could speak.

Henry said, "They will make camp for now and move at first light. I overheard some conversation that suggests they are going to split up. Two are going to the Mission, and I think they are going to deliver some orders – I did not hear where or to whom." This would be a problem, because JJ and Henry could not split up, and whilst there was two scouts coming towards them from Guruwe, it did not seem right to let them go. They were on home ground now, and it seemed the main group were headed to the Zambezi down the Rukomeshi riverbed, so JJ proposed they follow the two and dispose of them quietly – he had his bow and Henry had a silencer – then they could easily catch and overtake the main group. Henry agreed, but said they had to set a time limit, after which they had to turn back for fear of losing the main group. It was unlikely they would travel very fast, but maybe there was a chance that they would divert off the route; again, unlikely, but possible. They gave themselves a maximum of two hours after any split of the group.

They then went back and found the group already settling down, with no guards posted until they had eaten. There was then a two-man guard posted, which they guessed would be changed at midnight. They dozed themselves, but smiled when by 0200 all were asleep, but they at least had weapons to hand. At 0400 the group awoke and heated water to make a maize meal porridge from the left over sadza from the previous night. At 0500 they clasped arms, and the two going to the mission left the group, going back towards the crossroad. Interestingly, they did not carry any loot from the aeroplane, just their AK's and no supplies. JJ thanked Nyaminyami, and he and Henry began to follow the two men. Clearly the men were confident that there would be no people about on the track and were walking side by side, chatting away. After about 30 minutes had passed, the men stopped and one of them took his boot off, to remove a stone or something. Henry signalled to JJ to take up position on one side. He watched as JJ slipped into a stealth movement, with his bow and bolt already loaded. He was within 40 yards and signalled he would take the standing man. Henry was a little further away, but that was deliberate, so that he could cover JJ should he miss. He took aim at the sitting man, knowing he would shoot first, as arranged. JJ loosed the bolt immediately upon hearing the soft plop of the SVD. The man sitting just keeled forward without a sound as the SVD round thudded into him; the man standing let his jaw drop and then staggered as the bolt tore through his heart. He too dropped without a sound. JJ had a crazy notion that it was not enough, and had wanted to shout "That's for the plane!" The 10 massacred knew what was coming, unlike these two, who were dead before they fell, not knowing that they had been shot. It just did not seem fair. Unlike their usual routine, they did not wait to make sure, they ran up and quickly pulled the bodies some 30 yards into the bush at the side of the track. They checked their pockets and found a couple of envelopes which they thought would make the intel boys cream their knickers. They removed any military connections, including the ammo pouches and weapons. They left the bodies for predators to dispose of and buried the rifles.

They retraced their steps back to the crossroads and found that although they had been gone for two hours, the main group was not far ahead. The objective was now to overtake the group and get down to the Zambezi before them. They followed the group's trail down the Rukomeshi River, far enough to make sure they were taking the easy route down the dry beds, but with good bush cover to the Makuti side. Once sure, they cut across to the track leading towards Mana, and made good time down there before cutting back to the Rukomeshi, on what would be the opposite side to the guerrillas. They kept on going and right on 1500 the *whup-whup* came, a K-car this time, not directly overhead but well within range for the radio.

JJ called in, saying, "Group split 7 and 2, 2 dead, 7 for Zambia, best guess between Rukomeshi and Chiawa. Crossing probably tomorrow night."

The pilot acknowledged and said, "Good hunting."

They made it to within a mile of the Rukomeshi confluence with the Zambezi, because the terrain at that point meant they would have a superb vantage point of an incoming group and a decent ambush could be effected. They thought about booby trapping the narrow passage but decided against it because of the risk that animals might set it off, alerting the guerrillas. It was now 2000 hours and black as hell, so JJ went to sleep, leaving Henry on watch. At midnight Henry woke JJ and went to sleep himself. By first light there had been no activity, and with the strengthening birdsong to help them judge if any party was coming, the two made it down to the Zambezi before 0600, having carefully ensured they left no traces of their stop. They also felt that it would have been foolhardy for even an experienced group to show themselves in daylight along the Zambezi, so it was a good bet the group would lay up through the day, partly to check if there were following soldiers and partly because the risk of chopper patrols along the border was high. Indeed, an Alouette made a pass following the river in the morning then doubled back, which JJ knew meant there was a message. The chopper would never radio units in the field for fear a transmission might be heard, giving away a position, so instead they flew where the unit might be and it would make the second pass so the unit could contact the chopper. JJ called in and was told the unit coming upstream from Kanyemba had been air-lifted to within 5 miles of the confluence and to expect two men within two hours.

He replied, "OK," and the chopper was off downstream, presumably to let the other unit know. Some two hours later, around 1030 hours, Henry heard the first of the identifying clicks and birdcalls. He answered, but both he and JJ moved apart and made sure they could cover a very wide arc of fire, just in case. One man appeared and came forward, and Henry greeted him, at which point both the man and Henry signalled to their partners it was OK. The four men moved quickly away from the open ground of the confluence and to a place where they could talk. Henry and Jacob knew each other, but JJ could not recognise Keith under the black paint; he did know him, but only by sight at the Salisbury depot. The four of them continued the search that JJ and Henry had begun; there were probably dug-outs hidden somewhere, because these boys had not been in a hurry, so either someone would come for them – not likely – or they had left their boats there on the way in from Zambia. JJ and Henry knew this area pretty well, so they decided that the bush and vegetation was sufficiently thick for concealment, with the bankside being reasonably accessible only in a few places. The river banks were often steep and difficult to get up or down, and if they were too shallow it would be an area that game came to drink, so there was the risk of things like hippos or even elephants dislodging or trashing any boats left. The other factor to look for was areas where the river would be sluggish, so it was easier to paddle across. The dam at Kariba controlled flow by only opening one floodgate at this time of year, and then only once a week, usually a Sunday, for 5 hours, so you really would be unlucky to be caught in any sort of swift flow. They found three dug-outs at the second of JJ's possible sites by 1300hrs, which gave them three hours to plan their ambush. They could not go to the boats, as that would leave tracks which even a novice would see. Looking out across the river to the Zambian side, JJ could see they were about 400 yards downstream from Tsika Island, which would be the most probable place they launched; however, that would be a paddle upstream, so it would be easier to start off upstream, then let the current do the work and land them on another promontory slightly downstream, across from where they were now. As far as they could tell, there was no hippo pod opposite. Ideally, they would have preferred to be over on the Zambian side for the ambush, but that would be risky given the time they would have to be there, risking discovery by the Zambians. The ambush had to be by the boats. This was not entirely ideal, as they could not cover the river if they decided to swim, but that was unlikely given the croc population and the chance any singular hippos, given the absence of pods. Still, there were other things to prepare for, like if they arrived as ones and twos, how to maximise use of claymores, and where to site themselves to cover each other and cover the full arc of fire.

They had pretty much worked out how to set themselves up and where to place the claymores. They would use the claymores to cover any escape route upstream, both above the bank and below, by the river. Henry and JJ would be positioned together, just a couple of yards apart, directly opposite the entrance to where the dugouts lay, with Jacob to their left and Keith to the right, both 50 yards from them. Keith would be first to see the group and would effectively come in behind them. He would convey by the clicks and hoots when in position behind. JJ and Henry would move from the bush towards the point where they could see the dugouts, while Jacob would remain to the left and cover the angle. Keith would hold fire until he joined JJ and Henry. For maximum surprise, JJ and Henry would have to begin the ambush with the bow and the silenced SVD. They hoped to kill 2 to 4 of the group before there was any reaction. By 1700 they took up their standby positions and waited, prepared for a long vigil, possibly 10 hours. They had agreed among themselves that they were not looking to take a prisoner unless a safe opportunity presented itself; after all, Henry had the letters he and JJ had taken off the bodies of the men they had killed at the crossroads nearly two days ago now.

Just past 0100 hrs JJ heard some new clicks and hoots, adding to the general symphony of noise, and then the noise began to stop and start again just in front of them. Their night vision equipment let them see that a group of seven men moved quietly and stopped in front of JJ and Henry, not more than 20 yards away. Hushed tones, then a torch appeared as the point-man of the group, still wearing an Air Rhodesia captain's hat, began to lead the group towards the river and their boats. One of the group remained behind, as if he was the back door sentry. The others made their way the few yards to where the boats lay and began to talk amongst themselves. The watchers could see that the group was relatively lightly armed, with only four of the group carrying AKs. The other three seemed to be armed with pistols only, so JJ made a mental note that they must have cached their arms along the way. They would have to look for the cache after the firefight.

Just two hours later, as the shimmerings of first light began their assault on the darkness, converting it into a gloom, the sentry joined his comrades, allowing JJ Henry and Keith to move forward into their places, whilst Jacob remained in his night position. It would only be moments now before the ambush was triggered. Then the four were astonished by a real stroke of fortune that fate dealt them. Suddenly, as JJ and Henry were beginning to aim, the first soldier, the one with the captain's hat, screamed, jumping back from a dugout with what looked like a snake hanging from his cheek. The others, to a man, turned and looked at their comrade, standing still, open-mouthed. JJ loosed his bolt, Henry shot twice, and then Keith opened up and JJ loosed a second bolt. All seven were down and still, except for the snake victim. Henry fired into the bodies to ensure they were not feigning. Jacob came down to them and they strung out, moving down to the boats. Only the snake victim moaned, and Keith quickly despatched him, taking the hat. They pushed the bodies into the water, allowing the current to take them and knowing crocs would soon find them, and the tigerfish would be on hand to clean up. Even if any bodies made it through unscathed and landed on either shore, the word would spread like wildfire among the villages, adding to the rumours of the Rhodesian forces' apparent invincibility. They checked the dugouts for any more snakes before dragging them further into the bush. Jacob disabled the claymores that had been set to cover an upstream breakout, and they retreated towards the Rukomeshi confluence before full light. They embraced each other and promised each other a few beers next time they met off-duty, knowing full well it was unlikely. Keith and Jacob would resume their patrol down along Mana and back out towards Kanyemba. JJ and Henry would retrace the group's steps towards the crossroads to try and find any cache recently used or set up. By midmorning both units were on their way. Henry took the lead, picking up the trail easily and, judging by the depth of boot imprints, it was clear that they were already travelling light. They were soon up through the narrow pass, but had to slow, as there might be booby traps set by the group to discourage and kill any pursuers. Just beyond the narrow area, Henry stopped and held up a clenched fist. JJ stopped and waited, moving the safety catch on his AK to the off position.

Obviously, Henry did not like the sign in front of him and was trying to work it out. Then he came back towards JJ and softly said that there was soft ground and the footprints had stopped being regular in file and had a mixture of forward and backward prints. He suspected a booby trap and proposed he would drop his kit and move forward slowly at ground level, probing with his knife. At one point he gesticulated to his right, having seen signs to that side. JJ immediately moved to that side and began a step search of the ground, mid-line and eye-level. 30 minutes later, Henry had unearthed a Russian-made mine, and JJ found 2 claymores directed at waist-level for anyone on the path who would have moved at the underfoot mine. They disabled all three devices and reburied them, deep enough not to bother anyone. They marked the spot as best they could and noted the position. They found a corresponding sign showing deviation off the trail a few yards further on and concluded that was the end of the trap. Still, it was with some trepidation they took those first steps retracing the group's steps, this time with JJ on point. Some 100 yards on they came across a major departure from the trail, which lead them into a small area that clearly had been their camp for the previous stop. The trail from the crossroads direction showed deeper footprints, signifying that more weight had been carried by the group coming to this area, yet lighter on leaving. The cache had to be close by. It took them another few minutes, but they soon found the dump. It was larger than normal and contained substantial arms, as well as a handheld Russian ground to air missile launcher, but no missiles. They needed to get the info to Karoi for a unit to come and lift the haul, as they guessed the importance of their find. They figured that although there was no prearrangement now for the flyover, as there had been for the two days previously, there may well be another flight down the river to get more news, and Keith would tell them about the letters and the route JJ and Henry were taking. They settled down and decided to camp there for the day, as it was near evening. Around 1630 they heard the familiar *whup-whup* of an Alouette coming up the Rukomeshi and JJ quickly radioed up, saying they had found a major cache of weapons, including a Strela missile launcher. He gave his ground reference and requested a unit to come and take charge of the cache. The pilot said he would relay his request and fly back down the Rukomeshi within the hour. It was already dark, and they knew it would likely be the morning again before they were contacted.

Sure enough, it was at first light that the chopper returned, and he brought a friend with him. When JJ called him, he was advised to stay put and that a unit of 6 were going to land close by and join them to take charge of the cache. Within an hour six personnel came blundering down the trail and looked surprised when a blackened JJ suddenly appeared and motioned for them to follow. He led them off trail and to the cache site. Henry appeared, again from nowhere, and said hi. The unit were surprised to see how large the cache was and began to chatter on the radio they brought with them, obviously to a bigger unit coming in on the Mana track with a couple of Unimogs. Henry and JJ were told they were to go without delay out to the landing area they had just used themselves, and a pickup was arranged for midday.

The chopper that met them had orders to go straight to the South Salisbury camp, where they were first congratulated by their CO and then debriefed by Army Intelligence and Special Branch. They would learn later that the missile launcher was used in the downing of Flight 825, and the letters they took from the pair headed towards the Mission were clear orders to certain sympathising tribal chiefs to attack a number of European farms using cached arms. Those sympathisers were identified, and the information they provided gave locations of several arms caches.

CHAPTER 12

Ndole Bay 1986

An open safari cruiser appeared with six passengers and their luggage for the out flight. Jasper and Sophie, Jonty and Paddy, and Paul and Donna waited while the cruiser was emptied, and then took their seats to be taken to the actual lodge, which was effectively the terminal. First of all they had to watch the ritual of the passengers pointing out their luggage before boarding and the cruiser driver standing in front of each engine whilst the pilot started them, with a very small looking extinguisher should there be a fire. Once the two engines were running, the plane turned and trundled off down to the bush end of the runway strip testing its flight surfaces and rudder before turning to line up for take-off over the lake. It looked a terribly short runway. The plane held, racing its engines up almost to full power for what seemed like minutes before the pilot released the brakes. The plane leapt forward like a scalded cat and was already hurtling past the gazebo. They watched almost in horror, willing the plane to lift free of the strip, knowing there was little chance it could stop itself from falling straight into the lake should anything untoward happen. It was definitely a case of getting it right first time, every time, and the pilots did, with the plane lifting up just as it came to the end of the strip. It hung in the air, flying a few feet off the lake surface for a few hundred yards, before finally climbing and banking left back over the land towards the south.

The breeze forced by the cruiser driving was welcome, if only for the two minutes it took to reach the lodge. Once there, Paul took charge of the luggage and got it loaded into a 25-foot banana boat for the final leg of their journey to Ndole Bay lodge, some 15 miles round the coast. Paul had actually finished with fishing for the season, and had already sent his gang to pick up his cruiser and take it back to Ndola, but apparently a group of fishermen had run a boat at speed into a rocky outcrop in an inlet leading to their camp. Two had died, and the Zambian police had asked Paul to have a look at the wreck and determine if there was any mechanical failure that may have caused the accident. Everyone knew that the group had left the Kasaba Bay lodge bar well-oiled and simply took the wrong line into the inlet at night while trying to line up on their camp lights, but Paul had to check. He had built the boat in the first place. Paul signalled everything was ready and they all went down into the boat. As the driver set off, he pointed over to the island, more a sand bar, just ahead, where they could see a big black-looking crocodile sunning himself. Paul said he was over 20 feet, making him a monster, and indeed he proved it by standing up. Truly, he was the biggest croc Jasper had ever seen; he stood at least 3 feet high as he walked, then slithered into the lake. He was thought to be 75+ years old and regularly patrolled this bottom corner of the lake, being sited over a range of 50 miles. Jasper's antennae were twitching, as the driver just did not seem to fit his role, and he noticed a weapon when the man leaned back to squeeze the fuel pump in the line to the motor. He made sure he was close to the back and resolved to jump on the driver if anything odd happened.

Everything about Tanganyika was big. The lake itself was among the deepest in the world; it really was like an ocean, and it made Kariba look silly. No wonder the kapenta here were bigger than Kariba, and they were the ones used to stock Kariba; the tigerfish were of the gargantuan species and the Nile perch can grow in excess of 300 pounds and 6 feet long. They settled down for the hour's journey and once out into the lake it seemed even bigger. With the regular slapping of the hull as it charged through the waves, it was possible to feel a little nauseous, and indeed the frequency of the waves was much shorter than at sea, about 19 to 20 feet, hence boats should be bigger than that to prevent over-pitching. Like Kariba, they would find the seventh wave seemed to be bigger. Sophie, with her captain's hat, certainly would not want to be caught in a squall out here and it confirmed for her how important it was to be aware of any lake's foibles and moods. As they came towards the land and Ndole Bay lodges, they could see roan antelope down at the shore, emerging out of the bush, which seemed to come right to the edge, and then they were there. They could see water cobra swimming around the jetty, reputedly more venomous than their land cousins; definitely no swimming.

They were shown to individual lodges, each of which consisted of a large room with a big double bed and ceiling fans, with a bathroom and shower at the back. The bed had mozzie nets and a small fridge with bottles of water in it. There was one of those Ali Baba laundry baskets, and if you left your dirty washing in the morning before you went to breakfast, your washing would be done and returned ironed by midday. The bar and restaurant was in a main central lodge, which was where everyone met after freshening up. As they sat chatting over beer and nuts, a twin engine Cessna came over the lake from the direction of Tanzania and clearly was coming in to land close to the Lodge. Jonty said there was a bush strip a few hundred yards away and that this would be the man they had come to meet.

Jasper asked Jonty, in a discreet moment, "Why are there six men above and beyond normal staffing, all of whom look like military men?" He added, "And the boat driver had a concealed weapon."

Jonty smiled and said, "You've noticed, and that's cost me 50 bucks, because I didn't think you would spot them. Now I have to tell Tony he was right about your instinct. They are there because Marshall is an important wheel and protocols have to be abided by."

In a few minutes James Marshall, flanked by a man who seemed to melt into the shadows, strode into the lodge, dressed almost like his interpretation of a big game hunter, complete with leopard skin band around his hat. The shorts, knee length socks, and double-breasted khaki shirt actually just looked out of place.

Sophie said to Jasper, "A pith helmet would have been better, or golf gear." Jasper shushed her. Introductions made and drinks in hand, it fell to Jim, as he told everyone to call him, to make general conversation and present his credentials before dinner. They learned he had a wife and three children; the wife stayed with him in Nairobi, the kids at schools in Britain. He had been the Chief Conservation ambassador for the UN at first, and despite having been published on environment vs. man themes, he had become passionately involved, if not obsessed, with elephants. He had asked for the specific role of the UN's policeman regarding ivory exploitation and had been accepted with open arms. He had been given a wide-ranging brief to police the poaching of ivory and progress prosecutions for poaching and its trade through the International Courts of Justice. The difficulties seemed to pile up, as most of the ivory seemed to go east, and China was blocking many prosecutions. The trade was undoubtedly into China, from Asia and Africa, but through the satellite friends of China or western enclaves like Hong Kong and Macao. The big culprits were in the Koreas and China, so stopping trade in Hong Kong was not going to achieve a lot. Since China was a member of the UN Security Council, the UN had to tread carefully for fear of disturbing what China felt was her sphere of influence. It had taken a few years and some distinctly underhand alliances between Interpol and selected officials in certain countries, but they were now beginning to make progress. Since Paul and Donna were present, no mention could be made of the real purpose of Jim's presence other than he was interested in talking to people like Jasper who were involved in elephant behaviour and their effect on environments. Over dinner, the main star of which was some beautifully but simply prepared Nile perch, they talked a lot about Jasper's elephant surveys and his conclusions. At one point, when Jasper was relating how important elephants can be in tribal lore,

Jim interrupted as if a penny had dropped, and enquired whether Jasper was related to a well-reputed anthropologist called Frank Jackson, down in the University of Natal. When Jasper nodded and said Frank was his father, Jim was delighted, and said he knew Frank and his work having met him several times. The conversation moved on and when Sophie's exploits, not as the businesswoman of Osprey Safaris, but more as a Kariba captain and fisherwoman became known, Paul began to tell stories of his fishing on Tanganyika and the two of them began to talk boats. Sophie described the Osprey and Paul was impressed, as he knew the boat type and the hull makers. He did say that she and Jasper should come out tomorrow with him and Donna to check out the wreck and then jokingly added that they could do some proper fishing, not the Kariba stuff. Sophie accepted but Jonty cut in, saying that unfortunately he, Jim, and Jasper were to meet about the detail of elephant surveys in Zimbabwe, but maybe Sophie would go.

Paul then said, "Well if you three are tied up, it will be my pleasure to take all three ladies off into the blue yonder," adding with a wink, "Girls, what goes on tour, stays on tour. These guys will never know what they missed."

Well-fed and thirsts slaked, the get-to-know-each-other session was now complete. It would save a lot of time tomorrow and allow the whole day for their discussions. Saying goodnight to each other, they all went off to bed and shortly the camp's generators were shut off. Silence fell like a brick wall and then, as the night orchestra gained its confidence, the noise of the night slowly took over. With the array of stars and a very distinct Milky Way dominating the sky, it was very romantic if you were in that mood, despite the croaking of frogs. The couple, like all couples on holiday, were certainly in the mood.

After Jasper and Sophie had made love, he lay with her head in the crook of his shoulder and stroked her hair, asking, "Are you trying to wear me out? You've become quite amorous lately?"

"Are you complaining? I don't believe it, did you want me to stop?" She laughed, and could feel him almost blushing but then he surprised her by asking if she was trying to get pregnant. "Would you mind if I was?"

Again, she was a little surprised when he answered, "No, I would not mind at all, in fact its time you were, before you become a dried-up old prune!" She punched him none too gently and then said she had stopped her contraception a month ago. Now he felt brave enough, and once more he need not have bothered, but he said, "Look, I want to be a father now, and I have to admit it's scared me, particularly where we live. I want your promise that when you are pregnant, I want you out of here and down in Durban until the baby is born. We'll get your parents over; I am sure my Mum and Dad would be delighted to have them and you. Seriously, if I am going to do this job for them, it should be easy enough for me, but I don't want the worry of your presence. Please do not give me a hard time over this, I promise I shall be careful."

She propped herself up on her elbows and said, "I'll go whenever you want me to, but I need your promise that you will not take risks and you will take Henry as back up. You have to be around to look after me and our family." And so that was that.

The next morning, they awoke to the lapping of waves on the beach and lay in bed watching out of the front of their lodge as the sun came up over the lake. There was the usual soothing symphony of insect and bush life noise in the background, except for the shrillness of frogs croaking, which thankfully seemed to weaken as the sun began to poke up over the lake. It was almost as if the water on the horizon was holding onto the sun, stopping it from rising, and then suddenly it broke free and began its climb into the sky. At the same time a new symphony of noise took over with birdsong being the dominant instrument, finally shutting up the croaking of the frogs. Another dawn had announced itself, another day in paradise it seemed. They showered and dressed, strolling hand in hand along the beach and dodging the waves that lapped ashore before heading up to the main lodge for breakfast. Paul's cruiser was tied up by the jetty where they had landed, and already the boys were loading fishing gear and cool boxes with both bait and cold drinks. Already the sun was hot, and they had to stop and put on their flops on for the sand was hot enough to burn their soles.

Once inside the cool lodge, they took juice and fruit from the buffet and sat. They were joined first by Paul and Donna, and then Jonty and Paddy, and finally by Jim. The waiters were on hand to ask how they wanted their eggs, bacon, and toast. Coffee or tea was continuously offered, to the extent they were almost scared to drink their cups because they would be refilled instantly. Once breakfast was over, the staff brought packed lunches, which were sent down to the boat for the boat party. Paul said he wanted to get underway, so could the girls please get their hats and whatever sun-creams/blocks and potions they may need and meet him down at the jetty. Jonty and Jasper both took their wives down, saying their goodbyes and waving them all off with the usual "Have a good one!" Jonty anticipated the question and assured him that there was no danger to their wives.

They turned and walked back to meet Jim before moving over to another lodge which had been prepared as a meeting room. Jim's companion, who had not been present last night, was finally introduced as a personal bodyguard, Jim being seen as a threat in that shady world of ivory trading. Jonty added that there was a squad of Zambian secret service men about, and it was only then that Jasper began to realize the gravity of the meeting and why it was held in so remote a spot. He had a nagging feeling that the photography job back home was not going to turn out to be his only contribution, and that for some reason he was being interviewed. He would tread carefully.

Big Decisions at Ndole Bay 1986

Paul cruised out of the bay, then opened up the twin Mercury90 units to get the cruiser on the plane, and off they went towards Kasaba Bay. The girls were chatting amongst themselves when he called back to Sophie and asked her if she would not mind taking over, as he wanted to go below and prepare his wet suit and air cylinder. First, he got on the ship to shore and called the Zambian Lakemaster, identifying the boat and that he was en route, Ndole Bay to the crash site, giving an ETA of 20 minutes. He then gave them a reference from the charts to indicate where he might consider fishing after he checked out the crashed boat. He would confirm on reaching the fishing areas and on his return to Ndole. The Lakemaster acknowledged and confirmed the frequency he should keep the radio on. Paul said that the authorities were rigid on you keeping in Zambian waters and that you did not stray into Zairean or Tanzanian waters without permission or notification. He gave her a point on the land ahead and just told her to aim that way. He added there would be no underwater obstructions and they were too far out for hippo. So, Sophie was at the bridge, playing with a smaller cruiser than the Osprey, but one that rode the waves more than sailed through them. Paul was back as she neared the shore and saw the inlet where the accident occurred, spotting the wreck on some rocks 10 yards offshore. As she came off the plane, and the boat sunk back into the water, Paul asked her to slowly move over towards the wreck while he went and sat on the bow to spot for her. Donna was set the task of dropping the anchor over the side on his shout. Sophie followed Paul's hand signals just off the idle and knocked the linked levers into neutral as Donna dropped the anchor. It was not deep and as the anchor bit, the boat settled with the onshore current some 10 yards the lake side of the wreck. Paddy went to the cool boxes to find some drinks, wine for her and Donna, but Sophie went for plain cold water.

Paul kitted up, but before he slipped over the side, he produced a pistol, which he gave to Sophie in case of baboons or cats coming across the rocks once he was over to the wreck. He went over and no sooner was he on board the wreck than baboons appeared out of nowhere, coming down the trees to the shore, screaming and showing off their considerable canines. Whether they could see Sophie had a gun or not, they didn't get on the rocks, so Sophie didn't need to shoot. Fifteen minutes later Paul emerged from the wreck and went over to have a look at the exposed keel. With that, he swum back over and got back on board. He said he had seen enough and asked Sophie to start up and get out of the inlet. She jiggled the throttles and by first backing up in the direction of the anchor got the girls to pull the freed anchor up and stow it on board. She gave herself some room and backed out into the middle of the inlet, said goodbye to the raucous baboons, and moved out into the main lake, getting the boat quickly onto the plane to reduce the drag.

Paul stowed his gear and came back and took over the controls and headed further towards Kasaba Bay before cutting into the next inlet where, surprisingly, what looked like a small factory was situated. He headed over to the jetty and tied up.

Jasper, Jonty, and Jim sat inside their meeting lodge, where the overhead fans whirred quietly, providing at least a cooling draught which just about enough to stop sweating. Jim's bodyguard sat on the veranda. Jonty kicked off, explaining that Jasper had been suggested to be recruited as part of the team by his Zimbabwean colleagues when they were discreetly approached for participating in Operation Tembo. This was based on Zimbabwe wanting to be as distant as possible, therefore diplomatically shielded. Jasper was known as the local elephant expert, an ex-Selous Scout to boot, therefore, utterly deniable by the politicians in the event of any difficulty. Apart from Sophie and possibly Jasper's old Selous partner, only two people in any of the Zimbabwean official, or unofficial, state organs knew or would know of his participation.

Jonty went on, "It's as tight as it can be, and his bush skills can only be an advantage. I would recommend we bring him in."

"I agree," said Jim, "but before we go on, I need to ask you to confirm that based on what you have been told about Operation Tembo, you are willing to join us. We will of course pay you, but you would not be as available to participate in your current activities, though I understand your wife and partner could practically run the safari business anyway. There would be no official appointment at this stage and you would only be identified as a consultant, so there would be no need for anyone else in my organisation to know who you are or, more importantly, what you are doing."

Jasper instinctively knew he wanted to be part of Tembo, but did not want to seem over-keen or as though he had not thought things through. He replied carefully, "Of course I want to do it, and I will find the Zimbabwe cache, photograph and gather the evidence needed, as was outlined by Tony and his boss I presume. My inclination is to join you, but before I say for certain, I want you to know that we are trying to start a family, so I have to consider that too. I will probably have to give up the safari business because frankly, our lifestyle and environment around Kariba is not ideal for a family. I do want to stay involved with the elephants and their habitats, but perhaps from another base. I would suggest I would like to see this current operation through. If we still like each other, then I can join, but that's the best I can do for the moment." He sighed and wondered if he had become over-cautious.

As Paul and the girls walked towards the buildings, Sophie noticed an array of what seemed like insulated containers that had been fitted with refrigeration units and hitched up to gennies; clearly they were being used as cold stores. Chris de Beer came down and greeted them. He was part owner, part manager of the fish plant. He had two boats that went out into the lake and caught Nile perch on lines, which were then filleted and frozen. When a unit was full, a horse would bring up an empty container and take the full one away. The idea of the individual generators was that they could keep their contents frozen even if the horse broke down or was held up at border crossings, for this fish was destined for South Africa. Chris offered them lunch, which they gratefully accepted, and a quick tour round the factory, which really was a row of tables and a crowd of woman filleting by hand. Only the fillets were exported; the remainder of the fish was sold to a canning factory in Ndola, mainly for the domestic market in Zambia. Paddy knew of the Ndola factory because Jonty grew tomatoes and haricot beans for them, as well as beef for their star product, corned beef. The corned beef was an international brand and differed from the South American version in that it was unextracted and in a round, not square, tin. It was held to be the best, being unextracted, which Paddy said meant no gravy generated in the process was used for other products.

Lunch was of course some perch fillets, which, with a simple salad, satisfied everyone. Donna said it was nice to drop in there because Chris was always delighted to see people, probably because he had never been able to persuade any girlfriends to come and stay for any length of time, and he was in danger of becoming a recluse. Chris asked Paul if he had been to the wreck yet, remarking that only idiots would get fired up and risk a night trip, especially at speed. He had been part of the party which had retrieved the two bodies and signalled for air ambulance to come for two others who had broken limbs and chest injuries. Paul agreed they had been stupid, but neglected to say that he had found a couple of discarded cigarettes, one jammed behind the throttles, which suggested that not only may the men have been inebriated, but they may also have smoked some dagga, probably

Malawi gold. There was probably no need to publicise that, as it would not help anyone now, so his report would conclude that no technical fault with the engines or props were responsible for the crash. Whether the police publicised the fact that the men had been drinking and simply misjudged their speed, entry, or both, into the inlet at night was their call, not his. Paul paid for two cases of fillets for the restaurant and he would pick them up on the way to the plane tomorrow morning. With that they left, and Paul said they would maybe try a little fishing on the way back.

Jim was very happy with Jasper's reply, and indeed thought it was a mature reply, showing that emotion could be controlled, and he was thinking much further ahead than just the next phase of Tembo. He looked up at Jonty, who was also happy, and they nodded at each other.

"Let's get down to business then. How much do you know so far, and what do you think we are asking at this stage? I'd like you to tell me so I can see how much you have understood, not assumed."

"Well, I know that you believe around 30 tonnes of ivory has been brought from Zaire to a bond in Kapiri, controlled by two North Korean diplomats who are based in Harare but are also accredited in Zambia. I assume it is brought through in small lots from Katanga province via Ndola. I know that a similar amount is supposedly coming from the Luangwa, probably in dribs and drabs also to the Kapiri bond. I am led to believe that yet another 30 tonnes are coming from Zimbabwe, from a cache that is currently established in Hurungwe. Half of that is from Wankie and the remainder from my patch. I know that we have labelled the Korean diplomats as Kim A and Kim B and they are working with a Brigadier in the Zimbabwean Army who has recruited an unknown number of ex-combatants to get and move the ivory. We believe that because some vehicles and two containers have been booked for 18 or so days' time, that will be when the Zim shipment will be moved to Kapiri under diplomatic tags. Tony and Ken are certain the two Kims will accompany or be in close attendance, as they have notified the foreign affairs people they are going into Zambia in that time frame. I assume they will supervise loading of all ivory, probably around 90 tonnes, probably 6 containers all diplomatically tagged, then hand it over to the Chinese management on the Tazara for transfer to Dar. Its due to be met by a Chinese freighter that you think will dock in Dar at the same time. I have to find the Hurungwe camp, secure photographic evidence of the Korean involvement and the ivory itself. My only contacts will be with Jonty for the Zambian SB and Tony for the Zimbabweans. My role is to get Zimbabwe off the hook with their Korean supporters to make them look good with the world, and I am completely deniable if it goes wrong. I assume you will not allow the ivory on board the ship and I assume that there are other reasons why I have been pointed towards you. I have to say I am not entirely sure that I am not a potential scapegoat or indeed being set up as one."

Jim smiled and said, "A little bit of paranoia is not a bad thing, but in this case I believe you to be safe in that I know, Jonty knows and as you say you have the credentials that you're on the elephants' side re: their conservation. I know the man you met personally as Ken and his involvement at UN level has been demonstrated by your government agreeing to assist my offices in prosecution of both poaching and ownership of ivory via Ken's department. He is your country's top Intelligence Officer, despite his colour. Your President is no fool and ensured he retained him at Independence."

This was news to Jasper, and though he had suspected the man was high up, he did not realize how high. He also would not accept that Tony would double cross him, so with Jim's assurances, he dismissed one of his two questions.

Jim continued, "I have understood that you are an authority on elephant behaviour, particularly in the Zambezi valley, but most of your work seems to be unpublished, other than in addenda to your Parks and Wildlife journals. Can you tell me why and, given your background, your father, why did you change from the anthropology side to the 'animal' side? Will you stay a hunter, a conservationist, return to academia or what? Will you still be running a safari business?"

Jasper smiled to himself, thinking, now we are into the interview part, but what for exactly? He would play along for now and see where this led. He began, "My father began taking me with him on his field trips in the late sixties and at first I was fascinated by the cultural aspects of tribal life that my father was documenting. I literally was absorbed by the culture, but of course I was not party, like my father was, to tribal life before the Kariba dam. I was viewing more the adaptation to environment than the actual cultural changes. Anyway, it was enough to set me off down the anthropology road and I suppose I had dreams of trudging the length of the Zambezi and discovering how the river made or influenced the cultures of the various tribes along it. I was interested in any distinct differences or similarities in habitats along the river's length to that of Kariba lake, and how animal populations adapted. There was an opportunity looming in that the Portuguese were building Cahora Bassa downstream of Kariba, so perhaps I would be able to complete my father's work." Jasper stopped to pour himself a drink of water and went on, "I was spending a lot of time up at Kariba and on the Zambezi down towards Mana, and increasingly I was left with some of the African helpers and researchers who began to teach me names of plants, animals, how to recognise spoor, dung, what to look for when tracking and when to back off, which plant's fruits were useful, to recognise various trails; just total bushcraft. I was totally hooked and even changed my degree, because I figured it was the habitats that drove everything locally and nature was the key to life. I was drawn into wanting to know how nature with its slow inevitable pace adapted to the sudden sharp changes that that either occurred naturally or were indeed man-made, how balances were restored. I was just a devotee of the bush. However, I was rudely interrupted by the gathering pace of our war, which, in turn, was a rapid change to the environment, especially the fauna, so in a way it would be another avenue to explore. I think fate played its part, and meeting Andre Rabie gave me the ability to learn more about how to use the bush to survive, actually how to live. I learnt skills which are probably a compression of what man had to learn from when he came onto this planet."

Jonty cut into Jasper's discourse, saying, "Jim, you may have heard of the Selous Scouts? Jasper was one of the few, I don't think he would tell you, but his tracking skills and knowledge of animal behaviour are beyond a science, they're an art form."

Jim spoke in a more official voice and acknowledged he had not known that Jasper was an ex-Selous, and said, "That kinda explains a few things and takes care of the past part of how you got here. It also tells me why you can handle the photo-shoot down your end."

Jasper continued, "I have only just begun to think about the future and Sophie and myself want to start a family; neither of us is getting any younger so we need to change a few things. For one thing, despite my love of Kariba, it is not a climate for that. It's hard on the women and children, so I do not expect we shall continue to live there, and I shall give up Osprey soon. I do fancy trying to return to researching how animal behaviour is adapting to their changing habitats, being a sort of spokesman on behalf of the animals. God knows they will need one as we continue to fix things that aren't broken in the name of progress. I don't think I'll ever do that from an ivory tower, pardon the pun, so I hope I can still get my hands dirty so to speak. I am not at all sure about being a full-time teacher, certainly not at school, but possibly and only occasionally, at University. By the way, I would like to get together with others, particularly those who have studied elephants, to compare notes and see if we can trace similar behaviour and how change affects them. Perhaps we can learn how to look after what we have left!" With that, he stopped and thought, I've actually said what I want to say about the future, but strangely he felt glad he had now plotted a course, something to follow.

Paul headed out into the lake after leaving Chris and the fish factory, and started towards Ndole Bay, passing the inlet with its wreck, and started his fish sonar to see if he could find a shoal of perch, or even a shoal of kapenta, which would certainly attract both perch and Tanganyika's gargantuan tigerfish. It was hot, still around 40°C, and with the glare off the water it was essential to have sunblock on and wear proper polarising sun specs. The water would be cool in comparison, at about 25°C surface temperature, though much cooler below the surface. Tanganyika was considered to be the second largest and deepest freshwater lake in the world, after Siberia's Lake Baikal, holding about 16% of the world's fresh water. When considering its general size of 420 miles long, up to 45 miles wide, with depths ranging from about 2,000 feet to a maximum of almost 5,000 feet, it could hardly be anything but an inland sea. The sides fell away very rapidly, almost immediately, so you needed a lot of line on big reels if you got a fish on.

Paul finally found a site he was happy with and let the cruiser drift across a small bay. He baited up three rods and let the girls loose. Paddy soon got fed up and chose to join Paul on the bridge, leaving Donna and Sophie to pursue the fish. Both looked as if they were experts, which of course they both were, and it was not long before both had bites and were reeling in. Both had caught small Nile perch, about 4-pounders which seemed a lot heavier when reeling in. Donna had checked Sophie's reel and said she had been at about 50 feet, and the deeper you went the heavier the deadweight would seem. She explained they spliced different coloured line on the reels so that they had an idea of depth. The first 100 feet wound on to the reel was black line, then next a red, then yellow followed by light green and finally standard transparent line. She shouted over to Paul and asked what the depth was; he looked the depth-finder and shouted back that it was about 150 feet. She said the bottom would be about halfway down the light green line as it came off the reel. She also told Sophie that bringing fish up from deep should be done slowly, just like a diver, to allow the fish to adjust to the pressure change.

"If you come up quickly it would look as if the fish has turned inside out, with its innards coming up through its mouth."

They caught a few more perch which went into the live well; they would be appreciated by the workers back at the camp. By now all the girls wanted was to shower and grab a nap before the evening, so Paul stowed the rods and started for Ndole.

Jim Marshall stood, stretching his limbs and looking Jasper straight in the eye, and said almost dramatically, "I believe we can do something together. I was hoping you would not turn out to be a zealot but more of a passionate realist, yet I suspect your time in the Special Forces has taught you to control emotion. No doubt you are thinking ahead and that's what I wanted to hear from you."

Jasper relaxed, happy that his second concern was clearly important, not only from his own point of view, but also from Jim's. It was true enough he thought that he probably preferred animals to most people, they were far more honest than people. He waited to hear what was going to come.

Jim continued, "As you have worked out, I am not so much concerned with the current operation between you, Jonty and your Zim people, but I have to look for someone to take over my role as coordinator of the UN's investigations and prosecution division. I do not think this is a role for some comfy bureaucrat looking for glory, but for a younger man who can get his hands dirty, as you say, a man who not only knows literally how nature thinks, is passionate and above all can keep his cool, a fundi. You will see things that will churn your guts, yet you will have to appear almost dispassionate, otherwise your enemies will tear you apart. You do not have to be competent in international law; in fact, better you are not, then you will not drown in all the flotsam designed to stop you. You will have enough legal experts at your disposal anyway. I want someone who hates the office desk, because your enemies will do everything to keep you there, someone who can ignore bureaucracy but deliver. I will be there to watch your back. Have I read you right?"

Jasper looked at both Jim and Jonty, smiled and, without hesitation, asked, "Where do I sign?"

Suddenly it was as if all tension evaporated, and he shook hands with Jim and then Jonty, who whispered "Makorokoto," – congratulations in Shona – then, "How about a beer?"

"Excellent idea," boomed Jim, "then let's get down to the current operation. We can go over the details of your appointment later, but I would say one thing which is not compulsory in any way: think carefully where you want to be based. I would advise you do not live in an area that is where the animals are, you could be at unnecessary risk, better you just come into those areas, but you did say Kariba was not likely to be home for much longer. Go anywhere, that's the beauty of your role, make the office come to you. There, that's it, now where's that beer."

CHAPTER 14

Making Plans Ndole Bay 1986

With the clinking of glasses, they toasted each other and sat down to get on with the business at hand. Jonty kicked off, "We do know that about 30 tonnes of Zairean ivory has been funnelled through Ndola from Lubumbashi and on to the Kapiri bond rented by the Kims. We know that the couriers of the ivory have taken it from the forest caches around Ndola, and this has been mostly as single tusks. A local haulage firm has been identified, more specifically the drivers who pick up the ivory. There are about 10 of them, but we will only get to determine if the owners of the trucks knew what was going on when we pull the drivers in. We have maintained surveillance for six months and have enough evidence, but with only dribs and drabs being moved at a time, it is possible that the owners of the company do not know. We don't, however, have any evidence that the Kims have had anything to do with the organisation and acquisition of the ivory in Zaire, other than the provision of bond at Kapiri. They are not accredited to Zaire and, as far as we can determine, they have never been there, so we assume other Korean involvement from Zaire diplomats or through third parties unknown to us." Jonty paused to drink, and went on, "The Zambian ivory is stashed at Musoro and is being moved in five-ton loads twice a week down the main eastern highway to Kapiri. They have been doing this for the past month and we have the full evidence we need to prove the involvement of the truck owners and drivers. We know the truck owners have organised ordinary Zambian villagers to poach the ivory and have solid photo and audio surveillance of these owners and the Kims' from their meetings in the Pamodzi Hotel. The Zambian ivory will be completed next week and we have notice of the bond booking a 40-foot container and two

20-foot containers for two weeks' time, and the generators at the bond are running full bore; we assume this is to air the raw ivory as well as disperse any smells. This leaves the Zim operation. We know that the Kims have had contact with an army brigadier whose identity is known and whose family have a contract haulage business. In fact, they request the same brigadier as their security, according to protocols. We know that the Kims have given notice of travel to the Zim and Zambian authorities for 18 days' time, so we pretty much know when that ivory will be moved. Two horses and containers are booked to coincide with that timing. The brigadier has recruited ex-combatants as well as some army personnel, with two trucks under his command which he has used to shoot some 200 elephant in Wankie and bring that ivory to the Chirundu camp. The other 15 tonnes is being obtained in the game areas around Chirundu and is being carried to the combatants' camp. They will load the containers and in the meantime guard the cache. Jasper is scheduled to go into the bush locate the camp, provide photo surveillance, and wait for the Kims. First prize is to get pictures of them attaching diplomatic tags to the containers. We think they will drive the next day and get to Kapiri before nightfall. The Zim authorities will close down the combatants and take care of the brigadier. The photos of the Kims attaching tags at Chirundu plus our pictures at Kapiri will allow the Zimbabweans and ourselves to insist on the Kims repatriation and to be served with International Justice Courts warrants. Our intention is to allow the containers to be transferred to Tazara for potential shipment to Dar."

Jim took over at this point, dealing with the outcome of the ivory. "We have a major operation which may or may not be entirely legal, but it will serve various agendas. Firstly, we need the containers to be loaded onto the Chinese ship, which is due to leave Shanghai in about a week's time, bound for Singapore. It will discharge several containers of Chinese-made electrical goods, probably destined for that city's Orchard Road dealers. The ship is then due to Bandar Abbas in Iran with machinery, probably arms, before crossing over to Mombasa with electrical goods, taking on some soya beans before it comes to Dar es Salaam. We cannot move on the ivory until it has been loaded onto the ship, and then we will use the Tanzanian army to execute an international warrant. At this stage, the Tanzanian authorities will know nothing at all and will be served the warrant for immediate execution. The warrant will be in the name of the World Wildlife Fund (WWF) and the United Nations Environmental Programme (UNEP), and Tanzania have subscribed to both organisations. Since the wholesale slaughter of the elephant population has been proven, they have become a leading member in trying to make the ivory trade illegal. We will pinpoint the containers, which we believe will have no diplomatic tags once loaded, so that the Chinese would have deniability, and the ship will be arrested as it leaves harbour. That way China can do nothing but comply in a public condemnation of ivory poaching, given its position in the UN and its Security Council permanent membership. As far as the Kims are concerned, we believe that they will remain in Zambia for the period that their travel documents say. They always have before, and they are accredited, so we think they will stay."

Jonty came back in, "We will watch them – in any event they will have to have a Zambian Protection Officer with them, and if they do leave prior to their end date, we will at least detain them until the ship is loaded. Zimbabwe have made clear they need to be at arm's length from the Koreans and are then diplomatically able to support any criminal charges. Once the ivory is loaded, we can then use the evidence of the Kims at the bond, the fitting of diplomatic tags – Jasper your shots will be needed – and we charge them with performing criminal acts on foreign soil and demand they are charged in international and UN laws. What will happen is they will be recalled under diplomatic immunity and disappear, their families too. We will try to interrogate the Zairean transporters, who of course have no diplomatic immunity, but apart from activities committed in Zambia, it will be difficult to persuade them to give up any bosses in Zaire. We may have to wait until the Zaire authorities get them, but by then they will be long gone."

Jim then asked if anyone had any questions. This time Jasper came in and said, "I have: what, if any, is the back- up plan§, if for any reason the ship gets out of Dar with the containers? Surely, for your purposes, delivery to the dock and the ship's manifest shows intent which allows for Chinese deniability?"

Jim smiled and said "Well, you might as well know from the start that there are other factors to be considered. True, the dockside should be enough, but we need to have insurance where the Chinese are concerned. They have shown signs they want to join in with the rest of the world but remain insanely jealous of what they call 'spheres of influence'. Basically, our hand in ensuring their cooperation regarding ivory is so much stronger if the consignment is onboard when they are stopped. Without insinuating the Tanzanians would deliberately foul up the mission, yes, there is a backup which ensures the ivory never gets to the east."

Jasper sighed. "That does not sound good for someone; let me guess, America or maybe Russia would like for China to get a bloody nose."

"Partly right, but our biggest supporter for stopping wholesale slaughter of the world's elephants is the USA, and they will take responsibility for the cargo never reaching the East. You won't believe this, but should the ship get away from Dar, a US submarine will launch a team of American Navy Seals who are all black and Arabic speakers to act as Somali pirates and take the ship during darkness. The 3 officers and 15 crew will be set adrift, and the ship sailed towards the Somali coastline, where it will be sunk with the ivory in deep water. The sub will pick up the team, and they were never there. Within six hours a British warship on its way to the Gulf, due to pay a courtesy trip to

Mombasa, will coincidentally come across the Chinese crew and pick them up. Their story is that they saw a distant fireball and headed for the area to determine if it was a ship and then to look for survivors. They will land the survivors at Mombasa. You can guess what the final backup is if the team fail to take the ship." Jim looked at Jasper with raised eyebrows and asked, "Does that help? Anything else?"

Jasper nodded, sat back and thought then said, "Do you know, I am not sure I would always be able to understand the politics, and I don't like the idea that we may have other goals than stopping the slaughter of the elephants in the first place."

Jim simply said, "As you said, the main objective is to prevent decimation, even extinction of the elephants, and always will be for your role. In this case we really are acting knowing that elephant are already dead, and we have used the potential stocks of ivory to close down a main route of organised poaching. I'm afraid that any conservation is always going to be political, given that politicians are the spokesmen of the people and are really the only ones who can fund it and transcend borders. That is why I want you to take charge on the ground, be the detective and the analyser. I shall deal with the politics and diplomatic issues."

Jasper felt more at ease and replied, "I can live with that."

Jim went on, "Look, I will pass onto you and introduce you to those law and order contacts I have made. Jonty is one, and no doubt you will find others, people that you can trust, and I have to guess your previous role for your country has in many ways taught you how to judge people and their sincerity. I hope I am not frightening you off. It won't be easy, it'll even be heart-breaking at times. I cannot deny it will be challenging, but that's why you will want to get up in the morning." Jim stopped and said "Maybe you guys need a comfort break, I know I do. Let's make ourselves comfortable and stretch our legs for a few minutes, and start back up in 15 minutes, say. I believe the girls are back listening to the chatter there. I think we will need another hour tops." With that they went out into the late afternoon sun, still having to squint against the shimmer of the lake's surface.

Jasper and Jonty met Sophie and Paddy as they were walking up from the jetty and duly asked how they got on. They then walked their partners back to their lodges. The fishing trip was a success, it seemed, and with Paul having seen the wreck, they had done all they needed to do. Sophie started to tell Jasper about their visit to the factory, but all Jasper could say was that he had some exciting news, but he would be another hour with Jim. Sophie said that was OK, as she wanted to go and shower and change, so he was despatched and told to hurry back so they could swap stories.

Back in the meeting, Jim once again opened and said he wanted to put into perspective just why they had such a mountain to climb. It was simply the value that people put on ivory regarding items such as the traditional gifts of dagger handles, hair trinkets, chopsticks, and the simple beauty of carvings. The sinister aspect, that of clandestine arms, was an important factor, as no hard cash was necessary to purchase those arms by currency strapped countries in Africa. Ivory provided no trail for accountants to follow. There was and remained an important cultural aspect with these gifts. Raw ivory had a value on the black market of anywhere from £150 per pound to £500 per pound. With average weights of tusks ranging from 200 to 250 pounds per elephant, there would be around 10 to 12 elephants needed per tonne of ivory. Unfortunately, there wasn't much large ivory anymore, and with killing of barely adult elephants, tusk sizes and therefore weights had reduced, meaning more elephant had to die per tonne.

So, as Jim began to say, "30 to 36 elephants died to provide enough tusk to be valued at £1 million. This one estimated shipment of 90 tonnes would be valued between £65.5 and £124 million; therefore, gentlemen, this 90 tonnes represents almost 1,100 elephants. There is a lot of money in this trade, and there are no winners, just losers. Worst of all, there is no real knowledge of how much ivory is already in the hands of the carvers. They simply inflate their holding stocks, which have never been verified. That will be another problem for us to look at." He continued "We have a two-pronged attack to fight the problem. The first, which I have been doing and you, Jasper, will take over, is against mass poaching, but the second side, which I will be able to concentrate on, will be education. If we can show the locals that the elephants are worth more to them alive than dead, then they will start to look after them. Tourism, for instance, pays millions to see these animals, so if we can get some sort of continuing income to the tribes in an area of habitat, they will see the benefit of keeping elephants alive, rather than a one–time kill. In fact, they will be lucky if they get £50 for killing an animal."

Jasper was certainly getting more excited by the minute, as he realized he was going to part of something that had a real chance of flying, and possibly delaying, if not saving a species from inevitable extinction. Maybe that's why America was contributing so much, remembering their slaughter of the Plains bison.

Then he got another example of how far America was willing to help: Jim opened his briefcase and brought out a series of aerial photographs, casually saying, "These are for you, Jasper, they may help."

It took a few seconds, but slowly he began to recognise the Zambezi, and picked up they were a series of satellite photographs, the first four being general to the Chirundu area, then some super close-ups of two areas circled on the first four photographic charts. He recognised the area where there was a failed, derelict sugar farm, but around some of the sheds he could see what appeared to be men in camouflage.

"How on earth did you get these?" was the incredulous response from Jasper.

"Oh, they came from the Pentagon, we have our sources. I'll introduce you after this is over. It will be your contact to use. Can you understand them? I have some notes to go with them." Jasper nodded, listening to Jim explain that Ken had asked him if they could divert a satellite over the Hurungwe area looking for military activity or a camp. Apparently, he gave two known army and security camps so they could be discounted, and the satellite made 6 general sweeps on its passes from Kariba to Mana. The analysts went over the pictures and highlighted two possible areas. The satellite then made two passes each with maximum resolution and produced the pictures in Jasper's hands. They would save a lot of time that would have been spent in searching the whole area trying to locate the cache. He could not get over the fact that a satellite could take pictures of such detail from that distance above the earth. Of course, what the satellite produced was not the pictures in hand, but the digital output that was transmitted back went through some NASA type gadgetry to produce graduated photo-maps of the sort Jasper was looking at.

Jim said, "You need to make what notes you need to, like coordinates and any detail you can see, such as how many men, but the pictures have to go back with me. I can tell you that the analysts think that apart from the eight men that are on camera, they believe that the pattern of movements around the camp suggest up to double that number of men, best guess probably 12 in total. The building to the left of the main sheds appears to be used as a bunkhouse. The road seems in reasonable condition throughout its 10-kilometre length, so that any lorry should make it OK. The place seems to have been chosen well and certainly is suitable. Now, gentlemen, anything else? If not, let's freshen up, get back to the ladies and enjoy a super evening here in the bush."

CHAPTER 15

Death Throes 1978–1980

Following the downing of Flight 825, there was a flurry of revenge ops which mostly consisted of air strikes and raids on the various camps inside Mozambique, but perhaps the most imaginative was the so-called Green Leader, or Operation Gatling. This was perhaps reported somewhat glamorously by the international press and did boost the morale of the nation. In the end it gave the enemy a bloody nose but could not save a country which would die, not because of military defeat, but for political expediency. The Green Leader episode involved a coordinated strike on three terrorist camps in Zambia using the Air Force and Army Special Forces. The aircraft crossed into Zambia below radar and arrived at Lusaka, telling the tower that they were controlling Zambian airspace and their jets would destroy any Zambian aircraft that attempted take-off. They also went to great lengths to state the incursion was not against the Zambian people but only against the terrorist camps within Zambia. During the period of action, no commercial flights were allowed into Zambian airspace, largely to the amusement of the incoming pilots. All targets were hit and eventually the forces departed back across the border. Famously, control of their airspace was given back to the Zambians by Green Leader. Lusaka tower had to endure the jibes of commercial pilots asking for Green Leader's permission to land. Back in Salisbury, banners and graffiti quickly appeared, supporting 'Green Leader for President'. As the year moved into 1979, a second Viscount Flight, 827, the Umniati, was hit, again after take-off from Kariba, killing all 59 on board. It was becoming more difficult to stop incursions and the number of guerrillas inside the country was increasing. Though it was not thought that the country would suffer a military defeat, the prospect of a long drawn out guerrilla struggle was just not on. The politicians tried to delay the inevitable by negotiating with moderate African leaders to bring into the world a new composite nation, which would suffer a cot death before its first birthday. In the end, the leaders of the guerrillas took control, and a new nation was born, finally ending the dying throes of the old nation. Rest in Peace, Rhodesia.

JJ and Henry were not involved in any more cross border raids, being considered to be more valuable in the Kariba-Mana-Karoi area, as indeed their success rate proved steady, both in terms of body count and arms cache finding. They were involved in the tracking of the group that shot down the second Viscount and initially picked up their tracks. However, on this occasion, the group split up almost immediately, and they could only point others in the directions taken. The two they continued to trail had clearly headed for Zambia immediately, and had already crossed the Zambezi when JJ and Henry caught up. They were not empty handed, however, as they discovered a new arms cache that the two they were tracking led them to. The last few months of their tour were more concerned with identifying arms caches and setting up of meet and greet ambushes as terrorists came to stock or stock up the caches. The guerrillas were now crossing the Zambezi at any time and in greater numbers, so the two-man unit became most effective in laying ambush at known cache points.

The end of the Selous Scouts came swiftly, after their founder and Major, Reid-Daly, resigned his commission. He had become aware that he had a 'mole' and offices, telephones were found to be bugged. He began to give no information out about his troops and indeed their service records began to be destroyed. The Selous had always kept their own service records, allowing no copies at all. By the end of 1979, only 4 months later, the Selous Scouts had disappeared into the mists of history, with only their more senior officers identifiable. These few 'took the gap' to South Africa by the time of the April elections, for they

knew they would be in line for detention, and probably elimi-
nation, as ex-Selous Scouts. The South Africans were extremely
jealous of the success of the Scouts and made it known that they
would be welcome in 'white South Africa', but clearly the apartheid state was not a popular option for the black Scouts. Most
of the black scouts managed to drift away to the TTL's and lose
themselves there; a few did indeed go to South Africa together
with their white partners to continue army life. The majority of
the whites left for South Africa or to countries where they had
passport rights, but a few, like JJ, decided to stay. When JJ and
Henry came to decide what to do, both had agreed they would
not 'take the gap' and go down South, either to their forces or
just as individuals of a lost tribe. Henry really only had one option, and that was to re-join his family in Matabeleland. Despite
the briefness of their parting, both knew the bond that existed between them which was stronger than any faith or culture.
They were boets, brothers. With that Henry was gone. Jasper
returned to Churchill Avenue and re-established his links with
the University.

A final word should be said about the Selous Scouts, demon-
strating their magnificent record, even though it became a lost
cause. Throughout the war the Scouts lost 30 men out of their
total number of almost 1,500. Within their borders, they were
credited with up to two thirds of guerrilla deaths, either due to
direct action or the indirect action of calling in the army. The
number of guerrilla deaths outside the borders is unknown, but
is thought to be in the thousands.

They had done their job, but the life had gone from the body
they tried to save.

CHAPTER 16

Plans 1986

Jasper practically floated across the sand to his lodge, and he was clearly on cloud nine when he began to speak to Sophie, almost not knowing where to begin. She could see his euphoria and just put her finger up across his lips and then kissed him until he was calm. Then she sat and listened. He told her about the job he had been offered, the chance to continue his behavioural studies and coordinate big time efforts to stop poaching and the trade in ivory. He could help nature to repair itself, its habitats, its very environment and get areas of safety established. He was excited by the resources at his disposal, he was... He stopped suddenly, realising Sophie was laughing, not at him but with relief because she had thought that he might be very disillusioned by Jim showing a potential for conservation but with Greenpeace mentality. Then she was slightly alarmed as she looked into his face and saw turmoil in his eyes. She thought, I have hurt him with my laugh.

"What is it my love? I was laughing because you are so happy, I promise I was not laughing at you."

He said, quickly, "No, I know, but there is a downside, maybe." That look was back in his eyes.

Sophie said, gently, "Out with it, Jackson, come on man!"

He looked at her and slowly said, "We may have to move out of Kariba and Osprey. I know that it means as much to you as me. It is because of you that we have got to where we are."

She took hold of both his hands and said, "Look, I love you and that means we both have to be happy. But I will be happy with just you, so whatever you want to do is fine with me. Anyway, I think I may be about to have a different baby to look after." He was on the ball and immediately understood. He kissed her and asked, "Are you sure?"

"Pretty much, I'm a fortnight late and I normally am regular. I actually feel different, so I would bet on it."

Jasper said, "That makes it much easier. As soon as we get home, I will get on to Mum and fix you up for Durban. We can get your folks over. This solves my worry that you would be here as I finish this job; I really do not want you around when I go on surveillance. Jim has satellite photos of where they think the base will be around Chirundu, its amazing, do you know they can see a man from all the way up there, and I will have access to that and police forces and…"

"Whoa there, you need to slow down for me, in fact why don't you start with what you went through in your meeting? I'm glad I went with Paul, Donna and Paddy, I can see you're excited. I think you have accepted a job with international objectives, but you aren't making too much sense, so take a breath, have a beer and tell me slowly."

Jasper took a breath, said, "You're right, OK," and began to go over the days meeting. He told her the whole thing, his doubts and now his hopes.

Sophie kept quiet and listened but had to stop him eventually to say, "It's dark, and maybe we need to go for dinner." He had not realised the time. Sophie was happy because now she knew his real purpose in life would be fulfilled and through that, she would be fulfilled.

After he showered quickly and changed, he and Sophie strolled arm in arm over the sands to dinner. Jim was clearly telling some stories of fishing in America and matching stories with Paul. He shouted across, "We were getting worried about you but am glad you're here now. Save me from making up too many stories!"

Everybody laughed and drinks were poured, Jasper noticed Sophie was only on tonic water and hoped that no-one would comment or joke, as they had both agreed they wanted to be absolutely sure, and anyway they wanted family to know first.

After dinner, everybody sat outside on the veranda with their drinks and coffee. There were several red lights around and Jonty pointed out that insects tended to avoid red light, so it was a good way to have light, albeit not a bright light. Using standard white lights at each end of the veranda, it left a largely insect free area to sit in. Paddy said she would remind him when they got home so he could do the same.

Jim regaled them with some stories of his various flights into the bush, having to land amongst herds of gnus one time and having to circle while some buffalo wandered on to the strip and actually lay down. He was low on fuel and was pretty much had nowhere to go, so in the end he thought he would buzz them, but that did not faze them, they just kept on chewing cud. The man who travelled with him finally got rid of them by leaning out of the cockpit window and discharging a firearm; they took off at a rate of knots. They actually hadn't seen Jim's plane because the strip was a couple of hundred yards back into the bush, so was not visible. Sophie asked the question as to what plane Jim had and was it his. He replied that it was indeed his, having bought it three years ago from a farmer in Kenya, he himself had qualified as a young pilot in the USAAF in the late sixties, in time to fly in the Vietnam war before the ignominious end of that war. He was qualified on both fixed wing and helicopters and loved his Cessna around East Africa. He kept it at Wilson airport by Nairobi.

Then Jasper learned something that left him speechless. He was listening to Sophie and Jim discussing specifications of his aircraft in such a way that he quipped, "Darling, you sound as if you are a pilot yourself, I did not realise you were even interested."

She replied quietly that he had no idea, but yes, she was a pilot, firstly as a gyrocopter; she gained a Private Pilot Licence on a single-engine Cessna 210 and then graduated onto a Cessna 421 twin. She had done this when she was a rescue nurse back in New Zealand. The silence was deafening, but they all laughed as she took Jasper's hand, kissed him, and said, "It just never came up."

He resisted asking what else he didn't know about his wife; after all, she did not know all he had done. Although she had some idea of his time as a Scout, he had spared her much of the detail of his exploits on the dark side. Jim toasted Sophie and told Jasper that she must refresh and re-rate because he would find that very useful in the future. Paul cut across and asked when Jim was leaving, maybe he could let Sophie have a go, but Jim said he would be leaving as early as possible as he was due in Arusha that morning. Donna said jokingly that she thought pilots could not drink for 12 hours before they flew.

"Nonsense," said Jim, "The rule is very specific, you must stop drinking 8 feet from the plane." Everyone roared with laughter and had another drink, except Sophie.

The next morning as they sat down to some breakfast, they heard the roar of engines and saw Jim come over the lodges, do a circuit and then waggle his wings, saying goodbye before turning towards the rising sun and the Tanzanian side of the lake. Paul said he had sent his crew and the trailer round to Kasaba Bay so that they could use the cruiser to take them back and not have the uncomfortable ride in the banana boat. They would have to get going soon, as he had to call in to Chris's place to pick up two cases of Nile perch fillets for his restaurant which he would take back on the plane. They all went back to their lodges and packed before meeting up at the jetty where Paul's boat was moored. As they loaded up, they all turned around and agreed that the lodges were indeed a superb getaway from the world, and as long as there were places like this, people could find themselves relating to nature, albeit in a fairly luxurious manner. A true sanctuary!

Paul took his boat out into the lake and headed for the fish factory, radioing ahead that he was underway. Twenty minutes later the boat came alongside the jetty at the factory and, whilst the boys held the boat steady, two 40-pound cases of deep-frozen fillets were loaded on. Hellos and goodbyes said, and with Chris waving them off, they back out and headed for Kasaba Bay. Paul's crew were waiting for them at Kasaba Bay and immediately unloaded the baggage and the fillets, taking it up to the check-in desk in the lodge. Paul took charge with the flight person and presented all six tickets and loaded their personal bags. The six bags weighed just on 60 pounds, so they were going to be overweight by at least 20 pounds. So, as the fillets were put on the scales, Paul put his toes under the lip of the scales and held it below the true 40 pounds to 30 pounds. This meant that there were no extra charges, and, as Paul said afterwards, he had also found out that there were no further passengers, so he could not ask to use up their allowance. In any event he had not exceeded the plane's weight restrictions, for the extra two passengers would have been allowed 20 pounds each. Paul then went down to see how his crew were getting on, found they already had the boat on its trailer and were in the process of tying it down securely and locking the engines off, ready for a rough ride at least to Kasama before more reasonable road surfaces were available. He gave them some Kwacha for food and overnight lodgings and said he would look for them by midday tomorrow; with that he said goodbye and re-joined the group. Within five minutes, they heard the engines first, and then saw the Zambian Airways HS748 doing a tight circle over the lake before diving into the bush. It was out of sight, but they heard the noise of the engines, props going into reverse for what seemed a long time. Since they heard no bang it was safe to assume the plane was down safely. They got on board the safari vehicle and trundled off to the strip.

When they got there, the plane was at the gazebo, unloading eight passengers who seemed to be a German party. As soon as the luggage was off, Paul made sure his fillets were loaded quickly to get them out of the sun. As they boarded, Sophie said this must be a different aircraft as the paper was not stuffed in the portholes and the linings did not look new. The stewardess was the same, however. This time they got the benefit of the remarkable take-off procedure from the inside, rather than watching from outside, and were mightily relieved as the plane left the strip without any lurching and smoothly gained height, slowly at first, out over the lake before turning towards the south and then onto its heading for Kasama. They landed, took on an almost full plane, no chickens or goat, and headed on for Ndola, landing right on schedule. Paul and Donna said their goodbyes quickly, grabbed their fish and left for the restaurant. Jonty got his twin cab, got the bags put in the back, and the four of them left for Suma Calo. They talked about Ndole and how it was a hidden gem of a getaway and must be heavily sought after but Jonty said that it had started out as just a fishing camp, and was initially set up for the government as a base for scoping out the lake as to how best the lake's fish could be exploited. It had been decided back in the early 70's that it should be left to some chosen people to develop the fishing so that it remained sustainable. The fundis of the time decided that their corner of Tanganyika was too much of a security issue, in that the area was too large and remote to police effectively. Typically, they instead retained control in strategic areas by building lodges with airstrips and allowed fishermen to come for the exclusive experience. They were able to build camps in the bush for the army, which were rarely seen but nevertheless were present, as a deterrent to the bandits from the north on the border with Zaire. They allowed small communities of indigenous fishermen to thrive so that the kapenta could be harvested for the people's protein. The bigger Nile perch and tigerfish were good business for the lodges to offer their visitors. In a rare show of good sense, the new politicians deemed only one fish factory for the export grade of Nile perch would be allowed. This would ensure that stocks were not overfished, so no great development for the area was necessary and the region's remoteness became its security. There would be enough people around to be the nation's eyes and, by retaining control of key lodges, backed up by a discreet army, it made for a buffer zone on the northern flank. Ndole was useful for having secret and international meetings in a relaxed atmosphere.

As they pulled into the farmhouse, they were met by Paddy's mum and the two youngsters, Jonty Jr and Dorothy, both keen to see Mum and Dad. Paddy took the children and went off into the house with her mum. Jonty took Jasper and Sophie through to his study, and when tea arrived with some sandwiches, the three sat down to eat. Sophie offered to leave, but both Jasper and Jonty stopped her. As Jonty said, she already knew what was going on, and he could see Jasper shared with her, so it was in the job's best interests if she was in the loop. Besides which, she might see flaws that were too obvious or simply missed, a sort of devil's advocate. She already knew most of it.

Firstly, Jonty asked what equipment had been given to Jasper by Tony, mostly to check the camera was night rated infra-red as well as standard, and that there was a satellite phone. As it was confirmed, Jonty gave him another number to call, direct to himself and asked what his call-sign was. He suggested it would be simplest if he and Tony used the same one, and Jasper could see the sense of that, so he gave him 'William Tell'. Sophie asked why, because she did not know about his prowess with a crossbow, and Jasper told her that it had been one of his specialist weapons during the bush war. She had seen a crossbow in the storeroom where he kept his hunting gear, but thought it was more of a toy from his youth.

Jonty had not known either, but then went on, "Do you need any other weapons, particularly untraceable ones?" Jasper did not and he simply shook his head, thinking to himself that he had at least one of his own caches which was never recovered and one old enemy cache which he and Henry had simply booby trapped and 'forgotten' to debrief on, given the speed of their de-mob. They went over what he proposed to do. Having been given the satellite intelligence, he and Henry would quickly confirm it was the site and then they would remain until the ivory came and the two Kims arrived. First prize was getting shots of the Kims applying diplomatic tags on the containers once loaded. Pictures of them being in camp during the loading would do, but then they needed a photographic record of the containers going through the Border post on the Zimbabwean side, and then Jonty's men would do the same on the Zambian side. They would continue the photo surveillance all the way to and at the bond in Kapiri. Since all photos would be date and time stamped, they would become prima facie evidence. Jonty did not ask what would happen to the load camp in Zimbabwe, nor what the arrangements were as to wrapping that end up. Sophie shuddered inwardly, because she pretty much could guess that none would remain alive, and just hoped Jasper was not too involved. She knew better than to ask, and if he were in any doubt, he would tell her anyway. Jasper asked about the brigadier and where any arrests would be made, sensing that Tony and Ken would rather the Kims were arrested in Zambia. No doubt they would claim diplomatic immunity. The brigadier was relatively easy in that he would be along with the Kims, but as a courtesy security man on behalf of the Zimbabwean government and not in any diplomatic function, so he would claim no knowledge of the true reason for the visit and would be escorted and handed over to the authorities at Chirundu. It was hoped to arrest the Kims in Zambia, but that could not be done ahead of Dar and at least the delivery of the containers to the quayside. The plan was dependent on how long after the despatch from Kapiri the Kims would stay in Zambia. According to their schedule they were due to be in Zambia for seven days, after which they believed the containers would have been booked onto Tazara. The rail would take between 24 and 36 hours, providing no major event occurred on the line, so the diplomatic tags should ensure the delivery to docks within 24 hours. The Kims would be arrested at that point. If they should appear to be moving to a border, SB officers at all posts would be instructed to detain them.

Jonty then said, "If necessary, they will be invited to meet with our President, so we are confident we can delay any early departure. If they attempt an unauthorised departure through any border, my men will stop them, and in that case no diplomatic immunity can be claimed. I have already requested your assistance in the guise of a fundi on elephant tracking for our anti-poaching squad seminar and Tony has given a go ahead – dates to be confirmed, but they will coincide with the week after the Kapiri despatch."

Jonty then said they had to work out how Jasper was already in Zambia so that no connection could be made to him as the loading operation at the abandoned sugar farm was going on. Jonty went away to have a discussion with Tony on a secure phone, leaving Sophie and Jasper in the study.

She came across to him and snuggled up and said gently, "I know this means a lot to you and obviously there is going to be risk, no, I am not going to make you choose me or them at all, and I know you will be happy in the UN job, so I am only going to ask two things. Firstly, after this so-called photo surveillance and the Kapiri follow up is over, I need you to say you will be the boss in future and not partake yourself in actual dirty ops, no more sitting waiting to get photographs of armed dangerous men, no more putting yourself in danger. Coordinate it, plan it, drive it, but others execute the work."

"And what's the second thing?"

Sophie said, "I love you, and I suppose I always will, but I need my husband to look after me and my baby, not be a memory, no "Mrs Jackson, your husband was a great man. I want you, not the memory."

He took hold of her tightly and said "Of course. I love you and I promise on the baby's soul that I will not be active other than following elephants, not people. I want you by my side and reminding me that my family always comes first in whatever I do. Anyway, I'm no use in the role if I don't show leadership, and that does mean letting the others do their jobs. I have to be around to be the backup."

She sighed with relief and said, "Attaboy," sealing their bargain with a kiss.

Jonty returned and cleared his throat diplomatically. "Wait till you have kids, it's not so easy to have cuddle and kiss when you want to, you'll see. Now, Tony tells me he can have your Zimbabwe passport stamped at Kariba to show a departure date whenever you need, so when you get back, ring him and he will tell you who to see at Kariba and leave the passport with that person. It will be sent to me so I can get the appropriate corresponding stamps here. When you have finished at the loading base, you call me on the satellite phone and give me the OK to pick you up. I will have a chopper on standby and can fly along the Zambian border, and we will just deviate for 30 seconds and cross over, pick you up and bring you to Kapiri. You need to show me exactly on this map where you want to be picked up."

"What about Henry, if he is with me?"

"No problem, he comes with you and I'll arrange to get him back to Zim after we are done. I am sure we can use him as well. I think the easiest thing is to take him to Siavonga and have you pick him up in your boat; you fish offshore and I'll have a boat to bring him over to you. We'll probably board you to tell you off for drifting into Zambian waters and one less of the boarders will get off your boat."

Jasper looked at the map, found the sugar farm and saw that the area where the sand bars were that he and Henry had staked out some many times were within 3 miles and had good visibility for the chopper. X marked the spot and with that they went through for dinner. For once they all sat and chatted without any reference to elephants, elephant poaching, ivory trading, policing or prosecutions, just about this and that, comparing their lives in Zimbabwe and Zambia, and the usual putting to rights the ills of the world. Not surprisingly, all of them felt tired. They had been quite intense over the last two or three days and were happy to retire reasonably early. As they went to sleep, both Jasper and Sophie knew a big turning point had occurred and their lives were going to change substantially, yet both were excited to take up the new challenges.

The next morning, after a superb breakfast of fresh fruit, bacon, eggs, mini steaks and toast, a rather full but satiated pair said their goodbyes – Jasper and Jonty knew it would not be long for them – and finally set off for home by 1000 hours. They stopped at the Pamodzi for a cold drink and a comfort break before continuing down the road to Chilanga, then Kafue, over the bridge where no photographs were allowed and made it to the Kariba turn mid-afternoon. An hour later, they were through Zambia's border post, driving over the dam wall and up the hill to the Zimbabwean border post. Five minutes later they were on their way through Kariba, and thirty minutes later they arrived home.

Jasper left Sophie to deal with Francis and Barnabas, and as he would have to wait till Henry got back later, he booked a call through to his parents in Durban. He was pleasantly surprised and was put through to the La Lucia number five minutes later. He enquired after everybody's health and then got to the point: they were hoping that Sophie was pregnant, and he wanted to send Sophie down to Durban fairly soon so that she would spend the confinement down there. He did not have to explain that Kariba was not an ideal climate for a woman, let alone a pregnant one. What a question, his mother virtually shouted down the phone, of course Sophie must come as soon as possible, and she would contact Sophie's mother and get them to come over at least before the birth, if not sooner. Jasper tried to suggest he would pay for tickets for her parents to come from New Zealand, but Marika said he would do no such thing, she would sort it. He said that it would probably be within the next two weeks and Marika cut across him and said she was happy to send the company plane for her. Jasper had forgotten she was a Joubert and that had many privileges. They decided that he would phone with a date.

Sophie came through and he told her that as soon as she had sorted out the calendars and the store's ordering sequences, he would hand over the lot to Tony's firm to handle. He would probably send someone to take over here and set up how to run it with Henry; he would speak to Tony tomorrow. Sophie asked how long she had before he and Henry would begin, and when he said one week, she nodded and began to weep. Jasper was immediately distressed and shushed her holding her and stroking her hair. She said she was just scared of what lay ahead. He was not; Nyaminyami would be on his side.

CHAPTER 17

The End Game Begins

Henry and JJ sat well into the night, first with bringing Henry up to date, then with what their role was going to be. He went on to explain how they were a small part of a larger operation. He went on to say that it was probably going to be dangerous and killing was probably on the agenda. This time it was a war on men who would destroy the heritage of the nation, and it would be every bit as frustrating as their last war together. JJ told Henry that after this action, he would be taking up a post away from Kariba, to pursue the men who profited from the trade in ivory and bring them to justice in world courts. He would understand if Henry did not want to join him on this surveillance mission and made it clear that the handing over to Henry of Osprey Safaris would happen anyway. He had already signed it over and Tony would help him with the business side for as long as was necessary. Henry was quite emotional but refused to let JJ do the job alone. JJ told Henry about the satellite photo-charts he had seen and that the old sugar farm/plantation near to Chirundu was thought to be a base where the brigadier had set up ex-combatants. Henry stopped him, asking whether it was the same brigadier they saw not too long ago at the airport with the Koreans. JJ nodded. Henry went on to say that he would not be surprised if the sugar place was a base, as he had heard rumours of a camp from the locals when he started the last safari. They said that there was a secret base nearby and that locals had been warned by armed men to keep away from the general area where the old sugar place was. He went on to say that there were stories that the elephant had gone away and there were dead animals in the Hurungwe. Army trucks were going into the bush and coming out with strong smells of death about them. Henry thought that would be raw tusk, and maybe game meat, in view of what JJ had just told him. He had also been told gunfire had been heard, and he too noticed an absence of game, from the Zimbabwe side till well past the sugar place. JJ told him that Willie du Preez was concerned about the elephants, particularly Marta. Henry had not seen Marta for quite some time, though that was not necessarily unusual. They might go out as if they were checking on the canoes tomorrow afternoon and have a recce as soon as it got dark. They had a beer together, as it was getting dark, and soon Sophie came to say Francis had dinner whenever JJ was ready. They finished their beers and Henry said goodnight and went off to his family. Over dinner JJ told Sophie what he and Henry had gone over and that they would go and have a look tomorrow.

When they were going to bed, Sophie said she was now sure she was between 6 and 8 weeks pregnant. JJ was genuinely happy, and he told her so. About 0200 hours the peace of sleep was shattered by the phone, which was unusual. When Jasper picked up it was the doctor at Kariba hospital, who enquired if Sophie was there.

Jasper passed the phone to her with a quizzical look, but he could only hear Sophie's noises of understanding before she said, "Hang on, I need to speak to Jasper, do you want to phone me back in five minutes?" She put the phone down, turned to Jasper and said "There's an emergency; a client of Lakeview Safaris, a Yank, has collapsed with what seemed like heart attack. It's not a heart attack, but the doctor is sure that the coronary arteries are affected, and some lesions have appeared on X-ray. The doctor's no cardiologist but is certain the man needs surgery. The fellow's wife has organised a medevac flight, but because of the hour there is no nurse available till 0900hrs, therefore the plane would not be here until 1030 hrs. The doctor here cannot go but he knows I was an emergency nurse back home so he wants to know if I can go. The flight is waiting to take off from Lanseria and will come and pick him up as long as a nurse is available to return and transfer the patient to a Pretoria clinic."

Jasper immediately said, "You must go; in fact, its fate, or rather Nyaminyami has been kind. Take a bag of what you need and your passport, credit card and you have my mother's number. My love, I want you to do your good Samaritan thing and then go on down to Durban. I'll ask Mother to organise the company plane for you to Lanseria, and that will be opportune for me so I can get into this and get it over with. I think this will be best, and I can make the break and come to join you, no lingering, trying to hang on here. In the meantime, you start thinking where you want to live, anywhere with good airline services and communications, I'd prefer not to be in Africa, but we can see how serious Jim was."

The phone rang and she took the call. Jasper heard her say yes and ask what time, then she put the phone down. She said better she pack a bag now because the flight would be ready for take-off from Kariba with the patient by 0630. She went and showered, got her most important belongings together – Jasper would have to bring the rest when he came – and was ready to leave by 0530. Jasper got the cruiser, put her single bag in the back, and she came over, looking all professional, as if she were going to work. She had her jewellery, credit cards, and passport in her handbag and jumped in. He drove quickly and they were there in 20 minutes and were met by the doctor and the ambulance. The doctor took her bag and passport and suggested that they say their goodbyes because he had to brief Sophie on meds and prep for the journey. He would then introduce her to the patient and his wife, then there would be no time. He said five minutes max, so they only had time for Jasper to say he would ring Marika as soon as he got back and make sure again that Sophie had the number to call when she handed her patient over. He told her to ring his mother from the clinic and give her a time for the plane to meet her at Lanseria. There was just time for a lingering kiss before the doctor was back. Jasper waited till he saw Sophie and the patient's wife walk over to the little jet with its red cross markings. Sophie turned and waved, the doors shut, and the jet was off to the end of the runway, taking off fast, gaining height quickly and slowly turning to the south and on to Joburg. As he rode back to Osprey, he said a little prayer and thanked Nyaminyami for the stroke of luck. Now he could concentrate fully on the job in hand.

As soon as he got back from the airport, he called his mother. Marika was alarmed when she heard Jasper's voice and immediately asked what was wrong. He had to calm her before he was able to tell her about the medevac plane and that Sophie was on her way with a patient to Lanseria and he wanted her to be picked up and taken to Durban. He told her what he and Sophie had agreed, and that the request arose for her to fly down as a nurse, so that made it easier. He said that Sophie would probably have to go to the clinic with the patient in Pretoria, Eugene Marais clinic he thought, and when she debriefed, she would get back to Lanseria and ring Marika. She told him not to worry, she knew people at Eugene Marais, and she would contact them now and get them to pick up Sophie. She would send the plane to get her. He said he would get in touch soon but would leave Sophie to explain what was going on. He hung up and then took the phone Tony gave him and went outside, used the number Tony gave him, and gave the call sign 'William Tell'. The phone re-routed and Tony answered.

"Hi, no names please, how are things with the neighbours?"

"Fine, plans are complete with options covered. My pal and I start this p.m. to confirm the site we believe to be the one of interest and go from there. I have another matter. I believe you can tell me where to leave the document requiring a stamp, but first I have to tell you my partner left this a.m. using her professional skills on a mercy mission out of Kariba. I have made the necessary arrangements for a stay over, so I need your office to send a person to look after the books and decide how my pal will need any help. Probably need someone for a few days to take charge, say till D-day + 7, immediate control, then how to transfer calendars and books to you at later date. Can you assist?"

"Will have someone temporarily today p.m., please pick up from afternoon flight and your document can be given to him on his arrival. Do you need anything else, data or equipment?"

"I need bags to be sent to Durban, will give details on arrival, otherwise no. I expect to complete by D-day + 7 and will plan to be available for further 3."

"Understood and good luck, keep safe." Tony broke the connection.

Henry Jones Wilson the 3rd, Americans always seemed to be "junior" or "the third," looked up from his cot into his wife's eyes to see the fear, fear for him, and tried to make light of his sudden collapse, saying it must have been something he ate and it had disagreed with him. He could see the anguish in her eyes, and her comment that the antacid tablets weren't as strong out here was a little too forced. Then a most radiant face with the sweetest of smiles leaned over him and said she was not to worry, stop frightening everyone and let her take his pulse. Just for a second, he thought, I am dead, and I've gone to heaven. Then he realised, or rather remembered, where he was. He asked her name and thought, what a lovely name, Sophie, and gently floated off into sleep. Sophie told Mrs Wilson that the journey would be easier for Mr Wilson if he slept. She had hooked him up to the monitor so that there was a constant watch on his heart output, blood pressure and breathing. The doctor at Kariba had briefed her that Wilson had arrived unconscious, but when he awoke there seemed to be no neurological effects. Despite Mr Wilson seemingly recovering, the doctor thought he was going to need some valve repairs, possibly a bypass or, as the doctor suspected, a multiple bypass. He seemed stable and should be monitored closely, kept quiet and allowed to sleep. The plane was properly equipped with a heart monitor, paddles, anti-coagulants, and adrenaline, so in the event of problems during flight, there was every chance positive action could be taken. Sophie settled down to watch and listen to the patient and the monitors. The co-pilot came back and spoke to Sophie to say they were 30 minutes from beginning their descent, and ask if there was anything she needed to tell the ambulance crew meeting them regarding emergencies. She shook her head and told the pilot that monitor readings were acceptable, the patient was sleeping, and no nausea had occurred. They touched down smoothly and didn't even wake Wilson the 3rd. The jet rolled out and pulled over into the medevac area, where the ambulance was waiting. She supervised the un-strapping of the patient and put the last five minutes of the monitor readings on the stretcher for the ambulance crew. An immigration officer came on board to stamp her passport while the doctor, who came on with him, asked how the patient had fared through the flight, had a look at the print out Sophie had provided, and made a quick examination before accepting the patient. As the stretcher was taken off, the doctor said thank you and invited her to continue the journey in the ambulance. She sat with Mr Wilson, who had awoken, somewhat bewildered, as the ambulance pulled away and asked for his wife and his Sophie. Once he saw them and spoke, he became calm and was quite cheery for the 30-minute journey to Pretoria and the private clinic his insurance was paying for. At the clinic he was wheeled away, but not before he and his wife thanked Sophie for looking after him. She wished him well, for it was not usual in her world to see a 50-year-old need emergency treatment, bypass surgery, or even, possibly, a transplant.

As she turned to try and find the reception, a young man came towards her and asked, "Mrs Jackson, Mrs Sophie Jackson?" She nodded, nearly putting up her hand and saying "here." He said he had a message from the Jouberts and asked her to follow him. They went into an office behind reception and he picked up a phone and dialled before saying, "Mrs Jackson, I have Mrs Jackson here," and almost apologetically handing the phone to

Sophie. Marika asked if she and her patient were well, then went on to say that the Company plane would be waiting for her at Lanseria around midday, and that young De Bruin would get her back to Lanseria in time. Marika would be at Virginia airport waiting for the plane's return, and she would keep lunch for her. Sophie looked a little bemused and asked the young De Bruin if there was somewhere she could freshen up. Of course, there was, and he asked for his manners to be excused and led her to a private room. He said she had time to shower if she wished, as they had an hour before he would take her back to Lanseria. He would organise some coffee in the meantime. She realized just how much the Joubert name meant, and that clearly it was a case of who you knew that made things happen in South Africa. When she had refreshed herself and found her way back to young De Bruin's office, she was grateful for the coffee and fruit offered.

A girl came into the office and said, "Meneer De Bruin, the car is ready."

"Baie Danke," replied young De Bruin and, carrying her bag, he led Sophie out to a waiting Mercedes, where he opened the back door for her, then got in beside the driver. On the way back, she looked out at some greyish green bush before they were back in an urban environment, and she wondered how long it would be before there would be no way of telling where Joburg stopped and Pretoria started.

When they arrived at Lanseria, the car went directly to the charter area and stopped by a handling office shed. There De Bruin got out and went into the office. He was back after two minutes and instructed the driver to move over to the hangers on their left. Outside the hangers there was a white jet standing, not unlike the Medevac plane, and the car pulled up by it. De Bruin gave the man waiting Sophie's bag, who took it into the plane and gestured for her to follow rather than speaking, as it was noisy.

She turned and shouted, "Thank you!" to De Bruin as he was getting back into the Merc. He waved and the car drew away. As soon as she got inside, she was shown to an extremely comfortable armchair seat and the door closed. The co-pilot asked her to belt up, said there were drinks in the side cabinet, and disappeared into the cockpit. The plane was on the move and on the runway within a couple of minutes and they were up, up and away in what seemed like an instant. Sophie began to doze and must have fallen asleep, as she woke up when the intercom came on to say they were about to land at Virginia airport, and ask her to please fasten her seatbelt. Sophie was fully awake by the time they were taxiing, thinking, How on earth will I ever fly in steerage class again. The plane stopped, the co-pilot came through, opened the door, and let down the steps. He took her bag, helping her down, and took the bag over to the car where Marika was waiting. She got out and kissed Sophie, asking if the flight was OK. She bundled her into the car and they were off on to the M4 to La Lucia. They were home in minutes.

Jasper began packing up the clothes and personal items that he and Sophie would want to keep. He managed to fill three suitcases, two holdalls and his army kitbag; he would have to make more arrangements for his hunting rifle and pistol, but that could wait. He caught up with Henry and they decided what weaponry they would take with them tonight, given they were in surveillance mode. JJ said he would take his hunting rifle with night scope and the special camera; he showed Henry the SVD with silencer and he could swear Henry's eyes lit up. They would take the side arms and the night vision gear, and they would just recce. Henry went off to sight the SVD in and JJ went to the airport to pick up Tony's person. There was no need to identify them, as it was obvious: a youngish man, in a suit, collar and tie, and sunglasses just had to be the man, and sure enough he came straight over to the Osprey bakkie with his bag and briefcase. He introduced himself as Jani Vermeullen, a Chapman associate. He tore off his jacket and remarked that it was very warm. Jasper said he hoped he had brought T-shirts and shorts, but they could fix him up with something if he had not. Jani had very little warning and was not sure how many days he would need. He dug into his briefcase and pulled out an envelope marked for JJ, handing it over. The letter read:

"J, this introduces Jani Vermeullen. He is a competent accountant and scheduler and also has a second role specific to me. He knows only that you are engaged in elephant surveys for the government. You may give him the passport. Please show him your diaries, schedules, and books for the business. He will spend several days and must meet H, as he will be linking the business. We can then run the business with H from here, though meetings will be at Osprey. If you need extra supplies, ask JV. He will also take control of baggage issues. T."

"Right, let's get you to Osprey and get you set up. I'll show you the office and my wife's system. I have to give you my passport, Tony says you'll sort that. Also, I have some bags which need to be sent and delivered to an address in Durban. I'll introduce you to Henry, who will be the main chap once we have finished the survey. He broadly knows how the business operates, but he is not an office man. We have deliberately stopped any canoe safaris for the next month, but Barnabas and the boat, also called Osprey, have a charter on the lake this week. After then I have made sure he's got no further charters for 3 weeks. Any questions?"

Vermeullen asked, "What time are you leaving today, and Tony said you may want some special supplies?" Already Jasper liked the man, he did not need to make conversation and was a listener.

When they got back, Jasper called Henry, quickly briefed him as to the extent of Jani's knowledge, particularly the upcoming time, and the three of them went to the office. Henry and Jani shook hands and spoke a little in Ndebele, and Henry was clearly a bit more relaxed and comfortable after that. They showed JV the books and Henry told him how the canoe bit worked and what he knew of the boat safaris. JJ left them to it to make sure Francis was briefed to look after Mr. Vermeullen and let him know that he and Henry would be leaving shortly for a day or two. He went back to the office and found the others in deep concentration, going over Sophie's systems.

He broke in, saying, "Sorry but who is on site that can take us in an hour's time to drop us at Mongwe Road end?"

JV said he could do it; he knew the area a little as he had been seconded to Karoi and then Chirundu during his training with Tony's other side, and he said it was surely better Osprey staff were unable to say anything definite, other than that they were checking safari sites. It made sense, and that was agreed. JJ and Henry left to get their gear; Henry took the SVD and 50 rounds, plus a CZ75 pistol and the night vision gear, while JJ took his 375 H&H Winchester Safari Express, hunting rifle, a pistol, the IR camera, with two extra lenses, one a wide angle and one a telephoto, and a bottle of Scotch. They did not say anything to JV, but they would supply themselves with any other weaponry from at least two caches they had left from the war. They left Osprey just before dark in a plain bakkie, without Osprey markings. JV was driving. Henry warned him that it was not unusual to meet elephants on this dirt road, or even buffalo, so he would need to keep his eyes peeled on the way back. When they hit the Makuti-Kariba road, JV turned right, noting the mile marker so he could turn in on the way back. The road was clear, and they made it up the escarpment to Makuti, turning left towards Chirundu and heading back down the other side of the escarpment. Twenty minutes later JV slowed and said the Mongwe Road end was coming up on the right.

JJ said, "Don't stop, go on by a few hundred yards and turn round."

As they came up to the road end JV cut the lights and stopped. Henry and JJ got out and took their rucksacks and weapons and were gone across the road and on to a trail opposite the Mongwe turn. They sat for a few minutes after JV drove off, just to let their eyes get accustomed to the darkness and their ears to the local insect and animal life. They looked at each other and went through the old habit of a quick prayer to Nyaminyami.

Opposite to the Mongwe Road end was a track which, in fact, was an elephant trail, many years old, still in use by Marta. Using their night vision scopes they slowly moved away from the road and got much deeper into the bush.

They stopped after a couple of hours and, after keeping silent for a few minutes to allow the habitat to absorb them, Henry said quietly, "No animals, it seems."

JJ agreed and thought that was unusual; "I expected to at least see impala and eland, and it's not at all noisy."

Henry was more concerned that if the animals were quiet – he had not heard even a lion or chattering of hyena – they might suffer a sudden charge by a buffalo. He wanted to do a 360-degree sweep at 50 yards. He took the left forward sweep and JJ the right backward sweep. They would use the night vision gear and each make a circle, crossing the track, before meeting back up. They would be specifically looking for grazing animals, or signs of the animals, and use their click and whistles for recognition.

Forty five minutes later, they got back together, and JJ said, "It's as if the place has been deserted by the animals." About a mile further on they began to smell the unmistakable stench of dead meat. They followed their noses, clearing by clearing, and as daybreak began to filter down, they came across first a youngster and then twelve elephant bodies in almost a circle, with a calf in the centre. At least nine of them had been butchered for their tusks. The youngsters only had rudimentary tusks. They circled the area to make sure they were alone before Henry approached the bodies.

As he returned, JJ simply said, "Marta?" and Henry nodded.

When he spoke, he said quietly, "I fear there will be more around in Charara . I had a look into the park when you were up North, and though not deserted, there are fewer animals for sure. The buffalo were very skittish, and I saw no lion spoor, but there was plenty hyena and jackal sign. Now that I think about it, there were a few marabou storks, not that usual in that area."

"The undertaker bird? That must mean something, what the fuck is going on?"

It was unusual, thought Henry, to hear JJ swear, though he could well understand why. They had hunted together before many times, some animals, but mostly men, who were armed and just as determined to kill them. It was now daylight, and JJ went and photographed the scene. He had always been able to control his emotions when he came across or even participated in the killing of people, but this scene tore at his guts.

He turned to Henry and said, "Let's head for Du Toit's place and hide up for the day."

Everybody was a winner in La Lucia; Sophie had taken a home kit and confirmed what she already knew: she was pregnant, about 10 weeks. Marika was fussing away, and she for one would enjoy this pregnancy. Jade, Jasper's twin and, by a fraction, his elder sister, was also arriving within a couple of days, though without her husband. Still, the good of that was they would have their own doctor in the house. She had also got Mrs Mitchieson on the phone, and so Sophie got to chat with her Mum and they arranged for her to come over for a visit, which was fairly easy since Sophie's father, Alan, was Air New Zealand's engineering manager at the airline's base in Auckland. He would be able to get complementary tickets for Sophie's mum, Stephanie, via Singapore Airways. So, Stephanie would come shortly for a short visit, and both she and Alan would come over for the birth.

Once Sophie had settled, she took the chance to bring up the real reason for her coming to Durban. Marika had not thought that Jasper had told her any more than he had to on the phone, so she told Frank that they would have to wait until Sophie was ready. She sensed there was a little turmoil in the girl's mind, and that she was not entirely happy. Sophie sat them down and said that there was a good chance that Jasper would be leaving Kariba for good and they would be looking for a home elsewhere.

She went on, "The business has been good to us and has made us a reasonable nest egg, but Jasper does not think that Kariba is the right place for us to bring up a family. He has had a job offer that will allow him to indulge a passion. You will probably know that he is all bush and that the animals, particularly elephants, are his raison d'être, and that he has been doing a lot of survey work regarding habitats and their management for Parks and Wildlife. He has become involved with an international poaching operation, working very secretly as part of a joint Southern-Central-Eastern African-UN operation. Its real hush-hush. When it's over he'll become a sort of policeman for the UN. I don't like his bit at the moment, it relies on him and Henry doing a lot of what they used to do, though it is a tracking and photograph job. We can live anywhere we want, as Jasper will be coordinating operations and not conducting them, and can spend time publishing papers, so I am looking forward to that. The safari business will be run by Henry as a majority partner, with Tony Chapman, our lawyer; you might remember him, he was with Jasper at school. That's about it."

Frank was especially pleased that his son was still interested in academics but Marika shared Sophie's current concern. She, of course, hoped they would settle in South Africa where she could spoil her grandchild, the first of a few, she hoped. Unfortunately, Jade and her husband Thomas had not had children – the biological clock had run out for them.

CHAPTER 18

The End of the Beginning of the End Game

JJ and Henry moved quickly and quietly towards the river south of Chirundu and arrived at the back of a compound and some shacks just opposite Bolt Island, which was home to the legendary Piet Du Toit and where they stored their motorised canoes.

Du Toit was thought to be born around the turn of the century, long before even Chirundu was there. His parents were thought to be sorts of missionaries from the Dutch Reform Church. It was probable that at least one of his parents was of the Griqua people, a result of integration of early European settlers and local Khoi people of the Cape. Certainly, he would be shunned by just about everybody, could barely read or write, and probably had several black wives, numerous children, and was feared for what many locals thought was magic. Piet became known for long Safari walks into the bush across the river, and it truly seemed that lions and crocs were frightened of him. Even buffalo and hippos had been known to turn away when Piet was out in the bush. He was a totally uneducated man, having only been taught by his parents to count and read, with the Bible being the only book he ever saw, yet he knew more about the animals, particularly elephants, than any University professor or fundi. He was given to rambling in his speech from time to time, which only added to the mystique and aura surrounding him. He was a formidable hunter, preferring a Mauser rifle to his father's Royal Enfield. How he got it was only speculation, but in 1920 two German so-called hunters shot an elephant after they had Piet call the beast into the open. Piet supposedly cursed them and their families and called a small herd of buffalo to kill them, and baboons carried the bodies to the river for the crocs to dispose of. Piet is said to have thundered verses from the Bible as their bodies were laid on the banks. Whatever the truth, Piet acquired new guns, and the Germans were never seen again. JJ was taken to visit Piet on one of his holidays by Frank, who had heard of the man and, as a scholar, was naturally interested. By then Piet was a fit but nevertheless elderly man, who no longer hunted but had taught himself taxidermy, and was eagerly sought to stuff trophy fish, birds, and animal heads, being acknowledged as the best. He took a shine to young Jasper and had taught him those things about tracking and animal ways that no books recorded. It was largely this that Andre Rabie had recognised when he described Jasper as a natural when recruiting for Selous Scouts. Jasper always tried to look in on Piet when he was in the area and did so even on a few occasions whilst on ops with Henry. He called Henry 'a savvy Schwartz, a good boggar.'

Henry whistled a bird call and was rewarded by a roar and "Bloody Schwartz and bring the boy with you." They slipped in past two ridgebacks who barely gave them a glance, but had they tried to go in without a greeting from Piet, they would be very different dogs. They were lion hunting dogs, so they would not be easily intimidated.

When they got into the shed Piet called home, JJ handed over a bottle of Scotch and Piet nodded, asking, "Why you boys dressed and carrying guns, didn't think you need them on the canoes?"

JJ said that they were not on canoes but looking for a gang of poachers. He then said, "We found Marta and her family riddled with 7.62 mm ammo probably AK 47's."

"Aach no, man, why? Where did you find them?"

Henry told him and was not surprised to see a tear in the old man's eye. Piet said that he had noticed the animals were not as relaxed as normal, they were nervous, though he had not been able to get out as he was finding it more difficult to move around now. He needed his sons, but they wouldn't be back for another day. He told them that Willie du Preez had been round, and he was worried about Marta and all the jumbo up to Makuti.

"I told him that the army was stopping people from going beyond the road to Jecha Point, towards the old sugar place, and he should look there and get them to help."

JJ told him softly that what he thought was the army, was not the army but renegades using army equipment.

Piet nodded and said, "Presumably they will turn Willie away before he gets to the place. My boys say they have a roadblock half mile beyond the Jecha turn. What are you planning?"

"We want to wait till late afternoon to go have a look and take some pictures. We need to get evidence and follow the fat cats, maybe up into Zambia."

"Man shoot die bastars and be done, feed the crocs like you used to."

JJ said he would be doing just that if need be, but he needed to get the big bosses first. He then asked if there were any dug-outs that he and Henry could use, as that would be the best way to get down the river beyond Jecha. Piet said he could organise that, the boys would feed them, and that it was best they got some sleep. He would wake them by 1700. He left them and soon a breakfast of meat and sadza arrived. They ate and then one slept while the other watched, then changed over.

Piet came back around 1600 and said there was a dugout and two paddles down the front. "Don't worry about bringing it back if you have to travel otherwise."

When it begun to get dark, they went down with Piet to the river and got themselves into the dugout, put their night vision gear on, rifles ready, and pushed off as soon as it was dark enough. They floated slowly just steering with the paddles, keeping tight to the bankside. They floated through the bridges and round past their canoe launch point and on past Jecha. They found a suitable inlet to land in and dragged the dugout up out of the water into some reeds, where it would be out of sight from the river itself. They pushed up to the top of the bank to be out of reach of any crocs and adjusted to the bush. It was quite different from being on the river. Henry reckoned they were no more than a mile from the sugar buildings, and by 2000 they could see and hear activity ahead of them. They circled carefully to check for outer and inner guards or trip wires, but found only two men on the east side of the buildings and one on the west side where the dirt road came in. There was fresh soil turnover at the back of the main sheds, which looked and smelt like a latrine area. There were two army covered 10-toners parked at the entrance, which JJ got good shots of. The rest of the men seemed to be congregated outside cooking food, with some going back and forth into the first shed. There was a guard on the two doors of the centre bays of the big shed, which presumably held the ivory. So far JJ had shots of 4 guards, 2 army trucks, 6 men either cooking or just chatting. All wore army type fatigues. JJ decided it was not worth the risk of trying to get a look inside the shed, it being guarded, and in any event the odour of dead meat was faintly in the air. There was a channel were sugar cane stems would have been washed, and he guessed this where the tusks would be cleaned, at least, so that the cargo would not smell at least till after it crossed the border. Maybe they could get pictures in daylight of the tusks being washed. It seemed food was ready, and three canteens were filled, with one man taking two to the east side for the guards presumably, and another man taking the other canteen to the westerly side. The cook filled out a further 10 canteens and put two alongside the fire. That meant 14 were to be fed with 3 out of sight. JJ thought the two being kept warm would be probably for the roadblock crew, which he expected would be two men, so there was probably one other man unaccounted for. One canteen was picked up by the cook and taken to a small shed alongside the main shed, where he knocked, the door opened, and a hand came out, taking the food. That was probably the leader of this mob; he probably liked his privacy.

JJ withdrew and found Henry, who had been covering him. They agreed on 14 men, 4 guarding here at the site and probably 2 guards on the roadblock. The only weaponry they could see were the AK47's most of the men had with them. The ivory may well be here and was almost certainly in the main shed. Henry thought that if they were washing the tusks to at least rid them of any remaining flesh, they may well be leaving some out to dry in sunlight. Good point, thought JJ, and motioned Henry to start back-tracking when there seemed to be a bit of a commotion and lights could be seen spasmodically in the bush to the west. A vehicle was coming in down the road. JJ and Henry went back to see a Merc arrive, and it looked like the brigadier got out. His driver went over to the fire and began to pick at the remains in the pot. JJ moved back to his earlier position and got pictures of the brigadier, his car and driver. He felt Henry behind him, urging they should withdraw, but as he nodded something totally unexpected happened and froze them to the spot. The lone man whom they assumed to be the mob leader came out and dragged with him a battered person, completely naked, who had been tortured. Both JJ and Henry realized that the person was in fact Willie Du Preez. JJ put down his camera a with uncontrolled rage and un-shouldered his .375 H&H Winchester before Henry clamped his arm and shook him and his head. The red mist passed from JJ as quickly as it arose, and he picked the camera up and took shots that grouped the brigadier, mob leader and the bloodied frame of Willie. The brigadier was shouting at the mob leader and probably berating the man when he suddenly took out his pistol and shot Willie through the head. JJ shook, but with controlled rage, knowing there was nothing they could have done without blowing the whole op, and in any event, the fight that would ensue would have been unplanned and might go either way. They had a lot of evidence on film now, so they withdrew quickly, knowing now that they would not call in CIO but would deal with this mob themselves.

They managed to get back under the bridges before full daylight and decided to leave the dugout there and went back through the bush to Du Toit's compound. They slipped in and were greeted by Piet and two sons. They told Piet where they had left the dugout, and one of his sons slipped away, saying he would get it. Piet then asked what he knew already, and JJ, getting Henry's approval, began to tell him what they had found, however even Piet was visibly taken aback when JJ got to the part about Willie. JJ then promised that he and Henry would be going back when the ivory was to be loaded into containers, which would be in around 7 days, then to be taken through the border and to meet the big bosses. Piet thundered he cared little for the containers going north, those elephants were dead, but the men at the camp had to pay in blood for the elephant and Willie. JJ said no, he wanted the big men, but he agreed the men at the camp had to pay, and not in jail, pardoned by decree in a few years' time. He promised Piet he would take care of it.

"You know who Henry and me were, what we did?"

Piet nodded. "I know, but me and my boys can do this."

"You can't, please Piet, I have to let the containers get filled and go so I can get pictures of the top men in Zimbabwe actually involved. These guys will follow the trucks and meet the big bosses in Zambia and the international cops together with the Zimbos and Zambians will be arresting all involved. But I have to get the pictures first, otherwise there is no evidence. Please Piet, let Henry and me take care of these guys?"

Piet thought, and said, "OK, we will do nothing till the trucks cross the border, but you must let us help. I have the two boys, I taught them, they know the bush and can get to within 10 yards of an eland. I have guns, rockets, mines – I need to do this for Willie, for me, for Marta. I beg of you."

Henry spoke for the first time. "We could do with someone to come from the roadblock end, take out the roadblock if it's still there, cover the south whilst we take the east and river."

JJ saw that it was a compromise which he thought they could live with, and frankly he had to stop Piet from showing his hand too early. He also thought they could move more readily if they could pick up weapons at Piet's place without having to wait for night to cover themselves. He finally nodded and agreed to the Du Toits' help. He did insist that he needed to plan this, and there would need to be a meet later in the week once JJ had found out when the containers were due. JJ said he needed to get back to Osprey, so could Piet get one of his boys to go to the motel and ring Vermeullen to organise pick up at the drop off point between 1200 and 1300 hrs. That would not raise any suspicions, as there were occasional calls between Du Toit and Osprey about their canoes, and it would mean JJ and Henry would not be seen and were never in the area. This was done, and JJ determined that they could leave the SVD and night gear with Piet, and that there was a spare AK47 and ammo, plus 4 to 6 claymores. Piet said that he had plenty, including RPGs if they wanted; he had made a collection from the war days. That meant they could use the compound as a base, so it was decided that a safari would be due no later than 7 days, as this was the initial date for the Kims' leave of absence papers from the capital. They were dropped by the Mongwe road end and managed to slip into the bush without being seen. As JV arrived, turned where he had three nights ago and slowly pulled into the Mongwe road, the boys jumped in the back seats of the double cab. JV turned and set off for Makuti. They were home within the hour.

After a shower and a clean-up they met JV at the villa and sat down to review what they had found. The films used were given to JV, who would get them processed and have a copy sent to Zambia. The death of Willie du Preez would however remain a Zimbabwean matter. They made no mention to JV of their meeting and collusions with Du Toit, and JV assumed they had gone there as that was where their safari canoes were stored. All they needed was the date the two containers and horses were to go to Chirundu. JV had confirmation from Tony that the trucks were to leave the capital in five days, the day before the Kims' leave of absence, so it would seem that loading would be on the sixth day, with an early transit through the border on the seventh day. The brigadier had booked three rooms at the Makuti Clouds End motel for the evening of the sixth day. The Kims would consider the Chirundu motel a shebeen.

On other matters, he had already consigned the cases and bags packed by Jasper on their way to Durban via air and for trans shipping via the Sunday flight to Louis Botha in Durban for collection by consulate officials for delivery to La Lucia. Tony had advised that any guns would be best left with Henry.

They had a timetable of sorts and JJ decided they would start a safari check-out run in four days, and that JV would report. What was unsaid was that they would have an extra day with Piet and his boys to plan their end. However, they sent word to Piet to expect them for the safari excuse.

Jasper used the satellite phone that evening, first to call Jonty to provide him with his timetable regarding the shipment crossing the border and expecting to arrive in Suma in one week. He then called Sophie. Everything had gone to plan with the medevac and her transfer to La Lucia, courtesy of the Joubert company plane. She was indeed pregnant, so Marika had got her a private obstetrician, and in any event, Jade was on hand, so she was well looked after. He told her that he had packed pretty much all their personal possessions and knickknacks and they would be delivered. He asked about her parents and she said her mother would be coming soon. He then said that he hoped the whole thing would be complete in about two weeks, so he would join her then. He told her he loved her, and that started a whole performance of loves and kisses which he had to finally put to an end.

Later he drank a half bottle of Scotch and wondered how long the memories of yet more blood would take to heal or at least live with. What frightened him most was his preparedness to pronounce guilt and execute the sentence; what would he ever be able to teach his kids?

CHAPTER 19

The End Game: D-day MONDAY

The next three days Jasper spent with JV and the business books, and he became more relaxed as he saw how patiently JV was taking Henry through the main economics of the business. He was pleased to see Henry being serious and clearly interested. He spent a lot of time planning how they were going to get their pictures and then the subsequent action with the Du Toits. He mused about taking the tranquilizer darts and rifle; their intention was not to take prisoners, but they might have a use, especially as the odds could be 7:1, though with the Du Toits that could be between 5:1 and 3:1. Normally on their ops JJ and Henry would accept large odds, but would narrow them first before a main ambush. However he figured he and Henry would take care of the camp, striking from river and easterly direction, though he expected once the loads had left, there would be no need for the two east-side guards, nor the main shed. He couldn't be sure, but the roadblock might be unmanned once the loads left. If they were still manned, the Du Toits would take out those two and then come down the road to cover any potential escape. If unmanned, they would attack from the west into the camp area of the buildings. He would work out recognition signals when they went to the compound. His plan was to neutralize the guards silently, if they existed, with his crossbow and/or tranquilizer darts. The problem with the tranquilizers was solved when he called Tony and asked whether the tranq dose was lethal. Tony said yes, otherwise they could not knock down a man. He hung up and realised they would be as effective as his crossbow. Later, in the dark, he took the tranquilizer gun and one of the two boxes of darts and started at a target place at 30 yards.

He called Henry, and said, "Try and hit that target." The rifle was equipped with a night scope and JJ went to stand some 5 yards to the right of the tree with the target. He wanted to hear how quiet the gas gun was and how much impact a dart had at that range. Henry first shot was barely audible and hit the tree with a discernible thud. They both went to check that the dart had stuck and discharged. Henry had aimed dead centre and the shot was about 1 inch high and 1 ½ inch to the right. He adjusted the scope and the next 3 darts were within an inch diameter around the centre. They went to 40 paces, and that was still good, but at 50 paces the drop was significant and the dart did not remain stuck, not that that was a train wreck, as a body is much softer than a tree. Henry was confident he could hit an area one inch in diameter from up to 40 yards, but only a general body hit at 50 yards. He had used 9 darts out of the 12 in the box. They decided to take it, as it may help to cut the odds before any firefight; in any case it would complement the crossbow. The good thing was they now did not need to spend time trying to locate and equip themselves from their caches, which would have increased the risk of being seen in the area. To cover their tracks, JJ organised for one of Henry's guides would take a canoe downriver to the second night stop, where he would be met by the Unimog. It was sold to the staff as a test to make sure standards were being kept. If he had an early start and used the motor, he would comfortably make the journey well before 1600 hrs. The Unimog crew would stay 2 nights before coming back with the canoe to Osprey, and not Chirundu. Now the hard part was waiting two days before the plans could go into action. He went over and over the plan and its options until he could not wreck it anymore and had countered any deviations.

Come the appointed morning, he made his usual prayer to Nyaminyami, as did Henry, and they put their kitbags in the back of a double cab and took off at first light heading to Chirundu. Vermeullen wanted to drive them, but JJ said no, as he may be noticed and have questions asked about a stranger driving the

Osprey truck. JV understood, and the normal driver took them. They arrived at the compound to unload and sent the driver back. With the guide, they got one of the motorised canoes out of the shed and got him launched and on his way. Then JJ and Henry joined Piet and his two boys for breakfast. JJ went over his plan in exhaustive detail, and the boys listened carefully. For the first night and the next day they would photograph the camp and the arrival of the containers, then the subsequent loading of the ivory. He expected the Kims to arrive before nightfall and tag the containers so that they could move up to the lorry park for an early passage. The Kims and the brigadier would follow and spend the night at the motel at Makuti; the Chirundu motel was not in the Clouds End league. They too would make an early start, to drive the 20 miles to catch up with the trucks at the border. JJ and Henry would jog the 12 miles to Chirundu and take up bush hides around the lorry park to take pictures of the trucks and hopefully the Merc at close to 0600hrs. JJ fully expected that the brigadier would be on hand to ensure the first trucks through were the two carrying the diplomatic tags; therefore he would be there at 0530 to ensure smooth passage. Since the trucks were diplomatically tagged, they would only take as long as the paperwork and copies took to be stamped, 10 minutes maximum. They would only wait till they got shots of the trucks at the office and the brigadier and the Kims in the Merc before withdrawing to the dry pan half a mile from the motel, where Marta and her herd had used to dig up water in the dry times. The Du Toits had to be at the pan by 0630, and the four would drive to the Jecha Point road, where they would hide the bakkie. The two Du Toits would take up position to cover the roadblock men, if they were still in position, before proceeding to the western entrance of the camp. JJ and Henry would retrace their steps coming out, but slightly deeper because of the light, before getting to their previous vantage point to the southern side of the camp.

The ambush would be co-ordinated to start at 0800 hrs, with JJ and Henry firing first. The Du Toits would carry bolas and AK

47s. Piet bragged proudly that both boys could hit with knives at 15 yards, so the roadblock guards would die silently. JJ went over the disposition of the men as they were when he and Henry had spent the last night watching and photographing. He said he would take out as many as they could using the tranq gun, crossbow, and the silenced SVD. Hopefully, they would be on fairly even odds then, except he would expect the apparent leader to remain in his shed and try and hide. Everyone seemed to be clear that the first night was for photography only, and the day would see the containers and horses loaded with the diplomatic tags put on and the trucks moved up to the border post for immediate transit when the post opened in the morning. The brigadier and the Kims would leave behind the trucks and, after their night stopover, follow the trucks through the border and on up to Kapiri. The gang would presumably have some beers and roast meat that evening before intending to clear up the following day. The bodies would be left as they fell, and the Zimbabwean security forces would take charge after 1200 hrs to prevent knowledge of any event, other than an army manoeuvre, becoming public. As soon as the firefight was over, the boys had to get out and away to prevent capture. They agreed simple recognition calls, though the Du Toits were confident that Henry nor JJ would see them and know they were there. Then they rested and had a meal of warthog, marinated in port or sherry, and sadza, snoozing till the light became less intense. They kitted up – weapons, night gear, claymores and camera – shook hands with the Du Toits the African way, and took the dugout in the same way they had a few nights earlier. Both completed their ritual prayers, silently asking Nyaminyami for his protection, and then floated away downstream as the quickly darkening night began to cloak them, keeping them safe from any eyes. They arrived at the camp to a sudden furore, and the reason became apparent as the containers arrived and reversed up to the main shed. JJ loosened his rucksack as quick as he could and started taking pictures while Henry stood guard with the SVD. Then, once he had shots of the trucks, they began to count men, including the two drivers, to check their dispositions. The two drivers disappeared into the first shed with the man who seemed to be the leader. There was a single guard at the camp's west perimeter and one on the main shed. With seven men in view, they had to assume two at the roadblock and two on the eastern perimeter. Henry slipped away but was soon back, confirming the two to the east. JJ took more shots, but it became apparent there was going to be no more activity that night, as the evening meal began to be prepared. They stayed, taking more pictures of the camp and shift changes. As the men settled down for the night, Henry motioned for a withdrawal and led JJ about 50 yards towards the river, to a spot which allowed them to be hidden from view but still monitor the area by the trucks. JJ nodded and they agreed to a 2 hour on-off for the remainder of darkness and the same throughout daylight, moving back to their other vantage point once darkness fell again. D-day had come to a close.

CHAPTER 20

End Game D-day+1: TUESDAY

JJ and Henry were both awake, having snatched what sleep they could, by the time the night began its losing battle with the light. Accompanying that defeat, the symphony of the night was also being superseded by the growing dawn chorus. Before light won and full daylight had established itself, men began to waken and move to the area behind the main shed which they had designated as a latrine. They then washed themselves in the old cane washing troughs at the front. Two men prepared breakfast and as soon as they were finished they went up the road to the west to replace the roadblock men, who appeared back in the camp some 15 minutes later. They seemed to be taking a long time, so it began to cross JJ's mind that maybe the Du Toits had been unable to wait; it was with some degree of relief that he saw the two men come into view. Similarly, the two easterly guards came in, but were only replaced by one guard, and he only went to the edge of the sheds. Henry motioned that maybe all hands were needed to load containers, and that seemed sensible to JJ. They continued to watch, and at last the main shed doors were opened; for the first time they could see several hundred tusks. They were looking at the remains of 360 or more elephants. JJ took sufficient shots and then waited till the men started to load the containers. The two drivers stood with clipboards, counting in the tusks that the human chain was passing along. Clearly it was hot work and there were several stops for drinking from the well, so it was late into the afternoon before the trucks pulled away from the sheds into the main body of the camp and the doors shut. The men then washed themselves and the drivers brought 6 crates of beer out of their cabs. The two men who had done the cooking got their fires going and began preparing a meal. By now, darkness had fallen, and both JJ and Henry moved back to their forward position and waited for the brigadier and the Kims to arrive. They hadn't waited long when the Mercedes 320 appeared and the brigadier and the Kims got out. JJ had hit the motherlode and began taking shots of them standing by the trucks. Obligingly, they all gave plenty of opportunities to have full face photographs taken. The Kims were clearly uneasy and just wanted to get on with it. They studied the two clipboards, opened the backdoor of each container and, using their torches, checked the cargoes. They then watched the shutting and locking of the containers before applying the diplomatic tags, and gave a bundle of documents to each driver, presumably manifest declarations of diplomatic bag transfers to Zambia. All was recorded on camera. The Kims just wanted to get away and strode back to the car, calling the brigadier. He was having a last word with his leader, before joining them in the car. The two trucks started up and trundled up the road with the Merc following. There was a brief, wait and then beers were opened and everyone but the roadblock guards got stuck into the beer. The cooks also shouted the sadza and nyama was ready, and very soon men were dancing with beers and meat in hand. This suited Henry and JJ well, as they could identify if there were any non-drinkers whom they would have to target first. As it happened, they all appeared to be enjoying themselves and could be clearly heard asking for their money. The leader said no one would be paid until they cleared the site tomorrow and returned the two ten-tonners. With that they went on enjoying themselves, laughing and joking, talking about their women, tomorrow, and where they would go. They finally went to sleep around 2300, leaving only one man on token guard, who fell asleep himself within the hour. Normally this would have been an ideal time to attack, but they could not risk that the brigadier might pop in on the way in the morning. They had to be sure that trucks and Merc had gone over the border, so they set off to get round the roadblock and then used the main road to go to Chirundu. They took only the SVD, their side arms, their pistols and the camera, so, travelling light, Henry and JJ jogged, only getting off the road when they saw headlights.

CHAPTER 21

D-day +2: WEDNESDAY

They made it to a quiet lorry park, having used their skills to avoid being seen, and selected a spot where they could observe the exit and entrance to the border post offices. It was only 0200, so Henry took an hour's nap before allowing JJ to have his nap. Both men were fully awake by the dawn, and right on schedule, as JJ had predicted, the Merc appeared at 0520 hrs. The two trucks pulled out of line and proceeded to the Customs barrier. The brigadier got out, and in that moment, JJ snapped him and one of the Kims in the car. At 0545 a customs official came to the trucks with the brigadier, checked the tags, making a note of them, came back to the barrier and raised it, allowing the two trucks and the Mercedes through. The trucks stopped outside the immigration offices and went in from one side, whilst the brigadier, his driver, and the Kims went in from the car side. JJ snapped away and was happy with the shots. Within seconds the Kims came out and got straight back into the car. The driver came back next, then the brigadier appeared again, but from the truck side. JJ kept snapping and continued until both trucks pulled away, the Mercedes behind them, on the entry to the road bridge. It was 0605 hrs. The lorry park was now alive with drivers, all jockeying to get in line for the customs barrier, and nobody paid any attention to the two men in camouflage, one with a rifle, who slipped into the bush. Henry doubted if they had been seen, but army activity around Chirundu was such that even if they were seen, it would cause no alarm. They made it to the pan by 0645, 15 minutes late, and saw no sign of the Du Toits. For a moment JJ thought they may have gone ahead to do the job themselves, but a bakkie appeared as if by magic and the two got in the back and pulled a tarpaulin over themselves whilst the bakkie took off at speed. At 0700 the bakkie stopped and they got out, with one of the Du Toits, the elder, with his finger to his mouth. The other drove off to hide the truck. The elder Du Toit motioned them to follow and walked silently towards the roadblock. He indicated he would circle behind and for Henry to go right as he had the SVD. JJ was to stay. As he waited, he took out his pistol because he felt a change close to him, and sure enough the younger Du Toit appeared. Then Henry and the elder Du Toit appeared and nodded, no guards. Henry and JJ agreed on 0800 as ambush time, and with that left the Du Toits to get to their own positions.

Full daylight soon came, despite an overcast morning, and Henry melted away and circled out of sight to a point between the eastern end of the camp and the main sheds. JJ just managed to slink up to his position with five minutes to spare and organised his weaponry. At 0745 hrs Henry became aware of the changes around him and guessed the camp was waking and eating. At the same time, JJ saw a group of 10 in the front area, sitting having tea, with the leader in his shed as expected and the token guard on the west side. Two men were heading towards the back side of the sheds, presumably to the latrine area so he knew they would be picked up by Henry. Henry had taken the tranquilizer gas gun and the darts and slipped away to around the back of the main shed, checking that there were no guards at the east end. JJ guessed he was going to catch the missing two at their toilet. At 0800 he loosed his first bolt, taking the westerly guard in the heart. The man barely twitched and just slumped a little further into his chair. None of the others noticed anything, although there was a small pool of blood staining his shirt which might be seen later. There was, of course, no later for the rest. He reloaded and shot the cook over the fire, who fell forward, causing all sorts of confusion. By the time some realised and started to reach for their weapons, JJ had already dropped the bow, picking up the AK47, and started to shoot with short bursts into the camp. Immediately the Du Toits opened up from two positions, so the men in the camp were effectively caught in a lethal cross-fire. Within 30 seconds 13 men were dead, including the 2 caught with their pants down. As soon as he heard the first burst, Henry shot the first man with a tranq dart; he simply tried to stand, as if he had been stung in the backside, but fell. The second man looked over in astonishment and was in full squat, simply falling over. As he tried to stand, he too got a dart and sat down, keeling over. Henry was impressed with the tranquilizer, whatever it was. There was also no blood. Henry raced round to see 11 men scythed down in a manner reminiscent of Operation Eland. The Du Toits both appeared, and JJ had to stand and wave them down, pointing at the first shed and holding up one finger. The leader was holed up and keeping his head down, perhaps hoping no one would notice his absence. There was silence and it took about 30 seconds for the cicadas and their friends to start slowly before regaining full volume. Next, he saw the younger Du Toit appear by the shed with what looked like a snake in his hand. He dropped the snake in the window frame and retreated. Suddenly and explosively, a man burst out of the shed and started to run, then his feet seemed to trip each other up and he crashed to the ground. There was a bolas wrapped around his legs. The Du Toit who held the snake was on him in a flash and, with one slash of a fearsome looking knife, cut the leader's throat. He stood up and watched the man gurgle, spraying a fine red mist which fountained once, then dropped as the man died. That accounted for fourteen, but nevertheless JJ had the du Toits take the west and south sectors while he and Henry went east and north to check for any sign of any others. There were none, of course, and 30 minutes later they met back at the sheds. JJ went into the first shed, cautiously because of the snake, as he wanted to check for any documents. He found a portmanteau and grabbed it and got out quickly, realising the snake was probably long gone anyway.

Henry came up and suggested they collect the guns, but Jasper said, "No, let the Du Toits have anything they want." They declined as they had sufficient weapons cached anyway. They went over to the dead men, however, taking some of their weapons and discharging them into the bodies before dropping them, so that it might look like two or three turned on their comrades. JJ retrieved his two bolts and had a brief discussion with Henry to decide whether there was any point in Henry going into Zambia. Since everything had gone to plan, with no emergency retreat needed, they agreed it would be better that he would leave with the du Toits and go back to Osprey to continue working with JV as normal. He would be on hand to look after the place. He would tell JV that all went well, and that JJ had gone over to Zambia with the photo evidence. He would not make any mention of the du Toit involvement, but hand over the portmanteau of documents they found. They said their goodbyes and the three left to retrieve their bakkie whilst JJ made the call to Jonty on the satellite phone, gave the call sign and told Jonty that he would be at the agreed RV point by 1130hrs before breaking the link. He set off to get to the rendezvous early, to check the area out before the pickup. He put the films of the past 36 hours in waterproof packaging and put them safely away. He arrived at the area of the RV and made a recce upstream and downstream, finding nothing to worry him, although he did almost bump into a small group of buffalo. They looked at him and sniffed before deciding he was harmless, and they sauntered off into the undergrowth in search of shade. He found a niche which was shaded, checked for resting crocs, and settled down to wait. Now that there was a little time, JJ could feel his heartbeat slowing as the adrenaline wore off, and the start of a bit of a headache. That was soon forgotten and, about noon, he heard the whip of rotors and saw a Zambian helicopter fly by upstream. Five minutes later it was back and hovered opposite his RV site. JJ stood and the pilot allowed the chopper to drift over and brought it down to just above the ground. The man at the door waved him forward, and JJ threw his rucksack and bow in and then jumped himself. As he jumped an arm shot out to grab him and the chopper was already gaining height and back on its side of the border, before flying along to the Kafue river confluence, then towards Lusaka and north. Inside the chopper, a man gave him a note, which he found was from Jonty. It simply said welcome to Zambia, and that no one on board knew who he was, just that he worked for the President's office. They would bring him directly to Suma Calo, probably a two-hour flight. He shut his eyes and tried to sleep despite the clattering of the rotors, which he thought were noisier than the old G-cars. He must have dozed, because it seemed like minutes before he realised the change in rotor noise that meant they were descending. He looked out the main door and recognised the farmhouse, though they finally landed out of its sight. He got out, greeted by Jonty, and grabbing his bag and bow they ran away from the chopper, which immediately rose and disappeared, leaving everyone covered in a film of red soil dust. He put his kit in the back of the bakkie and climbed in for the short ride to the house. On the short journey to the house, Jonty managed to tell him that the Merc was at the Pamodzi for lunch, and the two trucks were just north of Lusaka heading towards Kabwe and were being discreetly observed by Special Branch.

Jasper told him, "I've some great shots of cargo being loaded, the two Kims both checking cargo, and finally of them attaching the tags. I have the films, can you develop them and send copies to Tony? Have you received any of my first lot?"

"No, Tony wanted to know if I wanted copies, but I said the camp and its layout were not really needed; we need the incrimination of the Kims' and the brigadier's direct involvement. You have those, so we have all we need for prosecution. I shall offer copies to Tony, but he may not want them – deniability. By the way, apparently an army training exercise has gone wrong near to Chirundu, some idiot issued live ammunition and 14 men have died. Now, get yourself into the house and have a shower, bath if you like. Leave your kit and my boys will wash it, in the meantime I've left out some shorts and a shirt which should fit for now. Get some sleep. We will talk after."

A grateful Jasper luxuriated in a warm bath, scrubbing himself down, and then lay down on the bed and went to sleep. He slept till the following morning, waking only once around 2300, having a drink, going back to bed and falling asleep instantly. It was already light when he woke.

CHAPTER 22

D-day + 3: THURSDAY

He joined the family, who were already sitting down to break-fast. Jasper went round and kissed Paddy on the cheek, saying hi, and then went by the kids to say hi to them. Paddy's mum was not down yet. He sat down and allowed the maid to bring him a plate of sausage, bacon, and eggs, with toast and marmalade. Though this was not his usual fare, he suddenly realized how hungry he was, and he got stuck in with a hearty relish. The coffee was extremely pleasant, and when he asked, Jonty said it was actually from a plantation in Zimbabwe, in the Eastern Highlands close to Chipinge, a place called Southdown. It was really a tea plantation but grew coffee and macadamia nuts as well. Once breakfast was over, he and Jonty walked over to the farm office, where, at last, they were alone.

Jasper handed the films over to Jonty, so that he could get them developed, and asked, "What's the story now?"

Jonty looked at his watch and said, "The trucks arrived at the bond compound last evening around 1700 without any deviation, except at a truck stop, where the drivers ate one at a time, the other watching the trucks. No one interfered with either truck according to the surveillance teams, so they were cargo intact. The Mercedes arrived at the bond to check that the lorries had arrived, checked the tags and left to a safari lodge where they had booked in for three nights. Speaking to Tony earlier, he had been told that they found 14 dead men, apparently as a result of some grievance or other they opened up on each other. They have sealed the site for now, and once the arrests have been completed, the army will claim an innocent mistake by a junior armourer allowed live ammunition to be issued, and in a mock ambush in the bush a number of men had tragically died. All in all, Ken was pleased with the result, so I am told to pass on: Well done."

JJ was not so sure, as he realized that the whole episode of the camp had come back too easily to him, like second nature, despite the passage of seven or more years. He had no doubts, though, about the execution, because that's what it was. It was not a war of mankind as such, but it was nevertheless a war. He hoped his soul was not tainted beyond redemption.

"What's next?" he asked.

"Before we do anything else, you have to be sworn in as a security consultant for game management, so that you can legally carry weapons. You have been registered as a consultant to the President's Office, so I need you to sign this document, which is your reply to our President's personal letter of offer to you."

Jasper read the letter and asked if that was actually the President's signature. He saw the pained expression on Jonty's face and said, "Just kidding."

He was astonished to hear Jonty say, "Of course its genuine, we have to keep it legal in case of any court cases we become involved with. You, of course, have credentials including a diplomatic UN passport, already filed by Jim Marshall, who incidentally asked where to send them to. I said that Durban would be best, and you need to give me an address so he can courier paperwork."

Jasper gave his parents address and told Jonty that Sophie was already there. He related the story of the medevac, and then thought he should tell Jonty or at least Paddy that Sophie had confirmed she was pregnant.

"Man, that's great news, Paddy will be delighted, and I am sure Jim will be too. He sees a family as a guarantee that you will keep out of the fieldwork directly and drive the bus, but not forget the destination. Anyway, we will get a call through to Sophie later and you can warn her about the documents coming. Now, I have been advised that the freighter left Bandar Abbas this morning and is due to dock in Dar in four days' time. That will mean the containers will be filled with the Zambian and Zaire ivory today tomorrow, and we expect transfer to the Tazara rail by tomorrow evening. That should get the containers to Dar the day before the ship docks. I'll take you by later so you can see the bond and the railhead in daylight, and then we'll go and observe tonight."

"Supposing the transfer to Tazara goes ahead tomorrow, what do I need to do after that? As I see it, I have completed my part of Operation Tembo regarding Zimbabwe."

Jonty said, "You are an employee/consultant of an appropriate UN agency, currently on secondment to the Zambian Security Services generally, the Special Branch specifically. I spoke to Jim about this and he is happy for you to remain with us for the next two weeks and oversee arrests with us. I would agree with Jim on this simply because you do not want to be seen as having had anything to do with the takedown in case of any retributions. It has been confirmed that your post has been filled, but you have not been identified yet. He needs to talk to you about nationality and he will be calling you this morning."

An hour later the satellite phone rang, and when Jasper answered he was a little surprised to hear Jim. He thought he would ask Jonty later about how he knew that number, as even Jasper didn't know it, but Jim cleared up the issue by saying, "Hi Jasper, I got the number from Jonty and have transferred the phone to the UN. I spoke to Ken about it. So that phone is our only means of communication for now. Get Jonty to show you how to engage the scrambler on it. You use it as you must and don't worry about the charges, they will come to my office. I am sending some numbers through to Jonty, which you will need, as well as the phone's number, which you can give out to those you want to, people you trust. Now, I have an address in La Lucia for you temporarily and will send, by courier, your letters of appointment etc and credentials, care of your wife. Best you ring her and warn her. Now I would prefer to keep your name out of the general lists until we finish this operation, and I would prefer you stay in Zambia and observe the arrests. Make sure on the UN's behalf they are carried out properly in the name of the International Court. Can you do that?"

"If you think so, then of course I will. I am not familiar with Dar and the detail of your dock operation or your contingencies, so I could potentially be a hindrance. I was told never to be afraid of doing the outrageous, but always with caution."

"Great, I'd expected that. I will pick up surveillance as the train crosses into Tanzania, Jonty will see it to the border, and hopefully we will tie up Operation Tembo in Dar without the extra help. Get Jonty to give you a full copy of the pictures and arrest warrants. Anything else, any questions?"

"Not any at the moment, other than when we'll meet to get me started?"

"Assuming we complete this job in the next few days, I will need to process paperwork, a week at most, and then I want to come to Durban to see you and to see your father again. I guess that would be in two or three weeks at the most. Look, Jasper, as you said in Ndole, let's get this done, and then we can get you organised and properly introduced to those people you will need to know. You can call me anytime; if I am not available, I'll call you back the instant I am. I've nothing else at the moment, so good luck with your arrests in Zambia. Cheers."

Jasper just managed to get in, "Good luck in Dar," before the connection broke.

He turned to Jonty and said Jim wished them good luck with their end, and then remembered, "Hey, how do I engage the scramble on this?"

Jonty told him that it was simply a four-digit code of his choosing, but it would only work with another phone similarly equipped. Jonty showed him how to do it and left him to put in his code. There was a knock at the office door, and a gentleman in a suit and tie came in and was introduced as Johnson Museka. He obviously worked with Jonty, who clarified that he was one of Special Branch's lawyers, and would witness and swear Jasper in for his secondment with the Zambian Security Services as a consultant. Jasper signed the letter Jonty had given him earlier, repeated an oath of allegiance to uphold the Zambian Legal Code whilst in Zambia, and signed an undertaking not to divulge personnel nor methods. That done, he was then given a permit to carry firearms and weapons of war whilst in the service of the President, whilst in Zambia. Museka was unsure how the crossbow fit into the licence, so he wrote an amendment to include sporting weapons and reminded him that he could only operate in the presence of a member of Security, never on his own. His Zimbabwean passport was also handed over, with stamps to show he had left Zimbabwe two days before the camp incident via Kariba and entered Zambia. He was also given a script of his lecture delivered to the Security Forces personnel, plus another due to be delivered in the week. He shook his head in amazement at how things were fixed and the speed at which it had happened. Museka left them and Jonty suggested that he used the office phone to speak to Sophie, to provide a record of proof that he was in Zambia if ever needed, but obviously he must be careful as to what he told her; better she did not know much about the operation anyway. Jonty then excused himself, as he still had the farm to look after and had to go around with his manager. He told Jasper that sometimes, like at present, he wished that Paddy was more involved in the farming business, like his Sophie was – not that he was really complaining.

Jasper picked up the phone and dialled for Durban. After what sounded like a thousand whirrs and clicks, a strange woman's voice came on the line, "Hello, the Jackson residence."

"Hello, could I speak to Sophie, Mrs Sophie Jackson please?"

A huge guffaw came down the line, "Good God, is that my little brother?" Of course, he recalled, Jade was due in Durban.

"Jade, heavens above, it must be a few years now."

"Just a few! We'll catch up soon, and you can tell me how on earth you managed to con a lovely girl like Sophie into marrying a beetle merchant like you. Anyway, here is the poor deluded girl, talk to you later."

Sophie came on the phone, gushing kisses, and wanted to know he was OK. She was missing him badly, loved him and wished he was there. He had to stop her, and she would not listen to him until she got him to say he loved her, knowing he would be turning beetroot as he said it. Finally, she asked, "When are you coming?"

He told her, "I am with Jonty and Paddy, they send their love and congratulations. Now, listen, I will be here for about a week, then I need two days back at Osprey before coming on to Durban. If you need me, I am going to give you a number, and you can call me anytime. If I can't answer, I'll call back as soon as possible. Now, there is some paperwork regarding my job, another passport, and some other stuff that Jim Marshall is sending down by courier, care of you. He himself is going to visit us in about three weeks, so you better warn Dad that he is coming."

Sophie cut in and asked, "Are you OK? I presume you and Henry have no injuries and you have no risky stuff to do."

"No, I am only an observer here in Zambia, and maybe a photographer. Henry is OK and back at Osprey, going through the business with the young suit that Tony sent up to understand the system. They will do the calendar and bookings, plus the accounts, leaving Henry to run Osprey itself."

"Jasper, look after yourself, I love you and need you." He gave her the satellite number and rang off.

Half an hour later, Jonty returned and said, "Let's have a quick bite of lunch, and then we can go and familiarise you with the territory around the Bond and the railway station. I need to see my men, and they need to know who you are."

Jasper was hardly hungry, so he had a cup of tea and a sandwich rather than the full buffet Paddy had organised. She did not feel offended, simply saying, "You will get it again tonight."

It was getting quite heavy and thundery when Jonty and Jasper headed out, with one of Jonty's men in the back. He was a silent man, completely atypical of the Bemba tribe, but Jasper could see he was very watchful and quickly saw that he was wearing shoulder holster, so he bet himself that this would be a bodyguard, amongst other things. The way he sat, held himself, and took in his surroundings belied the way he was dressed in shorts and T-shirt and a dirty torn jacket. He would be mostly taken for being a boss boy from the farm, a driver, or a messenger boy, and indeed he looked the part, but Jasper knew he was very much more.

He asked Jonty if it was normal for his farm hands to be watchful and armed, at which Jonty laughed and said, "Charles, he has spotted you." Then, quietly to JJ, he said, "He will be embarrassed that you spotted him so quickly, but then you have had to be aware of people, and you never lose that do you?"

Jasper turned to Charles and said, "I mean no disrespect, but my training makes me look at everyone with different eyes." Charles allowed himself the briefest of smiles and nodded.

Jonty then laid out what he wanted to do and that was firstly to let Jasper get a feel and lie of the land of Kapiri Mposhi as a whole, the area around the Bond, and then the station area, so that Jasper was not in entirely foreign environment, and secondly to make sure that his men were properly briefed and introduced to Jasper, so that if and when action occurred they would know who was who. At the junction with the Ndola road, Jonty turned south and headed for a compound that appeared to be a police camp. Once inside they made for some central buildings, parking at the back. Charles slipped out and communicated with what appeared to be paramilitary personnel. They saluted and opened a door to allow Jonty and Jasper into a warren of offices. Clearly Jonty had rule of the roost, and Jasper did wonder how it was that a white man could command what amounted to black officers in a country which had had Independence for quite a few years. He resolved to ask once they were alone, though he supposed that they had the same issue as the Scouts; Ken, Tony, JV, and Willie, rest in peace, were all examples where the new black masters recognised they needed people in certain positions to be free of tribal affiliations. He was introduced to both officers and the rank and file who were involved in Operation Tembo, and he was surprised as to how he was welcomed into their midst. It seemed that the two containers from Zimbabwe were parked within the Bond, and all day yesterday there had been a high degree of activity and noise coming from the Bond warehouse. The SB surveillance could not get into the Bond compound without endangering the operation, but they surmised that the forty-foot and two twenty-foot containers were being filled, ready for transfer to Tazara. They would be moved to the special park at the Tazara container area and would first be loaded onto flat-beds, possibly as early as tonight. Assembly of the following day's scheduled train would begin tonight. The two Zimbabwean horses were still there and would be used for the short distance to transfer the containers. All that remained for the Zambian team was to get pictures with the diplomatic tags on, and first prize would be to get the Kims doing it.

Jonty decided that they should go and drive by the Bond compound and the route to the station container area. They did this using a marked police van with special panels, so that they could observe without being seen. The two of them got in the back and Charles drove. Now, he became quite talkative. They drove to the big solid gates that were the only entrance to the Bond warehouse, and Charles stopped the van to call over the two policeman on guard at the gates, who informed him that there was a lot of activity inside, but there had been no traffic in or out. Virtually opposite the Bond was a double storey block, and Jonty said it would be there that they would be able to see into the parking areas in front of the Bond warehouse at least, but that would have to be at night. They drove on to the station container park and Charles went off to talk to Customs, who were unaware of Operation Tembo for security reasons, but were well used to SB officers coming to check on container movements. When Charles returned some 30 minutes later, he had news. As he was talking to the Customs people, the Chinese manager had come in and advised that they were expecting 5 containers, four twenty-foot and one forty-foot, under diplomatic tags of the Democratic People's Republic of Korea in the next intake for the Dar train. The Chinese manager asked for their co-operation to ensure they were passed through as quickly as possible, so that they would get loaded first and secured. As always on these occasions, he left some tokens of his gratitude for their assistance. It was not SB's preserve or intent to interfere with age old practices, but it was useful to know, and use if necessary, in the future. Charles merely reported that the usual gifts had been donated to Customs Officers, the main news being that the containers were to be moved tonight. Jasper had been surveying the location and now asked how the container park was secured and by whom, particularly at night. Customs looked after the compound using a squad of paramilitary drawn from the police. For the time being the squad was made entirely of SB men, but they could not risk an international incident with the Chinese management, so they were only instructed to keep a watching brief. However, they would be keeping a photographic record without risk of discovery, at least of the containers and their tags.

Jasper asked to see any plans for the station yards and container parks, but Jonty had to advise there probably weren't any, as the whole building of Tazara was essentially a Chinese gift to both Zambia and Tanzania. Local labour was used, but all the surveyors and engineers were Chinese, and there was no communication between them and the home engineers. He asked what provisions had been made as far as escape routes, should there be any disaster. Jonty said all three roads to the south, north and east were covered by roadblocks, which would be able to contain any truck escapes, as well as cars. Charles would swing by all three to check on them on their way back to the camp so that Jasper could see. When they came to the first one on the Ndola road north, Jasper almost laughed. It consisted of a few traffic cones to make a single lane, with an unarmed police officer in the road waving vehicles to slow down before either stopping them or waving them on through. He did notice men stationed both sides, about 100 yards from the policeman, and understood they were there to shoot any vehicles who failed to stop. What he did not see or notice that there were another two men stationed further out, but completely off the road, who would only appear if they heard shots, so even those feeling lucky enough to break the first ring would have little chance of escaping beyond the second group. He then began to look at the maps and asked what the likely escape routes were from Kapiri. Jonty and Charles both agreed that heading for Ndola was the only real option, as that part of the Copperbelt was very close to the Zaire border and there were many forest trails that could reach into Zaire without any border crossing points. It also gave options to go cross country through national parks to Angola, which would probably smuggle the Kims on to friendly shipping. Jasper thought that, based on having seen the Kims in the bush, it was clear they were uncomfortable, so he suggested they would more than likely run for Zimbabwe, bearing in mind they would know nothing of what had happened in the camp after they left. He would bet that the Kims and the brigadier would feel much safer within Zimbabwe, the Kims because of their immunity, and the brigadier because he had no idea he was already marked by the Zimbabwean CIO. Jonty was not so sure but would inform Chirundu and Kariba posts to stop any attempt at crossing over by the trio, in spite of any diplomatic immunity. The Immigration people would need some hours to validate the diplomatic status of the Koreans, and would have to inform Jonty's office anyway. In the meantime, surveillance would continue, but the roadblocks would remain in place for the duration.

It was getting dark, and the heat outside was really oppressive, so everyone was very thankful for the air conditioning in the vehicle. They headed back to the police camp and offices, getting inside just as a thunderstorm broke. The lightening was fearsome, big broad bands of blue light bridging to the ground so frequently that it was like daylight for several seconds at a time. There was a din of big cracks and whistles and a lingering but harsh rumbling. Then came the smell of earth, announcing the arrival of the rain, hurtling down, making pock marks in the soil before it flooded. It was impossible to see more than a few feet ahead. The violence of the storm seemed much greater than those Jasper saw around Kariba and Mana, and through the almost deafening sound of the rain on the roof, he made comment to Jonty that this would not help any decent photography. Jonty replied that these storms rarely lasted more than 20 minutes, and that the frequency of strikes was probably due to the high metal ore content of the earth in the area; indeed, from Kabwe up into the Copperbelt proper. He was right – the storm stopped just as suddenly as it started, and, despite a full 2 inches of rain having fallen, the run-off was quick leaving a much fresher atmosphere, heavily charged with ozone. Jasper was glad that it would take several minutes to drive to the Bond to allow his eyes to adjust to the darkness. He had kept his eyes shut and avoided looking out, but despite this, he was aware of the massive changes in light, which meant he and Henry would have allowed at least 30 minutes to pass if they were on a night bush op, even if they had night vision equipment. Still, tonight was about observation, and the team had to get pictures of the containers and their tags at the very least. Getting the Kims attaching tags would be the cream on top and make the case unanswerable. Jonty brought out some dark, golf-type shirts and loose trousers for him and Jasper, a black webbed utility belt which could take Jasper's pistol and knife, plus a couple of spare clips of ammo, and finally a black cap. He handed out a black wax stick to blacken faces, which he said incorporated an anti-mosquito repellent. A camera similar to the one Jasper had was produced; Charles would take pictures as well, plus there was already a man with another camera watching the Bond. Between them they hoped to get sufficient shots. A radio message came through to say that the Kims had arrived with the brigadier and the Zambian protocol officer, who was left in the car with the driver at the gates. This was normal procedure, as protocol indicated that the containers and the Bond were subject to a diplomatic situation, where the Bond was temporarily Korean soil. They went out and got into the vehicle Charles, now dressed as a Customs official, brought round, and off they went to their observation post overlooking the Bond area. This time they drove past the Bond gates and cut off behind the double storey building by way of a lane running up the back. They slipped into the building and made their way to the top floor, slowly, without lights. As they came into a room two others were already there and said they had taken pictures of the arrival of the Kims and got good shots of them entering the

Bond compound. From their vantage point, Jasper could see the two Zimbabwean containers, but could not see very far into the Bond warehouse – still, sufficiently far to see three other containers which had obviously been backed in, so getting pictures with tags might not be possible. That would have to happen at the railway yard.

Suddenly the two Zimbabwean horses started up and reversed the two containers they had brought round so that they could drive out of the yard. Jonty said he would take Charles and follow, and that Jasper should remain at the Bond site with his men there. Jasper nodded. The horses moved out and made off in the direction of the station. The Bond gates closed as they left, and the trucks were followed by the Mercedes, but with just the Protocol officer and the brigadier. Jasper could see the Kims moving about inside the bond, and hoped they would stay there, as he had no means of following if they left. One of Jonty's men's radios flashed, and he talked into it before handing it to Jasper, saying Jonty was on the air and showing him the hold down key.

Jonty said, "Jasper, the trucks are in the yard and are unhitching. We believe they are returning for the other containers, and we will be able to get good close ups of the tags as they enter the yard. I am leaving Charles here to do that and am returning, ETA five minutes. Over and out."

Jasper replied "Roger," and handed back the radio.

Jonty arrived back in time to see the two horses return and be admitted to the Bond compound. He reported that the Protocol officer was with the brigadier and they were in Customs handling the paperwork for the Zimbabwe-registered containers. This was just a record which had to be done anyway, despite any diplomatic tags. Charles was known around Customs and would not be out of place, simply one of the staff on duty.

The two horses reversed into the warehouse and were being hitched up to the forty-footer and one of the twenty-foot containers. Clearly the plan had been to use fewer horses to avoid any local chit chat, so only flat beds had been necessary, which had the containers already on them. Jasper looked at his watch and noted it was midnight.

CHAPTER 23

D-day +4: FRIDAY

It was not possible to get any shots of the tags being applied, as it was occurring at the rear of the warehouse and there was no way they could get in to the yard unseen. Jasper, who was used to working alone or with Henry only, was struggling to adjust to a larger team approach. He was used to reacting to the situation and initial pre-planning, which would take out a lot of risk areas, but he did understand he had to trust other people to do their jobs, as indeed he was going to experience in the future. He was using this surveillance as a learning curve, but he was in a foreign environment and he figured that was what was making him uncomfortable. He was used to trying to put himself in the mind of his adversaries, and he was not confident that the Kims would remain in Zambia for long. They may well want to be back across the border in Zimbabwe, which was their main accreditation nation after all. Their diplomatic immunity would save them there, with the worst-case scenario being that the government could request their recall to Korea. That, of course, was not what the President had wanted from Ken, so Jasper could only hope Tazara would work this morning and the train would depart today for its normal run to Dar and the Chinese ship. The sooner the arrests could be made and the Kims apprehended, the happier he would be. He asked Jonty if there was any further update from Jim on the ship, but the answer was it was all on schedule and should be docked by the following day. One of the men called them both over as engines were started and the horses edged the containers towards the gates. Jasper saw the second lorry stop and one of the Kims started to go over to it, having waved what looked a goodbye to the other Kim, so Jasper began taking pictures and got a series of Kim A getting into the cab with the driver. Kim B appeared to be staying behind. Already Jonty was on the radio and speaking with Charles, telling him of the development and to try and get shots of the Korean, especially if he was at the tags.

He turned to Jasper and said, "I shall go to Charles and keep in touch, we must not lose either one."

Jasper replied, "I think it's just sensible precautions that they are taking. The brigadier went with the Zim loads, now Kim A has gone with the next load, and I'll bet Kim B will come with the last container. If he leaves before one of these men here can go with me and follow, I'll need his radio and for him to say where we are."

Jonty agreed and spoke to the men, but, like Jasper, he expected Kim B would join the other Kim and the brigadier to ensure the containers all passed to loading. Jonty turned and said "If they do as we think, I'll send a car for you, as I need these two to stay and complete photography of all the people in the Bond. Otherwise you will have to follow with my man. Keep by the radio."

Fifteen minutes later Jonty was on the radio to confirm arrival of Kim A and the two containers. Jasper took more shots of Kim B, but obviously he was waiting for a horse to return and pick up the last container, which was probably already tagged. Half an hour later Jonty was back on the radio to say one horse had dropped its container and was making to leave, presumably to collect the last container. Kim A had linked up with the brigadier and they had great shots. It was now becoming light, with the advent of dawn, but there was very little in terms of the usual insect and bird chorus evident, certainly nothing like he was used to. The horse duly arrived back at the Bond and manoeuvred to hitch up with the last container. Once the hitch up was complete, seven men came out to the truck. Jasper was taking shots, along with Jonty's man, and then Kim B came from the warehouse, spoke to one of the men, and handed him a package, which looked like payment. He then got into the cab and urged the driver to get going. Jasper got on the radio and said the last container and Kim B had left, after what he thought was payment to the crew at the Bond. Jonty told him to come down to the alley and a car would be there in 5 minutes. It was full daylight when Jasper got to the hideout by the entrance to the Customs yard at the station. The last container had just gone through; in fact, it was still outside the office. Jonty had got good shots of the truck with Kim B in it on the way in and of the diplomatic tags on the container. At 0600hrs the five containers began to be loaded onto flatbed rail cars under the guidance of a Chinese manager, who appeared very friendly with the Koreans. By 0900hrs, all five containers were loaded and, using a long-range telephoto lens, Jasper was able to get a few shots of the Kims with the containers. He felt that it should be sufficient proof, given all the other pictures, and the guilt by association – especially of the two Zim containers – was tight. He need not have worried; when Charles came to the hide, he had taken several pictures at a closer range against all the containers, and he also had a golden nugget. No one had known or ever mentioned that, because of the Bond arrangement before delivery to the station, only the Zim containers had tags already verified at a border crossing, i.e. Chirundu, so all that was required for those was a visual check to ensure the tags were intact and their numbers tallied with the register at Chirundu. However, the other three had to have the issuing authority present when Customs declarations were made. Charles had managed to get a copy of manifests and the tag numbers through the Customs office without being challenged. All that remained was to see that the train actually left Kapiri. With a huge sigh of relief in their hideout, the train left at its allotted time of midday, which meant it should arrive in Dar anytime between 1000hrs and 1800hrs the next day. It was scheduled to arrive at 1000hrs, but with track maintenance and the odd breakdown, it was not unusual for the journey to take up to 30 hours, hence the 1800hrs time. Jonty had people on the train to record stoppages, but mostly to watch for any activity about the tagged containers during any stoppage. It was the duty of any country to provide security in the form of armed guards to protect diplomatic cargo, and Jonty had his people with the armed escort. They would report whilst within Zambian territory, and Jim had people from Tanzanian SB who would take over from the Zambians at the designated border stop for the train. These guards were actually necessary, as bandits were not beyond robbing containers by stopping the trains; however, that activity was more likely on trains headed to Kapiri, as those would have more luxuries. The trains going to Dar tended to be metal, mostly copper, containers. That seemed to be that as far as the Zambian part of the operation was concerned, other than to roll up the chain of poachers back to the Luangwa and Zaire routes. There was a quietly optimistic mood in the vehicles as they made their way back to the police camp, where Jonty suggested they all take a shower, get comfortable and meet back up in an hour. It was nearer 1400 hrs when they had completed ablutions and been served some meat and maize pap, nschima with an onion and tomato relish. Jasper had not realized how hungry he was and polished his bowl off, to the admiration of most of the men. When Jonty caught up with Jasper, he told him that he had reported the last 24 hours to Jim and given him the tag numbers and sent the films to his labs for printing. Jim was well pleased with their end and wished them luck with the arrests once he gave the word. He thought Jim was already in Dar, because he said he could see the Chinese freighter. A message from the Chinese manager at Kapiri must have been received by the Chinese Consulate, because they had already told the ship to dock before tomorrow night. Jonty guessed the Americans were decoding messages for Jim. Jasper said the sooner the better, because he felt that the Koreans would bolt for the Zim border as soon as they could, he would if it was him. He was glad that Tembo seemed to be progressing at speed and they should be able to wrap this end up the moment the containers were loaded, two days tops. Jonty also confirmed that the brigadier and the Kims had arrived at the Safari Lodge and were clearly celebrating their efforts of the day. Surveillance would advise when they left and track them back to the Pamodzi, where they were due to stay for seven days.

It was getting dark again and the regulation thunderstorm was due to roll in, so Jonty chose to wait at the camp before getting on the way home. As soon as the rain stopped, Jasper, Jonty, and Charles left for the farm, arriving there by 1930hrs, much to Paddy's relief. They went to the office to check on messages when Charles dropped a bombshell which brought the anxiety levels back up to the high level of the previous few hours and shattered any partial euphoria of a job well done. Jonty had noticed that, despite the smoothness of the operation over the past 24 hours, Charles was even more taciturn than usual, but even he had not expected the next revelation. Charles revealed suddenly that he now remembered where he had seen the brigadier before, and it had been bothering him to the extent he thought he should mention it. Ten or eleven years ago, Charles was a policeman, and had been deployed to assist Customs and Immigration on the Zambezi, ranging from Kariba to the Kafue confluence. One night he had been with his friend at Chirundu, who was due to take a Zipra commissar downriver, along with a second boat, to a camp from where there was to be a guerrilla incursion into Zimbabwe. It was a well-used camp for guerrilla fighters crossing, according to his friend. He invited Charles to come along for the ride. The commissar arrived at the border post after dark and was taken down for embarkation. He was carrying a package. Nothing was said as they moved off and the commissar sat well forward on his own, seemingly keen to get his mission over with. The two boats ran downstream for some time before pulling in. The commissar got out, talked to 6 men, handed over the rather large package and returned to the boat, indicating he was done. They then turned about and went back, leaving the other boat at the camp. The brigadier was the commissar. The immediate question was obviously whether there was any way that the brigadier may have recognised Charles at the rail-yard.

"Definitely not," said Charles, as he would have seen signs, and besides, Charles had worn a black balaclava, as was the norm on any night river operations. He was 100% sure that it was never off during the presence of the brigadier. Jasper tended to agree that there was no way the brigadier would stay in Zambia if he had recognised Charles, so suggested that Jonty might want to make his surveillance teams doubly vigilant for any deviation from the programme, either by the Kims or the brigadier. Jonty nodded and said he probably could put his own Protocol Officer with them, which should not alarm them as it was normal to change PO's every two or three days to prevent any suggestion of favours and favouritism occurring. Though this was a potential banana skin, Jonty and Jasper realised it was almost a red herring. Jasper, stirred by some memories, asked Charles if he could remember anything else about that night. Charles could recall they arrived back at Chirundu and the commissar literally jumped off the boat and disappeared. His friend told him several weeks later that several days later, they had found a badly damaged boat with two rotting corpses some five miles further downstream beyond the camp they had taken the commissar to. The boat was identified as the one they had accompanied downriver that night, so it was assumed the dreaded Skuz apo had caught the group. It had upset the 'chiefs' at the main guerrilla base, Westlands farm, near Lusaka. Jasper smiled inwardly, as he clearly remembered his and Henry's 'meet and greet' with this group, but he kept that to himself. It was near enough midnight by the time they all went to bed.

CHAPTER 24

D-day +5: SATURDAY

Jasper woke to a beautiful morning, a completely blue sky with the sun already well clear of the horizon. He showered and went down to breakfast at about 0800hrs to find Paddy, Jonty Junior and Dorothy already finished and a hot breakfast waiting for him. He ate with relish and, taking a coffee, walked over to where the office was. Jonty was on the phone but waved Jasper to sit.

When he put down the phone, he said, "I let you sleep, hope you got the benefit."

"Yes, thanks. Any developments here or in Dar?"

Jonty replied that the train was on schedule to arrive around 1400 hrs. The containers would be off-loaded and put into the customs yards by the evening. He said, "Apparently that means the containers cannot be moved before 0600hrs tomorrow morning, because nothing, including any diplomatic immunity, can open the Customs yard after 1800hrs. There is also a ban on heavy traffic moving during darkness, as most of their accidents occurred at night. Quite clever really. Jim is still hopeful that the containers will be moved to the dockside tomorrow, so expects the freighter to dock by lunchtime. He will make the arrests as soon as the containers are loaded, if the tags are taken off before the freighter moves away. He will advise us immediately. Now, about the Zambian bit; we have the haulage firms concerned and about a dozen drivers under observation, and we will pick them all up through the night as they are asleep, probably 0400hrs. If you want more details, I can take you through it, but I suspect you're after the Kims current whereabouts. They have just left the Safari Lodge heading for Lusaka. We expect them to get to the Arakan Barracks just off Independence Avenue by midday, where they are due to present the army with 10,000 pairs of boots and 5,000 army camo uniforms. They will attend a luncheon before arriving at the Pamodzi on a five-day booking for them and the brigadier. We will keep definite watch 24hrs with instructions not to allow them to drive south. Any move onto the Chirundu road will trigger holding procedures. The day after, they are due up by Mpongwe to donate seeds to the rural community, which we have to watch, as it's not all that far from the northern border. Sundays are big church and party days with the people, its family time. That should be all the time we need before Jim's OK."

Jasper nodded, but could not shake his gut feeling that the brigadier and Kims would try to get back to Zim before the schedule. He shared this with Jonty and was adamant, that's what he would do. There was no advantage to staying in Zambia until the freighter sailed, better to be in Zim, their prime accreditation nation. He was willing to bet that the brigadier would have already marked out an alternative route, and that was certain to be the old jump-off point he used to deliver the political sermon to the guerrillas about to cross over. Men, idealists when they have nothing else, were essentially lost once they got their ideal and grew lazy. They would revert to the way they knew, and the brigadier knew the way across the Zambezi.

Jonty stared at him for a while but then decided Jasper had not survived a nasty war by ignoring his gut feelings, so he simply asked, "What do you want to do?" Jasper said he wanted to talk to Henry and get him to cover that area as soon as possible, so Jonty said, "You need to talk to Tony first," reaching for his phone, and dialled before handing the phone to Jasper.

He heard Tony say, "Hello Jonty."

Jasper said, "It's me, I'm using Jonty's phone. I need either to talk or get a message through to Henry now now. Listen, I am concerned that the Mercedes three may try to return home outside of schedule and cross the river. I am certain I know where and I need Henry."

Tony said, without hesitation, "Stay where you are. I'll get back to you in fifteen. Tell Jonty I will need to speak to him as well." He hung up. It was a tense quarter of an hour, but to the minute the phone rang, and Tony spoke. "Vermeullen has Henry with him. You have your phone, use it, switch it on now."

Jasper handed the phone to Jonty, who continued to talk to Tony as he switched his phone on. Seconds later it rang, and he spoke to Jani. Next, Henry came on and said hello. Jasper said, "Henry, I may be wrong, but my gut says not. I think that the Mercedes three are going to try and cross over where we took six and then the last lot with Keith and Jacob. The odd one of the three has the knowledge of that place, as he was a preacher and gave men their last sermon before we met them – you understand."

Henry cut in, "I know where you mean, and you are talking of the three at the airport. What do you want?"

"I want you to stake out the place from tomorrow night, maybe for three nights, and suggest you have at least bolas with you. Confirm?"

Henry spoke quickly, "Understood, where will you be?"

"I will be right behind them to make sure they don't back out. Our guest nor anyone else needs to know any detail."

Henry just said, "OK, don't forget Nyaminyami," before breaking the connection.

Jonty was still talking to Tony, but looked at Jasper and mouthed "OK?" Jasper nodded and heard him say that Jasper had finished and with that put his phone down. He said, "I hope we can get them arrested without trouble, but your back up plan cannot hurt. Tony said they cannot be allowed back into Zim. Are you all right with that?"

Jasper said, "It will be taken care of if it becomes necessary," knowing he had ordered a death sentence the moment he told Henry to use the bolas. No-one but no-one would know he had told him to use the Du Toits with that reference to a bolas, and there was no way they would let the men who ordered the deaths of Marta, her herd and especially Willie du Preez live.

He did have a further request of Jonty, and that was for a dozen crossbow bolts with hunting tips, as he only had six left with him. That took another phone call to get his people to get round the shops and hunter societies.

Paddy knocked on the door and asked whether they wanted a tray for lunch. Jonty said that might be better because they were waiting for calls, and Paddy said OK, she would send over some rolls and fruit with the houseboy.

At 1400 Jim rang on Jasper's phone and advised the train and the tagged containers had reached Dar and were being off-loaded at the customs yard as he was speaking. He expected they would all be off and stacked in the diplomatic cage by 1500 hrs. He had information that horses had been ordered to the cage for Tuesday morning, but he did not know by whom yet, and was a little concerned. The freighter was lying offshore and was due to enter the harbour berths on Tuesday, which did not seem to make sense; why wait for another two or three days? Jim asked Jasper for any observations, and he replied that he thought this might be an attempt to be sure that the coast was clear, though he had to agree an untraced source of booking for Tuesday was a worry. His instinct almost suggested that the bookings might be a misinformation and he said that Jim should watch any movement of the freighter to enter ahead of the posted schedule of Tuesday. Jasper also suggested that if it were him, he would stage a diversion, bring the freighter in, or use a dummy ship, and take the containers out directly. That way the containers could be away and well into the Indian Ocean before the given schedule. The key would be the containers and when they moved. Jim harrumphed and then said it was possible, and his people would maintain their watch on the Customs yard. He was sure, though, that there was only one exit and entrance to the yard, so it should be straightforward to watch that point. He also did not want to bring the Tanzanians in too early, at least not before the containers moved, as he knew they were heavily dependent on the Chinese workers and management for the dock operation. The risk of Jim's unit's presence could easily be leaked, and sufficient obstacles thrown up to prevent the containers confiscation and arrests, or, at least, enough delay to allow shipment to take place. Jim also asked Jasper to report any schedule changes or irregularities in the Kims programme, as this may be the result of tip-offs from Dar, then hung up.

Jasper related the bits that Jonty had not picked up, and he in turn got on the phone and ensured full surveillance was continuing regarding the Kims. His teams reported that the presentation of boots and uniforms had been completed and the luncheon was just ending. Jonty was visibly becoming nervous, because it was evident now they would have to wait till Tuesday at least, and the longer the surveillance period became, the higher the risk of some 'embuggerment' factor occurring became.

A vehicle drew up and Charles came in, carrying a box of twenty hunting crossbow bolts. Jasper was delighted, as he recognised the make, and said, "Where on earth did you get these?"

Jonty said, "I have a couple of farming friends who also hunt, and luck had it that one of them has an interest in crossbows."

The phone rang and Jonty listened before replying he wanted a debrief from the Protocol Officer and for the teams keeping a watch on the Kims in the Pamodzi to be on their toes. He said, "They must not move outside the hotel without SB following and keeping up with communications with me." He sent Charles to the police camp to monitor radios and to radio him back here on the farm. He and Jasper would sleep in the office tonight. He wanted reports every hour, even if nothing had changed, and a watch must be kept on the car and its driver.

Paddy arrived and requested their presence for dinner across at the house, adopting a stance that suggested a battle line had been drawn. Jasper could see this and was too late to stop Jonty from saying, "Ah, Paddy darling, can you fix a couple of plates for us, I am afraid we need to stay here, all night for that matter."

At least Jasper was prepared for the response, which came with the ferocity of the Antarctic winter, and managed to step outside into the warm humid night just in time to avoid the dreaded hundred mile an hour silence. This was of course only a prelude to the storm that was brewing both outside and inside the office. It was either stay out and get wet or brave the inside.

He chose the latter and opened the door, trying to say, "Paddy, it's my fault, I need to keep in touch with the operation." He couldn't believe that he said that, and was already cringing at the polite but piercing reply.

"Do not say another word Jasper, you are a guest, but this man of mine has forgotten his family all day. I, of course, understand but the children do not. Why can't we see Daddy? You could at least come and spend a few minutes with them before they go to bed. Fix your own plate."

Jasper tried again and said "Jonty, why don't you go and eat with your family, I can look after the phones and come get you if there

are any developments. You could bring me back something."
That seemed to regulate the temperature, and Paddy and Jonty
ran across the yard to the house. The phone rang; it was Charles
to relate a "no activity" report from the Pamodzi, and that the
brigadier and the Kims were at dinner. The driver was engaged
with a female and looked as if he was settled in. Jasper acknowledged and hung up. He wondered what was going on in Dar.

Jim Marshall was in Dar and beginning to worry that Jasper's
scenario may well be a distinct possibility. For now, he had not
alerted the Tanzanian Security Services, because he knew there
was likelihood of leaks to the Chinese, so he was relying on a few
well-chosen people in Customs and Immigration and one individual in Intelligence for information. He looked at the time and
saw it was nearly midnight – Tanzania was on GMT+3 hours,
one hour ahead of Zambia – and that meant there would be no
traffic in or out of the Customs yard till 0600 Sunday at the very
earliest. He settled down and briefed his team of watchers and
then began to doze.

Jonty came back about an hour later with a steak and salad roll and
a beer. As he handed them over to Jasper, he began to apologise,
but Jasper just waved him away, saying he was learning valuable
marital lessons. He related Charles's last report and with that, the
phone rang. This time Jonty took his man's report. There was
no change and the brigadier and Kims had retired for the night.
The two now settled down for the rest of the night, but neither
managed to sleep, just doze while they waited for the hourly confirmation of no activity.

CHAPTER 25

D-day + 6: Sunday

It was 0600, and Jonty stayed on in the office allowing Jasper to go and shower and sit down to some breakfast. When he came back, Jonty did the same. He was able to eat with the kids but had decided that they should go into the camp and relieve Charles. Anyway, he needed to be in direct touch with his teams, which would be much easier at the camp. Jonty rang Charles and told him they were coming in and asked whether there was any movement from the Pamodzi. Charles said the Kims had gone down to the breakfast lounge at 0700 and were joined by the brigadier and the new Protocol Officer at 0745. The driver had washed the car and gone to the service station about 100 yards away to fill up with petrol and was now waiting to be called. Shortly after Jasper and Jonty arrived at the camp, Charles left, and the news came through that the Kims had left the Pamodzi in the Mercedes with the brigadier and the PO making for the Great North road on their way to their appointment at Mpongwe. Confirmation then came that they were headed north from the surveillance vehicles.

It was nearly midday in Dar, and the sun was nearing its zenith, making it extremely hot and humid, when things began to happen. First Jim got a message from his man in Intelligence that the freighter had made an emergency call advising they had a crewman who appeared to be having heart attack on board and wished to enter the harbour to hospitalize the man. This, then, was quickly followed by the watchers reporting that three horses with flatbed trailers were entering the diplomatic area. They had begun loading the five containers.

Jim told the watchers he was on the way, but that they must follow the trucks if they left before his arrival, and to get as many pictures as they could safely. On his way there, he phoned up Jasper to tell him it was looking as if he was right after all, and gave him a quick sit-rep before hanging up. He made it to the yard in time to see the lorries parked outside the Customs office whilst the paperwork and the diplomatic tags were checked. He would get that paperwork later, but now he and the watchers had to follow the trucks. It became apparent they were not headed for the docks, but into the industrial area, and indeed the trucks pulled into a yard on the Saza road. The gates were closed, but not before they caught a glimpse of men standing around each truck with what looked like sprays. The watchers split up, with one lot going round the block to check for other entrances and exits. The other watchers parked their van back a little and walked slowly past the gates and on to the next plot. The guard there sat in a little box, wearing a threadbare shirt with epaulettes, torn shorts, and pumps. The watcher parted with some shillings and managed to establish that it was a paint spraying shop for lorries. When Jim heard this, he knew what they were doing was spraying the containers before the containers were taken to the freighter. His other team now reported the freighter had docked; a man had been stretchered off into an ambulance. However, no-one from the ship had accompanied him, and now there was a bunkering barge alongside refuelling the freighter. Several containers were being offloaded to the side of the berth. According to the forward manifest, there were 10 containers coming off and five, 1 x 40ft, 4 x 20ft to be loaded. They reported the loading containers were not yet on the dockside. Jim phoned Jasper again to update him of the new developments, warning him to now become very watchful of the Kims as he expected the freighter to be loaded in the next hours and the ship to sail on the tide by 0200 at the latest. He was going to target an arrest warrant execution and impounding of the containers anytime between 1900 and 2200 ZULU hrs.

As he hung up, he got a message from the watchers in Saza road that they could smell paint and hear the spray guns, and did he want them to take the risk of trying to get pictures? It would have been good to get pictures, but he did not like the risk and since the watchers confirmed no other exits, he thought, we'll follow the trucks as they leave the site. He instructed the watchers to follow the first trucks out carrying a forty-foot and two double twenty-foot containers and get shots of the yard once the gates were opened. Jim returned to his vehicle in Saza road and settled down to wait. At 1800hrs the watchers who were taking turns walking past the gates reported that the noise of sprayers had stopped, and with darkness falling everybody became edgy. About 40 minutes later the gates were opened and a huge bit of luck came Jim's way. The first two trucks had to reverse out, and this allowed good close shots showing the tags on the back containers and, better still, that the yard was not big enough to hold decoys. The final truck managed to turn around in the yard and drove out forwards, catching up with the other two to complete the convoy. This time they headed for the docks and Jim contacted the Tanzanian Security Services to have the warrants he held executed, advising them to meet him at the dock gates within 15 minutes. He stressed the seriousness of the smuggling offences, which would reflect badly on Tanzania if the warrants were not executed. He gave the numbers of the warrants for checking. He knew it would take some time to check, but normal practice was that local police, and sometimes army, would be used to seal the dock entry and exits whilst credentials were processed. The last minute nature of informing local authorities was not unusual, and signatory countries had agreed that it may be necessary to ensure a complete arrest, and besides it did protect them from any possible finger-pointing in the event of failures. The three trucks entered the docks and Jim and his people stopped to await the local police. One of his teams of watchers had been located in the docks by the berthed freighter all day, so, short of the trucks driving into the sea, the catch was perfectly lined up. The police arrived and began sealing the gates to stop all traffic, including Jim's vehicle. Within five minutes a senior officer appeared and asked for Jim's documents and, on looking at them, brought Jim into the office. He was frosty at first, but on taking a phone call from someone who must have been very senior, he waved Jim over and took a detachment of army men, and drove round to the berth at which the freighter was moored. While they drove, Jim explained briefly about Operation Tembo, and that he also had a team photographing the freighter.

Jim could see the off-loaded containers stacked at the side of the berth, with five brown containers sitting on the berth. As he was approaching the berth, the ship's hoist was being attached to the forty-foot container by a Tanzanian crew overseen by two Chinese men. The army detachment drew up and ringed the berth. Jim and his escort approached the Chinese men. He introduced himself and asked who was in charge of the loading. One man visibly became anxious and tried to turn away, but was stopped by the officer accompanying Jim. The other Chinese man was quickly identified as the senior logistics officer for the dock authority, and he immediately began to shout about the unlawful intrusion and the possibility of an international incident. Jim patiently allowed the tirade and then if would not cause more of an incident if the great Chinese nation were found to be carrying poached ivory consignments on behalf of other countries? After all, had China not signed the international declaration banning the poaching of ivory worldwide? The logistics officer calmed immediately, and said of course his country would not be part of such a shipment, and he was after all just a man doing a job, helping the Tanzanian authorities to become efficient. Jim asked for the container to be opened, but the logistics man said it was not possible to open diplomatic cargo.

Jim's radio crackled and he listened, then said, "Thank you, over and out." He now turned to the other man, who claimed he could not understand when asked who he was. The logistics officer interjected that the man did not speak English but was the loadmaster for the freighter. Jim then asked the logistics officer to ask his countryman why there were no tags on the container about to be loaded. The logistics man listened to a stream of invectives that the loadmaster was shouting out before silencing him and turning to the Tanzanian officer, telling him that clearly the tags must have been knocked off during the removal from the trucks, and could he please stop this intrusion. The Tanzanian official simply said the container had no diplomatic tags and was still on Tanzanian soil, therefore legally it could be opened to check its contents against manifest. He went on to say that, of course, the fact that Mr Marshall had photographic evidence of the tags being deliberately cut off just shortly before he arrived justified the request. He was sure that if the tags had been cut off, it had been done so without the knowledge of the port authorities.

The logistics man was clearly shocked and thinking quickly. He bowed slightly and said "Of course." Jim then said there would be no need to search either him or the loadmaster, as clearly, they were being duped themselves, and it would not be necessary to impound the freighter. Both men seemed to relax. There was still a tension in the air as the Tanzanian officer broke the customs seals and locks on the container and Jim himself dared not to look as one door was swung open. The relief was palpable, because indeed the container was full of tusks, but there was sadness in Jim's heart for the elephants that had been slaughtered. He took final pictures and then left it to the Tanzanian police and army to open the other four containers. He stood back and phoned Jasper. After that call he called his American contact in the CIA to thank him for introducing him to the watch teams and tell him to stand down the submarine alternative.

Jasper and Jonty spent the morning receiving the surveillance teams' reports of the travel and subsequent arrival of the Kims to the Mpongwe sports field and the erected marquee there. This would be a major event for the community and the party spirit was completely dominant. Everybody was full of expectancy and fun; the atmosphere was very infectious. The whole community seemed to be there, but only the various village elders, Ministry of Agriculture officials, alongside their Minister, and invited guests from the diplomatic community were seated inside. The gathered crowd were displaying their best clothes, the women in the traditional very colourful full-length, wraparound printed cotton dresses. Bright oranges, reds, greens, and yellows were most prevalent. Their menfolk had on shiny suits, pseudo patent leather shoes and trilby type hats, and all were carrying carved walking sticks. There was roasting meat on grills made of fence wire resting on oil drums that had been cut longitudinally and rested on welded angle irons. The drums had holes in them for aeration and used the local fuel of charcoal. Alongside were several cauldrons on log fires cooking the maize pap, or nschima, and a tomato, cabbage, and onion relish, to which large dollops of peanut butter were added. The general hubbub of people chattering away to each other and the wonderful, enticing smells from the cooking added to the overall happy atmosphere. There would be no time for petty quarrels and squabbles, now was for genuine fun to be had by one and all. A grandstand and podium had been erected and the province police band was playing. A programme of welcome had been arranged, which meant the Kims would have to be seated on the podium while school children performed some songs led by girl majorettes, twirling and tossing their maces up in the air and catching them before repeating the process. This, then, would be followed by traditional dancing. The police band played on in the African style of jazz, alternating and even adapting other music to their mixture of instruments, mainly brass and marimbas. Then the Kims would officially hand the seed maize packs over to the local chief for further distribution among the people as gifts of the people of the Democratic People's Republic of Korea, amidst loud cheering and clapping. A vote of thanks for the generous gift would be given by the Minister, and then a specially chosen young schoolgirl would present a carving and stone sculpture to the

Kims for their Great Leader. There would be much ululation by the women as a mark of respect and gratitude. Both national anthems would be played, and the party would begin. The Kims and all the big wigs would go and be served luncheon by a professional caterer in the marquee, whilst the people would feast on pap, roasted meat and relish. A local farmer would have given a couple of steers and the brewery beers and soft drinks, but it was the traditional Chibuku-type maize beer that the men went for first. They would queue up to have their plastic buckets filled with the thick whitish, pungent, sour-tasting liquid. Once fed and fired up, the men would begin to dance among themselves to the music of a local mobile disco unit, never spilling a drop of their precious beers no matter how unsteady they became. It would perhaps be ad nauseam for the officials, but it would be a major party for the people and it would be rude to leave too soon.

It was around four o' clock that the Kims and the brigadier began their return journey to the Pamodzi.

The welcome phase of the Mpongwe event was in progress when Jim first phoned Jasper to tell him of the ship's early port entry and the collection of the containers from the Customs. That certainly ramped up the tension in the office, but all that Jonty could do was believe his teams were doing their jobs. With Jim's second call regarding the painting of the containers, what the smugglers were doing now became more of a discussion point, but as Jonty said, it smelled to him like a seemingly needless layer being added by the Chinese to ensure that they were sufficiently distanced from any wrongdoing.

That did, however, get Jonty to redouble his checks on the cover for a bolt by the Kims, knowing they would not be able to stop news of the arrests, if they were effected tonight, from getting out for any longer than 24 hours. It was gone 2300 when a euphoric Jim rang to tell them of the success in Dar; he repeated a warning nevertheless that the Chinese Consulate would probably know within the hour and would contact the main embassy in Dodoma immediately, so they would have the ability to contact their Lusaka embassy by morning and thence the Kims. Jasper thanked him and offered congratulations before promising to keep in regular communication regarding how their arrests in Lusaka were going. Jonty said they now had to get down to Lusaka to get to the Pamodzi and arrest the Kims.

The latest reports had indicated that the Kims and the brigadier had gone to bed, so Jonty made the instruction that they must hold the Kims if they tried to leave before morning. He himself would be with them in two hours. He turned to Charles, who had arrived back earlier, and told him to get on with the plan to arrest the haulage company owners and drivers, while he was going to Lusaka to arrest the Kims. He collected the files containing the photos taken by Jasper and the surveillance photos taken at the Kapiri Bond and rail-yard, and with that he called for a vehicle and he and Jasper got in the back and were quickly on the road to Lusaka. As the driver sped along at high speed, Jonty used the radio to get the teams at the Pamodzi to disable the Mercedes, just in case there was a sudden dash in the night. Midnight came and went before they passed through Kabwe.

CHAPTER 26

D-day +7: Monday

It was approaching 0200 Zulu when they drove down Church Road, past the Pamodzi entrance and down the almost half mile over Independence Avenue into Chimanga Road where Police HQ was located. The duty SB officer said that there had been no movement from the Pamodzi and that the brigadier's Mercedes had been disabled by deflating two tyres, one front and one back. They both went to the communications room so Jonty could speak directly to his people at the Pamodzi. They had men on all entrances, exits, lifts and on the floors above, below and on the floor that the Kims and brigadier were roomed, awaiting further instruction. Jonty said he would personally be there in 10 minutes to effect the arrests. He told Jasper that he would have to remain at HQ, as it would be better if the Kims and the brigadier did not see or know anything about Jasper. The photographic evidence that Jasper had collected on the Zimbabwean side, including the murder of du Preez, would be added to that of the surveillance at the Kapiri Bond and Tazara railway, and was more than enough to arrest the men. He would contact him shortly once he and his men had made the arrest and taken them to another holding point at the Arakan Barracks, where the donation of boots and uniforms had taken place two days before. He quickly explained that the Democratic People's Republic of Korea Trade Mission would probably be alerted by the Chinese Embassy as to the events in Dar. They would most likely try to advise the Kims at the Pamodzi and then come to Police HQ looking for their officials. Jonty left with a detachment of officers and requested the duty man to advise the head of SB so that he in turn could forewarn the Minister of Foreign Affairs.

Jasper settled down and waited in the comms room so that he could listen to the arrest operation as it happened. There would be onsite recording as well as an open channel to the comms room so that a second recording could be made. This was normal practice in instances of arrest overriding diplomatic immunity, for the safety of both the accused and the arresting parties. Technically the arresting authorities could only hold accused persons until they were advised by the home nation that the immunity aspects were waived. In cases where overwhelming evidence is presented and murder associations are made, it was very unlikely that the home nation would not waive the immunity. Generally, their defence would be that the accused will have acted without the knowledge of the home nation and in their own interests.

At 0305hrs the radio crackled into life and Jasper could hear, quite clearly, "This is the Zambian Security Services on behalf of UN agencies and the International Court. Stay still."

Then Jonty's voice came on. "I am Assistant Chief Commissioner in the Zambian Special Branch. I have warrants to hold Kim A ... and Kim B ... together with Brigadier X ... of Zimbabwe on charges of transporting poached elephant ivory from Kapiri Mposhi to Dar Es Salaam, by use of the Tazara Rail Authority, to be shipped as diplomatic cargo to a destination in China."

The immediate reaction from the Kims was an angry response: "All evidence is fabricated and aimed to discredit the Democratic People's Republic of Korea and a direct contravention of the Geneva Conventions covering diplomatic staff."

Jonty replied, "Nevertheless I am authorised to take you into custody whilst we provide our evidence to your Government and also to those of the People's Republic of China and the Republic of Zimbabwe. You will all be taken to a detention area while contact is made with the Governments involved. Please follow me gentlemen."

There were a lot of fairly severe invectives shouted by the Kims, and Jasper learned later they had to be restrained before they could be taken and driven off to Arakan Barracks. Jonty came on another radio to say he would take the two Kims, the brigadier and his driver over to Arakan and leave them in separate rooms guarded by the army and some SB officers before getting back to Police HQ. He thought he would be about 90 minutes. In the meantime, he asked Jasper to arrange a set of photos in chronological order from the loading camp in Zimbabwe including the execution of Willie, the tagging of the containers, and their passage through the border post, right up to the loading of the train on Tazara.

Jasper asked if he could inform Jim and Jonty replied, "Affirmative."

With the time at 0530 in Lusaka, which meant 0630 in Dar, Jasper phoned Jim and was surprised to get a very wide-awake Jim, keen to know how they got on. Jasper told him that they had taken the Kims and the brigadier with his driver from their hotel beds, and they were now with Jonty at an army camp until the diplomatic immunity issue could be finalised. He told Jim that they were preparing a photo evidence set for both the Korean government and the Chinese government representatives to get immunity waived. It would only be the Zim cargo at this stage, but it would be backed up by at least the pictures to include the Luangwa and Zaire ivory. Jim broke in and said he would tackle the Chinese Embassy in Dodoma to heavily impress the Chinese that they had photos of the containers in the process of loading and of one of their nationals cutting off diplomatic tags. He would make sure that they should contact their Lusaka embassy for further photographic evidence, so he asked Jasper to tell Jonty he must get that set to the Chinese soonest. He knew they would want to retreat from the affair, and they would put pressure on Pyongyang to waive immunity. He was going to allow the Tanzanians to announce the discovery of poached ivory and its prevention from being shipped out of Dar after it had been transported by Tazara. The identity of the poachers and freight would be withheld for the initial announcements. He said that this was going to turn out a job well done.

"Keep me in touch."

Jasper sat down with the files and began to get the photos in order, which did not take long as they were already pretty much in order, and soon he had three complete sets. He was just finishing when Jonty strode in with a smile on his face.

"You should hear the language, hardly befitting a diplomat, they used words I have not heard, but it's just bluster. They are rattled and the brigadier is strangely quiet; he knows the game is up, and I think he will talk very easily. I think they have or will shortly realise how serious this is and the likelihood that their countries will denounce their activities. Can't say that I can feel any sorrow for them at all, and I regret that this is one time I think the law should be forgotten, when animals are simply slaughtered for the whims of art aficionados."

Jasper nodded glumly as he remembered around a thousand elephants had died and said, "Don't encourage me, death may be too easy an option for these guys, and I don't think Jim wants that."

Jonty added, "You might be surprised as to what Jim may think, but a publicising of this affair may be more effective in the long run."

Jasper then related Jim's request that a set of photos be given to the Chinese embassy in Lusaka so that between the two embassies and Beijing, the Chinese would get a fright and disown Pyongyang over this. Without waiting any further, Jonty first got on the radio to Charles to confirm the arrests and to activate the arrests of the haulage companies and drivers. He then helped Jasper to finish sorting the photos into 3 sets. He then put one set into a large manila envelope which bore the crest and legends of the Republic of Zambia, together with a typed note requesting that the photographs be passed onto the commercial attaché. He called for a driver who was despatched for the urgent attention of the Commercial Attaché, despite the early hour. He reminded the driver to get an official receipt for the package. Jasper asked why the photos were not sent to the ambassador directly, to get a quicker response, but Jonty explained that ambassadors would only be approached directly by the Minister of Home Affairs, all other matters being put over to the ambassador's secretary. Since this could be a more prolonged route, given the unknown tasks or status of the secretary, it was much more likely that by sending it to the Commercial Attaché, it would reach the ambassador almost instantly, particularly as there was a hidden threat to any commerce between the two nations. It would seem as though the Zambian government were trying to advise the People's Republic of China of actions that had occurred without their knowledge but with the involvement of their nationals, who may well have been unknowing of the true nature of events. Hopefully, the photographs would have been seen by the time the embassy officials in Dodoma contacted them. Anyway, Jonty had followed the correct protocols so that both the ambassador and the Zambian Minister of Foreign Affairs were kept at arm's length officially. In any event, the Minister was being brought to Police HQ to be briefed and was due any minute. The Minister must have listened to Jonty explaining to Jasper, and it seemed on cue that he walked in and sat down, asking to be updated. He had already been receiving reports about SB being involved with an international poaching ring, but without knowing any detail or indeed of the identity of the players. Now he listened carefully to Jonty outlining the Luangwa and Zaire lines of poaching, including the involvement of Zambians, and then the Zimbabwe line, including the murder of a wildlife ranger. He offered the Minister a set of photographs, and he began to study them carefully whilst Jonty explained the scale of involvement of the two Kims.

The Minister then asked about the veracity of the pictures, to which Jonty replied, "We have the man who took the pictures with us Minister. May I intr –"

The Minister held up his hand and said immediately, "Please do not introduce your colleague," turning to Jasper and saying, "That is for political purposes, but I assure you that my country recognises the efforts you have personally made on behalf of this international operation. I wish to shake your hand, as no doubt our President will." He held out his hand and the two men shook warmly. The Minister went on to say, "You know many in the world call us dumb Africans, and in certain things we are perhaps behind others, but we are not wholesale slaughterers of defenceless animals for a few bits of bone. When we kill elephants it will be for a purpose; when our lives or crops are threatened. We do not seek tusks for vain reasons, and we would use as much of the beast to feed our people. For that they call us uncivilised, but I disagree; our reasons may be many, but never for money – that has been taught to us by our so-called betters in the world." He turned to Jonty and asked what he had done so far.

Jonty explained he had delivered the same set of photographs to the Chinese Commercial Attaché here, whilst the Chinese in Dodoma have been advised by the UN coordinator regarding the use of Tazara and a Chinese vessel due to be used in shipping. He went on, "The UN coordinator, who is an officer of the International Court, effected the discovery of the 90 tonnes of tusks in the containers on the dockside, with pictures of the North Korean tags being cut off prior to loading. As you see, we have clear view of the tags right from Zimbabwe to the Bond in Kapiri, then the addition of further Korean tags to the other ivory and their participation up to loading of the train. I believe the Tanzanians will announce the uncovering of a plot to ship 90 tonnes of ivory through Dar later today, but of course no mention of countries involved."

The Minister laughed and said, "Perhaps we will not be such dumb Africans after all. Our Chinese ambassador will not be looking forward to my summons later, especially when I suggest that it must have taken extremely clever planning by their own allies, the Koreans, to be able to deceive their friends. I shall enjoy his discomfort; I would like to say outright that they are in it up to their necks with the North Koreans, but I have to be diplomatic. He will, nevertheless, know that we know. I need a set of these photographs for my meeting."

Jonty indicated that one was being prepared, along with a summary of the whole operation, with certain names omitted, primarily any foreign advisors and local informers. The Minister nodded and then asked what was to happen to the Kims. Jonty said they would remain in Zambian custody until diplomatic immunity was waived, then they would be charged with organised poaching and despatch from Zambia of ivory, which would allow time for extradition to the International Court's jurisdiction.

The Minister thought the North Koreans may not accept that and demand their people back to be dealt with by themselves, "and we all know what that means for the poor bastards. The big losers will be China, loss of face and all that." He declared a job well done to everybody, including Jasper, and saying "I shall enjoy my day," he and his aides swept out.

Jonty and Jasper both almost burst out laughing as he went but managed to remain respectful, at least in front of the others. Jonty soon brought the office back to reality, telling everyone that they were only finished with the operational phase and now they needed to prepare for the questioning of those arrested and get all the previous weeks work properly documented. He instructed that all surveillance teams should take two or three days off now and catch up on sleep and see their families before reporting back for duty. He got onto Charles up in Kapiri to be brought up to date and to release the surveillance teams they used for the

Bond and station. He listened carefully as Charles reported the arrests of the Luangwa haulage company owners and the drivers with no issues. The Zaire connection was more difficult in that they had got 8 out of the 10 drivers who ferried the tusks from the forests, and a few of the couriers, but the haulage truck company used and its management were still under surveillance. They would remain so until the SB could get evidence from the arrested drivers as to which, if any, of the bosses were involved. Charles thought they may be lucky to get a quick result, maybe 50/50, but he would know better by tomorrow. Jonty thought that they should not waste too much time trying to arrest remaining minions and rather concentrate on sweating those drivers to see if they could get corroborated statements pinpointing any bosses. He would see Charles tomorrow.

He turned to Jasper and said, "I have to stay at least today to make sure the reports are written and to be told when I can start my interrogators. You are welcome to stay with me, or I can arrange for you to be dropped back to the farm and you can get some rest. You can set Paddy's mind at ease and let her know we have been successful, but not too much detail."

Jasper chose to go back to the farm, and within five minutes was settling down in a car and driven at speed back to the farm.

Jasper had arrived back at the farm just after lunch, but Paddy's cook did some mixed grill for him, and he went out onto the veranda to call Jim. He brought Jim up to date with the arrests and his pseudo-anonymous meeting with the Zambian Foreign Affairs Minister, and let him know that Jonty was now in the process of preparing to interview the Kims et al as soon as diplomatic immunity was waived. Jim said that he had delivered his indictment to the Chinese authorities in Tanzania and the Chinese ambassador was currently at the Tanzanian Foreign Affairs Bureau, being questioned as to whether or not they were involved in the transportation of poached ivory knowingly. Given the radio traffic between Dodoma and the embassy in Lusaka, Jim felt that immunity would be waived immediately and that the Chinese would offer all help to the Zambians and Tanzanians to bring the matter to a successful conclusion. Jasper said that he was going to bed now to catch up on sleep, and he would leave Jonty to keep everyone up to date. Jim laughed, said something about youngsters not being able to keep up the pace and hung up. Jasper went to see Paddy, gave her a shortened version of events as to what her husband was doing, and went off to bed.

Shortly after Jasper went to sleep, as Jim predicted, the Chinese ambassador in Lusaka advised that the North Koreans had withdrawn diplomatic immunity for the two Kims and had requested that the Chinese act on their behalf in the matter. The note read:

"It is clear that the Kims have acted on their own behalf and tragically have succumbed to the great Western disease of consumerism and greed. Though this was abhorrent and not at all representative of the Korean People's behaviour, Western agencies are to blame for constantly tempting Korean individuals with excessive and constant provocations."

A duplicate note had been sent to the Zambian Foreign Ministry.

The Chinese Chargé d'Affaires in the embassy had been delegated by his ambassador to deal with the Zambian officials to conclude the whole sorry business. As this was going on, and the Chargé d'Affaires, one Mr Xiong, was beginning to sit down with the Zambian Minister, the news came through that the Tanzanians had made an announcement to the UN and the world's press that they had managed to foil a plot to ship 90 tonnes of elephant ivory via the Tazara railway and through the port of Dar Es Salaam. Clearly Jim had managed to up the ante by allowing the Tanzanians to score the brownie points on the stopping of the shipment, but he had also managed to keep the identities of people and nations out of the official spotlight. The Tanzanians were only too happy to share in the success of Operation Tembo and take charge of displaying the whole 90 tonnes of ivory to the world's press.

Mr Xiong had begun the meeting demanding that the two Kims be released into his custody for their return to Pyongyang, so that they could be tried by the North Koreans. That the Kims would hardly want this was irrelevant, but the Minister said it was not possible now, anyway, since the crime of transportation had occurred on Zambian soil and therefore became Zambian jurisdiction. Even then it may be that Zimbabwe would demand their extradition regarding the 30 tonnes poached from Zimbabwe. Mr Xiong said that the People's Republic of Korea, as well as the People's Republic of China, did not wish for the world to know about their nationals having succumbed to temptations, for fear of political point scoring by their enemies. He went on to say that surely their friends, the Zambians, would understand this, and the PRC would undertake to guarantee that these men would be tried, and justice would be served. An aide knocked and entered the room passing a note to the Minister. The Minister smiled and said that if it had been left to himself, perhaps it may have been possible, but this was a UN led operation that had been active for many months and the warrants issued were for the International Court. Furthermore, he had just been advised that the Tanzanians had, in fact, released the news of a successful operation regarding the poaching. It was now impossible for Zambia to prevent the affair from being handled by the International Court.

Before Mr Xiong could consider a reply, another aide entered, but this time passed a note to Mr Xiong. He read this, and then stood and bowed to the Minister. He had been advised that immunity was being waived and he was to drop the demand for transfer of custody. Instead, he would ask for the Minister to publicly confirm that there was no involvement of the PRC in the sorry matter of the poaching in Zambia. They shook hands, and Mr Xiong left.

Jonty got the call from the Minister that immunity was waived, and he could formally charge them using the International warrants. He also issued a warning to ensure that any questioning should be done without allowing any excesses that may occasionally occur with non-cooperative suspects. The State would be happy to have assisted UN officials in their fight against illegal ivory poaching. Jonty thanked the Minister and assured him no excesses would happen in this case. He looked at the time, 1800hrs, and guessed Jasper would be asleep so he phoned Jim to inform him he was going to formally arrest and charge the Kims and the brigadier with the poaching and transportation of illegal ivory, plus the murder of Willie Du Preez. He would begin the questioning after leaving them to digest the fact that immunity had been waived. Jim was not surprised that immunity had been waived and wished him luck.

Jonty made his way over to Arakan, where the men were being held. He then briefed his interrogation teams and reminded them they were acting on behalf of the International Court, so no rough stuff was to be allowed. He would first formally charge the men and advise that their immunity under the Geneva Convention had been waived. He had a telex which the Minister had been sent confirming the waiving, and got copies made to file and give one each to the Kims. He went to the room that Kim A was being held, entering to a stream of what he assumed to be Korean swear words. He sat down and allowed the man to finish. He withdrew a copy of the telex cancelling the diplomatic immunity and pushed it over the table. Kim A looked at it and sat down in disbelief and hardly heard the formal execution of the International warrant against him. This time his response that he would remain silent was very docilely given. The performance was repeated almost to a tee with Kim B; clearly both could not believe they were being abandoned, not only by their own nation but also by their great protectors, the PRC. Both recognised that they were dead, along with their families, whether they were deported or tried by the International Court.

They also became overwhelmed with a dread that the Zambians may be persuaded to look the other way while agents of the PRC would kill them. All hope had disappeared.

The position with the brigadier was different, however. He was well aware of his predicament, he made no attempt to bluster or pretend that he had no idea as to what was going on, but simply asked to see a representative of his government. This had been anticipated by Jonty, and he very deliberately placed six photographs of the shooting of Willie Du Preez and of the brigadier and the Kims during the loading and tagging of the two Zimbabwe containers on the table. He then showed the brigadier the telex confirming the waiving of diplomatic immunity for the Kims and suggested he would give the brigadier more time to consider his position. Nevertheless, he was obliged to charge him in accordance with the international warrants concerning the transportation of the illegal ivory across border into Zambia and using Zambian facilities, namely a bonded warehouse in Kapiri Mposhi and thereafter the Tazara railway. Jonty told him that because the warrants were from the International Court, his nation would be automatically informed of his arrest. In the meantime, he was going to charge the brigadier's driver with complicity in the transportation of illegal ivory and the murder. The brigadier became extremely agitated, suspecting that his driver would be the weak link and in fact would reveal much more as to the acquisition of the ivory in the first place, further incriminating the brigadier and the Kims. He also knew that Jonty knew this and almost resignedly hunched his shoulders, sighing deeply. Jonty then went and charged the brigadier's driver who, as suspected, offered to tell the whole story almost immediately once he realised that neither his boss nor the Kims were going to help him, and indeed he could be in a great deal of danger from them. He agreed to talk to Jonty's people, understanding he could not be freed, but his testimony would be a big factor in receiving a greatly reduced sentence. He had already started to give details of the elephant slaughter in Wankie as Jonty left to return to the Police HQ.

Back in his office he contacted Charles at Kapiri to be told they had found a third party whose name the drivers from the Ndola haulage firm had given as the person from whom they got instructions and payments. It turned out that this third party was none other than the accountant for the hauliers, who was able to run the firm on behalf of the two partners who ostensibly owned the company. They had only started to interrogate the accountant, but it had already emerged that the two so-called owners were only frontmen and basically received a wage. Clearly the company was formed for the purposes of smuggling anything at all across the border to and from Zaire. They would have to sweat him some more, but they may need to give him some leeway if he was to give up any contacts on the Zaire side. The Luangwa side was tied up and the main players had identified the Kims as the people with whom they had dealt. Jonty said well done and, realizing it was now coming up to midnight, suggested Charles get some sleep.

He thought at first he would waken both Jasper and Jim, but decided to let them sleep for a bit yet; in fact, he would try to catch a nap.

CHAPTER 27

Breakout: Tuesday

The interrogators had got nowhere with the Kims, who claimed they could not understand the language, knowing full well it would take some time to find a North Korean language specialist, who no doubt would have to come from a UN department. The brigadier remained tight-lipped, even when the interrogators asked him about Wankie, obviously having so much detail that only the driver would have known. There was no point in talking yet. The interviews had all come to a halt and food was arranged for the prisoners and the SB teams. The latter retired to the officers' mess to eat and consider their next steps.

When the door opened to the room in which Kim A was being held, an army steward carrying a tray of food and drink entered. The SB guard moved forward and motioned for the tray to be put down. As he reached for some food and his other hand for drink, Kim A suddenly jumped up, pushing the steward into the SB man and performed a karate move that put the SB man down. He took the steward by the neck, twisted and jerked until it snapped, and then, dropping the steward, kicked the SB man, who was trying to stand, in the throat, under the chin. He stepped over the body of the steward and hit the SB man with tremendous force just on the bridge of his nose, driving the bone up into the brain. The man was dead before he hit the floor again. Kim A searched him, taking his wallet and gun as well as a spare magazine. He opened the door, and seeing no one in the corridor, just a trolley with three trays of food on it, he walked along to the next door in that wing and opened the door. The SB man was totally surprised and had no option but to raise his hands in view of the pistol in Kim A's hand. He was rewarded with a rabbit punch from Kim B and was unconscious as he hit the floor. He was lucky; he would live. Kim B took his weapon, and the two then slipped out and rounded the corner in the building into the next wing. They opened the first door and found the brigadier. They overpowered the guard and Kim B broke the man's neck. They spoke briefly among themselves, and when the brigadier told them it was likely the driver had talked, they did not waste time to try and find him but instead looked around out the windows to see where they were exactly. The brigadier recalled that they were in the next block to where they were treated to luncheon on the Saturday, and figured that it would be easier to get out of the camp by climbing the closest fence. Even if they could find a vehicle and were able to crash the entrance barriers, their escape would be known immediately. It would be better to get out of the barracks and steal a car, making for the Zim border. The Kims agreed, thinking that if they could get back to Zim, then their embassy could insist that they had been the centre of a cruel, Western-led misinformation plot. This would have been designed to make both Zimbabwe and the People's Republic look bad, covering up that the West had prompted the poaching of elephants themselves. They slipped past a tool shed, the brigadier stopping long enough to find cutters and pliers, before finding a suitably desolate part of the fence which was poorly lit. It took less than ten minutes to cut a hole and slip through and out. They moved quickly, keeping as much as possible to the shadows, and managed to get onto some waste ground. This led them to Yotam Muleya Road and then along till they came to Chite Road. They walked up until they came to the outer edges of Lusaka Teaching Hospital. This was perfect, as there would be cars parked and easy exits. They got onto the grounds and decided that they would split up with Kim A, who was confident he could get into and start any vehicle, going off to look for a suitable car. Kim B and the brigadier remained 50 yards behind Kim A and walked slowly towards the car parks. Kim A disappeared into a line of cars and eventually they heard an engine start up and saw a Toyota bakkie move towards them. Kim B and the brigadier got in beside Kim A, who then continued round to the exit. There was a man in the office by the barrier, but the pole was in the up position for the exit side and the man did not even look up as they drove through and turned right onto Nationalist Road. This took them onto Independence Avenue, which they followed westwards till they came to the traffic circle that let them take the southern exit towards Chilanga, Kafue and Chirundu. They knew that they could not cross through the normal border posts, but the brigadier had remembered where, during the Chimurenga, he had taken comrades for night crossovers to Zimbabwe. He reckoned he could get them over at night, and they would not have too far to walk to get to Chirundu and safety, as they saw it. With that they drove south.

Jonty was awoken at 0200 by one of his men, who was clearly agitated, so much so that Jonty knew it was bad news. However, he did not expect to be told that the Kims and the brigadier had escaped from Arakan Barracks, having killed two SB officers and an army steward. Their present whereabouts were unknown, they could be anywhere within Lusaka and were armed. Jonty gave instructions for roadblocks at all exit points from the city and for border crossings to be warned of the three, particularly Chirundu/Kariba. He also requested all movements in and out of the Chinese Embassy be monitored, though he did not think they would go there. He phoned Jim and reported what had happened and that it was now a manhunt for murderers. Jim was disappointed, but not despondent, as by engineering this escape and committing murder they had pretty much proved their guilt, so the events were not altogether a train wreck. Jim asked whether Jasper had been told, and suggested perhaps his skills might be useful. Jonty advised that Jasper had suggested that they might use an old crossing place on the Zambezi, used by the brigadier during the Liberation War, and had made arrangements for that to be covered. Jim said he did not want to know any more except the end result. They ended their call.

Jonty first called the Minister at home and brought him up to speed, with the predictable outburst. The Minister then apologised and said he was disappointed that it had happened, and that three Zambians had died. Jonty then told him of what he had done so far, and that their advisor had suggested that the three might make a break for the Zimbabwe border using a crossing point on the Zambezi previously used by the brigadier in his Zipra days. The Minister asked whether this advisor was the man he had met, and on Jonty's confirmation, suggested he looked like a man who might be the solution.

He pointed out that there would be no joy in Zim if they got back; as he said, "We Zambians will have to do it." He told Jonty to use whatever resources he needed, including the armed forces. He would clear the use of Zambian resources with all that may be involved right away. It was now 0245, and he arranged a helicopter to go and pick up Jasper. He would ring Jasper to warn him, and then the helicopter would come back to pick up Jonty. He would brief Jasper on the trip to Chirundu.

He got Jasper, who was coming out of a long sleep, so he was fresh, and simply said he was needed to 'consult' in a manhunt, the Kims and the brigadier had escaped. He would explain everything once the helicopter had picked them up, and oh, Jasper should get kitted up. Jasper heard the chopper and was ready in camouflage, with his bow, pistol, knife, phone, and night vision gear. He got on board and asked the pilot to patch him through to Jonty. He told Jonty that if he was going into the field, he would need an assault rifle, preferably an AK, and some army worm. The helicopter landed at Police HQ forty minutes later for long enough for Jonty to get onboard with two holdalls, then taking off and heading south. It was 0430hrs and, once again, the sun had won its daily battle with the night.

CHAPTER 28

The Final Cut

As they took off and headed towards the Zimbabwean border, Jonty began to relate the whole sorry episode regarding the Kims and the brigadier. He was acting on Jasper's hunch and had bet on Jasper being correct in his supposition that they would run for Zim and use the old crossing point. The fact that they had murdered three Zambian men during their escape may sign and seal their guilt, but now it was shoot to kill for the three men. The pilot cut in and motioned Jonty to switch on his communicator on the helmet. He did so and listened. He nodded and spoke, though Jasper could not hear above the clatter of the rotors. When he had finished, he turned back to Jasper and told him a red bakkie had been stolen from the University Teaching Hospital during the night.

He said, "It would seem that such a vehicle was seen by guards along Independence early this morning heading towards the traffic circle bottom of Cairo Road, so I have to assume it got past our roadblocks before they were set up. A normal roadblock down about Chilanga has reported the vehicle as having passed through before they got the info, so they have a head start."

Jasper shook his head and said they would try and get to the crossing point before nightfall, so he would expect them to take the bakkie as close to the escarpment as possible. He said, "Can you get your people to start checking the areas around the road, say from the Kariba turn off?"

Jonty went back to the pilot and started talking. After five minutes he turned back to Jasper, and said, "They have found a matching bakkie just down the Kariba Road, apparently a bus saw it going off the road there but did not stop for fear of bandits. They reported it to the roadblock, which has now been set up at the crossroads."

"Can you get us as close to where the bakkie has been left as possible?"

Jonty went forward and spoke to the pilot. Ten minutes later they were over the bakkie, but the helicopter had to go back to the road to be able to land. On the ground, Jasper got out, as did Jonty with the bags. Jasper took a rifle and 4 army worm; army worm is slang for grenades, often detonated by army men in rivers or lakes to stun fish, which float to the surface ready for picking. Jonty took a rifle and his radio.

Jasper said, "Look Jonty, I work alone and anyway you would slow me down."

Jonty said he was on Zambian soil and therefore he was lending legality, and anyway by now the helicopter had lifted off and was heading over to Chirundu to await instruction. Jasper shrugged and went over to the bakkie to examine it. He then circled outwards from the bakkie until he found a trail, which clearly belonged to the three men.

He motioned Jonty over and said, "This looks as if they came down the Kariba road to throw us off. The trail is about two hours old and is headed back to the Chirundu road." They got a map out and Jasper pointed out where they were headed. He asked, "Can you organize transport, like a routine police truck, to take us in along the dirt track to where it crosses the Kafue, nearest to the Kafue confluence with the Zambezi? That will put us ahead of them and let us set up properly with Henry to 'meet and greet' them. They will not try to cross before nightfall, nor much before midnight as there is too much risk of being seen in daylight. Too many safari operators and fishermen."

Jonty got on his radio, but before he spoke, he quickly asked, "What about the chopper?"

"No good," replied Jasper, explaining that the chopper flying over may well alert them and change their plan. Twenty minutes later, a light police truck with a canvas-covered back arrived, and the two climbed into it with their gear. Jonty told the driver where they wanted to be dropped and reminded the driver to treat this as a normal patrol and to drive normally. They reckoned it would take a couple of hours, so if they wanted to sleep, this was their opportunity. Jonty did slumber, having only had about two hours in the previous 24 hours, but Jasper was fresh and stayed awake and studied the map. They stopped a couple of times to chat to people walking and ask if they had seen any foreigners, but no one had. At just after 0930 the truck ground to a halt without crossing the bridge over the Kafue. Jasper woke Jonty and both screwed up their eyes as they got off with their packs. It seemed terribly bright after the canvassed back of the truck and it took a minute or two for a degree of acclimatisation with the light and the humidity. Jasper led off, urging Jonty to keep up, but first he explained a couple of hand signals, like stop, go to ground, circle left and right, use your eyes, and back off. He reckoned they had a couple of miles to reach the confluence and then it would be another mile to the crossing point amongst the sandbars. Jasper shouldered his crossbow and carried the AK in his right hand. His ammo was in his backpack, along with his switched off phone and three grenades. He kept one grenade in his breast belt, along with a spare magazine for the rifle and one for his pistol. Four of his crossbow bolts hung from his utility belt, which also held his pistol and knife. He had blackened his face, as had Jonty, and both wore floppy hats. They kept to the bush alongside the river and made good time, startling a small herd of eland, who slipped away deeper into the bush. They came into view of the confluence area before 1100, but Jasper skirted the actual confluence, as there were some women washing clothes in the water just where the two rivers met. He first stopped Jonty, who was some fifteen yards behind, and pointed to where the women were, putting his finger up to his lips.

He then motioned Jonty to join him and whispered, "Look about ten yards beyond the flat stones the women are using to beat the washing."

Jonty knew he was being tested and studied hard. After about 30 seconds he began to discern a dark outline in the water, which seemed to be causing a slight ripple like a sunken log with water swirling around it. He nodded and mouthed, "Flat-dog." Jasper was pleased and nodded, then led on. They reached the crossing area before 1200, much to Jonty's relief, and while he was left in a small gully, Jasper said to give him five minutes as he circled round the disused camp area to check for any surprises, like old booby traps, and to decide which would be the most likely point of entry by the fugitives. He came back and moved Jonty closer to the river and its sandbars. To Jonty's surprise, Jasper was making some strange clicks and whistles. Within a few minutes he was even more astonished that he was picking out similar noises and squawks. It was as if Jasper were talking to someone – then he realized he was talking to Henry, who could not be far away.

A few minutes later a motorised canoe came into view, with two men apparently fishing, one a black, presumably the guide, and the other who was perhaps of unknown descent, but his skin was deeply tanned, perhaps a racial mixture. Once again, he was astonished as Jasper spoke clearly to the men as they drifted by, before they paddled in behind the first sandbar. Seconds later, Henry and the older Du Toit came into the gully and embraced Jasper. Jonty noticed he was greeted as JJ, not Jasper, who then introduced Henry, forgetting momentarily that they had met at Osprey before. He only introduced Du Toit as a friend; there was no need to let Jonty know his name. They chatted for a few minutes, bringing Henry and the friend into the picture as they knew it. Henry suggested that the meet and greet would go better from the Zimbabwean side, and in fact provide more of a surprise factor than hitting them on the Zambian side. This made a lot of sense, and though Jonty was a little unsure about whether they were taking prisoners, he realised none of the men had any intention of taking prisoners. He was actually relieved, because he knew it would be difficult to ensure the safety of the three, given the murders they had carried out at the Barracks, and in any case his President would rather loose ends were tied off.

They were able to get their bags and Jonty into the canoe, which then pulled away and across to the landing site on the Zimbabwean side. Within ten minutes it was back to pick up JJ and take him over. JJ recognised the gully, even though he had not been actually in it for a few years. It was a little more overgrown, and there was perhaps some more bush, but it was the same place. He realised that it was a big assumption that the fugitives would use the crossing, but he knew the way the brigadier was thinking and that the Kims would capitalize on his knowledge of the land and to get them into Zim. This particular crossing gave them fairly easy options to either walk out or hide until their people came to get them. He also thought that the Kims would kill the brigadier, as he would be the only other man capable of giving full details and the extent of the ivory poaching committed at their order. As soon as the Kims were confident of being able to make it back to their embassy, they would kill him, of that JJ had no doubt. Once inside the embassy they would be smuggled home and would remain as missing persons. Jonty had had another scare when he and Henry withdrew to the topside of the gully; suddenly, another man appeared beside him out of nowhere, who obviously was just a younger version of the friend he had already met. He did not have to be told this was another friend.

When JJ and friend arrived, he saw JJ nod and say "Howzit," to the other friend, who just nodded and immediately disappeared. Henry said he was their sentry. The four of them settled down and biltong was offered, as well as cold tea, both very welcome, and they went over the planning that Henry had done. As Henry saw it, they would stake out the gully classically, both sides and back, with one man moving forward to cover the river. He had changed this now JJ was here; the younger friend would actually be in the canoe, back a little from the site in case someone made a run to get back across to Zambia. The canoe would move round to a position in the river from which it would cover the various channels of the river as it was split by the sandbars. Henry's plan was to have himself and JJ initiate the kill with crossbow and Henry's silenced SVD.

The friends would take care of the brigadier; there was no doubt that he would die, but Henry suspected that it would be an innovative death. He explained to JJ that that was the price of their help. JJ cut in and made it absolutely clear that the primary objective was to kill the Kims and dispose of their bodies; no one must ever find them, nor could they be allowed to get into Zimbabwe and live. As for the brigadier, he agreed that the friends could take him. Henry then suggested that Jonty should literally be parked and not take part at all, given he was not a Scout, nor of the bush in the same way as the friends were. He meant no offence to Jonty, but he and JJ were a team, and the two friends were a team, and a stranger may introduce unknown, unacceptable risk. He also stressed that Jonty must understand that in this case 'meet and greet' really did mean 'meet and kill'. There must be no interference from him. Jonty nodded that he understood and said that death was all that would have awaited all three in Zambia after the killings in the Arakan Barracks. He hoped he did not sound too hollow, as he did believe in the rule of law, but on the other hand he was secretly grateful he had not been assigned a killing role. He was a bit concerned with what may befall the brigadier at the hands of the friends – he had thought about asking for him to be taken alive so he could be questioned, but knew that was off the table. The sun was well on its journey down, sometimes briefly hiding behind odd little puffs of white cloud, but still in charge. There would be, however, not more than a couple of hours of light left, so they had to find their hiding places soon, as it was possible that the fugitives could be close. If any of them were seen, particularly Jonty, the game would be up, and no crossing would be attempted. They arranged themselves so that JJ took the left-hand side of the gully and would be the first to fire. Henry took the opposite side so that he and JJ would minimise the dangers of accidental crossfire. The Scouts were renowned for their ability to define angles. Teams often would seem to be shooting at each other, but their training was such that two men could virtually cover 360 degree fire, but know precisely where their partners were and therefore avoiding hitting each other. The older friend was positioned at the head of the gully, and once JJ, then Henry, had despatched the Kims, his target was the brigadier. The younger friend would bring the canoe around to cover any attempt to cross back. They were, however, unsure how to place Jonty so that he was out of harm's way and also would not be able to interfere. The younger friend said he would take the Zambian murungu with him: that way he would be safe and out of the way.

JJ told all of them that this man Jonty must survive, so the right story could be told later. The younger understood and nodded. JJ turned to Jonty and said, "You must go with him, he will see that you are safe, and should anything happen to me and Henry he will make sure you get back to Zambia. We are now going to wait for as long as it takes, so I suggest you have a pee now and then hold it till it's over or pee your pants, do not speak or interfere unless he tells you, do you understand?"

Jonty nodded. He embraced JJ before turning and saying, "Good luck," then disappearing along with the younger friend.

Henry reminded JJ about Nyaminyami, but JJ had already remembered. They now gave their prayer together silently, as was their way. Both turned and nodded to the elder Du Toit, who nodded back, and all three went to their positions. Henry and

JJ communicated with their own click and whistle system when both were in their positions, so that they knew exactly where each other were.

Jonty sat in the front of the canoe and thought he was seeing another side to Jasper, and wondered if Sophie knew of his past, or rather, how much she knew. He had not been directly involved in the war, but he had been through a fairly hard school himself, and had used or stood back as various degrees of coercion were applied. Who was he kidding? He had used torture when he thought he had no other options and rationalized it to himself. He just had never seen or met anyone like Jasper, who was an academic on one hand, and a stone-cold killer on the other, and undoubtedly a champion for animals. He could only guess at the demons that Jasper must have. Little did he know how much of a saviour Sophie had become, and how much he and Henry needed each other when they were in the bush. He felt a tap on his shoulder and turned to see the younger friend point to his eyes and then into the reed bed they were in. He soon saw a sleeping croc lying not three yards away, and realized he was being warned or alerted to the fact. He nodded and turned his head, now wondering at how calm the younger man was, and seemingly at ease with his environment. Jonty was a man of the land, but he never was as in touch with it as these people were, nor Jasper and Henry. Perhaps the world would be a better place if everybody were in touch with the environment, but that would never happen; too much greed existed.

Darkness marched in and blacked everything out, but the longer Jonty looked into the night the more he began to see. He also began to hear the noises of the night and to see the magic of his surroundings. Surprisingly, he found himself at ease.

Both JJ and Henry had emptied their minds of anything other than the job at hand, as they could not afford any distractions of thought; it was why they had survived all their contacts during the war. They were both locked in and would remain so until action or the morning came. What went through either Du Toits' mind, would not be known to anyone but themselves, and perhaps their old man, Piet. A small moon appeared, and an eerie sort of light bathed the river, which, with time, allowed a degree of vision. Nevertheless, both Henry and JJ scoured the opposite bank with their night vision binoculars, looking for signs of activity. A few impala and eland came down to the water's edge to drink, quite nervously, constantly watching for predators. They were lucky tonight, nothing from the land nor the river attacked them during their drink, and soon they melted away into the thickets.

It was getting on for midnight when Jonty felt the tap on his shoulder, and, on turning, the young man's finger went to his lips. He cupped his hand around one ear and pointed over to the other side. He looked in the direction and could not see anything, but heard the sounds of people talking, indistinctly at first, then clearly enough that he could pick out a word or two. He was not surprised that it was English, as he realized that would probably be the common language between the Kims and the brigadier. He then thought he could make out the shapes of three men in the subdued moonlight.

Henry and JJ had picked up the changes in noise patterns some five minutes earlier and communicated with a few clicks. The elder Du Toit heard them and guessed there was activity on the other side. Using there night binos and the night sights of their weapons, both Henry and JJ saw the men come into view, and as they recognised the Kims and the brigadier they both felt their heart rates quicken momentarily. The fugitives were clearly unaware that they were being watched, and although they all had drawn pistols, the Koreans were arguing with the brigadier. The Kims were already looking the worse for wear, having torn clothing, no suitable footwear, and obviously a hard time travelling in the bush. They were close to rebellion but had responded to the brigadier's cajoling. Now they wanted to rest, but then began to shout again, despite being hushed, and worse was to come for these five-star jockeys. They began to realise there was no boat, and the only way to cross was to sandbar hop. The widest part of the river would be no more than five yards, but by choosing the right sandbars they could traverse the river in a zig zag, with only one wide fording, plus four or five small ones. The bigger problem was that even the brigadier had a fear of croc attack, but was trying to sound confident. They had small arms, and with speed they could cross island hopping. The odds were actually in their favour, as the first fording was the widest, and that would probably only alert the reptiles to a presence in the water. They could be well across the first one before they were noticed, and subsequent fordings would be needed to alert any croc reaction. Moving together, they could make sure they appeared like a large animal, a hippo for instance, buying themselves a few more precious seconds. They were probably in more danger if they hung about on the sandbars or split up. The Kims wanted to look for a boat, but the brigadier said they would be unlikely to find one, and the risks became greater the longer they remained in Zambia. As he told them, there was no war anymore, so they would not get any helping hands from the locals and would be reported, if they hadn't been already. The brigadier had some experience of the bush – certainly he was a fundi in comparison to the Kims – and he told them that his own totem was the crocodile, so as long as they stayed close and were with him, the crocodiles would leave them alone.

In tribal cultures, commonly practised in Africa, belief remains strong in a spirit world despite the best efforts of the missionaries. Even though many Africans have adopted Christianity, they have adapted to allow for both belief systems to exist side by side without conflict. The spirits of their ancestors still play a part in daily life even amongst what would be termed as 'civilized, educated people'. Men have to live in balance with their environments. It is a belief that animal spirits help to ensure that balance when they communicate with people's spirits, almost a form of internal and external yin and yang. As a man, you are given a totem dependent on, or at least associated with, your behaviour, and it is believed that the spirit of the animal will look after you, guide your actions. It characterises you and you characterise it. The crocodile is held to be fearless, has highly developed senses, like its hearing of its young whilst still in their shells, and its protection of its young by transporting them in its mouth represents fierce protection. Its ability to see through murky waters teaches that people can see equally clearly through the most ambiguous dreams or the most confusing emotions. Their armour plating and their habit of floating just below the surface, with eyes barely visible, indicates these people look but remain unseen. Their habit of attacking by ambush and storing their prey under water to rot enough to allow chunks to be torn off demonstrates preparation, making choices wisely and allowing those choices to take their course. If, however, the people who have been assigned their totem fail to characterise that totem, it will be considered that they are out of balance with their environments, and the protective element of that totem will diminish. Belief, particularly self-belief, can be extremely powerful. It is not uncommon for chickens with small parcels attached like a collar to be let loose in a village. The collar represents a man's bad luck, debts maybe, and the belief is that anyone who then kills the chicken for the pot will then take over the bad luck, freeing the original man from it. Despite the poverty and the apparent free meal, many such chickens survive for quite a long while, because people will avoid them. Such is the strength of belief, and the spirit world always comes to the fore during adversity.

The fact that the brigadier's totem was the crocodile meant little to the very despondent Kims. They had already decided that their exposure in the ivory operation was wholly the fault of the brigadier, and would have killed him had they not needed him, at least until they could arrange for being picked up by their embassy. They were so indoctrinated that they refused to believe that they had been abandoned by their nation and its powerful friend, namely China. Besides, they were tired, and had no idea of where they were, nor any idea as to how they would find their way out of this infernal and seemingly unending thickets and bush. They needed the brigadier for now, but that did not stop them from complaining constantly. They still wanted to look for a boat, or even make a raft, but as the brigadier kept on saying, they had to move, they already may have been seen or heard and their chance to cross would be compromised. He re-iterated that if they moved together and got across the first ford onto the first sandbar, they would be home and dry. All they needed to do was to make themselves as big a unit as possible by crossing as one. The brigadier said their greatest danger was if they hung about on the sandbars, and that once started, they must keep going and keep together. He said they must try and keep their weapons dry, because they might need them if there were crocs on the sandbars.

The crossing point the guerrillas had chosen on this part of the Zambezi was just before a bend, where years of flooding after a wet season would deposit silt and sand, gradually choking the river. This made it wider during flood, but shallower during the dry season. As the river found a sand bar in its way, where previously a full flood would simply wash over it and reshape, with the dam at Kariba now controlling outflow, the river was no longer the mighty Zambezi. As the lake filled there was little or no meaningful flow, so a few areas did begin the siltation process, and once full, all floodgates were opened, restoring but magnifying the surges of natural rainfall and wet seasons that the northwest of Zambia, Angola and Botswana experienced. Now water was controlled simply dependent on the lake levels, which had to remain above a certain level for the hydro-electric generators to work; after all, the main function was to produce cheap electricity for both Zimbabwe and Zambia. It was only after a period of drought that it was finally realized that there needed to be regular openings of the dam floodgates, especially in the dry season, to keep the river from choking itself. However, the flood plain had diminished, and where excessive siltation had occurred, the sandbars became features, with an almost delta like flow through and around them. There were many small rivulets through the sandbars before they all joined up again to form the major river the Zambezi was.

The brigadier spent some time in the poor light of the moon to plot a way through the maze of sandbars and rivulets. Once he had decided which way they were going to take, he was keen to do it before his own fears overwhelmed him, but as a man with some training in leadership of men he recognised the Kims were in need of a short break. He had driven them hard for a few miles in heavy bush and noticed their suffering, which he dismissed as potential weakness. He had spent quite a lot of time with them over the past five years and had watched them grow soft as they began to enjoy the luxury of superior lodges and hotels, and it was for that he had begun to despise them. Still, they had been good paymasters, allowing him to keep his own private army of a few old veterans on retainer. He decided that he would allow them no more than fifteen minutes rest before he got them moving. He could see that they had ripped their clothes and skin on thorns, which every piece of vegetation seemed to have. Their feet were cut and blistered, having thrown away their shoes, and their faces were beginning to suffer the attacks from mosquito bites; they needed to get their breath back. He left them for a minute, going back a short distance along the way they had come to satisfy himself they had not been followed. He had no idea that he was being watched, not from behind, but from ahead. He never for a minute suspected that, nor indeed any danger from the Kims. Time was up, time to cross.

The brigadier chose his spot to enter the river as well as he could. He had spotted that there was a hippo run, and although the ford to the first sandbar at this point was almost 10 yards, he figured there would be less chance of crocs hovering around that point.

They plunged in together and waded as quickly as they could, having to bounce nearer to the bar before feet found a solidness below and propelled them onto the first sandbar. The brigadier pushed along at a trot to the next stretch of water, and again they ran through three yards of shallow water and on to a small bar, which was like a stepping-stone to the next medium bar. They were now headed downstream for a short jump over a rivulet onto the biggest of the sandbars. It ran for forty yards back upstream, but that was going to bring them closer to the gulley on the other bank. They would have to come to the end of that sandbar and cross over to a similar but narrower sandbar, which again was a short wade across. They then had to run the length of that bar downstream to reach and jump over to the first of three smaller bars that would take them back down to their objective. These smaller bars were within a five-yard channel from the Zimbabwe bank, but the sides of the river were high and there would be problems trying to climb. They would be vulnerable to croc attack, so they had to run and dash through shallows until they got down to within a few feet of shallows by the gulley. The brigadier led the run, then jumped, stumbling across onto the dry land of the gully. He stood immediately and looked for any crocs with pistol at the ready, as the other two fell, almost exhausted, into the gully. He walked past them back towards the water, was satisfied, turned, and tried to get the Kims up. He left them on their knees and looked inland up the gully moving a yard or two away from the rising Kims, who were laughing, releasing the tension of their 150-yard dash. The brigadier too felt a huge wave of relief, and then his world fell apart.

He heard a swish and a soft plop and as he turned he felt a terrible pain as his right knee exploded, and as he dropped his weapon, reaching downwards, he felt a thump below his left leg at the same time as he heard a shot, followed by another. He fell with a scream before passing out. The swish he had heard was JJ's bolt on its short flight to the left-hand Kim's heart, the barbed head ripping its way right through and protruding from his back. The plop was Henry's silenced SVD sending its lead bullet through the head of the Kim on the right. Both men fell without a sound, probably not knowing they were dead. Henry and JJ both rose as silently as ghosts and came down from their hiding places into the gully, where they were met by the older Du Toit, who was on his way to inspect his handiwork. JJ retrieved his bolt and both he and Henry cut the clothing off the two Kims to leave their bodies naked. The clothes would be taken and burned, so that there was no possible trace that the Kims were ever in the location.

As if by magic the canoe appeared, having paddled out of the reeds when the shots that felled the brigadier were heard by the younger brother. As Jonty got out, he saw the stripped bodies of the Kims, but the moans of a seriously wounded man took his attention. He joined the others and heard the brigadier, despite his pain, curse and say, "Bastard Skuz apo."

"I think he means you," said the older friend to Henry and JJ. The two nodded and said that the Kims needed to be presented to the river for disposal.

Henry stopped JJ from pulling his pistol to finish the brigadier off by saying, "He's yours," to the brothers.

Jonty saw all this carnage, swallowed to make sure his gorge did not rise, and said offhandedly, "Is there any chance I can ask him who the contacts for the Zairean ivory were?"

The reply from the brigadier was predictable: "Fuck off, white bastard."

The younger friend then asked Jonty what he meant; was there other ivory?

"Yes, this man has been involved through them, the Koreans, with not just the ivory from Zimbabwe, but also from the Luangwa and Zaire, with over a thousand animals slaughtered at their request, just to pay for bullets."

The two brothers conversed between themselves and asked Jonty what exactly he wanted to know. Jonty said he wanted the names of top men who organised the 30 tonnes from Zaire. They nodded and picked up the brigadier, who promptly screamed. He was tapped on the head with almost a careful blow. As he lapsed into unconsciousness, the brothers loaded him into the canoe, along with the Kims' clothes, and the younger set off upstream. JJ wondered where, and then decided he did not want to know, being well aware that the brigadier would probably never see any human beings again in his lifetime. He erased him from his mind. Jonty then saw the older brother slice open the abdomen of one of the Kims and did not know what to think – images of barbaric rites, even cannibalism, went through his mind, but JJ then said quietly, "It's to ensure the crocs come for them." Jonty understood, realizing they were making sure the bodies would never be found, and shrugged his shoulders. Both bodies, with their guts spilled, were pushed off into the current, and Jonty was sure he saw one disappear in a swirl followed by the other. There were so many images running through his head that he really did not know what he saw and what he imagined. He realized that his and Jasper's business was now ended, and he must get back to Zambia. He spoke to Jasper and asked if he was going to come back to Zambia now, or was he going back with Henry? Since there were no live arrests, it was not so necessary for it to seem that Jasper was in Zambia anymore, having completed his supposed lectures to SB. His passport could be delivered anytime with appropriate exit stamps.

Jasper said he would stay and finish up at Osprey before going down to Durban, but told Jonty he must make no mention to either his people or Jim of the involvement of anybody other than himself and Henry. Jonty understood that Jasper was deadly serious and agreed immediately. Then he got on his radio phone and spoke to his people, giving a message for the Minister that the mission had been completed. He also requested to be picked up at the given map reference. It was beginning to get light when they heard a launch coming down the river, and it was the Zambian Border patrol. Jonty asked if they wanted a lift as he went forward to climb on the launch. Not hearing a reply, he turned around, but saw no one. Like ghosts, JJ, Henry and friends had disappeared.

Morning had come by the time he got into a car at Chirundu, which would take him back to Lusaka first, so that he could debrief to the Minister, of course, only what he chose to tell him. He was somewhat alarmed at how he had accepted, despite being a committed law official, the killing which was not revenge motivated, but simply the only way to ensure particular individuals could never repeat nor spread their actions to others. This was about trying to restore balance, and that trying was the basis of morality, especially in a world where law breakers were increasingly more protected than victims.

After the Minister, he was going back home to his family, who had suddenly become the most important thing in his life.

He had understood the meaning of the Selous Scout sayings, 'Those who die, die. Those who stay behind, stay,' and the motto 'Pamwe Cheti' – 'Together Only'. Few people could truly claim to try living with, and as part of, their environments, but Jonty had met some of them.

CHAPTER 29

Taking Stock

Henry and JJ were happy to let the elder Du Toit lead them out of the bush, and he chose a route which took them past the old sugar compound where they had recently cleaned up. There was no evidence of the compound having been used at all, other than an absence of bush. It would soon close in, reclaiming the land taken from it originally. The trio made use of the road up to about the point where the roadblock protecting the camp had been. Du Toit left the road and cut off into the bush to the right and over to the road leading to Jecha Point, and lo and behold, there sat the Du Toits' bakkie with a canvass canopy. All three put their kit in the back, and while the elder brother went to sit alongside his brother, JJ and Henry got in the back. Twenty minutes later they were pulling into the compound to a smiling Piet, who motioned them inside and sat them down. A huge brunch awaited them, which they gratefully attacked. Old Piet let them eat and then asked them to tell the story. Henry, of course knew little of Tembo, so it was left to JJ to tell the tale of the affair. He began with telling how Jonty had approached him to go on holiday up to Tanganyika, and how he had met with a man who worked for the UN. This man, an American, had set up Operation Tembo, which was to counter the major-scale poaching of ivory by countries. The operation was backed and supported by the International Justice Court system, where even leaders of nations could be prosecuted. This was probably meaningless to Piet, as he lived by a code that perhaps did not need the evidence of wrongdoing; just the knowledge was enough to effect justice. Maybe he was right, and if more people like him acted within their own communities, perhaps the world would benefit overall. JJ explained how ivory was in demand as carvings and in medicine, particularly in the East, and although China, one of the biggest users, had signed a world treaty to stop dealing in ivory, nothing much had changed. Africa, as always, would be involved with wars, and as long as that was the case, then nations who apparently befriended various so-called liberation movements could continue to demand payment for their material support. Most of Africa was poor, so ivory was one form of payment for the guns and bullets. The UN was trying to bring the end of huge-scale poaching, which was now threatening the survival of elephant species. The Koreans, who were ostensibly the friends of the Zimbabwean people, were based here and had organised almost 100 tonnes of poached ivory from Zimbabwe, Zambia and Zaire to be sent to Hong Kong. They had organised the supply of the ivory and transportation via the Chinese funded railway from Zambia to Tanzania. The evidence had to be collected if the world's nations were to be convinced of another nation's involvement so that justice could be given. That, JJ explained, was what he had become involved with, and now the last events were the final tidy up of the whole operation. The main cargo of the ivory had been watched all the way to Dar, and the big 'chiefs' had been arrested, except for those in Zaire. JJ left out any mention of the Zimbabwean authorities, or at least names, as he had left out Jim Marshall's name. He did, however, tell Piet that he had accepted a job through the American with the UN, which would make him a sort of world policeman for elephants.

"Ach, you could do well at that, but I fear men's greed will never change. Perhaps I will be dead soon, but I think so will the elephants, not long after me. One thing, young man, be careful of the Americans; they have become too fond of secrets, they forget the truth. They are men after all. Still, may God look after you and remember your efforts." He then turned to Henry and said, "Hey Schwartz, you will need help from time to time with your business, be sure you ask my boys eh?" Henry nodded both to Piet and to the two boys. Piet went on, "You'll want to go home now, do you wish my boys to take you or what?"

JJ thought about it and replied, "No maybe we should not be seen together just now. Can you get a message to the Vermeullen man at Osprey to pick us up where he did before, say in 3 hours?"

Piet nodded to one of the brothers, who left to go and contact Vermeullen. He said he had some work to do and left, saying, "The boys will take you to Mongwe, but be sure to say goodbye before you go." He and the other brother left the room.

Henry and JJ sat round and began to clean their guns and equipment while they waited. A woman came in and offered beers or tea; they took tea.

Two hours later, Piet came in with the younger brother and said that Vermeullen was on his way and the elder brother would take them to the RV. They said their goodbyes and a special thanks to Piet. As they were walking out, Piet said, "Oh the names your friend from Zambia wanted: I think he said Hooan and Geeang, I am sure though of the last one, a Moise Katumbi. Hope that helps, and do not worry, my eh, informant tells me the truth. Unfortunately, he has gone forever, his bones are burning in hell."

JJ said he was sure that his friend would be grateful, and he shuddered inwardly as to what might have happened to the now disappeared brigadier.

The pickup went smoothly and the two got in the double cab unseen, to be greeted by a smiling Jani and a "Howzit." JV realised that the two did not want to talk yet and settled down for the drive back up the escarpment and then the turn to the Kariba road and back down the other side of the escarpment. On arrival back to Osprey, Jasper was quick to say that he wanted a shower, then a few beers whilst he made some calls. He suggested they left any chats till then. Jani then dropped a bit of a bombshell, in that Tony was on his way up, and would be here for dinner. He also said he had asked that Henry should join them. Both Henry and Jasper recognised a summons. Henry disappeared to his family and Jasper to his shower.

Later, sitting on the veranda with a cold beer which Francis had brought, JJ phoned Jonty. He had obviously been sleeping, and sounded a bit drowsy, but he soon wakened up. He told Jasper that the Minister was satisfied with his debrief and wished for his thanks to be passed on. He was not pushed for any details, which he would not have given anyway, so no one was compromised. The Minister did seem happy, nevertheless, at making the North Korean embassy in Harare uncomfortable, as well as the Chinese one in Lusaka. Jasper told him that his own debrief would be tonight, but he would talk to Jim first, straight after this call. Then he made Jonty very happy, when he told him the friends whom Jonty had met at the river had given him three names, two who might be Chinese and one who was a Zairean. He gave the first two as he had heard them, 'Hooan' and 'Geeang', but that would be phonetic at best, and Moise Katumbi. Now Jonty became excited, because he recognised the prominent businessman's name. He said Jim would want those names and that Jasper must tell him. With that he hung up. Next, Jasper rang Jim, who also sounded as if he had just woken, which was not surprising as he told Jasper it was early morning in the US. He had returned for meetings with various people, including the UN Secretary General, about their latest success. Jasper then told him that the Kim and brigadier problems had been satisfactorily concluded without any official involvement, and expected Jim to be disappointed that they no longer had major players to put on trial. On the contrary, Jim was delighted and said no matter, the embarrassment of the collected evidence was going to achieve the same result but without the public humiliation. The Koreans and Chinese would be more willing to assist in clamping down on ivory trading, at least publicly. He believed that Operation Tembo had been an unqualified success despite no major International Court prosecution. However, there would be several local prosecutions which would nevertheless show or point to the international involvement. The international press would perhaps make the necessary connections, he thought. Jasper then told him of the names he had regarding the Zairean connections, which did seem to really excite him, saying that was the cream on the cake. He asked what they were and like Jonty, recognised Moise Katumbi's name. They finished off with Jim filling in a few details of the Tanzanian operation. Then Jim confirmed that he would be in Durban the next week, and they would have more time to discuss this case and the future. He added a further well done and broke the connection.

JJ desperately wanted to phone Sophie; he was conscious that he had been apart from her for around 10 days and did want to tell her about the successes so that he could keep his demons at bay. He knew he was still on a bit of a high, and now that Tony was coming to debrief him, he was having to stay on the high, and he wanted to complete the debrief, close the episode, 'Cheti'. He did not want to blow hot and cold with Sophie, he loved her too much for that and she deserved better, so he chose to leave the call until he had debriefed, and it was over. He needed to come down from the events of the last 10 days and get back to normal. The high of the chase and that of the kill were entirely different, largely because the latter was invisible and almost unknown to his mind. That was a legacy of having to shut out inner feelings, or make any moral self- judgements, just to be normal, whatever that was. It could be described as a kind of controlled schizophrenia, resulting from having to do what was necessary to protect a nation you were committed to, despite ultimately violating what you had believed was the right thing to do. There were no shoulders to cry on, they were chosen men, but then, that's precisely why there were so few casualties amongst that band.

It was almost dark, that time when light began to lose its daily battle and the onset of darkness became overwhelming, when Tony arrived, brought from the airport by Jani. Jasper and Tony spent a few minutes chatting with each other, observing the niceties, before Jani and Henry joined them on the veranda for some welcome beers. Francis had laid on an excellent buffet style dinner with some battered fish based starters and a pot of steaming curry with a pilau style rice, all self-service so that they could be alone. They decided to eat first and, once they had, Francis cleared away plates and served coffees.

Once finished, Jasper again took the lead and started with his meetings with Jonty and Jim Marshall at Ndole Bay. He described how he became aware of Operation Tembo and how he had agreed firstly with Tony – he made no mention of Ken – that he would get the evidence of the Zimbabwean end of the poaching of elephant ivory. Tony interrupted to confirm, mainly for Henry's benefit, that Zimbabwe had subscribed to the joint operation. They had found out about the involvement of diplomatic staff from Korea, and because Korea was held to be a friendly nation towards Zimbabwe, it would be difficult to punish a friend. Jasper then related the story of the assault on the camp. Tony then said that the story that had been concocted to cover this was that the army was conducting a training exercise at the location of that camp, which involved a team of commandos capturing the camp. Unfortunately, due to a simple mistake by a junior armourer, the commandos were issued with live rounds, and 14 soldiers were killed before it was realized, and the exercise stopped. There was also a civilian wildlife officer who had been at the camp, probably doing a routine check on wildlife numbers, and was caught up unintentionally. That story was utterly believable and, on its release, provoked no comment either internally or externally. Tony said the site had been cleaned up and once again left abandoned. Jasper deliberately made no mention of Piet Du Toit and his sons, whose involvement only he and Henry knew of, along with Jonty, who was sworn to secrecy. Henry noted the omission, of which he approved. Jasper then went on to relate how he was choppered up to Kapiri by the Zambians to join Jonty and his teams, discussing his cover story, the surveillance of the transportation of the ivory, and the arrest of the two Kims and the brigadier, explaining how they escaped and he, Jasper, was brought down from Kapiri to track the fugitives and, guessing they would head for the old crossing point, organised for Henry to stake out that crossing point while he and Jonty tracked the three, going over the 'meet and greet' operation, and how afterwards they got rid of the bodies into the river for the crocs to finish the job, so no identifiable remains would ever surface. Finally, he explained that Jonty had returned to Zambia with names of the Zairean contacts which the brigadier had given up before he expired, while he and Henry went back to Chirundu with the motorised Osprey canoe that Henry had used to get downriver. They then got the people who look after the canoes to contact Jani for a pickup. Jasper had covered the main story, that the objective that neither of the Kims had returned to Zimbabwe had been achieved, without any potentially awkward diplomatic issues arising. Zimbabwe could not be blamed for the loss of face that both the PRK and PRC might experience. The brigadier's demise was a bonus, as it put distance between Zimbabwe and the affair. He would have been killed by the state anyway, and now he had simply disappeared.

The brigadier's driver was providing evidence of the operation slaughtering the Wankie elephants; the people involved, army equipment used, and transfer to the Chirundu area. Jonty had said he would provide the testimony to Tony and, after a shortish sentence for involvement of transportation of illegal goods, he would be released back to Zimbabwe authorities. Tony and Jani may have suspected that the whole story had not been told, but Henry and Jasper had completed a dirty job superbly and had met the objective that the President himself had set. Tony declared himself and his service satisfied and delivered a genuine thank-you and congratulations on behalf of a grateful nation. He raised his beer bottle and toasted both Henry and Jasper in turn. They started into another few rounds of beers and whiskies, discussing this and that, before Henry stood and said he needed to go and see to his family and bid everyone goodnight. Jani, too, decided it was time for bed, and anyway he and Henry had quite a bit to do tomorrow, as they would be due to restart taking clients within a few days.

Jasper and Tony sat out, quietly drinking, with Tony interested in what Jasper's new role would entail, whether he would be back at all, where he would live and what was he going to do as a father. Clearly Jasper was excited by the prospect of the new job, but apart from leading a team to target major ivory smugglers, he was not sure as to how much autonomy he would have and exactly to whom he would report. He wondered if it was the IJC or the UNEP, WWF, or even the UN itself. All would be dealt with next week when Jim Marshall came to Durban. Tony asked where he intended to live, realizing it would not be Zimbabwe; would it be America, where the main funding was? Jasper said he would have to work that out with Sophie and consider how the job demands would dictate. He told Tony that Jim had at one point advised him to live anywhere but where the poaching took place, so he guessed it would almost certainly be Europe. Neither he nor Sophie fancied the States; New Zealand was a possibility, but it really was a long way from anywhere. And yes, the big event would be the baby, and then where to get education.

Still, he thought that for once he knew where he was going in his life, because up to now pretty much everything he had done was a result of letting it happen. It had taken nearly 40 years, but he could use his bush experience and academic training to an end dear to his heart, helping to keep an environmental balance on behalf of the flora and fauna. He had been a warrior for man, and now it seemed he need to be one for the animals, trying to minimise the effects of man's excesses. He realized he was becoming quite maudlin and approaching the first stages of getting drunk, so he switched the conversation to how Tony and Chrissie were getting on. Now it was Tony's turn and he dropped a bit of a bombshell: he and Chrissie were planning to get married before their baby was born – Chrissie was around 3 months pregnant, similar timing to Sophie, and he had not enjoyed his parents cajoling him, even accusing him of fear every time he and Chrissie saw them. It was only right, and he was actually looking forward to it himself. Jasper called him an old dog and laughed when Tony said that in the future Jasper might need a lawyer on his team – Tony would also have to consider if Zimbabwe was the right place to bring up a family. They finished the bottle of Scotch and were both well under the influence when they went to bed. Jasper decided now was not the time to phone Sophie.

CHAPTER 30

Tying up loose ends, perhaps?

It was already daylight when Jasper awoke, but still early. He was in surprisingly good shape given all he had drunk last night, suffering from a thirst but not the headache. He went to the kitchen and began to make coffee. He was berated by Francis, who came in at 0600 hrs, for not having called him earlier. It was his job to provide food and drink for the boss. He walked out to the side of the house, where he could sit and watch the early morning sun climb up and over the Hurungwe hills on its way west. Francis brought him some coffee and left the pot, along with a cold pitcher of water and glasses. He drank his first glass of water in a gulp to slake his thirst before pouring himself a cup of coffee. He remembered the coffees he had drunk in the mornings with Sophie, and decided not to wait beyond 0700 hrs before he rang. He did not know exactly when he would be able to leave, as it was the weekend coming up and he wanted to walk round his patch, say goodbye to a few friends, his neighbours and the staff at Osprey. He would probably get Tony to get him booked through to Durban for Tuesday. As he counted the minutes to 0700, Tony came round, and Francis took away the old coffee to fetch a fresh brew for Tony and Jani. He asked what they all wanted for breakfast before disappearing into the kitchen. Jasper said good morning to both and said he would join them shortly, but he wanted to go and phone Sophie.

He went round to the other side by the pool and dialled Durban on his satellite phone. The number rang and a domestic answered it. When he asked to speak to Sophie, he was politely told that Miss Sophie was still in bed, and could he leave his name or ring back in an hour. He smiled and insisted that Miss Sophie should be woken, as it was her husband was calling.

After what seemed to be an age, he got a tentative, "Is that you darling? Where are you? Are you OK? I love you, I miss you, when…"

"Hold on love, slow down. It is me and I have missed you every day you have been gone."

He heard a sigh of disappointment as she broke in, saying, "At least tell me you're finished and you are coming."

He said, "Yes, I've finished the job and am OK, and so is Henry," anticipating her next question. He went on to say how he got back to Osprey yesterday and was debriefed by Tony last night. He went on to tell her he wanted to say his goodbyes to friends and staff, so he would hope to be on his way by Monday to be with her Tuesday or Wednesday latest. He did then say he would tell her all about his adventures, as he called it, when he got to Durban, but he had got one bit of good news from Tony, which was that Chrissie was about 3 months pregnant and they were going to get married soon. He decided not to tell her about Willie Du Preez till he was in Durban.

He was telling her he loved her just before ending the call when he heard Jade's voice in the background: "If that's my younger brother, tell him to pull finger and move his arse down here."

Sophie said, "My sentiments entirely." He hung up and re-joined Tony and Jani for breakfast. He felt so much better now he had spoken to Sophie, and with some food in his belly, he was keen to get on with the day. Tony said he would have to leave shortly, so he needed to know Jasper's plans.

That was easy. "I'm going to spend today and tomorrow saying my goodbyes here and in town, so I want your people to get me on a plane to Harare on Monday p.m., then on the morning flight to Joburg on Tuesday with a connection to Durban."

"OK, you'll stay with me Monday night and we'll get you to Durbs on Tuesday. I'll make sure that any paperwork you still need to sign will be with me. What about your passport, have you got it?"

"Yes, but I have no exits from Zambia, just an entry, I did not exactly exit via any border post. Jonty was to date it to prove I was in Zambia giving those lectures."

Tony said, "Don't worry, I'll sort it, give it to me and you will have it back for Tuesday. Anything else?" Jasper said there was his rifle and crossbow, which he wanted to take with him. "Best you leave the rifle, your Zim certificate is not transferable, so the South Africans won't let you have it; anyway, you don't know where you will live yet. The crossbow you can take as hold luggage." That seemed to cover it, and Tony drew Jani aside to chat with him. Then he came to say goodbye, and Jani took him off to the airport for the 1005 hrs flight back to Harare.

Jasper decided to use the rest of the day to go into Kariba to say goodbye to the people in the Wildlife offices, and felt really guilty at having to pretend he knew nothing about Willie's death. He moved on to several local suppliers of foodstuffs and fuels, as well as a couple of safari lodges who helped each other out when overbookings or other mishaps occurred. On his way back he called in on his neighbour, Sid Brown, and spent some time with him, with a beer as the sundowner, and explained how he and Sophie were starting a family and he was starting a new job regarding the investigation of international ivory poaching. They talked a bit about the ultimate futility, but nevertheless it was important to try and take care of the whole environment. Sid asked about Osprey and its future, and Jasper told him how Henry would assume control and run the operations while a management firm of lawyers would ensure the business side. He was about to take his leave when Sid asked about Jonty and his interest in the canning of pineapples. Jasper could only say he had not heard from him since his visit, but he thought he was genuinely interested, so no doubt Sid would hear from him when he was ready. They shook hands and Sid wished him all the best for the future.

He was back in time for Francis to serve dinner and sat with Jani, just chatting and looking up at a big sky, with the stars and the Milky Way particularly prominent. He was surprised that Jani knew some of the constellations, and that he knew how to extrapolate a line from the back two stars of the Southern Cross and then use the perpendicular to show North. He himself had been taught how to navigate by the stars, but he always used to joke, "How on earth could you see the sky when in thick bush or thickets?" He hoped that Jani would only have to use any bushcraft skills he had for pleasure, and not in any nefarious way. There was a flash and trail of a meteor across the sky and Jasper laughed at himself for making a wish. He would remember to tell Sophie sometime. Jani was beginning to enjoy the life at Osprey and would look for excuses to spend more time at Kariba. They went to bed feeling fairly content.

The next morning he spoke to Jani at breakfast, saying that he was going to take Barnabas and Henry out onto the water, perhaps up the Sanyati Gorge, and have a braai, and asked if he would like to join them. So the four of them got on the Osprey and headed out towards Matusadonas and up the Sanyati Gorge. They found a good mooring beyond the steepest sides of the gorge and set up the skottel braai. They cracked open some beers, put the pieces of meat on to sizzle and heated the relish Francis had previously made for them. They sat there just talking about everything, except the business or anything connected. They talked about the price of food, they talked about nagging women, that the government was getting to have too many chiefs, all of whom had to have new Mercedes, they laughed that they used these cars to pull ploughs in the rural areas. Then as more beer was drunk (Barnabas did not drink beer, but coke), they started to talk about how long South Africa could survive, and then moved on to right all the wrongs of the world. It was while they were eating their meat that they saw some elephant come to the water's edge, not 20 yards from them, and cross over to the other side. It was a small herd, a matriarch with a couple of sisters and an adolescent calf. They all sat in silence and agreed that that was a life of freedom, and maybe if men could only adopt the ways of the elephants and their family life, the world would be a better place. With bellies full and beers running short, they finally untied and let Barnabas take them back.

All three of them had to be woken when the boat was tied up. No mention was made of Jasper leaving, but they all knew that this was a goodbye, and they wished him well, as he did them, adding that if they did not run Osprey properly, he would send Sophie to sort them out. Henry and Barnabas rolled their eyes, as only Africans can, in mock horror, and they all had a good laugh.

Later that evening he rang Jim, just to confirm that he would be in Durban by Thursday at the latest. Jim told him he would travel at the weekend, so he hoped to be with them by Sunday. He looked forward to it. Then Jasper rang Sophie and they spent fifteen minutes just blowing each other kisses and making remarks full of innuendos regarding how they were going to say hello to each other. Jasper slept like a baby that night.

The next morning, Jani told him that he was on the 1700 hrs plane to Harare and that Tony would collect him from the airport. He was further booked on SAL/SAA Tuesday 1045 out of Harare to Johannesburg, with an onward flight to Durban at 1410, arriving 1520. He spent the morning walking around Osprey and the bush, as if the local habitat would understand the concept of goodbye, but he had to keep the balance for his own peace. After lunch he packed his two remaining bags, not forgetting his crossbow, and hoped he would see Osprey and the Zambezi again. Jani took him to the airport, and there was a tear in his eye, as all the staff had turned out to wave him goodbye, singing an African song of farewell. It was still ringing in his ears when they turned into the airport and Jani took him in, picking up his ticket from the desk. He boarded what looked like a new jet, a BAe 146 that the national airline had acquired for the President, but also for normal use outside of his requirement. It had the wings above the fuselage, so almost all the passengers could see the ground without the wings getting in the way. Take-off was fast and smooth, with the plane taking a route that went over Osprey as if it might be some sort of omen, but Jasper did not want to look anyway. Most of his life, certainly the important bits, happened there, and his second family was still there. He closed his eyes and dozed.

Forty minutes later, the plane touched down at the international airport, using less than a third of the length of the runway, cutting off well before the international terminal and beyond that the big corrugated shed that was the domestic terminal. Tony met him at the door as he entered and took his ticket stub, giving it to his driver. He and Jasper continued out to the VIP area to the car whilst they waited for the driver to collect Jasper's two bags.

They drove quickly back into town using Dieppe Avenue, along Cripps, past Colcom, and along Rotten Row before turning right into Samora Machel Avenue. The car turned in to the Supreme Court buildings opposite Third Street, and Tony said Ken had asked them to drop in. They entered the building, bypassing the reception, and turned along a corridor. Jasper noted they stopped by room Number 112. Tony knocked, waited, and entered when called. Ken sat behind a desk, surrounded by files and several telephones. He was replacing the red one as he stood, and then came round to Jasper with his hand outstretched. They shook hands and Ken motioned that they should sit down. Tony excused himself, saying he needed to check some information and that he would be back shortly.

Ken said he had been asked to speak to him, and just at that moment the door opened and the President himself walked in. He nodded to Ken, saying, "Ken, introduce me!"

Ken spoke quietly. "Mr. President, your excellency, this is Jasper Jackson, the young man who has assisted us in the unfortunate affair we were faced with."

"And I believe we could not have asked for a better conclusion. I know we were adversaries not long ago, so I do appreciate what you have done on our behalf. I cannot thank you publicly but wish to do so privately. I do so now on behalf of a grateful nation." He shook Jasper's hand, who was absolutely dumbstruck, partly out of awe and partly because, had he had the chance a few years ago, he would have killed the man without thought. He could only manage a quiet thank you. The President continued, "Ken tells me you will be working for the UN, anti-poaching. I am sorry we are losing you; despite what you might think, I still need men like you to develop this nation. I wish you well with the UN. Goodbye Mr. Jackson." With that, the President left the room.

Ken put his finger to his lips, then pointed to his ears and blinked, warning Jasper that ears may be listening. He sat again and said, "I am sorry I cannot join you this evening, but I have to brief the President tonight at Chancellor House on other matters. Tony will look after you. Now I've talked to Jonty, who is a changed man after your time together, and now begins to see that looking after the nation's best interests may force you to make unpleasant choices. Jim, on the other hand, was delighted, recognizing that, although there will be no high level prosecutions, the threat of public disclosure will be sufficient to drag concessions out of those who do not toe the international line. He sees it from his earlier background in the CIA, before he went to the UN. I think he too, like you, was part of some elite group in Vietnam. He is looking forward to working with you."

There was a knock at the door and Tony came in with some papers in hand. Ken said he had been telling Jasper about Jonty's reaction to bush-work, whereas Ken was completely relaxed about it, having been there before himself. Ken asked how Sophie was and said he must be keen to get to Durban. "I believe congratulations are due to you both, soon-to-be fathers. Remember, family is all. Now I am sorry, but I have to throw you out; I need to finish my reading before I go. Good luck and keep in touch." He shook hands, said "Cheers," and that was that.

Tony and Jasper walked back out to the car park, but this time to Tony's personal car. They got in and as Tony started the engine, Jasper was about to say luggage, but Tony forestalled him, saying it was in the boot. They left by the back entrance, went up Third Street onto Rhodes Avenue, along to the left before turning right at the robots up Second Street. They cut off up East Road and into Mount Pleasant Drive, finally turning into Quorn Avenue where Tony and Chrissie lived. As Tony stopped a domestic came out grabbed Tony's briefcase and Jasper's bags, whilst Chrissie stood at the door waiting to greet them. She was looking well and positively shining; clearly pregnancy was agreeing with her, though she said she was getting fat. She asked when Sophie was due, and Jasper had to confess that actually he did not know. Chrissie berated him, saying he was nearly as bad as her Tony, and that if she left the date of their wedding to him, she might have had the baby before they were married. They went in and the houseboy brought drinks.

When Tony remarked that one thing that he had noticed was that his wine bills had shrunk, Chrissie punched him playfully and shot back, "You, my boy, will find it hard not to notice me shortly as the bump grows. I shall enjoy having you do a bit of the running around after me for a change. Pity it will only last a few months, the running round after me will stop when I pop." They all laughed. Tony took his briefcase and went to his study whilst Chrissie showed Jasper the house and his room. She said that they would have to convert one of the back bedrooms into a nursery, but she expected that she would have to handle that. She left him to wash up and said dinner would be in an hour.

When Jasper came down Tony called him into the study and said he had two or three papers that required his signature, including a power of attorney regarding authorizing expenditures at Osprey. Another document was the deed of transfer, making Henry the managing director of Osprey Safaris with proxy for fifty one percent of the shares. He would control the use of annual profits less the purchase fees of USD30,000 per year for three years. A final payment of USD10,000 would complete the purchase of the business. Tony's firm would be paid for its role in management of the business up to an equivalent of USD10,000 pa fixed for the three years, after which Henry would renegotiate a new fee for any continued management services he needed or drop those services. Francis and Barnabas were awarded an annual bonus of five percent each of any profits after the initial USD40K had been deducted, but would be paid in local currency for as long as they worked at Osprey. Jasper signed off on the deal, Tony saying he had really given away his business and he hoped that Henry would succeed. Then he gave Jasper his passport, which now bore proper entry and exit stamps as well as matching entry and exit Zambian stamps. He also gave him his airline tickets, which would get him into Durban at a scheduled time of 1520. Tony then dialled the Durban number and, handing Jasper the phone, he left the room.

Jasper's mum Marika answered, and began to call Sophie, then simply asked when and went into excited mother mode as she heard 1410 from Joburg. She just had time to say she would send the car before Sophie came on the line. Then it was a series of sighs and kisses, so he was not sure she had heard that he would be there by about quarter past three tomorrow. He had to say, "Hey, calm down," several times, and when that did not work he said, "Sophie, what about the baby, you should not get excited."

She told him to stop being a worry-guts, "The baby is fine," and resumed her nonstop kisses and sighs. He did manage to tell her he was at Tony and Chrissie's tonight and Chrissie was keen to know when Sophie was due to see if they were near enough the same. Sophie said her doctor here in Durban had just calculated that she was fourteen weeks gone when she was examined last week. He suddenly remembered that Jim reckoned he would look to be in Durban on Sunday, so could Sophie tell Marika. After another bout of "I love you, I miss you and hurry back to me," he finally put down the phone, having played the old game of listening to see who actually put down the phone first.

He went through to the dining room and joined the others. He told Chrissie that Sophie was 14 weeks gone as of Friday past. Chrissie laughed, "You know, we could be on the same dates, wouldn't it be a hoot if we both gave birth on the same day? I bet you could get good odds."

Drinks were served and they sat down to dinner. The first course was Beira prawns done in garlic and chilli with wedges of lime. Tony had a contact in Umtali, now Mutare, who supplied a hotel, the White Horse, and who had a source on the Mozambique border, so he could get from time to time some of the best prawns in the world. It was followed by a roast shoulder of lamb, which was indeed quite unusual as there were few sheep farmers, but Chrissie's friend was married to a South Salisbury farmer who had sheep, so she was able to get some for the freezer every so often. They finished off with some fresh fruit and local ice cream before going out to sit by the pool in the cool of the evening. The houseboy brought coffee and a bottle of port, but only Tony and Jasper were drinking. They mused about the old days and, when Chrissie went off to bed, the boys began to remember some of their wilder nights at the Coimbra, the Park Lane, and of course the Archipelago, but that's all they were, just good memories. They did not really want to relive those nights, however magnificent they had been. They mused about friends, some killed, most left to either South Africa or Perth, Australia, and two or three still hanging on. They drank several toasts and decided to go to bed before they became too maudlin.

CHAPTER 31

New Beginnings Part 1

Jasper woke fairly early, went and took a quick dip in the pool and then showered and shaved so that he would not be told off for being scruffy. He went down to find Tony going through some papers and Chrissie in a dressing gown, telling the cook just tea and toast for her, no eggs and bacon. It was 0730 and a typical clear sunny day, so with plenty of time in hand, Jasper took the time to enjoy his fried eggs on toast and crispy bacon rashers. He kidded himself that the usual tray on the plane was inedible, so he had to eat well now. Ha ha. Tony said they would need to leave about quarter past nine, so if Jasper would excuse him, he would go and do some work in the study. Jasper went upstairs, took out what he needed for the flights and repacked his bags to fill in time. He was beginning to realize this was it, he was leaving the country that had been home for near enough 35 years; he had fought for it, but now he was about to turn away from it. He was in a quandary; he was not as remorseful as he thought he should be at leaving, and that surprised him. He had not expected to burst into tears, but thought he would have more emotion than he had. He just wanted to get away and get back to his wife.

He had also realized he was going to have to do some deep thinking about the new job, not so much having second thoughts, but needing to clarify his independence. He had not picked it up at the time, but it seemed that Jim was not worried about the prosecutions of the Kims having been lost, seemingly more interested in the leverage over the Chinese that the affair had produced. He had noted that Jim and Ken were no strangers to the world of spooks, Jonty and Tony too, with no one who was primarily a conservationist involved in Tembo. He needed to clear a few things up, because he was determined not to be a spook. He had spent too much time in secrecy and, worst of all, his covert operations almost always ended in deaths. He needed to leave that behind him, not continue in the same vein.

He was brought back to reality with Tony calling him, saying it was time to go. He went down with his bags and Chrissie gave him a small parcel for Sophie and the baby. Tony promised to keep in contact and to let them know when the wedding would be. After the hugs and kisses, he got in the car beside Tony and they pulled away, heading towards the airport. Tony drove straight to the VIP barrier, flashed a card and was saluted in. A man appeared, took Jasper's bags and followed them to the SAA desk. Whilst Tony took Jasper to the VIP lounge, Jasper's tickets and passport were taken and processed. The SAA plane landed and taxied to its stand. Jasper watched the people getting off, a mixture of businessmen, returning residents and relatives waving to the upstairs gallery. A crew of cleaners wandered out to clear the plane of rubbish whilst the luggage was pulled off onto small trailers. A farm tractor came out of the shadows and hooked up to the carriages and took them to what passed as a baggage hall. Fifteen minutes later, bags started to be loaded and Jasper was relieved to see his go on board.

A few minutes later a South African Airways official entered the VIP lounge, came across to Tony and Jasper and said, "Mr Jackson, we are ready to board you," handing him his passport and two boarding cards.

Jasper shook hands with Tony, no words necessary other than "See you," and followed the official out to the plane and found himself boarded at the front steps and sat in the first row. He looked at his boarding cards and realized for the first time that he was in Business Class both here and to Durban.

The Steward said, "Your bags are booked through to Durban but will be passed by Customs in Joburg. Someone will meet you and take you through Immigration and on to the departure lounge for domestic flights, I'm afraid we only have a business lounge in domestic, as we don't have any First Class cabins on internal and regional flights. I am sure you will be comfortable there. If you need anything, please ask. Now, can I offer you a drink?"

Jasper declined and closed his eyes. The cabin took two other businessmen, leaving three seats free. The back end of the Boeing 737 filled up quickly and the doors were shut, the Afrikaans crew were keen to get going. The plane went to the end of what was once the longest commercial aircraft runway in the world at 4.725 miles, spooled up and thundered down the runway and was airborne within half the length. It took off over the southern satellite town of Chitungwiza and headed south. Just under an hour later, they crossed over the Limpopo river into South Africa, just east of the border post at Beitbridge. Five minutes later they began a gentle descent into Johannesburg, arriving over the city fifteen minutes later. They passed the city to the west, did a 'u-EE' over Soweto and were on final approach. They landed past the terminal then took five minutes to run back and park on an outside bay. Everybody got off onto buses and were ferried over to the arrivals area.

As Jasper got off the bus, he strode up the corridors to where an official with his name on a board was waiting. He greeted him and took him through a side channel to get his passport stamped with a 6-month visa and then took him through to the rabbit warren of the domestic flights area. Once he was put in the business lounge, the official said he would be called when the flight to Durban was ready, and his luggage would be loaded, so he would need to collect it in Durban. Jasper thanked him and realized he was hungry, so he helped himself to a round of sandwiches and a bowl of a vegetable soup.

He had barely finished when he was called and off he went to Gate 54, handing in his boarding card and getting on the bus. He boarded another 737 and again he was in Row 1. It may well have been the same plane, for all he knew. The crew offered drinks and a copy of today's Natal Mercury newspaper, which he took to have a read. The plane took off on time and headed south west for Louis Botha airport in Durban. The flight was quick and they began their descent just south of Pietermaritzburg, heading for the coast at Toti, turning left and landing by 1505.

As the doors were opened, the wall of humid heat hit him. Harare was at 5,000ft above sea-level, Joburg was nearer 6,000ft, and now Durban, at sea level. He could not see Sophie among the waiting crowd in the upstairs gallery as he entered the baggage hall. His two bags were amongst the first to come through, and as he came through the exit, he saw her jumping up and down with someone else. It took a second before he recognized Jade.

Sophie ran across and literally jumped into his arms, and they kissed, then just hugged and hugged until Jade said, "Come on you two, we are blocking the exit. How about a kiss for your big sister?" He dutifully hugged and kissed Jade before an insistent Sophie wanted him back. Jade got the driver to take the bags and bring the car round to the terminal. While they waited, all three were asking each other questions, so no one heard anything. The car arrived and Jade got in the front and let the lovebirds get in the back. As they all settled down, he realized that it had been over ten years since he had seen Jade, but he would have to wait to chat with her. He thought he could feel there was some sadness in her; no doubt he would find out what, but now was a time for him and Sophie.

Now that she had him back and could see that at least on the surface he was fine, Sophie was relieved he was finally here. Now she could hang on to him, but she knew it would not be till much later before they could be alone. First there would be Marika and Frank to see, and they would have to talk, and then Jade, who had not seen him in years. Then there would be dinner, and drinks afterwards, before they could reasonably escape to the privacy of the bedroom. She hung onto him, though, as they got out of the car, only letting go as Marika opened her arms for a hug; a handshake was sufficient for Frank.

They all went through the doors and into the lounge, which looked out to sea. With the French windows open, it would keep fresh with a gentle onshore breeze. However, it was about 28 centigrade, and the air was heavy with humidity, so the windows were closed and the air conditioning on. Mum was first to ask about the new job. Jasper guessed that Sophie had told them something about it being hush hush, so he simply said he had played a part from the Zimbabwean side in tracking a poaching gang and that they had managed to arrest the ring leaders. Since it was an international operation involving another three countries, it had to be kept quiet so that as many of the top people who organized the poachers in all countries were arrested. The worst part for him was the realization that over a thousand elephants had been slaughtered for their tusks. They may have successfully prevented £100 million of raw ivory reaching the far East, but he would have preferred to keep the elephants. They did not know how big a dent this would cause to the trade; hopefully it was significant, but that in a way was going to be his job worldwide. He told them that the present co-ordinator, a Mr Jim Marshall, had recruited him to take over the role.

Jasper went on to say that the man "claimed to have met you, Dad, in the past, he said he knew of your work." He went on, "Anyway, he is coming down here this Sunday to talk to me, but he said he would like to renew acquaintances with you."

Frank thought for a few seconds and said, "I remember the man now, yes, he was interested in how tribal cultures might clash with the modern world. Nice man, and he seemed interested, something he was working on for the UN, but you know, I always thought he was probably CIA."

Jasper almost said he had wondered about that, and he knew that Jim had been involved with the CIA, but all he said was that they would know more about his job once Jim arrived. He then quite skilfully took control of the conversation, much to the amusement of Sophie, by asking Frank what he was working on currently, and when that became exhausted, he moved on to his mum, asking what little projects she had on the go. Marika had set up a small workshop at the family's main sugar mill to teach some of the Zulu women some of the elements of jewellery making. She said it was really an extension of their native embroidery and beadwork, but it did mean that the women could earn a lot more from their tourist sales. Already some of those earnings had been used to build a school and pay proper teachers to educate the children.

Finally, he turned to his 'big sister' and asked whether she was on holiday, or if there was some other purpose. Jade said they may as well all know that while she was primarily on holiday, hubby Tom, or Professor Huntingdon, was finishing up at the London School of Hygiene and Tropical Medicine before he could come out and join her in about 3 months. She had specialized in the last year on a little-known disease that had begun to show itself principally in the UK's homosexual community and amongst drug users. The disease had been commonly called AIDS, or Acquired Immune Deficiency Syndrome, for which there was no cure as yet. In South Africa, Uganda, and Zimbabwe it had been shown to be spread by heterosexual activity; indeed most cases were. AIDS was becoming recognized as a pandemic, with millions dying and hundreds of millions expected to die. The forecast, especially for third world countries, was that significant numbers of their labour forces would suffer and there would be a high number of orphaned children. The effects on their weak economies would likely be severe. She and Tom had accepted a proposal to work with the SA authorities, probably in Cape Province. She was to find housing and dot the I's with University of Cape Town in running a world research programme sponsored by the

UN. They needed to find out how this particular virus worked before they could begin to find out how to control it. So, they would both be working for the UN.

That brought a sigh of relief from Marika and Frank, who had thought that Jade and Tom may have succumbed to splitting up, maybe because of no children. Frank stood and called for a bottle of Pongraz, a local Champagne type, to toast the twins. He was delighted they both would be working for worthwhile causes. He then wanted to have another toast for Sophie and his as yet unborn grandchild, but Marika told him to behave himself for the moment. She was thinking more along the lines of trying to persuade her daughter-in-law to look for a home in South Africa, preferably Natal, so she would have easy access to her grandchild or grandchildren hopefully. Of course, she was delighted that her children were being recognized as experts in their fields, but she wanted, perhaps selfishly, all her family around about her and Frank.

The dinner gong sounded, so that put paid to Frank's calls for another champagne. They sat around the 8-place table made out of Acacia hardwood, with Frank at the head and Marika and Jade on one side, facing Jasper and Sophie. Marika had organized a starter of a partially hollowed out orange filled with prawns in a mild horseradish mayonnaise, followed by a fresh kingklip, a firm fleshed white fish which is actually of the cusk eel family. It is highly prized as a culinary fish course, so much so that the South Africans tend to keep it to themselves. A simple fresh fruit salad with an ice cream and sorbet finished off the meal, and the family moved onto the veranda to look out over the ocean.

The villa style house was a couple of hundred yards away from the shore, but in the cooler aspect of the breeze of the evening it was still possible to hear the breakers crash on the beach. Jasper noticed that the lighting on the veranda was a soft red, and wondered if this was Sophie's work, because he would have expected more insects and could not remember the red lights before. He touched her on the arm and pointed discreetly to the lights while asking with his eyes, she laughed quietly and nodded. Coffee was served along with a local cream-based liqueur, Amarula, which was the South African version of Baileys but based on the amarula, the fruit of the marula tree. It was almost apt in that the amarula was a favoured meal for elephants, with them coming from miles to eat fallen, fermenting fruit. Certainly, the big pachyderms are seen to sway about and occasionally seemingly stagger as they scoop up the fermenting fruit. There is no record, however, of whether the beasts have a babelas the next day; still, it would be prudent not to bother the elephants early the next morning. The view out to sea over the bay looked calm, with several ships at anchor, all brilliantly lit up, as they awaited their time to enter the port at Durban. The lights to their right were of Durban, out to the Golden Mile, the port, and on all over the district. The scene was relaxing, but not in the same way as sitting looking out over Kariba and its kapenta boats. The lights of the city and its surrounds meant that the intensity of the darkness, the depth of the night, was weak in comparison to Kariba, and consequently the stellar display of the night sky was less brilliant.

As the Jackson family sat in the warm evening, the contentment that often comes with a good meal, together with the relief of being together again as a family, gently washed over them, and the conversation turned to nostalgia. For Jade and Jasper, the memories were associated with Salisbury, not really Durban, which they only knew as visitors. Sophie listened intently, because she knew relatively little of Jasper's childhood or his teenage years.

Eventually the contentment turned to sleepiness, and Jade withdrew first, claiming she needed to call Tom. Then Marika, happy that her flock was pretty much around her, except for Tom, suggested to Frank that they should retire and let Jasper and Sophie be on their own. They left, and at last Jasper and Sophie were on their own. They made their way to their room, and now was not the time for any great conversation. It perhaps was only about three weeks since they last saw each other, but for them it may as well have been a year. The absence was reflected in their lovemaking, being intense but gentle, in view of her condition, followed by that deep sleep of utter fulfilment.

They woke when it was already light, and their first thought was for each other and to make sure that both were still there and last night was not just a dream. They showered together, as playful as any young lovers, before dressing minimally to be comfortable for the heat of the day. They took breakfast with Jade outside on the veranda before it became too hot and heavy, as it would in a couple of hours. Sophie excused herself at nine o'clock, saying she was going to phone her mum regarding when she was coming, saying it would be eight o'clock in the evening in Auckland. Jasper and Jade had just begun to talk about themselves and what they hoped the future held for them when they were joined by mum and dad. They had genuinely overslept and Frank was wanting to get away to the University to prepare for a University Council meeting due at eleven. He was taking Jade with him to meet the head of medical research in KwaZulu Natal. Marika was due to oversee a quarterly meeting of the Small Jewellery Manufacturers Association being held at the sugar factory. That would leave Jasper and Sophie alone and give them a good chance to talk about their future, and where it would be.

Sophie came back a few minutes later saying her mum, Stephanie, was due the following Tuesday on the Singapore flight into Durban. Her dad had got Stephanie a complementary flight for a 2-week visit. They would both come over for the birth of Sophie's baby. Once everyone had gone, Jasper and Sophie strolled down towards the shore and the hundred yards or so which was technically the Jackson's land, but while it prevented people getting to the beach through the property, they would be unable to prevent the few joggers or beach strollers. Still, the beach was empty, and they strolled to where some dunes came close to the high tide mark and sat down there and talked. Sophie began by asking where he would be happy to live. She accepted that New Zealand was too far away, so that, practically, left South Africa, America, or perhaps Britain, maybe Switzerland. He replied that he would not rule anywhere out yet, but first he was not sure that he could take on the job.

Sophie recognized the torment and now wanted to find out what was the cause but knew she needed to tread softly. She had learnt of his Selous Scout past and she knew broadly of the fact he had to kill people. She had after all, had to experience the dreams, the insecurity at times that the past brought. She guessed that perhaps he had been using those 'skills' again. She took his hands and approached the matter at a tangent by asking him whether or not they had managed to arrest the people responsible for the poaching, especially the Korean diplomats. When he said that they had arrested the Koreans and the army man, she knew a but was coming, so she allowed a pause while he got himself ready to speak and then listened. He began with telling her how Willie had asked him about the apparent lack of elephant, and Barnabas and Henry also confirmed lack of signs, how he and Henry found the slaughter of Marta and her herd. He did tell her about Piet du Toit, whom she knew a little given the canoe safari business, and how they then staked out the old sugar factory site and photographed the loading of two containers in the Kims' presence. He then took a breath and told her he had watched and photographed the murder of Willie Du Preez, being unable to stop it, before he and Henry followed the load to the border. He said that Jonty had then taken over surveillance of the load, and he and Henry, together with Du Toit's sons, went back to the camp, and in the firefight that followed all the poachers had been killed. He told her how he alone had been choppered to Jonty's farm and of the surveillance of the Bond warehouse where the ivory was assembled, how they photographed everything and saw it transferred onto the Tazara. He told her of what Jim had told him about the operation on the dockside in Dar and how that triggered the arrests of the Kims and the brigadier. He told her how he had a premonition and, based on info he got from one of Jonty's men, had Henry and the Du Toits stake out an old crossing point frequently used in the war, just in case, and almost inevitably the Kims and the brigadier escaped, killing several people, and disappeared. JJ explained how he took a chance and found a trail, Jonty used his resources and got them to the crossing point ahead of the three. He told her that they killed the men, not the detail, and how, subsequently, he had been thanked personally by the President himself. He fell silent and just squeezed her hands.

She waited, digesting what he had told her, before kissing him. She said that it was finished, and maybe now was the right time to direct anti-poaching and not be a soldier. He spoke softly, saying that he did not worry about the taking of lives when in just cause, that was something that had to be done if a balance with the surroundings was to be kept. He did worry that the job he had been offered, and that he had provisionally accepted, was not what it seemed. He had begun to feel used, and that the main objective of the job may not be to keep a balance between man and the environment. He had become concerned due to a dropped phrase by Jonty, Ken's remarks about Jim's background in CIA, and Jim's own lack of disappointment that there would be no prosecution, which made him think the motive had been political. In other words, it was little to do with the poaching, but more to do with the US wanting a hold over both China and North Korea. If he was only to be allowed to save elephants for political games, then his soul would indeed be damned; how could he be a father, what would he tell his children?

Sophie became angry, and she berated him for even thinking he could not be a good father, she knew he was a kind, considerate person, and because of what he had done, she could not think of anyone better placed to be a father. He knew far more about the badness in men, who better than he to teach right or wrong, and if he could do anything to bring about a better balance between the world of man and nature, he would do more than most. She then said she would understand if he refused Jim Marshall's offers, that was fine by her, but why not do the job if he wanted to, but tell Jim he would be no lackey.

"Make sure he knows you will not take on the job unless you decide what the job is. My guess is that they do want you, and maybe it is an afterthought they want you to be a spy. You know, it might be possible that you are assuming too much. Anyway, I love you, and whatever you do, as long as I am with you, that is all that matters."

Jasper listened to her and thought she was absolutely right, and decided yes, he would take the job, but on certain conditions. He hugged and kissed her, knowing she would support him. She would help him keep his demons firmly in the past. "Right," he said, "now let's consider where to live." They agreed that they had to consider the child or children, and living third world may not be the best, so that would leave North America, Britain, possibly Switzerland, because there were UN offices there, or New Zealand, despite its relative isolation.

Just then there was a shout and one of the servants came across to them carrying a blanket and a hamper. Jasper looked at his watch and saw it was nearly half past two; he had not realized that they had been out here for over four hours. The servant said madam was concerned that Sophie should not miss meals. They thanked him and sent him back to tell madam they would be back after they had eaten. He spread the blanket and they opened the hamper. There was a selection of fresh cut sandwiches, some cold game pie, and some fruit. There were also some cold soft drinks, including a beer for Jasper. As they ate and drank, America was discarded but Canada remained. Britain was a front runner, Switzerland was discarded as culturally wrong, and given air travel nowadays New Zealand and its colonial mentality began to grow on them. They would sleep on it.

It was four o'clock when they got back, parched with the heat and the effort of carrying the hamper back. Sophie went for a lie down and Jasper went to sit in an air-conditioned lounge with his mum. The boy brought in tea, which was welcome. His mother asked him if he had managed to discuss what had happened with Sophie. Marika liked Sophie and told, or maybe more warned, her son that he had a responsibility to be happy and make Sophie happy. She also told him that if he was worried about not living within the reach of Durban, because of course she would want to have all her flock close, he had to pick somewhere that was good for him and Sophie. Marika just wanted to have him happy, she would expect seeing her grandchild and any further children on a regular home and away basis. Jasper thanked his mum and assured her about grandchildren, but he did say he would probably not stay in Africa.

Marika said, "Don't forget New Zealand, it might be a bit isolated, but it may well be the best choice." It offered much for the future, was home to Sophie, and was perhaps not subject to violent political change. She feared South Africa itself was going to have to consider some form of political power sharing sometime soon if it were to survive.

As his mum went off to supervise dinner, Jasper thought he had better switch on his phone and see if there were any calls for him to return. There were none, but he thought that he must learn to leave the phone on in case of calls. He still had not heard that Jim was indeed coming on Sunday evening, but he was going to work out what to say anyway. Sophie would help him with that, but he must settle down and put down his thoughts on what was needed to first control, then eliminate, ivory poaching. He would need to become familiar with poaching in other parts of Africa, and especially in Asia. He had to work out the cultures of elephants, wherever they were, and determine whether similarities existed or not. Then there was the question of who was funding his activities and just how much would he be in control.

He resolved to have a chat with Dad; he had quite some experience of working for world bodies and was not actually the absent-minded professor he was sometimes labelled as.

He went up to their bedroom and decided to have a shower to freshen up. Sophie was not long out of the shower and was dressing for the evening, so he was left on his own till he came out of the shower. As he was dressing, he told her what his mother had said, particularly about considering New Zealand as a home. He said it was possible to get anywhere in the world in 24 hours, given how world airlines were expanding, and communications were served by telephone systems evolving. He wanted to let her know that he would not be against the idea, if that's what she wanted. He also wanted to say that there was a colonial spirit that existed in terms of getting things done that allied settler backgrounds. She positively beamed and did say that she was not sure about living in America or Canada, nor the UK, whose climate might sicken them. When he suggested the South of France, she thought that might be OK for a holiday, and he must get world travel allocations for an family holiday at least once every two years. He laughed and thought that was a good idea. They went down to join the others before dinner.

Jade and Frank had got back while Jasper was showering, so everyone was in the cool lounge and the three women got together, being served their choice of drinks by the house steward. Jasper was left standing with his father and asked him if they could spend a few minutes discussing a couple of things on his mind. Frank said it would be good to get a chat together and suggested that after dinner, the two of them would go into Frank's study and lock the door, so to speak. Jasper took a beer and wandered over to the window, looking out over the bay and the bright displays of ships anchored there, then looking towards his right to see the lights along Durban's golden mile and its neon displays.

He was joined by Jade, who said simply, "Beautiful, isn't it?"

He agreed, "Yeah, but it's not the bush. Mind, I haven't spent much time at the sea as they say, so maybe I'm biased."

They chit chatted and then Jasper asked her about the work she and Tom were going to do. He had not realized that the 'wasting disease' that he had heard various Africans talking about was either as serious as Jade had said nor as global. Jade explained how it had been first identified amongst San Francisco's homosexual community and then amongst drug users. The thinking had been that the drug users got it from sharing needles and the few incidences of female AIDS would be as a result of bisexual male partners. However, in Africa it seemed that the disease was almost entirely heterosexual. She clarified that AIDS wasn't itself the disease, but that its effect was to compromise the immune system so patients would actually die of other diseases like pneumonia or starvation. She explained that the basic thinking was that a retro-virus was responsible for the invasion and collapse of the immune system, but until they could properly identify the virus and its modus operandi, there was no possibility of finding a cure. Often the initial infection was not serious, and by the time it was identified, it was too late, and the patient was doomed. Here in the Cape, it looked like the University of Cape Town had found that a large percentage of AIDS sufferers had suffered from TB, so that was an opportunity to study patients earlier. He could see that she was excited, and though he had not understood all of it, it was clear that it was very important. He was glad for Jade, in a way.

Sophie came over and put her arm through his and told the two of them that Marika wanted everyone to go through for dinner. Once again, the ex-Joubert chef had prepared a wonderful dinner of melon and ham, followed by a Mozambican style peri peri chicken, and ending with a lime cheesecake. The peri peri chicken was perhaps more refined and not as hot as what Jasper had been used to at the Coimbra, but it was done so that you could enjoy the chicken, not just the fiery heat of the spice. After coffee was served, Frank announced that he needed some time with his son, some man time, so he and Jasper were retiring to the study and he did not expect any interruptions.

He said, "We may be some time, don't wait up." As they retreated, he told Jasper that he had always wanted to say that, not realizing how much amusement it was causing the girls. When they got to the study, he opened a cupboard and pulled out a bottle of 18-year-old Caol Ila single malt whisky, two crystal glasses and a matching jug of iced water. As he poured, he asked, "Now, I assume you have already found out about the birds and the bees, as evidenced by Sophie's condition, so what is it that you require me for?"

Jasper thought, where to start, and said, "Dad, you know how involved you always have been about tribal cultures, God knows there won't be anyone on the planet who knows more than you about African cultures. Well, I have begun to feel the same way, but about the balance of man with nature, and how man is corrupting that balance. Now, with this proposed job, I think it will let me try to get the balance in some way to tilt back, to allow the flora and fauna to live. The job I have just done regarding the poaching ring is only a small part of how I see the job. I am concerned that the only people I have been involved with in doing this job seem to be spooks, and maybe its other skills that I possess that they want me for. Your friend Jim Marshall did not seem that worried that three of the main instigators of the elephant poaching were killed during an escape bid. He was far more interested with getting the USA an upper hand over China and North Korea. I do not want to be a pawn in the political games they play, and I am not sure how to handle it."

Now his father spoke, "Son, first let me tell you that I knew about your being a Selous Scout, and I have a fair idea of what that involved. I am, after all, in the field of tribal cultures and how history is passed on via word of mouth. I assume these are the other skills you have. I wish I could tell you that there is a path for right and another for wrong. Right and wrong are beliefs at best, and tend to be pertinent to particular actions; by definition they cannot be judged except at the time. Now what it is that determines a right or wrong, I won't bore you with, but so far, we are only talking about two paths. Just imagine if you add several more paths, each with specific rights or wrongs, how many more degrees of freedom become involved, and soon what was a single path you should take becomes indistinct. Even worse confusion or chaos arises if you now have a power that deliberately forces the introduction of yet another path. Sometimes there can be a pure question of the greater good, but then you must first define that greater good. You cannot do this in a general way, but only for a specific action. You will need to always redefine the greater good with each objective you set yourself. Like your paths, there are many greater goods, but only one can apply at a time. Am I making sense to you, or am I confusing you?"

"I think I understand, the path only presents itself with the objective that's set, you have to be prepared to choose another if other information comes up or if an outside force comes into play."

Frank began to pour them both another drink and asked, "Let's go back a bit. Are you sure that you want to be a conservationist?"

Jasper nodded. "I don't see myself as a conservationist per se, more a protector of environments. I'm not silly enough to imagine that the habitats can be exclusive in terms of the flora and fauna, and I know that inevitably man will take away these habitats on any excuse be it mineral wealth, hardwood to be harvested, any greed even natural disasters. Nevertheless, I can work to slow that inevitability down whilst I try to educate, enforce legally if necessary, so there will be laws to make. I bloody know I can at least make a difference with the UN behind me; it probably won't be enough, but it would be a start. But I will not be a lackey at the beck and call of any nation who has a whim now and again. I perhaps see the ivory poaching as one of the paths that has to be gone down, but others can do that. I am happy to set it up, but I see it as largely more of an education job, long term."

Frank smiled and said, "I think you have sorted yourself out, now all I need to say is make a plan, put it down on paper, what you feel you can start with. Don't have too many objectives, and when you tell Jim, also tell him about your fears of being a pawn only. Don't assume he is all spook, because you might be surprised. I may be wrong about many things, but not usually about men." He paused, then said, "I think we may as well finish this bottle."

"Now that's a plan, Dad!"

CHAPTER 32

The Plan

The next morning, Jasper awoke to find himself alone in the bed with the curtains still drawn. He looked the time and saw it was almost 8 o'clock. He sat up and decided he really felt quite well, surprisingly so given he and Dad had finished a bottle of malt whisky last night, and it had been well after two before they had gone to bed. He showered and went down to get some breakfast. He did feel hungry and loaded up a plate with bacon, scrambled egg, mushrooms, and toast, before heading out and joining the girls and his dad.

Sophie smiled, blew him a kiss and said, "Hello sleepyhead." He grinned and said his good mornings, and asked if he could use his dad's study, as he had to sit down and write out his plans for the job before he saw Jim Marshall. Mum was going to do some gardening supervision, and Jade and Sophie were going to do some shopping and get something for Sophie's mum, whilst Frank was due at the University for meetings.

He finished his breakfast and took a refill cup of coffee with him as he went and sat down in his dad's study. Typically, old-fashioned Frank had a big desk, several filing cabinets, a separate telephone from the rest of the house with a telex machine, a typewriter of some vintage, a typical green desk lamp, and a big blotter. A carved jug held a range of pencils and two Waterman fountain pens lay in custom made boxes along with black and blue ink. There would not be any biros in his dad's study. There was a big couch and two comfortable chairs around a coffee table in the corner, and of course a door to a private toilet. Jasper fell quite at home and, taking a pad and a pencil from the jug, went to sit by the coffee table, but found that too low, so came back to sit at the desk. He started by writing down what he wanted to do. He thought that an all en-compassing aspiration would be good, something like *Securing the future for the elephants and their habitats to best reflect their co-existence with mankind's needs for mutual benefit.* This then would be the basis of his vision. He would secure their future by a mixture of first understanding the elephant world in terms of its needs, understanding Man's needs regarding the elephants, then working through education and involvement, especially at grassroots levels, of all involved parties, reinforcing where necessary with common global legislation and provision of enforcement resources where necessary. The other element that he felt would have to be addressed was that of funding, as the elephant ranges were generally in the third world countries, who often would not have excess funds themselves to finance his vision. He labelled the next page Threats to the Elephant', and began by putting 'save the elephant' in the centre and then made a spider diagram, citing the big issues with that. He was now in academic mode and was ruthless in only writing for five minutes. He knew from experience that 80% of his main ideas would flow in these first minutes, and thereafter it might take a further hour to exhaust the remaining 20% of the ideas. He had written six main legs, including international and domestic trade in ivory (ornamental, cultural and medicinal), human elephant conflict, habitat loss and break up of habitat, killing for meat, lack of legislation and subsequent enforcement and local over-population of habitat. Already he had found quite a few 'paths', in his father's parlance, to follow, and now he was going to complicate it further by trying to overlay those countries in Africa where elephants had habitats. He was well aware that he would have to complete a plan for the Asian elephants, but felt it would be more manageable to separate the two for now.

There were other priorities arising in Asia, stemming from the threats to his central vision. For example, some of the sub-species of the Indian elephant had suffered an imbalance of the male to female ratios due to poaching, resulting in severe reductions in the tusk gene dominance in males. Tusks only appeared in males anyway, so the loss of genetic diversity reduced even further the males bearing tusks. He would consider Africa first, before linking his developed strategies to the Asian sector, where appropriate. He would modify and adapt his potential strategies for Asia to suit, as he was sure that all would fall within the basic strategic sub-groups that were emerging, namely Habitat Preservation, Legislation and Enforcement, Education, and Funding.

His initial studies at University and his subsequent time in the bush made him at least aware, if not well-versed in understanding the elephant behaviours in Central, Eastern and Southern Africa. That would include Angola, Botswana, The Democratic Republic of the Congo, Kenya, Malawi, Mozambique, South West Africa, South Africa, Swaziland, the United Republic of Tanzania, Zambia, and Zimbabwe. There were quite a few other countries within Africa whose elephant behaviours he had not studied, but published information would exist and establishing contact with local universities should fill in any gaps. He listed these as Benin, Burkina Faso, Cameroon, Central African Republic, Chad, Côte d'Ivoire, Equatorial Guinea, Eritrea, Ethiopia, Gabon, Ghana, Guinea, Guinea-Bissau, Liberia Mali, Niger, Nigeria, Rwanda, Senegal, Sierra Leone, Somalia, Sudan, Togo, and Uganda. He sat and looked at these two lists and thought that there were quite a few 'paths' there to consider.

His mother came in and left a jug of iced water for him, asking whether he would be coming through for lunch or if she should send a plate through for him. He nodded and said that would do and did not even notice as Marika left.

He began to consider what strategies he needed to put forward to combat the threats he had identified. He went back to his Threats page and its spider diagram. He now made the priorities: Illegal Killing for Ivory and Other Products, Conflict with Humans,

Local Overpopulation and the Loss and/or Fragmentation of Habitat. These alone made the future for the African elephant insecure to the extent that Jasper knew some of the elephant populations would not survive. So how was he going to address this? Assuming he was in a role that was being backed by the UN, he would begin with the understanding element and have the UN resolve that the African member states must set up a programme of joint conservation policies, based on an exchange of proven management experiences of their own elephant populations. Jasper meant to facilitate constant dialogue between the nations. The common goal would be to establish sustainable elephant populations within their present habitats, preventing further loss of that habitat. He would have to suggest how sustainable populations could have or generate benefits along ecological, cultural, and economic lines.

Jasper moved on to strategies that would be needed to combat the illegal poaching for ivory. Firstly, he figured that there would have to be a set of laws, perhaps centrally enacted, which all elephant nations would cooperate on and adopt, so that there was one set of laws and one set of minimum punishments applied. This must include helping member states to strengthen their law enforcement agencies, including anti-poaching units, providing any additional necessary resources in terms of equipment, personnel, and education in conservation techniques. Jasper then wrote that Scientific Institutions should be funded to provide forensic techniques which could identify areas from which ivory had originated.

He did not notice that it was Sophie that brought him in some cold meats and salads until she kissed him on the top of his head. She asked how it was going and realized he was not in that much of a talkative mood and, judging by the amount of paper around and on the desk, he was busy. He promised he would call her when he needed a proofreader, and, with a proper kiss this time, she left him to it. He did not stop while eating, but simply carried on, putting his ideas on paper.

He moved on to deal with human and elephant conflict. This usually arose when a local community bordering or in a habitat range were negatively hit by elephants raiding crops or consuming scarce water supplies. Peoples who were subject to such severe competition could then die of starvation, lose their domestic stock, so communities would often seek an end to the conflict, resulting in the killing of elephants. This route can destroy the herd if, for instance, the matriarch is removed, and it does nothing to address the real problem of limiting the elephants' range. Mostly, in Jasper's experience, there was no definite deterrent to keep an elephant from going to a known source of food and water, so most measures to stop marauding elephants tended to be reactive rather than proactive. His suggested strategic approach had to be split into three parts. This would compromise of research of all known mitigation methods, traditional and non-traditional, with the most effective introduced continentally. Scientific Institutes must be funded to develop non-lethal technological solutions, such as using sound frequencies. Evaluation of the causes of particular conflicts could lead to relocating water sources, or their delivery, and provision of alternative feeds during hard times. The other side of the coin was, in all the vastness of Africa, was the space where humans chose to live actually the only place for them to be? Jasper believed that, at best, only a reduction of conflicts between elephants and humans could be aimed at, outside of a rigid adherence to habitats being limited to elephant only populations.

He knew that habitats, even if designated National Parks, could be subject to a political whim, so he needed to make a plan regarding the preservation of elephant habitats, but again he came back to logging of valuable hardwoods and/or mining of minerals. These were two areas that would prove very difficult to ask any nations to forgo incomes from. Regarding logging, it may be possible, he thought, that a fund could be provided, out of which the UN as a whole could literally agree on a value of the hardwoods and pay for that forest to remain; the UN would, in fact, own the timber. This would have support from conservationists generally, as forests had been shown to be 'the lungs of the earth', absorbing atmospheric carbon dioxide and processing it through photosynthesis. It was thought that the forests globally produced up to a quarter of the oxygen in the world, so they were very significant contributors, though not as large as the three quarters of oxygen produced by micro-organisms in the oceans. Nevertheless, due to this ability to convert or lock up the carbon dioxide, along with their roles in rainfall and climate patterns, forests are supremely important, so perhaps owning the timber could be an option. However, Jasper could only leave a big question mark against his bullet point concerning minerals. This would include metals and oil, and how you could stop that utilization was beyond him. That was for better brains than his to work out. However, against agricultural expansion, he thought that elephant friendly policies could be introduced. The education and involvement of local communities to show that elephants have a value to them may be a more profitable way to go. It would be important that a share of income from tourists was given directly to communities who were neighbours to elephants, rather than the tourist income benefiting those not living in the conflict area. Jasper thought this incentivising of the local people was the key to success. Clearly an education programme would be necessary, and careful application vital, but the central pillar would be the total involvement of the grassroots. His overall strategy would be to promote the development of innovative incentive schemes that increased benefits to the local communities, whilst trying to mitigate the cost to the community caused by elephants.

There remained two aspects that he felt would need to be addressed at the first opportunity, being associated with habitat control. The first was international, as elephants don't recognize man made or even natural borders, so where elephant ranges involved border hopping, this needed to be identified and common protection provided by the nations involved.

Secondly, perhaps more controversially, Jasper believed that culling, where habitats were judged as being unable to support numbers of elephants, should be researched more thoroughly than it was at present. On the face of it, controlling the numbers by a cull was to save and maintain an adequate habitat, but non-selective culling had resulted in the loss of the wrong members of the herd, in effect creating more undisciplined and rogue members within an elephant community. It also did not ensure that the strongest genes necessarily survived, and so the genetic pool was being artificially weakened. It would take detailed histories of all the elephants in any particular habitat to identify and pinpoint those animals least likely to impact on the future. Jasper conceded that, short of having some sort of radio collars with renewable batteries, full blood-work analyses of all elephants was impractical. However, other than targeting culling of whole families of elephants, including teenagers and calves, he had begun to favour no culling policies. He accepted more work had to done researching the effects of a no cull policy, but the belief was that as the habitat became unsustainable, elephants would die naturally due to starvation and drought, and would do so to balance the damage they had done to their habitat. The theory was that, as the habitat recovered, the elephants would once again begin to flourish, but the survivors would be the strongest and so would the gene pool. This was not unknown within other mammals, where in bad years natural abortions would increase or fertility would decrease, the difference being that elephants were on a much longer breeding cycle that other mammals.

Jasper realized it was beginning to get dark, but he wanted to finish his papers before bed tonight, and when Sophie came in with some tea for him, he said he was going to miss dinner this evening. She recognized that he was on a roll, as it were, and said she would bring him something he could eat while working. He checked back against his priorities concerning poaching, conflict with humans, local overpopulation, and the loss and or fragmentation of habitat. He felt he had suggested sufficient strategic approaches towards each of the priorities to warrant a start. He knew there were other things that would need attention, but he had covered the biggies. He was confident that he could commit himself to the coordination of the activities he had suggested. His interest was particularly in the education, right down to grassroots, the coordination of anti-poaching activities, and the research needed to prove sustainability. He also put down areas where the professional skills of others were needed, and of course resources he would need. The latter were more to do with contacts in law, law enforcement, university academia, technological institutions, wildlife institutions, international media, and secretarial services. He would prepare and deliver papers for any audiences that could help. The two big areas where he could only act as a support entity would be the diplomatic negotiation between nations that had elephant populations and those negotiations for funding the various anti-poaching units, education programmes, university research and technological developments. This would be, as he saw it, a sustainable funding involving all nations globally as well as foundations.

He now turned and examined his primary paper and tested it against what he knew of the Asian elephant story, and hoped that with minor changes it would generally cover the problems faced by the Asian elephants. He knew that poaching for tusks in Asia was probably less than in Africa, partly because only males bore tusks in Asian elephants, and then it was only by some species. The ivory, however, tended to be regarded as a better quality than tusks from Africa, and therefore there was a demand for Asian tusk. Jasper knew there was little hard, reliable data about the extent of poaching in Asia, but there was some information, as well as plenty of anecdotal evidence. He was interrupted by Sophie, who brought a steak roll with a bottle of Castle beer. She teased him with a mock hula dance, blew him a kiss and swayed out, bringing a smile to his face. He took a bite and a swig from the bottle and turned back to his action plan. Poaching for meat was rare, not least due to religious beliefs, but elephant hide was prized for both clothing and for furniture. Traditional medicine was also known to create a demand for elephant poachers to exploit. Nevertheless, elephant populations were thought to have dropped severely in Vietnam, Laos, and Cambodia, which Jasper of course thought to be as a result of war, spilling over from the Vietnam-American conflict only just over a decade previously. The main area of difference that Jasper surmised was the apparent imbalance emerging in the ratio between sexes. Any imbalance would eventually affect reproduction rates, leading in turn to a decline in genetic diversity. This would not bode well for ensuring healthy populations. Perhaps the lack of tusks in the male population was already an indicator. He thought that an addition to his action plan would help to cover this in research, but otherwise his paper would largely encompass Asian elephants with their African counterparts. He would have to do more work himself on the cultural aspects among Asian elephants in India and all the South East Asian countries to pinpoint difference in behaviours. That would take time, whereas the anti-poaching programmes could run alongside the African ones.

That finished his thoughts, and he would present that when he talked to Jim. He had decided that the best way to tackle the issue regarding being a pawn or puppet for the CIA was to put it on the table at the time of his presentation. Now he was up for another beer, and to ask his dad to read through his paper. He photocopied his scrawl and would give it to Sophie for her comments. He went through to join the rest for coffee and felt he had achieved something. He was shattered, and giving up his work to Frank and then Sophie, he went to bed. He went to sleep instantly, rather like he used to be capable of in the bush on ops, except now it was deeply. He never heard Sophie some three hours later, nor felt her cuddle into him. When he woke, she was already gone from the bed, and looking at his watch he saw it was nine o'clock in the morning. He had slept for eleven hours.

CHAPTER 33

New Beginnings Part 2

By the time he went down, breakfast was already gone as indeed were the family. The houseboy came and asked what he wanted for breakfast, and said toast, coffee with eggs and bacon would be quick, and that JJ could join Professor Frank in the study after he had eaten. The madams had gone into La Lucia. He sat and read the Natal Mercury, catching up on the latest news, before eating and finally going with his coffee to his father's study. He heard the clattering of a typewriter as he knocked and entered. To his surprise, Sophie was on one side of the desk, busy typing, with Dad reading and putting red marks with some comments on his first draft. Sophie was typing the sheets that had been 'corrected'. Frank looked up over his glasses and motioned for him to sit over on the couch and to be quiet. Jasper planted a kiss on the top of Sophie's head, and she smiled and briefly squeezed his hand before returning to the typing.

Finally, Frank passed the last sheet over to Sophie and said, "Son your English and grammar was appalling, but your content is fascinating and I think it's an exciting piece. I would certainly put it in the top pile. I hope you don't mind, but I have corrected the English and your wife is typing it up so that at least it will look professional. Oh, by the way, Jim phoned not long ago, and he will be arriving on Sunday night. He's staying at the Beverley Hills along at Umhangla Rocks and suggests you meet on Monday morning at the hotel. He is bringing some chap from India with him. He has some meeting in Durban at lunchtime, which may go on a bit, then we are all to have dinner at night with them at the hotel. If you allow me to make a final suggestion, I suggest you let me photocopy the script once Sophie is finished, and I will leave it for Jim at the hotel. He can read it before he sees you, so you won't waste time in your meeting." He then excused himself, saying he would be back in a few minutes. Jasper merely nodded but was secretly pleased his dad had cleaned up the presentation, and he was glad Sophie was typing it. It seemed only right that she was involved with it, as it was the basis for their future. He began reading the first three sheets she had finished and as he came to the end of them, she handed over the fourth sheet, saying there would be another half page. As he continued reading, he also realized how serious his paper was and how much he wanted to get started. He sincerely hoped that Jim would not disappoint him regarding the spook issue, but the fact he was bringing someone else may suggest there was going to be nothing to hide. Sophie had finished the last sheet and came over to sit with him on the couch while he finished reading. When he finally looked up, he smiled and asked rather apprehensively what she thought of it.

She chose her words carefully and said, "I think it's wonderful, and of course I'm biased, but if you can get this started you will achieve as much as anybody can. I am proud of you and love you so much." As he hugged her and kissed her, his father returned and said that he presumed they had finished. Jasper was momentarily embarrassed, like a schoolboy having been caught with his first girlfriend, but soon got over it. Sophie laughed and said she wished she had a camera to hand so she could have captured the look on his face. Frank took the finished pages and went over to his photocopier, making several copies. He took the top copy and put it in a large envelope, sealed it and addressed it to Jim Marshall, care of the Beverley Hills Hotel. He gave the original back to Jasper and suggested he kept the two remaining copies here in his filing cabinets, should they be needed. Sophie picked up another envelope and carefully folded the five sheets and put them inside, saying she would put it together with their other papers and documents. Jasper said thanks to his dad, who dismissed it as unnecessary and added that he was proud of his son.

Now, he had some other things to do, and he wanted them out of his study, suggesting they took a car and went exploring or stayed at home sunbathing, but warned them that if they stayed, Marika would organize them. He cocked an ear and declared it was too late, for he could hear the staff stirring, which could only mean that Marika and Jade were coming up the drive. He sometimes wondered how they knew, but know they did, clearly an in-built radar or the like.

They left the study and were strolling to the back veranda, holding hands, when mother and Jade came in, carrying the evidence of their morning shopping. Dumping the parcels, they shouted for tea and joined the lovebirds on the veranda. They began talking amongst themselves, clucking fussily, so Jasper thought, and he sat back thinking they were really quite fearsome in a gang, or whatever you called a collection of hens. He got up and left without any of them seeming to notice. He went into the cool of the lounge, picked up the Mercury again and decided to do the crossword. He had nearly finished when Sophie came and got him for lunch. Marika announced that they would all go to the Roma revolving restaurant along the Embankment tonight. It was basically an Italian restaurant with magnificent views of Durban at night as the restaurant revolved.

After lunch, Jasper and Sophie went for a walk, taking the two supposedly guard/attack German Shepherds, who in reality were more house pets though they were only allowed in the kitchen, rear lounge and the verandas. The two dogs were named after Zulu chieftains, Zulu being the dominant tribes in Natal. The eldest dog was named for Dingaan, the Zulu king who notoriously signed a deed allowing Piet Retief, the Boer leader, to settle in Natal. Dingaan then killed Piet Retief and his party of about 100 people during the celebrations for the signing of the treaty on the 6th February 1838. The Boers regrouped and later in that year, on the 16th December, they defeated the Zulus at the Battle of Blood River. That day became a sacred day in Boer history, being variously called the Day of the Vow or Day of the Covenant. The second dog was named for Shaka, the fearsome king who transformed the Zulu armies from a mediocre base into the most feared bodies of fighting men in black Africa. The two dogs were happy to run around chasing tennis balls, which they constantly brought back to be thrown again. They tended to go to Sophie, as she did make a fuss, and threw the balls each time. Jasper tended to hold the balls and tease them. It was about half past four when they got back, with two very happy but panting dogs who made straight for their drinking bowls before flopping down on the veranda at Sophie's feet.

That evening, Frank drove them all to the Victoria Embankment, parking alongside the Roma restaurant. It was a squeeze into the lift for all five, but they made it to the 32nd floor and were welcomed into the restaurant. The restaurant revolved once every 65 minutes and gave magnificent views across a well-lit Durban, which tended to make up for the average Italian cuisine, or at least Durban's version of Italian cuisine. The meal was well enough presented and tasty enough. The sweets, however, were excellent, and mostly instant heart attack material. Jasper hated the growing fad which called itself nouvelle cuisine and was intended to be healthy. He always thought that if you went out to dine, then you expected decent portions, not postage size bits and bobs. At least the Roma delivered edible food, and in portions that satisfied southern African bellies. Of course, nouvelle cuisine was healthy; so were starvation rations.

The next day Jasper took Sophie to see a rugby game; the Natal Sharks were playing Western Province at their home ground Kings Park. They sat amongst 40,000 people, all baying mostly for the Sharks, but a sizeable roar was evident for the Capetonians. He was about to start explaining rugby to Sophie and stopped, realizing she would have to be the only New Zealander who did not know about rugby. The all-conquering All Blacks were probably the best team in the world, but because of apartheid, they could not play against South Africa. The game itself was typically hard fought, the two packs seeking dominance over each other with very little wing play. The match ground out a victory for Natal, 9 points to 6 points, with no tries being scored. After the match they enjoyed a mass braai in the car park, often called the biggest barbeque in the world. The smell of meat being burned on charcoal fires really got the juices going, and a typical plate would have bits of steak, pork, and lamb chops, as well as the famous boerewors sausage rings, carefully basted with lemon juice and beer. There was a formidable array of salads, cold sultana rice, and potato mayonnaise, all washed down with wine and beer. Music blared out and everybody, whether they were Natal or Cape supporters, joined in. It was quite late by the time they got back to La Lucia and bed.

The next morning, Sunday, they came through to breakfast at nine o'clock to find Marika and Jade gone to church. Frank was there and rarely went to the Dutch Reform church, because he always thought that Marika only went to meet others socially, keeping up with the gossip. Jasper spent most of the day with Sophie, practicing his presentation and getting her to play devil's advocate and challenge some of his statements. He knew though, that despite already having accepted a role in the anti-poaching and prosecution of those major rings, this was his best chance to put together a programme to slow down the possibility of extinction and promote a sustainable approach to maintaining the elephant species. He went for a swim after lunch, and when Sophie joined him the two dogs trailed her to the pool and then raced around as she moved around herself. Tennis balls were brought and dropped in the pool for her to fling out. Occasionally one would fall in, but clearly it was a common event, and they would swim to the wide marble steps at one end and clamber out. Eventually they got out and showered in the poolside shower before getting back to the veranda to sit and snooze until Mum came to fetch them for dinner.

After dinner, the whole family sat in the cool of the air-conditioned lounge and chatted. They would have played cards, for

Marika and Frank were well known as a bridge player, but it was a Sunday and Marika was, after all, a member of the Dutch Reform Church. Jasper always thought that this meant no fun on the Sabbath at all. He had one more run through his presentation before bedtime.

The next morning, he and Sophie breakfasted early, and with her and Frank wishing him luck, he went off to the Beverley Hills hotel to meet Jim. He was clearly expected, and the reception directed him to one of their conference rooms.

He knocked and heard Jim call, "Come in." It was a smaller conference room, perhaps for a dozen people, but it had some video facilities. He shook hands with Jim, who then presented the man with him, Mr. Sanjeev Pradham, as an expert on anti-poaching in both the sub-continent and South East Asia. Jim asked how Sophie was and said that he was looking forward to meeting everybody in the evening. He suggested that they sit and have some coffee. When they were settled, Jim looked across at Jasper and said, "Thanks for your paper, we have both studied it, and though we were really here to tie up the coordinator of the UN's investigations and prosecution division, your paper opens up an entirely more complete approach to the problem, which caused us to set up the investigation and prosecution job. We think we have to take this back to New York and get it endorsed. We believe you have in effect given us the skeleton of what we should have done from day one. I have already sent a copy of your paper to the office at the UN and to WWF."

Jasper was inwardly ecstatic but he dared not show it, but did say, "After the Zambia job, I sat and thought about what we had discussed up in Ndole and thought that, as events showed, prosecutions for a variety of reasons may be diplomatically incorrect. In fact, I was not happy that I was possibly used as judge and jury, and that you, Jim, were not overly concerned that you would not have any prosecutions internationally. If this post is only about being a tool in some sort of game countries play with each other, then I have to tell you I will withdraw. Now I realize that there will always be some benefit to some country, whatever happens in investigations and prosecutions, but the problem is much bigger than can be solved by prosecution alone. It seems to me that whatever prosecution is set up, it could be hijacked by any country for what I will call a diplomatic whim. All my division, or part in this, would be looked at to see if someone could use the prosecution to their advantage; in other words, the elephants are incidental. Now if we tackle the problem of maintaining sustainable habitats and a strong gene pool for the elephants, and not just the poaching aspect, I believe we would be attacking the real problems that elephants face. That I want to be part of, if the diplomats want to play games with each other and use my work, so be it, but I and those I have on a team, must be independent. I will consider any requests, but I have to be able to say no, a veto if you will, as to what I take on. I will not be a de facto member of the CIA, KGB, MI6, BOSS, or whatever the Chinese call their spooks, the elephants have to be my boss. I really do not have much more to say and will understand if I ask too much, but if you and yours are serious about saving elephants, then I am in." With that Jasper shut up and went to pour more coffee. He offered to pour for Jim and Sanjeev, and both had another cup. He sat down and waited.

Sanjeev spoke first. "Well done, sir, you have hit it right on the head. Prosecution on its own is not making all that much of an impact. Perhaps the disappearance of main players may make a difference, but it will take time which the elephants do not necessarily have. Your linkage to local communities has been tried in my country and it has been mostly successful. I can arrange for you to receive the reports about it. I too am concerned about the elephants and I am also a policeman, but I can see that if prosecutions may well be too circumstantial, the easy route is, as you say, becoming judge and jury, which does not allow for publicity."

Jim now spoke, saying, "I think we can agree that investigation and prosecution alone does not do it for the elephants. You have probably reminded us what the real objectives are. No, I am no longer an active agent of the CIA, but I have probably been around diplomats too long to not understand how they operate. Also, my home nation is one of the biggest funders of the UN, and sometimes they try to remind me of my past. It would be wrong to say I can ignore the pressures entirely, but there are ways round that. I think we can swing an enlargement of the role, whilst keeping you in my bailiwick, that of International Justice. I am afraid you will be stuck in my domain, but with this poaching thing off my desk, I can ensure the diplomatic whims, as you call them, are dealt with by me. Now it seems to me we should work out your terms; I am sure I will get a positive from my colleagues at the UN, even if I have to remind them about some 'whims' that have never surfaced. How about your title as Director of Elephant Survival; you can make something up if you like, and then I need you to write your own job description. My divisional heads get paid USD100k, wherever you want, with all local living expenses paid. The local expenses include schooling and secretarial services. A further USD50k will paid, but only to a personal pension fund. Have you decided where you will live yet?"

Jasper shook his head but said he thought it might be New Zealand. "Neither of us fancy the US, Canada may be too cold, the UK too wet, and Africa basically too unstable."

Jim laughed and said that Jasper had a settler mentality. "You know, New Zealand would be OK, comms are good there and you can reach both Africa and Asia in a day, same for New York. Local schooling right through university, and Australia is a couple of hours by plane. New Zealand also has a strong conservation culture, which helps. Your UN passport is ready, but I warn you it is useful, nevertheless, to keep at least one national passport. I will need you in New York for a couple of weeks to introduce you to contacts in Law Enforcement and Intelligence. Sanjeev here is a commissioner in his force, but he knows many people in Asia, plus he controls a lot of the university research on elephants – don't ask, I do not understand that division of labour at all. So, a couple of weeks with him trotting round India and Asia will be needed. I expect you to take at least 6 weeks break every year, with at least one break of a minimum of 21 days. Now, can we agree that we have a deal based on the minimum post, as previously discussed, but with what we have here today?"

Jasper nodded and signed the appointment letter as Director of Elephant Survival, but with a gap as to his domicile. He shook hands with both Sanjeev and Jim. As they began to leave the room, Jim offered lunch, but Jasper declined, preferring to leave it to the dinner planned tonight. As they walked Jim asked about Jade so he would not appear a stranger, so Jasper told him about her and her husband's role, also funded by the UN, in the AIDS programmes being developed in the University of Cape Town. Jim nodded and said AIDS was getting out of control in many countries.

As Jasper was getting into his taxi, Jim suddenly said, "Oh, those names you gave to Jonty that the brigadier gave you, 'Hooan' and 'Geeang', have been identified as Huan and Jiang, both businessmen living in the Chinese consulate in Lubumbashi, and of course we knew about Katumbi, but well done to have made those connections. See you this evening."

As the taxi pulled away, Jasper wondered how much Jim knew about how they got the names. He decided that Jim would not care.

Dinner that evening at the Beverley Hills was held in a private room and was every bit as sumptuous as the furnishings. It also turned out to be a celebration, as Jim announced that Jasper had been accepted into a new role covering all aspects of the elephant survival objective. Jim was a perfect host and began circulating, speaking with everybody individually. He spoke with Jade for a while and showed he had considerable knowledge about AIDS. He even gave her the name of an orphanage in the Cape Town district, where they were feeding babies using donated milk powders so that comparisons could be made with normally brought up children. Finally, he gave her a name of a researcher in retro virus behaviours who might be able to help her and her husband, as he had already made inroads into the disease. When Jade remarked to Jasper later that Jim seemed a decent sort and knew quite a bit about her subject, he realized that Jim was in fact one of the world's great fixers. Sophie got the name of a man that Jim knew who had several aircraft who might be interested in being part-time pilots, should she and Jasper decide to live in New Zealand. Finally, Jim, Marika and Frank settled in a corner and chatted over old times.

Sanjeev had not joined them as he had relatives or acquaintances amongst the Indian community in Durban, but he had left some papers for Jasper as background on the cultural role elephants played in religion in India. His note explained that, unlike in Africa, man had trained elephants for all sorts of duties and rites, which clearly impacted on behaviour of herds. There was also a name of an eminent academic, a fundi, on elephants and their behaviours both in the wild and domesticated. Finally, Jim came back to Jasper and suggested that he needed to make a decision about his domicile and go get established before starting an induction programme. Sophie's condition would complicate long haul flights soon, and with the prospect of fatherhood in the next six months, Jim did not think the process of handing over contacts needed to happen straight away. There would be enough collection of data and information transfers to be undergone in setting up that he thought it could be done so that they kept him with Sophie until after the birth. He may have to put up with some visitors, however, but that would be part of his job anyway. They would keep in touch by the satellite phone.

With final handshakes and the usual "Don't let us leave it too long before getting together again," the evening came to an end. That night, Jasper and Sophie agreed that the baby should be born a New Zealander.

EPILOGUE

The next morning, Jasper met his mother-in-law, Stephanie Mitchieson, for the first time, and immediately saw where Sophie got her vitality from. He stood well back to give mother and daughter room to hug and kiss each other for what would be the first time in a few years. When the initial welcoming was over, she came over to where a somewhat anxious Jasper was standing and subjected him to a strong hug and kiss. She took his hands and looked into his eyes and said her daughter had chosen well.

Before he went through the drama of what he would call her, he found that she had that same ESP that Sophie had, and she forestalled him by saying, "Call me Steph." They finally got into the car, and with Sophie and Steph in the back seat, Jasper in the front, they set off for La Lucia to meet the rest of the Jacksons. Marika and Steph fortunately hit it off immediately and began making plans. Jasper was left alone and was gratefully rescued from the four women by his dad. The two of them retired to the study. He told his dad of their decision to go and live in New Zealand, and was not surprised to hear Frank say that Marika would be disappointed initially, but she had told him that it would be best that Sophie and Jasper did not stay in South Africa. Frank thought so too, as he could see big changes ahead which might not be as smooth a transition as had seemingly happened between black and white in Zimbabwe. He thought that a period of calm might well ensue depending on the black leaders emerging, particularly one Nelson Mandela, but then what? If the pattern of most independent African states was followed, South Africa may well start well, as it was the richest economy of all the sub-Saharan states, but it would slowly proceed downhill as people's needs and wants would have to be fulfilled. When the wealth was gone, there would only remain chaos. It certainly would not be a place for young children to be brought up.

Frank asked what flights Steph was going back on and suggested that Jasper and Sophie should also go to New Zealand on the same flights. Frank would have the University Travel Bureau get them on Business on Singapore Airlines all the way through to Auckland. Always practical, he suggested that Jasper ask Sophie what district she wanted to live in and perhaps get her dad, Alan, to put the word out to estate agents, so they had places to look at. After lunch Steph went for a lie down, so Jasper had the chance to talk to Sophie about where to live. She knew exactly where she wanted to be; either Mount Maunganui by Tauranga, on the Bay of Plenty, or Tairua, further round to the base of the Coromandel. They announced their plans that evening and received best wishes from everybody. Frank had been called back to confirm the seats had been booked on the same flights as Steph so that was great. The next day Jasper phoned Jim, who was actually in London on his way back to New York, to give him the news and to use Sophie's parents address whilst they house-hunted. He then phoned Tony and gave him the same address for now, so that he could be reached regarding any matters to do with the Kariba business.

Two weeks later, Jasper and Sophie, along with Stephanie, left Frank, a predictable tearful Marika and Jade to begin their new life. For Jasper it was a new country, normally not an easy task to get residence, but his UN status helped, as well as being married to a New Zealand citizen. He was sorry to be leaving his beloved bush, but he knew the best way to help that bush was from outside. For Sophie it was not really going home, because the circumstances were different; she was married, about to become a mother, and now she would have to make a home for her family.

They would find a property within a week of arriving in New Zealand, on an exclusive plot within sight of Mount Maunganui, which was redone and furnished by the time Sophie gave birth to a little girl, who was named Marilyn Stephanie Marika Jackson. A son, Marcus Ethan, would follow later. Sophie did meet up with the man that Jim knew, and she kept up her pilot's licences, but her other baby became a fifteen-metre ocean going cruiser, offering game fishing and diving safaris in the Pacific. Jasper spent a lot of time preparing much of the educational programmes, both for anti-poaching units and for local communities, whilst waiting for the birth of Marilyn. He would go on to implement his programmes and became feared by poaching ringleaders, but those are different stories. Alas, he found that short-term greed by his fellow man was the real problem that threatened elephants, and ultimately even the planet. If only Pamwe Cheti could be achieved, then many precious things might be saved to glory at. Ah well, just a dream. So, Jasper had become yet another of that lost tribe, perhaps unforgotten, but there seemed to be nothing left in his tribes' fiefdom that he could fight for. He now had a bigger fiefdom to fight for, but though he would have some great successes, he had that uneasy feeling that it would end in tears just like before. He only hoped the elephants would survive beyond his and his children's lifetimes. Perhaps the winds of time would gather up the lost tribe and its descendants and let their skills rebuild their habitat.

GLOSSARY

Kapenta: a type of fresh water sardine

Now now: 1) Southern African slang for soon, though it is often variable 2) expression of urgency, though it can mean anything from immediacy to an hour, as opposed to **just now,** which can mean up to 24hrs

Stoep: outdoor patio, usually under partial cover, attached to a house

Posi: Southern African slang for position meaning an unofficial moorage for a boat, usually in a natural part inlet

Rondavel: a circular thatched hut

Tigerfish: *hydrocynus forskalii,* freshwater gamefish with teeth, a relation of piranha

Chimurenga: black uprising in Rhodesia to achieve Independence for Zimbabwe

Selous Scouts: A Rhodesian special forces elite anti-guerrilla force named for famous hunter Frederick Courteney Selous 1851–1917

Wafa Wafa: secret training camp of Selous Scouts known for its extreme training, bushcraft and individual survival techniques. Attrition rates in training are high, often less than 5% survive selection. Wafa wafa is a loose translation from the

Shona language meaning 'Those who die, die. Those who stay behind, stay behind."

Shona: refers to the largest tribe in Zimbabwe and its language. The people are looked upon as farmers and with contempt by the Matabele.

Ndebele (sometimes synonymous with **Matabele)**: refers mainly to the language of the minority tribe and the language. Ndebele were offshoots of South Africa's Zulus who travelled north to escape the ruthless king Shaka

Sadza: cooked maize meal starch staple in Zimbabwe

Nshima: as above, but in Zambia

Mealie Pap: as above, but South Africa

Piri piri: a fiery spice chilli preparation, Portuguese in origin, particularly favoured for chicken or prawns.

Beira prawns: famous large prawns from the coastal town of Beira in Mozambique, easily obtainable before Zimbabwean Independence

Babelas: Term for hangover in Southern African slang

TTL's (or tribal trust lands): areas of land reserved for the native populations as opposed to commercial European farming. TTL's were of much poorer arability and capability than the commercial farming areas

Agri-alert: A radio warning system between commercial farmers in isolated areas as a form of neighbourhood watch in the event of attack by terrorists

Bakkie: Southern African term for a pick-up truck of up to 1-ton capacity. From Afrikaans. Similar to "Ute" in Australia and New Zealand.

Ops: military use re operations, sorties

Fundi: expert

Taking the gap: term used by ex-Rhodesians and continued by whites to describe emigration, usually to South Africa at least pre 2000

Kwacha: Zambian currency

Howzit: Standard white greeting in Southern Africa: "How are you?"

Joburg: Johannesburg

Kak: Faeces

Schwartz: normally derogatory reference to a black person

Nyama: meat

GMT: Greenwich Mean Time

ZULU: name of a South African tribe, also used to signify local time at location

UNEP: United Nations Environmental Programme

WWF: World Wildlife Fund

IJC: International Justice Courts –a fictional arm of the UN

Army Worm: slang for grenades, sometimes used underwater, allowing stunned fish to be picked up easily

SAL/SAA: Suid Afrikaanse Lugdiens or South African Airways

Kafue: a river in Zambia, a tributary of the Zambezi

Pamwe Cheti: Together Only – motto of the Selous Scouts

Skuz Apo: derogatory term used by Zanla/Zipra for the Selous

Zanla: Zimbabwe African National Liberation Army

Zipra: Zimbabwe People's Revolutionary Army

Jay W. Ess was brought up in Northumberland, England, before becoming employed in agri-industry in Scotland, where he met and married his wife, Nancy. He later emigrated to Southern Africa, spending time in Zimbabwe and South Africa, and travelled through Africa, India, Australia, New Zealand, and Ireland in a consulting capacity. Mr Ess has now retired to Royal Deeside, Scotland, to be nearer to his grandchildren. Some Stay, Some Die is his first published work.

The publisher

*He who stops
getting better
stops being good.*

This is the motto of novum publishing, and our focus
is on finding new manuscripts, publishing them and
offering long-term support to the authors.
Our publishing house was founded in 1997, and since
then it has become THE expert for new authors and
has won numerous awards.

**Our editorial team will peruse each manuscript
within a few weeks free of charge and without
obligation.**

You will find more information about
novum publishing and our books on the internet:

www.novum-publishing.co.uk